The Gathered Fragments of Us

Mireille Martinelli

THE GATHERED FRAGMENTS OF US

A Novel

Mireille Martinelli

If you're sensitive to these topics or in crisis, please consider your well-being and seek support if needed. Characters and events are fictional and do not depict real-life events or people. In case of immediate danger, contact emergency services or crisis hotlines.

ISBN 979-8-9941723-0-8

Mireille Martinelli

For my mom.

We lost you too soon. I wish you could be here to see this. I wish I could have called you and talked to you every day to share this with you. I'm so grateful for all you were and all you gave me. As I wrote this, I thought of you constantly. I thought of the times we would read together, go bookstore hopping, and talk about all our favorite authors and novels—bickering over who would get to read which book first.

Thank you for being the best mom anyone could ever dream of having. Thank you for giving me the most incredible example of what a mom is—my daughter will thank you for that one day. Though she will never know you in person, she will always know you in spirit.

La-La-Love-You

Content Warning

Content Warning and Disclaimer:

This story is a work of fiction and contains themes that may be triggering for some, including substance abuse, mental health struggles, family conflict, and threats to safety. It explores marital and parental challenges as well as traumatic events. There are scenes which involve law enforcement, medical emergencies, grief, and intense family dynamics.

Chapter 1: The Purse

~FELICITY~

The Dior bag gleamed under the kitchen lights like a beacon of everything wrong with my marriage.

I stood frozen in the doorway. The grocery bags were cutting into my fingers as I watched my stepdaughter, Macy, unconsciously trace her fingers over the embossed leather.

It was the exact shade of powder beige I'd sent him in the screenshot. The precise gold hardware I'd included and then texted to Caden weeks ago with the message:

Me: This is what I want for my birthday.

Me: Please don't send Lauren to get something for me this year. I just want this.

Me: Nothing else... Just this.

"That's a beautiful purse, Macy," I said, forcing my voice to remain calm and steady.

Caden's head snapped up from the end-of-summer schoolwork in front of them. His blue eyes widened with what was clearly panic. His voice cracked a bit as he said, "Oh, hey babe. Didn't hear you come in." His voice sounded gravelly, and his gaze darted between me and the purse. "We were just—"

"Look, Felicity! I found it today!" Macy chirped, innocently and excitedly holding the bag up for me to see. "It's the most beautiful thing I've ever seen. Dad said it was for the first day of school next month. You guys are the best! Thank you, thank you, thank you!!!"

Before she could hurry to me and 'thank me' for something I had no hand in—because it was my birthday gift, not her first day of school gift—the grocery bags slipped from my numb fingers.

"Shit." Caden jumped up as the bags hit the ground and a jar of my favorite tomato basil sauce shattered across our kitchen floor. "Felicity, are you okay?"

No, I'm clearly not okay. I thought them, but the words wouldn't come out—stuck in my throat instead. I stood there and stared at the mess the sauce had made.

My birthday was in one week. The purse--my fucking purse, the one thing I'd specifically asked for—was now in the hands of an eleven-year-old for the first day of school.

I coughed, unable to speak. Silently, I grabbed paper towels from the counter, tossing towels on the floor to contain the sauce before it spread any further.

My eyes were on the ground when I said, "Macy, honey, why don't you take your homework upstairs?"

"But we're not done—"

"Now, please." I snapped out. The sharp edge in my voice made both their heads shoot up from where they'd been watching me clean the sauce.

I sighed. My shoulders drooping, and I softened my voice. I looked up and gave Macy a small smile that should have shouted to my husband how much my heart was breaking. "You can finish after dinner. I just need to talk to your dad for a minute."

Macy gathered her things, clutching the designer purse like a security blanket. "Okay. Are you okay, Felicity? Is something wrong?" She looked back and forth between me and Caden, her head volleying.

"Of course not, sweetheart." The lie burned my throat. "Head on upstairs. We'll call you for dinner when it's ready."

Satisfied, she bounced out, the stupidly expensive bag swinging from her thin shoulder. A bag I had no doubt would be battered within a week by an eleven-year-old's carelessness. Not her fault though. She had no idea what Dior even meant. Nope—this was all Caden's fault.

"Felicity—" Caden started.

I shushed him and, once she was out of hearing range, I spat out, "Don't." I went back to cleaning the sauce up. "Just... don't."

"Let me explain," he said. I looked up at him in disbelief, but he couldn't help himself.

"I'd hidden it in the back of her closet. Since she was only going to be here for the weekend, I never thought she would see it." Yup. Like I thought—all Caden's fault.

I said nothing, yet he just kept talking. "She found it when she was looking for her old ballet shoes." His voice was shaking a bit. "She fell in love with it, kept going on about how sophisticated it made her feel, how the other girls would think she was so grown up..." He kneeled beside me, reaching for the paper towels. "What was I supposed to say?"

"How about 'That's Felicity's birthday present'?" I jerked away from his touch. "How about 'No, sweetheart, that belongs to Felicity? How about literally anything other than giving away the one fucking gift I have actually asked you for—in years!?"

His face went through a series of expressions—guilt, frustration, then I saw that defensive set of his jaw take hold, and I knew he wasn't going to listen anymore. He started putting the remaining groceries on the counter and said, "It's just a purse, Felicity. I'll go get you another one."

"Just a purse?" I stood slowly; sauce-stained paper towels clenched in my fists. "If it were just a purse, then why didn't you just tell her no?"

"You didn't see her face. She was so happy—"

"So, what then ... " The words exploded out of me, what felt like thousands of swallowed frustrations finally breaking free. "So, her happiness—God! When did my happiness stop mattering? When did I—"

"That's not fair—"

"Isn't it? Three anniversaries!" I threw the towels into the trash and slammed the top shut. " My last birthday! You forget so many of the milestones in our lives—the things that are so important to me."

Caden took a step toward me, and I stepped back.

"Do you get that for years you've sent Lauren to pick out my gifts because you can't be bothered? It's always great getting things from my husband that are sent care of his assistant." Sarcasm burned through my words, and I turned away from him.

Facing the sink, I started washing the vegetables for dinner. "The one time--the ONE time--I ask for something specific, you give it to your daughter because she looked happy when she found it?" Fed up, I turned the water off and started pulling things from the bags he'd put on the counter, simultaneously grabbing items from the fridge for dinner.

"She's just a child—"

I looked up. "That's right. And children should have boundaries, not just get whatever they want! They should have parents who teach them the difference between yes and no. Though, that's not really fair here since you didn't even say no—not Macy's fault on this. It's completely yours."

I spun to face him. "Why couldn't you say no? You're too con-flict-avoidant to set boundaries with Jessica, afraid to rock the boat and have to deal with things that could—God forbid—take you away from your work or get messy."

"It's because of Macy. I have to think of her when—"

"Yes! And you should always think of her. All I ask is to be remem-bered too! I'm an afterthought. I'm the person whose gifts you have your assistant purchase. Why do I have to fight to be cared about?" I uncontrollably hiccuped at that last. Damn it. Hold it together, Felicity.

He stood slowly, and I watched his CEO face slide into place--the one he uses for difficult meetings or recalcitrant employees. "You're being dramatic, Felicity. I'll buy you another purse. A better one."

I walked to the other side of the kitchen, putting the island between us. After effectively stowing and pulling out the groceries over and over and fussing around, I realized I'd created a mess in the kitchen—a bit like my marriage, I guess. I looked at him and saw he was still standing in the same spot.

"I can't believe you think this is just about the purse?" I scoffed. "It's about you just not caring. You don't seem to care that you gave away something that was meant especially for me—a milestone gift, if you will. You don't even—you know what? You've never even bothered to figure out what I actually wanted. Instead, I had to tell you." I'm so aggravated that I can't even keep my thoughts focused.

I was back to moving things around aimlessly—slammed the cabinet door and was moving around the kitchen, unable to stop myself at this point. "Then finally I found something that I really wanted. I mean... God! I sent you the details. Didn't that tell you how much it would mean to me? And you thought so little of it. Of me. That you gave it away."

I stopped moving, faced my husband, and felt my head and shoulders just slump. "Caden, don't you understand that it's about being so low on your priority list that a child's whim matters more than your wife's birthday?"

"I told you, she found it and—"

"You don't get it. Or you don't care to get it. Husbands protect their wives' gifts. But you'd rather I be disappointed than have to deal with Macy being sad for a couple of minutes."

"That's not what this is—"

"It is. That's exactly what it is." I was defeated. "Why is it okay that I have to sacrifice? That I have to walk into my own home and see your daughter with my gift. And you didn't even think about how I'd feel. You didn't even think to ask her to put it away until she went home."

His silence was answer enough. He hadn't even considered it.

I turned away, unable to look at him anymore. I could see my reflection in the kitchen window. I looked haggard. My hair askew. Makeup smudged and running from my tears. My slacks from work were splattered with sauce. When had I become this woman? The one who accepted crumbs while everyone else got the whole cake?

"I'll get the purse back," he said finally. "I'll tell Macy I made a mistake."

"Don't bother." I looked at him. Really looked at my husband. "You want to traumatize her by taking back a gift from her daddy? You want to make her think it's somehow my issue that she can't have the gift? Better yet, you want to give me something that you gave someone else? What could possibly be worse now?"

"Then what do you want me to do?"

"It doesn't matter anymore. You can't right this boat, Caden. All I wanted was for you to think of me first. Just this once." I reached into the junk drawer, grabbed a handful of Reese's peanut butter cups, filled my water bottle up, and headed for the stairs, exhaustion settling into my bones. Fuck dinner. Why should I cook tonight after all of this? Chocolate will comfort me tonight—he sure as shit won't be.

"Where are you going?"

"Guest room."

"Felicity, come on. You're overreacting—"

I stopped on the third step, looking back at him standing in our mess of a kitchen. "You know what? That's the problem. You think my feelings are an overreaction," I sighed. "Honestly, I think I've run out of words at this point, Caden. I honestly don't know how else to help you understand. And I can't figure out why I have to try so hard. I can't for the life of me figure out how—you know what? In the last fifteen minutes of us arguing, you haven't even apologized. Not even once."

"I'm sorry, Felicity."

"Don't bother. Too little, too late. Loses its effect if I have to bring it to your attention."

I went to turn away and paused. I looked at my husband. Really looked at him. In my staring, he started to shift his feet, uncomfortably fidgeting. "Do me a favor, Caden. My birthday is in just about a week. Tell me how old I'll be."

The silence stretched between us. He opened and closed his mouth like a fish. Pathetic. Finally, he replied, "Of course I know how old you'll be. It's insulting you'd even ask."

"Forty," I said with a sigh. "I'll be forty. Can you make sure you tell Lauren it's a milestone birthday?" With as much sarcasm as I could muster up, I continued, "That way, when she goes out to panic-buy whatever she has to pick for my birthday this year, she'll get me something just super great."

I climbed the stairs, each step heavier than the last. The crinkle of wrappers sounding with every step. I heard him call my name. But I didn't turn back. There was nothing else to say tonight.

Sitting on the guest bed, I looked around the room. Cold and impersonal. Finally, I let the tears fall. It wasn't about the purse. It had never been about the purse. It was about being invisible in my own marriage.

Chapter 2: Reckoning

~Caden~

I sat back in my chair, staring at the screen in my home office but not even seeing the words. I'd come downstairs hours ago when, at around three in the morning, I finally gave up on sleep.

I watched the clock tick over to seven a.m. While I'd hoped work would be a distraction, it wasn't.

Forty. She was turning forty.

Shit. Where had the time gone? Why didn't I realize it was this year?

I stood there like an idiot, unable to answer the simplest question about my wife. How could I not remember her age—as much as I tried to play it off when we were talking, we both knew I didn't know. Instead, I sat there and tried to do the math—useless.

My wife. The woman I love. The woman I swore to cherish. FUCK. Forty is a big fucking deal.

And I forgot.

How? When did I become this man? I knew I wasn't exactly detail-oriented in our marriage, but how had it gotten this bad?

My phone lit up.

Jessica: Caden! The bag you got Macy is amazing. She showed me last night when she got home and won't stop talking about it! She's planning her whole first-day outfit around it.

I stared at the screen, nausea rolling through me.

The Dior bag had been perfect—for once, I'd actually gotten it right. I'd saved the screenshots Felicity had sent. Gone to the boutique myself. Spent an hour making sure it matched the one she wanted. The saleswoman had smiled like I was some kind of hero when I went in a couple weeks later to pick up the final customized product. "Someone's very lucky," she said in that singsong way while carefully wrapping it up.

Felicity told me once she didn't want perfect. Just effort. I'd forgotten that. This time when I got her gift, I felt proud. In reality though, I shouldn't have. What kind of asshole gets proud that he knows how to follow directions? I put zero effort into her gift aside from the minimum of getting what she asked for.

Then, when Macy found it—I hate even thinking about the memory, but the whole scene kept replaying in my head.

I'd been sitting in my office, dealing with final things in preparation for the week ahead. Felicity was at the store, and Macy was upstairs in her room.

I looked up from my work when I heard her come into my office, and I froze when she asked, "Daddy, what's this?"

She held up the exquisite gift bag from Dior.

"Where'd you get that, honey?" Dumb question—I knew where she found it. Even remembering it now, I hung my head in shame.

"It was in the back of my closet! I was looking for my old ballet shoes and found it." Before I knew it, she was pulling the purse out of the gift bag. She gasped, saying, "I love it!"

"That's—" I'd started to say it was Felicity's.

"It's amazing." Her face fell. "It's sort of like one that Mom has. She always gets nice things," she said with a shrug.

That line. She always gets the nice things. Does Macy not?

I'm sure confusion is written all over my face. "Don't you get nice things too, honey? From your mom?"

"Ummm...not really." Her eyes went wide. "Is that why it's here for me? So, I can have something nice for my first day of junior high?! I KNEW you'd think of something!"

I should have said no. That was my moment. Should've told her the truth. I'd hidden it in Macy's closet, thinking there's no way Felicity would go digging there. And to be honest, the bottom of my eleven-year-old's closet is like a cesspool—unsure when her old clothes, shoes, and everything in between had last been cleaned, I thought for sure it would keep for a couple weeks. Stupid. Just stupid. Clearly.

But she looked up at me with those green eyes that kill me every time.

"I've never had anything this beautiful. Sophia has something like it—but not as beautiful. Nothing's this beautiful," the last words merely a whisper in awe as she stroked the leather.

"See how it looks," I heard myself say. What? Why did I say that?

Her squeal filled my office. She strutted around like a runway model, practicing how she'd carry it.

"This is really for me, Daddy?! Like really, really?"

And I fucking caved. Like I always cave. Macy was so young when her mom and I divorced that I've basically always been a weekend dad to her. I know it's not enough. Guilt was a difficult thing to contend with. She's such a good kid. Rarely complains. So again, I'd heard myself respond—almost like an out-of-body experience.

"Sure, sweetheart. It's for your first day. A new school can be scary, so I thought this could help."

Every word out of my mouth made it worse—I'm essentially rubbernecking at my own train wreck.

And now, here I am—sitting in a dark office alone. My wife is asleep in the guest room—definitely not speaking to me.

I don't know how to fix this.

I searched the Dior site again. That bag was a limited edition. Custom order only. I'd had to plan ahead for once.

I dropped my head to the desk—hard. Pain radiated straight through my skull. I deserved it.

I felt the buzz of my phone reverberate through my skull.

Jessica: BTW, can you do me a favor and pick up Macy tomorrow? Brad and I have something with a house showing, and I can't make it.

A week ago, I would've said yes. Would've rearranged my whole day to make it work. I only get to see Macy on the weekends, so if the chance comes up to pick her up, I take it. Even if I have to work, I've brought her back to the office—me doing work, her doing her homework.

Not now, though.

Me: No.

Jessica: WTF, Caden? Seriously? Since when do you say no?

Jessica: Well—since Macy needs things for school that you don't cover, I have to do extra work. This wouldn't happen if you weren't so stingy with support payments.

Me: We have a custody agreement. I pay what we agreed to.

Jessica: Required minimums don't cover reality, Caden. Do you know what private school costs these days? Her activities? Her clothes? Brad and I are drowning here while you live in your nice house with your perfect wife.

Jessica: Plus, Brad's business is going through a rough patch. Construction permits are taking forever and we're carrying debt we can't afford. I can't keep asking him to cover Macy's expenses when his company is struggling.

Me: If money's that tight, maybe we should talk about adjusting support.

Jessica: Don't patronize me. We'll figure it out.

I shut off my phone and opened my laptop. I can't deal with Jessica's BS right now with everything going on.

New email from Lauren. Perfect.

~~~To: Caden Barrett (CBarrett@BandRConsulting.com)From: Lauren Chase (LChase1@BandRConsulting.com)Subject: Flowers for Felicity's BirthdayMr. Barrett—Confirming flowers are scheduled for delivery to Felicity's office for tomorrow. I ordered a beautiful bouquet that should last the week for her birthday. I know you mentioned getting her gift this year. Is there anything else I can do to help?Regards, Lauren~~~

God. The flowers. I'm sure she'll burn them the second they arrive. I opened the email to reply.
~~~

~~~To: Lauren Chase (LChase1@BandRConsulting.com)From: Caden Barrett (CBarrett@BandRConsulting.com)Subject: Re: Flowers for Felicity's BirthdayMe: Can you cancel? I should be handling the flowers myself. Can you send me everything you've given Felicity over the years—every gift, reservation, note you've kept. And anything you know about my wife's preferences. All of it.~~~

Lauren responded instantly.

~~~To: Caden Barrett (CBarrett@BandRConsulting.com)From: Lauren Chase (LChase1@BandRConsulting.com)Subject: Re: Flowers for Felicity's BirthdayIs everything alright? Did I make a mistake? Please see attached preliminary file. I will provide the full detailed file tomorrow when I get to the office. —Lauren~~~

I fired off a response.

~~~To: Lauren Chase (LChase1@BandRConsulting.com)From: Caden Barrett (CBarrett@BandRConsulting.com)Subject: Re: Flowers for Felicity's BirthdayMe: No. Just send it.—Caden ~~~

The file was... embarrassing.

Turns out I've been having my assistant manage my marriage. Birthday gifts: always jewelry, always from the same two stores.

Anniversary: spa packages or weekend trips... most of which I probably canceled

Flowers: white roses, calla lilies, and wildflowers in the summer. Monthly rotational order signed "Love, Caden."

Restaurants: her five favorites, rotated on schedule

Additional Preferences: Chardonnay, Reese's Peanut Butter Cups, likes country music, not a fan of surprises

Not a fan of surprises. When did I stop trying to surprise her?

I scrolled further.

Reservation at new French place for next month—her suggestion.

Sent flowers for her promotion.

Disappointed with the tennis bracelet—try something else next time, include a gift receipt.
~~~

Disappointed. My wife was disappointed in a gift she received, and Lauren knew it. She was preparing a backup plan. Because I didn't know her well enough to get it right. Was it the gift she didn't like? Or the fact that it wasn't actually from me? And she knew it.

Ping. Another email from Lauren.

~~~To: Caden Barrett (CBarrett@BandRConsulting.com)From: Lauren Chase (LChase1@BandRConsulting.com)Subject: Re: Flowers for Felicity's Birthday

I should mention—Felicity's had a difficult quarter. The merger has been stressful. She's mentioned wanting a vacation.~~~

Even my assistant knew she needed a break.

When had I stopped asking her how things were going?

Regret broke my heart. I thought about her when I stood in the kitchen. Her shoulders were slumped—defeated. Voice quiet. "I've run out of words, Caden."

She was right when she called me out for not even apologizing. I'd been too wrapped up in my thoughts—thinking about Macy's happiness and my own defensiveness.

I picked up my phone. Scrolled through our texts.

Me at various times—"Running late." "In a meeting." "Order without me." "Lauren will handle it." "Can you pick up my dry cleaning?"

I sighed. I'm an asshole.

Then, I looked over responses or impromptu messages. Even the tone was different: "Love you," "Thinking of you," "Miss you," "Don't forget—dinner with my sister Saturday."I'd forgotten about the dinner months ago when Maliyah was up visiting from Florida.

"Fuck." The word echoed in the empty office.

I opened a browser.

How to apologize when sorry isn't enough... Romantic gestures for milestone birthdays... How to be a better husband...How to tell your kid no

Useless. Nothing useful for this specific kind of failure.
~~~

I pulled up the Dior website again. That perfect, powder-beige bag stared back like it knew exactly what it had ruined.

Macy's face lit up when she tried it on. She'd felt so grown up. But Felicity's face when she saw it on Macy—that was the look that's going to haunt me.

At work, I don't second-guess my decisions. At home? I bend. I soften. I let things slide in the name of peace and forgiveness for not being a full-time dad.

I grabbed my phone again and opened my messages with Felicity.

Me: I know you don't want to hear from me. But I love you. I heard you. I love you. I'll do better — «Delete»

Me: I'm going to fix this. I know — «Delete»

Me: I'm sorry. She just looked so happy wi — «Delete»

What could I possibly say in a text? I didn't even know what I wanted to say yet.

I had less than a week until she turned forty.

Mere days to figure this out.

Just days to become the husband she deserves instead of the one I've been.

Time to learn who Caden Barrett really is and what he stands for.

And maybe more importantly—

Time to humble myself. I refuse to lose the love of my life.

Me: *I love you* — «Send»

Chapter 3: Storm Warning

~FELICITY~

I woke up to a quiet that was so soundless it was almost deafening.

No footsteps. No voices. No TV. No clinking bowls in the kitchen.

I shivered. Why did we have two vents in this room? The AC had been running all night, blasting cold that hit me from head to toe. Matching the way I felt inside. There weren't enough blankets in the world to warm me last night. I thought of my sister and her constant need to be cold—the room was the perfect temperature for her.

I sat up, looking around the space. I'd furnished this room a few years ago. The bedding was muted blue and seemed dull now. The walls were dove gray with white trim. The furniture was a matching solid wood set painted gray. I'd loved it when I had made this room up. Now it just felt sterile—almost like a hospital room.

I shook my head. I needed to redecorate. I hate it now. Cold and impersonal. It was like a metaphor for what had become of my marriage.

I showered, dressed, put my face on. I felt almost restless instead of rested, but at least I looked passable. It would have to do.

When I went downstairs, Caden was already at the kitchen table. Laptop open, coffee in hand. Staring at the screen. He looked completely unfazed, like nothing had happened. Like we hadn't torn each other apart the night before.

He looked up. "Hey. You sleep okay?"

I didn't answer. I just looked at him and turned, walked to the coffeepot, and poured a cup.

There was a beat of silence before he tried again. "You working from the office today?"

"Yes."

"You need anything this morning?"

Yeah—for you not to have fucked up yesterday. But I held back. I didn't say it—he can thank me later. Instead, I just remained silent.

He leaned back in his chair. Clearly, my silence said enough since he didn't follow his question up.

The Dior purse was gone. Macy had obviously taken it with her when she left for Jessica's last night. I'm guessing she will probably never let it out of her sight. I wouldn't if it were mine—wait, it actually is mine. The gut punch I felt just thinking about it caught me off guard. I felt tears spring to my eyes. It's not about the purse, Felicity. It's not about the purse. I exhaled—okay... it's a little about the purse.

I took a sip of my coffee and turned to him. "You still taking Macy to that school thing this weekend?" I asked.

"Yeah. The ice cream social."

I nodded. "Good."

Another stretch of silence. I waited for him to catch on. Needless to say, he didn't.

I stared at him, waiting for the words that should have tumbled out of his mouth: "No, Felicity, I'm so sorry I completely fucked up already, and I know how much I need to make it up to you. So, I called Jess to take her because it's your DAMN BIRTHDAY and I'd rather DIE than drag you to a sticky-fingered kids' ice cream social when you should be wearing something devastating in a restaurant where the wine costs more than my first car." But did he say that? Nope.

The silence stretched between us like a rubber band about to snap. And his face remained blank. Oblivious. Fucking clueless.

I put my mug down and reached for a granola bar from the cabinet. Putting the bar in my purse, I stared at it. *Fuck it*—I reached back into the cabinet and grabbed the whole box. I looked him dead in the eye as I dumped all twelve bars into my bag. No idea why. I just didn't feel like sharing, and I wanted him to know. I dropped the empty box on the counter, still looking him in the eyes. *Take that!* Fuck, I feel petty. But. I. Don't. Care.

"You're not going to talk to me?" he asked.

"I am talking."

"Felicity—come on."

"What do you want me to say, Caden?" I looked at him. "That everything's fine? Say something to make this easier on you? My voice cracked slightly on the last word, betraying the exhaustion that had settled deep in my bones. I think I've done that enough."

I leaned against the counter and continued, "Cade, you screwed up. And I'm not going to sugarcoat it. It's not just a purse and I'm not just being dramatic. That's it. Full stop."

He shook his head. "That's not what I meant."

"It's what you said—just last night, in fact."

Silence.

I put my mug in the sink, hand lingering on the ceramic. "Look. I have meetings all day." I turned halfway toward the door, then back to him. "I'll be home for dinner." I paused, swallowing hard. "Or I won't. I don't know." My voice softened despite myself. "I'll let you know." I reached for my keys, gripping them until the metal bit into my palm. "Or maybe not."

I walked toward the door.

"I said I'm sorry," he added.

I stopped. "You said it after I told you to. And even then, you looked like you were swallowing glass. And honestly, sorry just doesn't cut it."

He stood up and made to move closer, approaching carefully and tentatively—like I was a wild animal. Damn straight I'm a wild animal—and he should definitely be approaching with extreme caution.

"I didn't mean for any of it to go that way," he finally said as he stopped walking. Good. I think he could tell I was two seconds from losing it on him.

"No, Caden. That's the problem. You didn't mean for anything. You didn't plan. You didn't think. You just reacted like you always do." I opened the door. "I've got to go."

"Felicity—"

"Nope...I'm not doing this now."

I stepped out into the warm air, my hand sitting on the doorknob. For a second, I pictured myself slamming it—the satisfying crash, the way the frame would shudder. Instead, I eased it shut with a soft click that felt both like restraint and surrender. Even now, I couldn't decide if I was being reasonable, avoidant, or whatever.

The elevator doors slid open with a whoosh, and I stepped out onto the twenty-second floor of BAC Banking International. Everyone knows that Mondays have a certain feel to them, and today felt like every ounce of Monday it possibly could. The hum of gossip, the clacking of keyboards, the smell of burned coffee already told me I was behind. I knew stopping for a venti latte would make me late—but honestly, I didn't care.

I forced a smile that felt like a bandage over a bruise and headed toward my office. My lips twitched at the corners, threatening to collapse. Part of me wanted to scream about it to anyone who would listen—make them understand the magnitude of his betrayal. Another part whispered that I was overreacting to a luxury accessory, that there were marriages surviving far worse. Both voices drowned in the relentless loop playing in my head: He gave my birthday gift to Macy... My customized, stupidly-expensive, ridiculously extravagant bag—to his eleven-year-old daughter who probably wouldn't even appreciate it.

"Morning, Felicity." Callie, our newly hired project manager and analyst, said as she handed me a stack of briefs. I haven't had much time to get to know her, but she seemed nice—if not a bit annoying. "Ethan asked if you'd swing by his office when you have a sec."

Of course, he did. I don't know if I have the energy to deal with nice people today.

I thanked her and headed for my office, dropping my tote beside the credenza. The Boston skyline was visible through my floor-to-ceiling windows, sunlight gleaming off towers and rooftops. The foot traffic below buzzed with movement, people going somewhere, doing something. I loved this city. I loved this office. Just standing inside it reminded me of how hard I'd worked to get here.

I blew out a breath and started to unpack my bag. Laptop. Files. An unnecessary quantity of baked goods to accompany my latte. I laughed softly when I pulled out the selection of granola bars. What the hell was I supposed to do with all these? They weren't Reese's, so the reality was they only had so much value. Reese's, I'd gladly go up a size for today. I tossed everything into my desk drawer where my stash of sweets usually landed for snacking, and connected my laptop to the docking station. All three monitors blinked to life.

Finally—something I could control.

A soft knock at my open door pulled me from my inbox—three rapid taps, hesitant but deliberate, the sound of knuckles against wood cutting through the artificial quiet of my sanctuary. I sighed, the exhale carrying the weight of more than a hundred unread emails and the impatience to go along with it.

"Knock-knock."

Ethan Hayes leaned against the frame, his crisp white shirt sleeves rolled precisely three turns up his forearms, revealing tanned skin stretched over the kind of defined muscle that comes from actual rock climbing, not just gym sessions. A thick silver watch glinted against his wrist bone. Most of the office called him McSteamy behind his back, and they weren't subtle about the way "work husband" rolled off their tongues whenever we collaborated. The office gossip mill thrived on speculation I had no interest in feeding.

I nodded toward the guest chair. "You summoned?"

"I did." He grinned, but his expression softened the longer he looked at me. "But first—happy early birthday. I know it's not until the end of the week, but I leave tomorrow for that conference, so I'll be out of the office, and I didn't want to miss the chance."

My pulse stumbled. My birthday wasn't exactly my favorite subject this week. "Thank you. But really, you didn't need to do anything. It's just another year."

Ethan tilted his head, one brow arched. "Just another year? It's not every day you turn twenty-one for the nineteenth time."

Without waiting for permission, he placed a small, carefully wrapped package on my desk—simple brown paper, tied with twine.

"Ethan..."

"Just open it."

I unwrapped it slowly. Inside was a worn—but in great condition—first edition of "*The Handmaid's Tale*"—the book I'd mentioned loving during our coffee conversation weeks ago. "You said it changed how you thought about storytelling," Ethan said quietly, looking almost shy. "I found this at an estate sale last weekend. The previous owner made notes in the margins, but nothing crazy—I thought you might find them interesting."

He rubbed the back of his neck. "Though now I'm second-guessing myself. Maybe you think that's annoying? I should have asked first. Open the front though?"

I opened the cover carefully. His handwriting was on the inside flap: *"For someone who sees the world in stories. —E"*

"This is..." I traced the aged pages. "This is perfect. But you didn't need to—"

"I know I didn't need to. I wanted to."

He sounded a little nervous, but there's no way he could know that the words were hitting me harder than he probably intended. Because all at once, the contrast was sharp: this man—this colleague—noticed the details my husband didn't. He paid attention. He remembered. He saw me.

I blinked quickly again, trying to pull back the tears that I felt coming. I closed the cover before my face gave too much away. "It's... wow. It's incredible. Thank you, but it's too much, Ethan."

He shrugged, but his eyes held more weight than his tone. "You're welcome, and it isn't too much. It's a big birthday."

I sniffed a bit and busied myself with sorting out the tissue paper, bag, and contents.

Then he asked: "Hey, is everything okay?"

"Of course," I said—too fast. I reached for the stack of files on my desk and straightened them like they needed organizing. "In other news, how's house-hunting?"

He accepted the redirect without a fight. "I saw a three-bedroom yesterday with ceilings so low I could barely stand upright in the kitchen. Apparently, that's a 'historic feature.'"

We bantered a little, both of us pretending the energy between us hadn't shifted with the opening of a book.

I gave him a grateful smile. "Thanks, Ethan. Really."

The rest of the day blurred. Meetings. Audits. A crisis-consult with a department head who thought yelling counted as leadership. Another who thought they could fire someone without consulting with HR first.

Normally, I thrived on cleaning up other people's messes. But today, my mind kept drifting to the raw markings under my wedding ring from where I'd been twisting it the night before—trying to ground myself with every turn.

At noon, I escaped to the lobby café. Another coffee with an extra shot. Quiet corner. Emails.

One reminder notification popped up: Dining reservation for two: Antico Forno. 7 p.m.

My heart stuttered. Dammit—I'd forgotten about our dinner plans. Part of me wanted to see him try to make things right, to show up with that earnest look he gets when he's truly sorry. Another part wanted to cancel, to make him feel even a fraction of the disappointment I've been feeling. Would he try to turn it into some sort of apology? Guilt dinner? Or would we just pretend everything was fine, like we always did?

I tapped the screen to open it, but I didn't delete it. I didn't cancel either. I just...let it sit there. Like the recent state of our marriage.

"Hiya," Callie said as she slid into the seat across from me, setting down her quinoa breakfast bowl with its artful arrangement of kale, avocado slices, and what looked like pomegranate seeds scattered like tiny rubies across the top. The earthy scent of it made my nose wrinkle—gross. Give me the sugary comfort of maple syrup pooling around a stack of pancakes or the buttery embrace of a croissant any day.

"Hmmmm," I said, voice disinterested.

I checked my watch three times in two minutes, but Callie kept talking. Part of me wanted to snap at her to leave me alone, while another part craved the distraction from my thoughts. I nodded at something she said about her weekend plans, hating myself a little for the relief I felt when she finally glanced at her phone and mentioned our upcoming meeting.

I checked my watch one final time, relief flooding through me at the excuse to escape. "We should head back upstairs," I said, already gathering my things.

The day dr*agge*d, but I survived it.

By four-thirty, thunderclouds had littered the sky. I shut down my laptop and packed up slowly, dread rising inside me. The dinner reservation still blinked on my calendar like a countdown I couldn't stop.

When I stepped out of my office, Ethan was waiting by the elevators, umbrella in hand. My stomach tightened—both pleased and unsettled to see him there.

"Heading out?" At my nod, he said, "Let me walk you down. Forecast says cats and dogs." While his joke fell flat, it still made me smile—hating how easily the gesture came, how I couldn't decide if I wanted him to leave me alone or stay exactly where he was.

We rode the elevator in silence. In the mirrored walls, our reflections stood side-by-side: his loose charm, my stiff shoulders. He spoke just before the doors opened. "You know, some people don't see what's right in front of them. That's their loss."

His words landed like a stone in still water. I blinked. Had I been that transparent? "Thank you," I managed, the syllables sticking in my throat. For the book? For seeing me when I felt unseen?

He raised the umbrella over both of us and walked me around the building and to the garage where I'd parked my car. I slipped inside, smiled, and nodded my thanks. Pulling out of the garage, I looked in the rearview mirror and saw he was still standing there. Watching. Waiting.

My phone dinged, and CarPlay reminded me of the dinner reservation—should I go?

But the question felt bigger than that.

It wasn't about dinner. It was about whether I still believed there was something left worth salvaging.

I didn't know what to do.

I watched the reminder fade from the screen as my finger tapped it away, then merged into traffic with no destination in mind.

Chapter 4: Stop Coasting

~Caden~

I arrived at work before anyone else had come in, badge tapping against the scanner with a mechanical beep. The floor was quiet, and I was glad for the silence.

I grabbed a black coffee and went straight to my office, not even bothering to check my phone. I already knew there were no new texts from Felicity. Not that I expected one. I hadn't earned one.

I sat at my desk, staring at the screen without seeing it. After about an hour, my assistant arrived, and I heard her moving around her desk and the area. Once she was settled, I pressed the intercom—time to face the music.

"Lauren? You around?"

"Yep. Be right there."

She walked in moments later, tablet in hand, eyebrows slightly raised. All business. Lauren is amazing. I stole her from my former boss when I started B&R Consulting. She had been working for him already for fifteen years when he retired. Rather than let her get away, I begged her to come with me to start my own firm.

Lauren has been my assistant now for over a decade, and I couldn't live without her. She's a grandma three times over now, I think, and right now I have a feeling like she may wring my neck.

"Everything okay?"

"No, can we go over a few things?"

She nodded, taking the chair across from my desk.

"I need to go through everything. All the personal stuff. Felicity's birthdays, anniversaries, flower deliveries—everything you've helped me with."

Lauren blinked. "You want a full rundown?"

"Yeah. No filters."

She was studying me for a beat before pulling up a file on her tablet. "Okay. You ready?"

"As I'll ever be."

I watched her scrolling. "Alright. You got the file I sent you yesterday, right?"

I winced. "Yes—let's go beyond that."

"Okay—let's start with her birthdays since hers is so soon. I've helped with buying her gift for the last three years. First year, you got her diamond studs. Second year, Tiffany pendant. Then the silk scarf. Last year was a Saks Fifth Avenue gift card because you didn't confirm sizing in time on the long-line coat that she'd mentioned being interested in."

"I gave my wife store credit for her birthday?"

"You did," she said, evenly.

I dragged a hand over my face, rubbing the stubble along my jaw. "Jesus."

"Anniversaries have mostly been spa packages or dinners. You canceled dinner two years in a row—once for the Houston trip, once because Macy had a fever. The spa was booked out by the time I tried to rebook."

"I remember the fever. I don't remember canceling dinner."

"You did. I called her myself the following Monday to help with rescheduling."

There was a lump rising in my throat. I sighed.

"She's never complained or said anything negative about any of the gifts or cancellations—at least not to me." Lauren said gently.

There was a long silence.

"Keep going."

Lauren hesitated. "You want me to review Jessica's gifts too?"

My eyebrows lifted. "Jessica's gifts? You've sent Jessica gifts?"

"Yes." She looked at me like I'm an idiot. "You asked me a while back to keep things cordial. Gifts from Macy for holidays and milestones. Nothing too big, but still meaningful—your words."

"And?"

"And... last year, for her fortieth, I sent a Cartier desk clock."

I blinked. "You what?"

"She turned forty. You were in New York, I think. You told me to handle it and do something special from Macy."

"A fucking Cartier clock?" My voice cracked as I leaned forward, knuckles white against the desk edge. "You're telling me I bought my ex-wife—my EX-wife—a goddamn luxury timepiece that costs probably more than a grand? For fuck's sake."

She flinched at my tone but recovered quickly, squaring her shoulders. "The receipt is in the system if you'd like to see it. You told me to handle it and didn't specify a price range."

I leaned back in my chair, stunned. "So Jessica got a Cartier clock, and Felicity got a Saks gift card and a recycled spa package?"

Lauren didn't respond right away. Then: "You want to tell me what's going on?"

"Complete fuck up."

Lauren's spine straightened, her lips pressing into a thin line as she clutched her tablet tighter. "I beg your pardon?"

My voice was low now. "No—not you. Me." I dug my fingers into my forehead trying to rub away the headache that was building. I couldn't meet Lauren's eyes. "Yesterday—like a moron—I gave Felicity's birthday gift to Macy when she saw it and thought it was meant for her. God, the look on Macy's face—she was so happy. But Felicity..." I swallowed hard, the memory of my wife's expression flashing before me. "Then, to top it off, I forgot how old Felicity was turning. Forty. It's forty. How could I forget that?"

I leaned my head back, squeezing my eyes shut. "And meanwhile, my ex-wife is sitting in her office checking the time on Cartier throughout her day." Bitterness flowed through me.

Yes, she's Macy's mom, but Cartier? What's next—a private island for her half-birthday? I don't remember 'luxury timepieces' being in the 'nothing too big, but meaningful' list of possible gifts.

"I'm sorry—can we go back? Did you say you gave Felicity's gift away? The custom-made purse?"

I exhaled, the sound hollow in my chest. "Yes—not on purpose. I mentioned that Macy found the bag. What I didn't mention is that I'd hidden it in her closet, behind all the crap she's collected over the years. I figured it would be safe there for the couple of days she'd be home."

I sighed, thinking it through. "What eleven-year-old goes digging in their closet? Mine, of course—since it just so happened she needed her ballet shoes." I rubbed my temples, feeling the headache pulsing beneath my fingertips. "But then she walks into my office and pulls out the bag—this stunning Dior bag in all its effing glory." I groaned. "Lauren, she was going on about how perfect it was. She was so happy. I just couldn't find the words to say no."

Lauren crossed her legs and narrowed her eyes. "And you thought your wife would just... what? Understand?"

I held up my hands, preemptively. "I know. She saw it when she walked in and actually dropped the groceries on the floor. There was Macy with the bag. And Macy started talking to her about how happy she was—even thanked Felicity, thinking the gift was from both of us. Fuck, what a mess. Then once Macy went upstairs... she let me have it. Deservedly."

Lauren's expression dialed back from pissed-off mom to deeply disappointed. Her voice softened, but not by much. "Listen, Caden—I haven't said anything before. I wasn't really sure it was my place. But I think it's time. After thirty years, with Mark, I've learned that if you stop showing up, the other person stops waiting."

I didn't even try to argue. There was no venom in her tone—just truth. Truth, I hadn't wanted to see.

"She said she's run out of words," I murmured.

"I'd say she's earned that right," Lauren said, leaning forward. "She's out of words, Caden. What Felicity needs isn't another promise or explanation—it's action. Show her that she matters."

I stared at the desk—jaw tight.

"You want to fix it?" Lauren asked.

I nodded slowly, feeling a painful ache spread through my chest. "I do. God, I do. I love her more than anything—I just... I'm terrified of it being too late."

"Well," she said, walking to the door. "You've got the week to prove it's not. I'd start there."

She paused, hand on the doorframe. "And for the love of God—don't delegate this to me. I believe in you. You love her. You've got this."

She walked out.

I was rubbing my eyes when her head popped back in again.

"One more thing—freebie. You've got dinner reservations tonight. Antico Forno, 7 p.m. I booked it a month ago—an anniversary makeup, just in case. Based on what you've told me, I doubt she'll show, but maybe you can figure out a way to make it count—If you've got it in you."

She paused at the door, then turned back with a slight frown.

"Actually, there is one more thing. Has Jessica been asking you about work lately?" I looked up from my desk. "Not really. Why?"

"She called here last week. Said she was trying to reach you about Macy's school schedule, but then she started asking questions about our clients. How business was going, whether we were busy this quarter." Lauren's expression grew concerned. "It felt... off."

"What did you tell her?"

"Nothing specific, obviously. I told her she'd need to discuss business matters with you directly. Probably nothing, but it felt weird.

I felt an uncomfortable twist in my stomach but pushed it aside. "Probably just making conversation. You know how she is."

"Maybe." Lauren didn't look convinced, but she shrugged. "She also asked if you still travel a lot for work. Even overnight. Whether you're ever out of town overnight."

"Could be it was because of her wanting us to take Macy maybe? But if it happens again and it still feels off, then just let me know."

"Will do." Lauren paused at the door, then turned back. "Actually, there was one more thing. She asked about our expense reimbursement process—how quickly we turn around travel expenses, whether receipts go directly to accounting or through me first, that sort of thing."

"Our reimbursement process? Why?"

"She said Brad's company was looking to implement a new system for their employees. Wanted to know how we handle things—do you submit expenses as you go or in batches, how long approval takes, whether we require original receipts." Lauren shrugged. "It seemed like a lot of detail for casual conversation, but maybe she was just being thorough for Brad."

I felt that uncomfortable twist in my stomach again. "What did you tell her?"

"The basics—that you usually submit monthly, that I process them and send to accounting, standard turnaround is about a week. Nothing confidential, but..." She trailed off.

"But?"

"I don't know. It just felt like such a strange conversation, you know? She was definitely focused and paying close attention."

"Yeah. Thanks Lauren. Keep me posted on anything else, okay?"

"Will do." And with that, she was gone.

I stared at the empty doorway for a moment, sitting in the silence—Lauren's words echoing in my head. Really though, Jessica is a problem for another day.

Right now, I need to focus on my wife. I need to worry more about figuring out where shit went wrong with us.

A memory hit me like a punch to the gut. Three years ago. We had the issue with the Pemberton contract.

Felicity had planned our anniversary dinner—not Lauren. Mistral at 6:30. I could still picture her that morning, humming while she got ready for work, mentioning how much she was looking forward to our evening.

Then at 4 PM, Pemberton's CFO called. The contract we'd been counting on—the one that represented nearly thirty percent of our annual revenue—was being slashed. They had reevaluated their office space with most of their workforce moving to remote. This meant their construction partnerships needed review and our bids for the new builds and renovations were being reconsidered. No capital for the space? No money for planned contracts.

I'd sat in my office doing the math. While we would retain the existing Pemberton work, most of those jobs were coming to an end. Losing the future contracts meant having to lay off Jake and several newer guys. I remember that Jake and his wife had just had twins.

When Pemberton's team said they could meet that evening to discuss salvaging part of the contract before they presented to their Board first thing in the morning—maybe keeping us on for specialized work instead of general construction—I didn't hesitate.

I'd called Felicity within a few minutes of getting off the phone with their CFO.

"Honey, I'm really sorry, I have to cancel tonight."

"Cancel?" The disappointment in her voice was immediate. "Caden, it's our anniversary."

"I know, I know. Emergency client meeting. I'll make it up to you, I promise."

"But I already—" She'd stopped herself. "Okay. Sure. I get it."

"I'm so sorry, honey."

"Yeah, okay. I have to go. I'll see you at home."

She'd hung up. I'd told myself she understood. That she knew how important this was.

I realize now that by not telling her why, I'd completely failed in that moment. I'd never explained how that meeting meant keeping a significant amount of revenue. That we were still bleeding money from the pandemic shutdowns, that this contract was the difference between keeping people employed and laying off several of our workforce. I didn't give her the chance to understand or even help me figure out another solution.

I'd saved part of the contract—managed to keep us on for the specialty millwork and high-end finishes. It meant only having to let go of one subcontractor and one employee versus the several that may have been impacted otherwise.

Meanwhile, Felicity had gone home and spent our anniversary alone.

When I'd gotten home at midnight, she was already asleep. The next morning, things had been fine with her. She asked how the meeting went and said she understood. She kissed me good morning, I apologized again but she brushed it off and never mentioned her disappointment again.

Looking back, I realize I'd let her brush it off. I'd been so relieved she wasn't angry that I'd never bothered to explain the details. I never told her I'd been trying to save people's jobs during the worst economic crisis of our lifetime. I failed to read between the lines and avoided instead of confronting the issue.

And then, I can't remember even having a makeup dinner. I may have—Lauren may even have scheduled it, but I honestly can't remember if we ended up celebrating at all. Damn it. I've been killing our marriage with a thousand paper cuts. Every forgotten anniversary, every missed dinner, every delegated gift—they weren't just disappointments. They were betrayals. My God, I broke her heart one forgotten event at a time.

Time to stop being the man she resents—and figure out how to become the one she remembers loving. Time to make damn sure she knows how much that man still loves her.

I thought about calling my brother Cash or maybe Danny or one of my other cousins for help—the Barretts and Doyles had always been there for each other during crisis moments. I pushed the thought away though. They all had a tendency to take over and this was something I needed to handle myself first before I bring in any reinforcements.

To start, I sent her a text, knowing I wouldn't get anything in response—not that I was owed one.

Me: We have reservations tonight. I know you probably won't come, but I'll be there regardless, just in case.

Me: I'm sorry. I know I haven't done a good job of showing it, but you are my heart.

Chapter 5: Left Waiting

~CADEN~

I sat at the back table of Antico Forno, alone, nursing my Pellegrino. With growing certainty moving through my bones, I knew she wasn't coming. In truth, I knew it before I even sat down, but I had to be sure. And I couldn't not be here in case she did show.

The server checked in—twice. I waved him off with a polite "just a few more minutes," though part of me wanted to admit defeat, to say, "She's not coming" out loud. He nodded and walked away, his eyes flickering between sympathy and judgment. I couldn't decide which was worse, or which I deserved more.

This reservation, while originally a makeup anniversary dinner, was now something else. A Hail Mary.

I watched the door for thirty-three minutes. Every time it opened, I looked up. Every time it wasn't her, my gut twisted tighter.

The couple at the table next to me was enjoying their dinner and each other's company. She kept reaching across to squeeze his hand, and he kept making her laugh. They looked like us, once.

Fuck, we used to grab dinner here all the time. It was a favorite spot when we were dating, then early in our marriage we found other places, but this was still a date night win. That was back before some of our special occasions got lost in the murkiness of my tunnel vision at work.

Sure, we still had date nights—pizza runs, quick Mexican—but the real occasions? They always got pushed to the sidelines.

I could almost see us at that corner table by the window—our usual spot back then. There was one time when Felicity wore this green dress, the one that made her eyes stand out—they were mesmerizing.

We'd been talking about something work-related, for the life of me I can't remember. I'm not even sure I was paying too much attention—probably something about someone doing something stupid at work…HR problems as usual. I just remember losing myself in her eyes.

I vaguely recall reminding her of how brilliant she was. I'd reached across to steal her hands from her wine glass, her playing with my fingers as we interlaced them.

She'd blushed—God, I loved making her blush. I'd lifted her hand to kiss her knuckles. She'd turned her hand and cupped my cheek.

We'd been interrupted by the server—making her blush even harder and reach for her wine.

For hours, we'd sat and talked. Drank and ate more food than any reasonable person should. I'm sure that we probably shut the place down since that wasn't uncommon when we came here.

I had glimpses of us leaving, an indistinct memory of a time when I was kissing her behind the restaurant—almost fuzzy with the picture in my mind, probably from the wine at the time, or because it was a frequent result of the many dinners we'd had here.

I can actually see her nails in my mind—pink polish. Funny how I can remember that. I can picture her glow, cheeks ablaze and eyes unfocused. Couldn't remember her age on demand, but today I could remember her fucking nail polish color.

I sighed, our sex life was great, but when was the last time I'd made Felicity glow? When was the last time she felt like the center of my universe? The last time I'd told her she was brilliant and then set about proving it to her.

I couldn't remember.

I sat alone now, the white tablecloth stretched before me like an empty canvas. Same restaurant, warm brick walls and flickering candles—but the man reflected back at me in the black screen of my phone as I checked the time felt like a stranger.

My thoughts were cut off when the server approached my table and asked if he could help me with anything—again.

"Can I get a few things to go?"

He looked eager to move me along. "Sure. Anything in particular?"

I ordered all of Felicity's favorites. The spinach gnocchi, the eggplant she used to insist no one made better. A side of broccoli rabe she always asked them to char it a little extra. And for dessert—instead of ordering here, I'll plan to pick up some cannoli from Modern.

As he walked away, I sat for another moment, imagining what this dinner could've been if I'd manned up sooner. If I'd seen her—really seen her—before she reached the end of her rope.

But this wasn't about what could've been. It was about what came next.

The drive home was quiet—no music. No phone calls. Just me and my thoughts.

I walked into a dark house when I got back, flipping lights on as I moved from room to room. The living room sat empty, and the hallway echoed with my footsteps. I made my way through to the kitchen, where the empty countertops gleamed cold under the sudden bright lights.

I unpacked the food carefully, transferring it to plates. The ones we chose when we got married. The matte ceramic ones she insisted were "modern but timeless." She was right. About those. About a lot.

One place setting that I put to warm in the oven. A glass with her favorite wine.

I didn't know when she would be home, so I set out candles and laid the lighter next to them. I may be an idiot, but at least I wouldn't burn our house down.

I didn't sit down. Didn't linger. Just folded the letter I wrote, slid it under the white dessert box where I'd written "Check the oven" on top, and left it all for her.

I wasn't asking for forgiveness. I wasn't demanding attention. I was simply leaving for her what should have been there all along—recognition, and the words I'd failed to give a voice when I should have.

Then I went upstairs to bed.

~Felicity~I didn't mean to get home so late. I'd left work without a plan—just a need to move, to not be home when the reservation time came and went. I parked by Carson Beach and walked around Castle Island until the dusk stole the light. I even drove the long way back on purpose.

By the time I unlocked the door, it was nearly nine. The house was quiet. But not empty.

The smell hit first—warm, rich, unmistakable—Italian. I blinked, stepped farther in. The light from the dining room spilled low across the floor. I turned the corner and stopped.

On the table there was a glass of wine. A pastry box that told me to look in the oven. From the oven, I pulled out one of our wedding plates. It was covered with all my favorites from Antico's—gnocchi, broccoli rabe, eggplant. I felt a sarcastic edge in my mind, thinking, well, at least he remembered that.

And under the dessert box I recognized from Modern Pastry—ten bucks says there are a couple of cannoli in there—sat a folded slip of paper with my name on it.

I picked it up with careful fingers, already bracing for too little, too late. As I opened the letter, I took a sip of wine and reached for my fork. May as well eat while I read. Heartbreak didn't mean I had to let this go to waste! On second thought, screw the fork—I'll start with the cannoli—a hands-on activity. Then I'll worry about adding in some vegetables after with the eggplant.

Felicity—

I know I've let you down. I know that showing up late doesn't undo what I've already broken.

I don't expect this to fix things. I just wanted to offer something quiet. Something without pressure. A table with your name on it, because you deserve that. You've always deserved that.

I forgot what matters. Somewhere between late office hours and broken promises, I let the most important thing in my life become an afterthought. I see that now. God, how I wish I'd seen it before. But I can't change the past. I can only beg forgiveness for it. I can only work to build a future where you feel nothing but loved.

I'm not going to ask you to believe just my words. I'm going to show you. Every day. With heart and actions. I'm going to show you that you are—and always have been—the love of my life.

I love you,

Caden

I sat down slowly, moving to the counter stool. My chest was tight, but my eyes burned with something warmer than anger.

No performance. No apologies laced with excuses.

Just food. A table. A letter.

I'm hoping it's something real—and lasting. I'm not sure where I stand in all this, but I can say honestly that, while I'm not walking away, I have no problem eating my feelings tonight.

Chapter 6: Remember the Fireworks

~FELICITY~

My eyes felt crusty as I came out of a deep sleep and my body was buzzing with the hurt of an emotional hangover. I swear I could feel my heartbeat in my teeth—if I didn't know better, I would've said I took down a couple bottles of wine last night. Meanwhile, I had only a glass.

I pulled up to a sitting position, and after a moment of steadying myself, I forced myself to stand. I swear I groaned as I almost waddled—heading toward the bathroom. When did my bones start to feel so old? Forty is supposed to be the new thirty, so this old-ass feeling in my body could suck it.

I straightened my spine, grabbed the edge of the dresser, and steadied myself. I reached up toward the ceiling to stretch my body out. Looking at myself in the mirror on top of the dresser, I spoke to the woman in front of me.

"Get your ass in gear, Felicity. You're not old, you're just getting started. Your marriage does not define who you are. You are a fucking beast and you will stand with fucking dignity."

I looked at that tired woman I saw reflected, and as I spoke, I swear she started to grow more determined. Almost fortified by the impromptu speech.

"That's right, Felicity. You will close out your thirties with a bang—with or without your husband by your side."

I reached for my phone. My fingers hovered, aching to text him. I opened my messages and started to type.

Me: Thank you for dinner last night. It was thoughtful.

Delete.

Me: The food was good. We should talk when you get home.

Delete.

Me: I read your letter. I don't know what to say yet but thank you for trying.

Too honest? Not honest enough? I had no idea anymore.

Delete.

Me: Thank you for dinner.

My thumb hovered over send. «Sent»

I set the phone aside and walked to the bathroom, frustration building in my chest. When had communicating with my own husband become so complicated? When had I started overthinking every word?

It had been gradual, so gradual I hadn't noticed it happening. Somewhere along the way, his responses to my attempts at connection had become shorter. More distracted. Until eventually, I'd stopped trying as hard.

I could see it now, looking back. The way I'd started editing myself. Keeping conversations surface-level because going deeper meant risking his distracted "mm-hmm" while he scrolled through emails.

The way I'd stopped sharing the little things—funny stories from work, random thoughts, dreams about our future—because he'd stopped really listening.

And then I'd gotten angry about his lack of attention, but instead of saying "I need you to put your phone down and actually hear me," I'd gotten passive-aggressive. Made comments about how he was always working.

Rolled my eyes when he missed details I'd already told him. Let silence fill the spaces where conversation used to be.

God, when was the last time we'd had a real conversation? Not about schedules or logistics or whose turn it was to pick up groceries, but an actual talk about thoughts and feelings and dreams?

I couldn't remember. And that was as much my fault as his.

I'd stopped fighting for us somewhere along the way. Stopped demanding better. I'd gotten comfortable with crumbs because asking for the whole meal felt like too much work, too much vulnerability, too much risk of being disappointed again.

But he'd stopped offering the whole meal too. We'd both just... settled. Into politeness. Into parallel lives that occasionally intersected at dinner or in bed.

Standing in the bathroom, looking at my reflection, I tried to pinpoint when it started. Maybe it was after the third failed IVF cycle, when we were both so raw and grieving that it was easier to retreat into our separate corners than to hold each other through the pain.

Maybe it was when his company started struggling and he disappeared into eighteen-hour days. Maybe it was when I got promoted and started staying late to prove myself.

Or maybe it was all of those things, layered on top of each other until we forgot how to reach across the distance we'd created.

I missed us. Not just the version of us from that July 4th—though God, I missed that intensity, that certainty that we were building something beautiful together.

I missed the way he used to look at me like I was the most interesting person in the room. The way he'd ask follow-up questions about things I'd mentioned in passing. The way he'd remember details about my day and check in about things that were worrying me.

I missed feeling like his favorite person.

But I also missed actually being his favorite person. Missed the way I used to light up when he walked into a room. Missed looking forward to telling him about fun little things instead of dreading another distracted conversation. Missed feeling excited about our plans together instead of resigned to them being canceled or postponed.

When had I stopped bringing him coffee in the morning? When had I stopped wearing the perfume he loved? When had I stopped kissing his cheek as I walked by him?

I'd been so focused on feeling invisible to him that I hadn't noticed how invisible I'd become to myself. How I'd shrunk down to fit into the smaller and smaller spaces that existed in between the moments.

My eyes dropped to my hands, and I realized I was holding something—white and folded. It was Caden's letter from last night. When had I picked it back up?

I opened it again and reread the line that kept echoing in my head: I'm going to show you that you are—and always have been—the love of my life.

I could almost taste the memory of a time when I really felt that.

Boston, July 4, 2018:

We'd arrived early—Caden insisted. Blankets, wine, snacks, Bluetooth speaker for the wait. He always overprepared, and I didn't mind it. It let me relax and go with the flow because I knew he had the details covered.

It was hot. Not unbearable, but enough that I tied my hair up and peeled off my sandals the moment we laid our blanket down near the Esplanade. It was early—as was necessary on the Fourth in Boston. The crowd hadn't fully settled yet, but he sat close, one of his legs stretched out behind me like a safety rail.

"You good?" he asked, offering me a chilled water bottle he'd packed in a tiny cooler like a dad at his kid's softball game.

I nodded, smiling as I took it. "You're very proud of this setup."

"Damn straight. Blanket real estate is no laughing matter."

I laughed, then leaned into his side, resting my chin on his shoulder for a moment. He smelled like sunblock and soap and just a little like the white wine sweating in plastic cups between us.

"You used to come here a lot as a kid?"

He shook his head. "Nah. My parents weren't into the crowds. Then later, with Jessica—she preferred house parties. Watching the fireworks on TV instead of being here in person. This is one of my firsts."

I hesitated. He rarely mentioned his ex without prompting, but there wasn't any bitterness in his voice. Just fact.

"What made you want to come this year?"

He looked at me then. No smirk. No joke. Just eyes that went quieter than usual.

"You," he said. "I wanted to be here with you. I wanted to experience this first with you."

The fireworks hadn't even started yet—hours to go—but something went off in my chest at that.

"Felicity," he said after a minute. "I know I talk too much. I make everything a joke when I don't know what else to say—but I need you to hear me on this."

He sat up straighter, pulling one knee toward him, his posture shifting into something more serious. He cleared his throat.

"I've never... wanted someone like I want you. Not just for now. Not for something casual or convenient. I want to build something with you. Whatever this is, it's not temporary to me."

I blinked. I hadn't expected that. We'd been dating a little under a year at that point. Things had been good—really good—but we'd never put it into words like that.

He rubbed the back of his neck, looking off toward the Charles. "I know that's a lot. I just... needed to say it."

Music started playing through the speakers along the river. Odd timing, but it felt like a sign. It screamed romantic so I went with it.

I slid my fingers over his, threading them together. "It's not too much," I said.

And it wasn't.

Not when it was him.

Hours later—after countless card games, a couple of bottles of wine, some funnel cake, and a lot of laughs—we stood side by side to watch the fireworks. Hand in hand, standing barefoot on our blanket like the hundreds of people around us. It was the most magical moment of my life.

Thinking back on it now, I asked myself 'Where did that couple go?'

Chapter 7: Departure

~CADEN~

I didn't sleep.

Not really.

I swear I could hear every creak in the house—every shift of the floor-boards made my ears prick, my stomach clenched. I kept waiting to hear her. To hear... anything. A door closing. A plate clinking against the counter. Even the sound of the dishes in the sink.

But there was nothing.

I lay in bed, staring at the ceiling, hypnotized by the ceiling fan spin-ning. The note I left—did she read it? Maybe she didn't. Maybe she came home, saw the table I set and the meal I picked out, and decided it wasn't enough. Hell, I wouldn't blame her. Couldn't blame her for it.

But I'd tried. And I meant it. Maybe too little, too late. But it won't stop me from trying.

It wasn't a grand gesture. It wasn't diamonds or a trip or a spa reserva-tion my assistant handled. It was me. Picking out her favorites. Writing that letter by hand with the chicken scratch she always made fun of—me writing in all caps like my father did.

I smiled at that. Briefly. Thinking about her teasing me over the years about how my writing was so bad, but she never had a problem reading it. Just another reminder of our vibe—but I'd forgotten even that too.

And I had forgotten. Somewhere in the last few years, I lost the only language that ever mattered—hers.

A knot formed between my ribs, twisting tighter with each breath. I used to know how to make her laugh. I used to know the little things that made her smile. That made her feel safe. Loved. Seen. Then work crept in. Slowly, then all at once.

I think I thought I was doing it for us. For her. For our future. A few years ago, the company almost folded—it changed everything. I couldn't breathe unless I was moving. Thinking back, I realized I didn't look away long enough to see what it was costing me.

Late nights. Missed dinners. One anniversary on top of another. That year was a blur of stress calls, emergency loans, restructuring. I fought tooth and nail to keep us from closing—from impacting hundreds of jobs—and I won. At least that's what I told myself.

But I came out the other side a man who had his name on the door but no clue what day his wife was born.

I didn't even notice her pulling away. Which I know isn't really fair since in truth I pulled away first. But it was unintentional. Reckless. Stupid.

At first it was subtle. Fewer inside jokes. Less spontaneous laughter. More closed doors. Shorter responses when I asked how her day was. Then eventually, she just stopped answering those questions altogether.

God, I hate myself for how long it took me to notice. But I see it now—clear as fucking day.

And I know what I have to do. There is no quick fix. Definitely not a fix by her birthday. I know I can't sweep in and try to charm her into forgiveness. She deserves better than that. What she needs is consistency. Intentionality. Sustained change.

So I'm going to remind her. Of what I know. What I love. What I've seen. What I've quietly noticed—every day, even if I stopped showing it.

I once heard it said that love isn't about how loudly you say it—it's about how well you live it. So I'm going to start there.

Steadily. Consistently. Undeniably. Until she believes me again.

~Felicity~

I was dressed and out the door before seven—telling myself it was because I had early calls. Really, though, I just couldn't sit in that house any longer. Not with the letter still on my nightstand and the weight of it lodged in my chest.

No makeup—honestly, I can't remember the last time I went to work without it—but I just couldn't bring myself to care. I didn't blow-dry my hair, just twisted it up in a makeshift bun. As soon as I was dressed, I ran downstairs, planning to take coffee with me.

I tore through the cabinets looking for my mug. Then went back through them again, heart racing now. Where the hell was my freaking mug?

My favorite one—the mug Caden got me after my promotion, when I'd cried in the car because I didn't think I was good enough. One side read: You are brave, bold, courageous, amazing, inspiring, and loved. The other had a cartoon pickle and the words "If in a pickle, flip." And if you actually flipped it? The bottom screamed: SEND HELP.

It always made me laugh. I couldn't explain why, but I wanted it to-day—needed it today. Maybe because it reminded me of when things with Caden were light and easy—when he knew how to make me laugh. When he cared about making me laugh.

And now? Gone. Like everything else that used to feel safe. I threw some coffee in the first to-go mug I could find since clearly, I wasn't going to find mine this morning.

Arriving at work, I sighed as I closed the door to my office. I dropped my bag on my desk and went to the windows, still holding my coffee. Sitting here thinking about everything—my marriage, our fight, our good times and our bad. Who were we now? We weren't always this couple.

Once settled, I tried to dive into my inbox, but I couldn't focus. My eyes blurred. Partly over the words, partly because my eyes were moist with uncried tears. I kept checking the time like it was last period in high school.

Ethan was out for the rest of the week—client meetings out of town. Normally, I'd enjoy the uninterrupted time to get ahead, but today it just made the day feel stark.

I sat back in my chair and stared out the window. Forty. A milestone I'd been quietly dreading—it wasn't about the number. It was about the feeling of invisibility. Of being forgotten.

Except now... I wasn't forgotten. Not exactly, I guess?

I couldn't decide what was worse.

Caden's letter still echoed in my head. The words had been right. Thoughtful. But one moment, one act on his part doesn't mean he deserves easy forgiveness.

What I did know was that I wasn't going to sit around waiting to see what he might do next. Not for my birthday. Not anymore.

I clicked over to my calendar and opened a new time off request. Thursday (half day). Friday (full). Reason: reclaiming my damn life...Okay that's dramatic. I really just put "Personal time."

I logged off before I could talk myself out of it.

I was home by noon. The silence in the house felt less oppressive this time—maybe because I had an energy that juxtaposed the silence.

I dropped my bag by the front door and made my way to the kitchen. It was still warm from the sunlight filtering through the windows. There were some dishes in the sink, piece of toast off to the side, and the garbage was empty with a new bag inside. I swear I was almost ready to forgive the whole thing—he took out the garbage without being asked. I smirked to myself. Just kidding, kinda.

I leaned against the counter for a moment, then walked to the office. Caden's office.

The scent of his cologne still lingered. I sat in the chair behind his desk and grabbed a notepad. The old-school kind—spiral-bound at the top, pages slightly yellowed.

I grabbed a pen. Paused. I stared at the blank page for a long moment, pen hovering over the paper. My handwriting started out careful, deliberate—cursive penmanship that seems to be a lost art in itself, but more meaningful in appearance than today's block lettering. As the words flowed, my script loosened and flowed with a natural curvature that spoke its own language.

The pen moved steadily across the page, pausing only when I needed to think about how to phrase something. When I finished, I set the pen down and flexed my fingers. I'd been gripping it tighter than I realized. I read through what I'd written twice, my lips moving silently as I traced each sentence. The words looked foreign in my own handwriting, like someone else had guided my hand.

I folded the page carefully, creasing each edge with precision. The paper made a soft sound as it compressed. For a moment, I held the folded letter against my chest, feeling its slight weight, before placing it squarely in the center of Caden's desk where he couldn't miss it.

I bought a last-minute ticket out of Logan and searched for just the right place. Once I found what I was looking for, I went upstairs, grabbed my carry-on down from the closet, and started tossing things in.

The packing felt strange—there was a mix of excitement and terror churning in my gut. What did you take when you didn't know what you were actually doing? Where were you even going?

I pulled out the dress I'd bought last year but never worn—the blue one with tiny flowers. It hugged my upper body and flared out. It screamed "take me dancing!" Today it was coming with me.

My hands moved automatically: underwear, pajamas, sandals. Anything that made me feel beautiful—my makeup, perfume, jewelry—you name it.

I stood in front of the bathroom mirror, looking at the woman staring back. Forty. Empowered. I'm going to own this birthday. And I look fucking good for forty. I deserve to laugh, take joy in my day, and feel free from the burdens of invisibility.

On impulse, I grabbed the red lipstick from the bottom of my makeup drawer. The one I'd worn on our first real date, the color that had made Caden stutter mid-sentence when he picked me up.

The suitcase zipped closed with a satisfying sound. Final. Decisive.

Walking downstairs, I paused at the front door. The house felt different already—I can't explain it, but it didn't feel so...broken. *I* didn't feel so broken.

I didn't look back as I locked the door behind me.

By 5:30, I was boarding my flight.

Only a few hours later, I had landed.

Stepping out of the airport into the Florida air, while heavy with humidity, my heart felt light with peace.

When my Uber arrived, I climbed into the back seat. Off to The Setai Hotel in Miami Beach.

This weekend was mine.

And I was going to savor every single moment of it.

Chapter 8: Love, Felicity

~CADEN~

I got home earlier than usual.

Meetings had bled into each other with me listening in like a zombie, not offering a single thing of use, until I finally gave up and came home, hoping by some chance I'd get to see Felicity. That maybe she'd want to talk. Or at least argue.

I walked through the door, tossed the mail down in front of me while I loosened my tie. Sorting through the mail, I absentmindedly opened the Visa bill and glanced through it, tossing it back on the table, but then I paused. Picking it back up, I noticed a vendor charge on the bill. Double checking, I saw it was my personal card instead of the corporate card. That's weird. I made a mental note to give it to Lauren to review and deal with.

My stomach grumbled at me that it was time to get some dinner. The house was quiet though, so I knew I would be eating alone. It wasn't the kind of quiet that feels peaceful. Instead, it felt like the kind that comes with an unexplainable foreboding.

Felicity's computer bag was by the door. Shoes tossed to the side. Her car was in the garage, parked next to mine.

Guessing she must be upstairs, I tossed some leftovers into the microwave and made my way to the office to drop off my bag.

That's when I saw it.

Folded on the desk. My name scrawled across the front.

Caden.

It was in her handwriting.

My stomach turned. I sat down slowly and just held it. No. God, no.

All I could think of was Schrödinger's cat—if I didn't open it, then nothing inside could be real. She couldn't be telling me she wanted a divorce. She couldn't be telling me she was done.

I must've sat there for an eternity before I finally gave in. I opened the note with shaking hands, letting my eyes adjust while a tear escaped in fear of what I could be facing. I leaned forward and took in the words my wife had written me.

Caden,

I got your letter. And the dinner. All of it. And yes, it meant something. It really did. But to be honest, it's not enough. Not for this moment. Not for today. Not for me. Though I wish it could be.

Though I think you already know that.

Yes, you remembered some of my favorites. Yes, you may have meant what you wrote. God, I hope you did. But this week—my birthday—it was too late. You've had years.

And that purse...it meant more than just the material it was made of. Not only that, I'll forever have to see it when Macy carries it—a constant reminder that I wasn't enough. I wasn't enough for you to choose me and my feelings. While I hate how petty that sounds, I hope you understand that this is not about being in competition. It's about being considered at all and, right now, I don't feel considered. I don't feel seen. I don't feel loved.

I'm not punishing you. This isn't payback. This is me standing up for myself. Speaking up for myself. Even though it hurts to do it.

I need space—real space—without expectations, without you trying to fix things with a gift or a grand gesture. Without worrying about how you feel or what you're doing.

So this weekend is mine. Mine alone. You are not welcome.

I don't mean that to be harsh. I just want to be clear: I don't want you trying to ride in and 'save the day.' You can't. Not today, and not this weekend.

I deserve this birthday. I deserve to feel full of life. To feel free. And I don't need anyone's permission—not even yours—to reclaim that. Even if it terrifies me.

I don't want to talk to you until I get back. Please don't reach out unless it's an emergency, but I will text you to let you know when I get to my destination safely.

When I get back, we'll see if I feel like talking.

I want you to know that I do love you. I've never stopped. The choice to celebrate me is not about my love for you.

Right now I need to take a moment to love myself.

Love,

Felicity

I read it twice.

Then a third time.

And each time, something inside me cracked a little further.

She was right. God, I hated that she had to leave to make a point. I hated that I didn't even know where she was—anywhere in the world, really. I'd waited until it was too late to try. I'd treated her like an afterthought.

And now she was claiming what she should never have had to fight for in the first place: Her happiness. Her time. Her damn birthday.

I let the note fall to the desk and dropped my head into my hands. The emptiness of the house echoed her absence. And her words echoed in my chest.

She wants no contact.

Just space.

I wasn't used to feeling this powerless. But I knew I'd earned this silence.

And now, all I could do was wait—and start the long road of proving I'm still worth coming back to.

Chapter 9: Letter to Myself

~Felicity~

Room service arrived at 8:00 a.m. as I'd ordered for the last two mornings. I've always been an early riser, and it seems that even vacation can't change that. I wasn't hungry, but I knew I needed something, or I'd be hangry before 10—while I ordered more than I'd ever eat for just breakfast, the tray was filled with things I could pick at through the morning.

I squinted, staring into the almost blinding ocean. The waves crashed in patterns that looked too beautiful to be real. I sat in the lounge chair off to the side of the wide balcony. My legs were pulled to my chest, arms wrapped around my shins, chin resting on my knees. Escaping from my life had felt necessary, but my time here had felt different than I'd imagined.

I'd come here for freedom—for space.

Maybe naive of me, but I didn't expect the grief to follow me here. It pressed in like a second skin, even as I tried to peel it away with ocean views and room service mimosas. One moment I'd feel weightless, almost free—then suddenly crushed by what I'd lost over the years. Part of me wanted to call him. Part of me wanted to throw my phone into the ocean.

There's something about turning forty that makes you take stock.

I picked up the hotel stationery, half as a distraction, half on instinct. This was no Hilton notepad. This was thick, creamy, embossed stationery with the hotel's name in faint gold. I slid my fingers over the embossed logo, and I swear it was like real gold. Couldn't be, though—right?

Looking for a pen, I found one tucked in the leather folder next to the room service menu. The weight of it surprised me—solid metal that pressed into my palm with unexpected gravity, as though even this small hotel amenity not only understood the heaviness I carried inside, but also knew how to help me let it out.

I went back to my seat on the balcony, and I started writing.

I didn't write to Caden. It was a letter to my sister. Or to friends. Not to anyone in my life.

To me.

This would be a letter to myself—or the woman I hope I still am in ten years. Or maybe the woman I'll finally become.

<u>Letter to Myself, July 2025 – Miami</u>

Dear Me—the me of 2035 (as long as the world is still turning...):

If you're reading this, and I hope you are reading it, I pray you're somewhere warm again. Maybe your hair is a little longer. Maybe it's not (though please don't have given in and cut it like your mother did once she passed the age of 45).

Maybe you finally learned to stop apologizing for taking up space in this world—for being you.

I'm writing this from the balcony of my hotel suite where I've watched countless turquoise waves crash against the white sand so far below. The humidity and heat cover me like a blanket and even this paper dampens from it.

There's a breeze blowing through, carrying the scent of coconut sunscreen mingling with the citrus from my untouched mimosa. Somewhere down the beach, I can hear Latin music beating a rhythm making my foot tap.

I'm alone. It's my fortieth birthday weekend, and I left home with nothing but a letter to Caden. I didn't tell anyone where I was going. I just booked a flight, the hotel suite, and flew away.

Think back to this time and remember what it felt like—the need to belong to yourself for the first time in a long time.

You know what happened this week. There's no way you've forgotten. You probably still flinch when you think of the purse—maybe Macy even still has it. I imagine you haven't forgotten how quietly your heart cracked when you realized he gave it away without a thought to you or your feelings.

Maybe by now you've forgiven him. Or maybe not—maybe it was the last straw for you two. I don't know—only you do.

But this letter isn't about the purse. Or even about him.

This is about you.

You've been through so much. Sometimes I wonder how you've carried it all and still managed to smile at the sunrise.

You and Maliyah lost your parents far too young—two girls left alone in their twenties to make a way in life. Mom with her warm heart, who would sing "la-la-love you" like a lullaby and hold you close when you were hurting. Dad with his booming voice and Sunday breakfasts—always quick with an off-key song.

They taught you both that love was something given, not earned. They taught you that your strength came from within and from above. Somewhere along the line, you forgot that, though—working to earn love and affection.

Maybe by now you've finally remembered you were always enough. Always.

Then the infertility. That broke something in you that, as of today, you've been unable to glue back together—the pieces are sometimes unrecognizable. It felt like a betrayal—by your own body. The nights you cried after every test. Every appointment. Every month that passed.

All you've ever dreamed of was being a mother, being able to share the joy and love your own mother had surrounded you with. You've envisioned a life for yourself surrounded by yours and Caden's children. And after years, that vision still remains untouchable.

But you need to know you are not defined by the accumulation of failed IVF attempts. And you are not less than just because you haven't been able to have a baby—yet. I know you've tried to stand beside and with Macy, to be something soft and steady for her, but she has her own mom and you've always had to be careful with that relationship.

So again, you've stood outside of yourself—still unseen and still separate. Still waiting. Still hoping.

And then—there's Caden.

He loved you once. Fully, completely. He still does—at least, he says he does. I remember how he used to look at you—like you were the answer to every question he hadn't figured out how to ask yet. He made you laugh. He made you feel seen. And for a while, you let yourself believe maybe this was it. That after everything, this love would hold.

But love, like anything, needs tending. And eventually, he forgot. Or maybe he just got tired. Maybe you did too. The long meetings, the silent dinners, the anniversaries pushed aside for flights and fires. The promises you stopped believing.

Emotionally, it has all been too much. So, you let silence speak words you never said. You rode that silence into anger. And you didn't try. Neither of you really tried. You could have spoken up before now, but you didn't. He could have fought before now, but he didn't.

Now here you are. Forty. Alone in Miami. Eating overpriced breakfast and writing a letter to a woman who you hope no longer remembers the pain of what this felt like, but instead looks back on it as a catalyst for the strength she built.

Looking out at the endless ocean, I see possibility like nothing I've seen before. As impromptu as this trip may have been, my heart knows it will also be a balm to the soul. I chose me, and that has to count for something.

So what do I want to tell you?

You are not broken.

You are not forgotten.

You are not less just because someone else forgot how to love you loudly.

Your softness is a gift. Your fire is your own. Your worth was never dependent on anyone else remembering it. The trials of life you experienced are the building blocks for the strong woman you have become.

I hope you have found a way to settle your heart by now. That you've found it in that heart to forgive him. Not because he deserves it, but because you do. Because bitterness only eats the one holding onto it.

I hope you let yourself love again—whether that love is poured into others or allowed to flow back inside.

And I hope you still walk barefoot in the sand, that you smile at sunrises, ride rollercoasters, read books by the dozens, and live life without apology. I hope you found a way to settle your heart around giving life and that you have somehow found a way to make it all happen for you. I hope that in writing this letter, we are encouraged to do something different. Because it's time to remember—it is never too late. Don't let anyone tell you otherwise.

You made it through.

And you're not done yet.

With everything I have and with all of my love,

~Felicity

Chapter 10: Worth Every Penny

~Felicity~

The spa treatment was everything I didn't know I needed.

They called it the Master in Time, which sounded dramatic—but honestly, they weren't wrong. Basically a full day of self-care, from full-body exfoliation to a rich cream hydration aimed at turning back time. I can't say that it definitely reversed my age, but my skin glowed like it remembered how to breathe again—and I felt years younger.

The facial alone could've changed my entire outlook on life. Four different massages—each one designed to lift, tighten, and smooth. The collagen mask placed over my skin afterward sent me into an almost meditative state. I swear I emerged looking like someone who had slept for a week and had never had a day of stress in her life.

Then came the Thai foot reflexology, followed by a manicure and pedicure that made me grateful that I brought open-toed shoes just to show off the results.

It was indulgent. Over the top. Probably ridiculous.

And I loved every single moment of it.

Afterward, I laid out on the beach for a bit in a cabana—safe from the sun but alive with the ocean air. The cabana came replete with a misting fan and endless cucumber water. I sat with my Kindle, opening up my library of books and casually jumping from one book to the next—not really invested in a story but not really caring either.

By the time I got back to my room, it was nearly eight.

I almost didn't go out. I could've curled up with room service and a rom-com, called it a perfect night. But something in me whispered, *'Not tonight. Go. Get out of the room.'*

I stood in front of the hotel mirror, still wrapped in the plush terry cloth robe, my skin glowing from the day's treatments. My phone sat on the nightstand, screen dark. Part of me wondered if Caden had tried to call, what he'd thought of my letter. The thought made my stomach twist, so I pushed it away.

I opened the closet doors and stared at the limited options I'd packed. The blue dress with tiny flowers hung there, too formal for a beachfront bar. My fingers moved past the work clothes I'd somehow thrown in out of habit. Then I saw it—a simple sundress I'd brought. I'd almost left behind. Low back, soft fabric, the kind of thing I used to wear when I felt young and free. When had I stopped wearing clothes that made me feel beautiful instead of just appropriate?

I slipped it on and turned to face the mirror. The woman looking back wasn't the corporate executive who lived in blazers and carefully coordinated accessories. This was someone softer, more open.

My hair was a mess of sea-salt curls from the ocean air. Instead of fighting it with a brush or trying to tame it with product like I would at home, I just ran my fingers through it, letting it be wild and imperfect. I turned my face side to side, touched up my makeup, and smiled. I felt beautiful.

I checked my phone one more time—still nothing. I stowed it in my crossbody purse and walked out of my hotel room. Letting the door close behind me, I felt excitement bubble up inside—it was going to be a good night. I was sure of it.

The beachfront bar was exactly what I'd hoped for and exactly what intimidated me. It was alive with music and the pulse of the ocean. Lights strung through palm trees, laughter over clinking glasses, the air thick with lime and salt and maybe just a little magic. The outdoor area ran right into the sand, giving the illusion of almost being on a deserted island. I could see the back of the bar from my hotel room, so I knew the walk home wouldn't be painful at the end of the night. This place was perfect.

Standing at the entrance, I felt myself pause, suddenly aware of how long it had been since I'd walked into a bar alone. At home, social events meant Caden and I attending corporate functions or dinners. I can't remember the last time we went bar hopping and it felt strange to just walk in.

A couple brushed past me, arms wrapped around each other, laughing at some private joke. They found a table near the water, and I watched the man pull out the woman's chair, saw her reach across to touch his hand as they settled in. I saw myself and Caden in them. Not the us of today, but the us of yesterday—when life was carefree and the kinds of problems we face today weren't even in our imaginations.

I forced myself to walk in and move toward the bar, aware of the eyes that followed me—not unfriendly, just curious. A woman alone often drew attention, and I felt exposed in a way I hadn't experienced in years. At home, I was Mrs. Barrett, Caden's wife, the HR Executive. Here, I was just Felicity, and I wasn't sure who that was anymore.

The bartender was mixing something complicated for another customer, shaking a martini with theatrical flair. Music pulsed from speakers hidden in the palm trees—something Latin and infectious that made my hips want to move. I could smell the aroma of grilled seafood wafting from the kitchen, mingling with the buzz of animated conversations that rose and fell around me.

I slid onto a stool, ordered a mojito, and let the night air wrap around me like a cloak. The mint and lime were sharp and clean, the rum warming me from the inside. For the first time in months, maybe years, I wasn't thinking about tomorrow's schedule or what needed to get done the next day.

That's when I noticed them.

A group of seven women, tucked beneath the string lights at the corner patio table. They were radiant—laughing with the ease that comes from deep friendship. I envied them and their carefree night they clearly had ahead of them.

I ordered an appetizer and tucked into my mojito.

"You here solo or waiting on someone to join you?" The bartender asked.

"Solo. Just visiting for the weekend."

"All alone?" I heard from just behind me. I swiveled on my stool and found one of the women from the table standing there.

I smiled. "Guilty."

She looked at the bartender, "Juno, we'll take another pitcher. Put it on the tab?" With a nod, she turned toward me.

"Well being solo here is just not allowed," she said, looping her arm through mine. "Come meet the bad decisions committee."

I laughed, collected my mojito, and tagged along with my new, but very necessary, bad influence.

Upon arrival at the table, I got the rundown of the crew—Tanya, from Miami, Janet, and Tiff both from West Palm, Mercedes who lives in Orlando, and Rina, who is from a place called Melbourne. Then there was Olivia and Pam both from out of state—New York and Vegas respectively.

All different ages—ranging from mid-thirties to mid-fifties—a more eclectic group of women I'm not sure I remember ever meeting. A teacher, a chef, a hotel manager, a retired scientist, and one who just shrugged and said "consulting." They all seemed to be from different backgrounds, to look at them, they were a mosaic of beautiful colors.

Apparently, they met over ten years ago at some women's wellness retreat, hit it off, and from there a tradition was born. Once a year, every year they come together for a weekend in one of their cities—live, laugh, drink, whatever the weekend calls for.

I sat down and instantly felt like I'd stepped into a secret club, but one where I was immediately let in on the secret. They didn't ask me to explain all my woes for why I was there alone. They didn't ask my job title or my marriage status—though I'm sure my ring said it without words. They told stories that made everyone laugh.

Tiff complained about a song being stuck in her head which led to all of us singing it—loudly and off key because Mercedes was convinced that singing it would "kill the ear worm." Needless to say, it didn't, and we all ended up with it stuck in our heads for the rest of the night. But it made us laugh that much louder and harder.

Plates of Cuban sliders, fried plantains, garlicky shrimp with mofongo, and the best damn empanadas I'd ever had, were brought to the table in rounds along with each round of drinks. Mojitos turned into mango mojitos which turned into strawberry mojitos, and so on it went. I'm sure you get the picture. By a couple of hours in, I was blitzed and wasn't sure I had ever had as much fun as I was having with these ladies before.

At some point, Janet grabbed my hand and pulled me toward the patio's makeshift dance floor. We danced barefoot in the sand, hips swaying, arms up, salt air clinging to our skin. I was spinning and laughing so hard that my side ended up hurting—I drank and laughed through it.

When the bar finally turned on the overhead lights, signaling closing time, we booed like kids past curfew. Phones came out, numbers exchanged, and promises made—half-serious, but given this group of ladies, I think maybe more real than not.

I walked back to my hotel barefoot in the sand, opting for the oceanside walk instead of using the sidewalk out front. My sandals dangled from my fingers as I swung them by my side. My hair now piled on top of my head, curls escaping and sticking to my face and neck.

It was after 3 a.m. when I finally crossed the threshold of my hotel.

And I felt alive.

Not as someone's wife. Not as someone waiting for an apology or trying to hold everything together.

Just me. Felicity.

Joyful. Exhausted. Glowing inside and out. I hadn't felt this light in years. Not because my problems disappeared—but because for once, they weren't the loudest voice in the room.

And as I stepped into the elevator, grinning to myself, one final thought made me laugh out loud:

This entire weekend was about to cost more than that damn purse.

And worth every penny.

Chapter 11: The Confession

~CADEN~

Stillness embraced me.

It was so quiet when I woke up—and not the good kind. Not the kind where the house is still because everyone's sleeping in, and I get a moment to breathe before the chaos of the day starts. No. This kind of silence was louder. Emptier. It felt like absence. Like grief. Like the moment you realize something sacred has left the room and you don't know when, or if, it's coming back.

Her side of the bed was still made—all except for her pillow, which I had hugged to myself nightly in her absence. Last night, I realized her pillow no longer smelled like her, so I stole the one off the guest bed where she was sleeping. They say you don't know what you've got until it's gone. Who would have thought scent was one of those things that lingered—along with the pain from its absence.

I sat up and stared down at my feet for a while. Poised on the edge of the bed, I couldn't make myself stand. Rubbing my face, my hand came away wet—tears? I hadn't even realized I was crying.

My stomach clenched as if I'd been punched. It was her birthday—and she was alone. I knew she was in Miami since her travel confirmation emails came to our shared email account. I wasn't sure why she picked Miami, but I couldn't help but hope she was safe. Every time she charged something expensive on our cards, we both got notifications as part of our bank's settings. And with every notification, I found myself relieved to know that she was safe.

I threw on a hoodie and walked downstairs, grabbing coffee more for the ritual than anything else. I kept it black, seeing as the bitterness suited me this morning. It's going to be a busy day for me, and I need to get moving. No more wallowing. Real change had to happen.

I glanced up the stairs—Macy. Here for the weekends, I knew she was still sleeping. I hadn't told her much—just that Felicity was out of town for the weekend. But now, thinking about the purse, about what it symbolized, I knew I couldn't keep her in the dark.

It wasn't fair. To Felicity. Or to Macy.

As I walked up the stairs, my phone pinged with a text.

Lauren: Jessica called again with some questions.

Damn it. I really don't have time for this today. Resolved to get more details later, I shot off a quick note to Lauren telling her we could talk through when I was back in the office.

Finishing my ascent, I stopped at Macy's door and knocked lightly. "Mace? You up?"

A soft murmur from inside, then, "Yeah."

"Can I come in?"

Again, "Yeah." She had the crack-of-sleep voice and that faint edge of attitude I've come to expect from an almost-twelve-year-old.

I cracked the door open, the hinges protesting with a soft whine. Macy lay curled like a comma in her unmade bed, one pale leg twisted in the lavender comforter that had slipped halfway to the floor. Her chestnut hair splayed across the pillow in wild tangles, and the blue glow of her phone cast eerie shadows across her face, illuminating the dark circles beneath her eyes. "Sleep okay?" I asked, leaning against the doorframe.

She shrugged without looking up, her thumb still scrolling mindlessly. "I guess. Tired still." Her voice was sandpaper-rough with sleep.

I sat on the edge of her bed and took a breath.

"I want to talk to you about something."

Still scrolling, "okay."

"It's important. Can I get your attention?"

She looked up from her phone. "Everything okay, Dad?"

"Yes, and no, honey. I want to talk to you about the purse you found in your closet."

Macy sat up and looked at me. "Okay."

I blew out a breath, feeling my shoulders sag with the weight of my confession. The morning light slanted through Macy's curtains, illuminating dust motes that danced between us. My coffee sat cooling on her nightstand, forgotten. *Damn, this was hard.* Necessary, but so hard. How do you find the words to tell your daughter you've been a complete moron? That you've hurt someone you both love?

"You know it's Felicity's birthday."

"Yeah, Dad, duh."

"Okay, well, it's a big birthday. She turns 40 today."

"I know, Dad. I thought this was about the purse?" She says with eyes open, genuinely confused. Which tells me I'm doing this all wrong.

"Okay, so it's her birthday. Remember when you found the purse?" At her nod, I continued. "It was hidden in the back of your closet. You only found it while looking for your ballet shoes, right?"

"Yeah, Dad. Wha—" Macy's eyes widened until I could see white all around her irises, her mouth dropping open in slow motion. "Oh my God—"

"Macy -"

"OH MY GOD. Oh my God, Dad. No! Oh my God!!!!" Her hands flew to her mouth, fingers splayed across her cheeks, nails digging into skin that had gone from sleepy-pink to ghostly pale in seconds. "Dad," she whispered through trembling fingers, "are you about to tell me that was Felicity's birthday gift?"

"Yes, honey. It was."

Eyes starting to water, she leaned forward. "Oh. I guess... I didn't even think it was Felicity's? Oh dad. It was in my—she always uses a black purse—dad! Why was it in my closet??"

"Sweetheart, it's entirely my fault." Inching closer to her, I reached out to her shoulder. "I thought your closet was a good hiding spot. I was really dumb when I hid it. I just—when you saw it, you were so happy holding it, thinking it was for you. I completely failed and, instead of telling you the truth, I said yes."

Macy was full-on crying now, hands covering her face.

"I'm so sorry, honey. I didn't mean for this to happen." I ran my hand through my hair, feeling the weight of my mistake like a stone in my chest. "It was a gift she had asked for, something she actually designed and picked out her—"

At that, her face shot up. "What?! You mean she knew what she was getting?"

"Yes honey. She did."

"But Dad, that means she knows I have it! She saw me with it that night!" Yelling now, she jumped up from her bed. "Why did you let me take it?"

"Honey, I—"

"Why did you let me think it was mine? Let Felicity see me wearing it?! Dad! She knows I have it! She knows! I thanked her for it!"

"I know, honey, that's why I—"

"Dad! She must be so upset! Is that why she is gone? Did she leave because of me?" Macy's tears started to flow again.

"No honey. Not you. She is not mad at you. Please don't worry about that."

"How can I not? Oh my God, Dad. I don't know what—how do I—? What do I—? What do I do? I feel horrible!"

She crumpled to the floor. Damn. I had no idea that she would react like this. I'm fucking speechless. Frozen. After a beat, I sat on the floor next to her and put my arm around her shoulder. "I'm really sorry, honey. I messed up. Now I realize that in trying to avoid hurting you when you loved the purse so much, I caused a bigger problem and I hurt Felicity. When she saw you with it, and she learned what I'd done, it broke her heart. She was sad because my actions showed her how little attention I'd paid to something that mattered to her."

Macy turned her body and buried her head in my chest. "Daddy. I'm so sorry."

My gut twisted. Even now, she was worried about someone else's feelings. She's better than I've been. "No, sweetheart. This is not on you. Like I said, honey—this is all on me. You didn't do anything wrong. I should've told you. I should never have given it to you in the first place. You know, when I told Felicity I would get it back from you, she was more worried about how you would feel in that moment."

Her voice muffled, "Really?"

"Mmhmm. Yes—she didn't want me to take back something that you believed I'd given you." I stroked her tangled morning hair, noticing how much longer it had grown. "I realize now that I should have just come to you right then and been honest—I mean, I should have never done it in the first place, but once I had, I should have just talked to you." My voice caught slightly, and I cleared my throat. "I don't think—I don't think I gave you enough credit. You're growing up, and clearly I've missed a lot." I pulled back just enough to look into her reddened eyes, seeing Jessica's features reflected there, but something uniquely Macy too. "I'm really sorry, honey."

Her fingers twisted at the edge of her shirt, pulling the worn cotton into a tight spiral until her knuckles blanched white. She stared down at the floor, her voice small but steady. "Yeah dad. You should have told me." She swallowed hard, a tear tracking down her flushed cheek. "Daddy, I love Felicity. She always makes time for me, even when she's tired after work—like when she helped me with my science project until midnight when it was due on Monday and Mom forgot to get the stuff to help me. I don't want her to be hurt because of something I did."

"I know, sweetheart. And I'm going to make this right. Not just with her. But with you too. I don't know how yet, but I know that talking to you was my first step."

She was quiet for a moment longer, then looked up at me with soft, thoughtful eyes. "Can I help you figure out what to do to make it up to her?"

I blinked. "You want to help?"

She nodded. "But you have to promise not to mess it up."

Despite everything, I smiled. "Deal."

And for the first time in days, I felt the smallest flicker of hope.

Chapter 12: Mimosas and Murals

~FELICITY~ I WOKE UP slowly, sunlight warming my skin—I'd left the curtains open. I wish I could say that I felt fresh as a daisy. I did not. I was definitely hungover. Burying my head in the pillow I found myself wishing I could be forty with my twenty-year-old capability to bounce back from a night of drinking. Groaning, I pulled myself out of bed and slunk to the bathroom.

Leaving the door open, I thought, No lights—definitely not turning the lights on in here. Climbing into the shower, I just let the hot water wash away the alcohol I knew was seeping through my pores. The massage on my scalp was surprisingly healing. I think I need an infusion of caffeine … and water. I should probably drink water, not just stand in it.

I went through the motions of getting ready. Deciding though that I would get breakfast out, I skipped room service and held off on taking something to help with my headache. I did, however, knock back one of the giant bottles of water they provide in the room. Just before leaving, I checked my phone and found messages from Caden.

Caden: I know you said no texting.

Caden: But I didn't want to let today pass without saying Happy Birthday

Caden: I realize everything I've done, recently and in the last couple years, hasn't told you this, but I love you. You are everything to me. I've done nothing to make you believe that. I wish I could turn back time, but I can't. So I will show you that change is essential to me because YOU are essential to me.

Caden: Enjoy your birthday. Call me if you want to talk. But I couldn't let you think that you weren't on my mind on this very special day. I love you.

I looked at the messages, reading them over again. My fingers hovered over the keyboard for a second. A thank you? A heart? Something easy and kind? But no. Not today. Today wasn't about us. So I left him on read and exited my hotel room.

Ten minutes later I slid onto a pastel barstool in a tiny café tucked beside the hotel. My fingertips traced the cool blue and white tiles of the counter. The barista pulled an espresso shot, and the aroma hit me like a physical force, popping my drooping eyelids open. When the server set down my Nutella French toast, I closed my eyes at the first bite—warm chocolate spreading across my tongue, the bread soft and gooey beneath my fork. I caught the server's eye, pointed to a woman three stools down nursing something orange in a glass the size of her head. "That. And coffee. Lots. Please." By my third sip of my mimosa and my second cup of coffee, my headache receded, and I could finally unclench my jaw. I felt human again..

Human—and obligation-free. No reminders popping up on my phone, calls to answer, no colleagues pinging me about yet another crisis. It was my birthday, damn it, and I had officially reclaimed it.

Phone in hand, I opened Google Maps and typed *Things to do in Miami.* For the first time in what had felt like forever, I could pick anything without factoring in someone else's schedule—or their opinion. The freedom tasted better than the French toast.

I settled on three things: Wynwood Walls, Pérez Art Museum Miami, and a sunset cruise. Zero sand, zero tequila shooters (probably), maximum touristy delight. A perfect farewell tour.

By late morning the Uber dropped me onto NW 2nd Avenue where color bled across every surface. Murals stretched to the sky: a neon jaguar stalking a queen; block letters screaming *CREATE MORE, CONSUME LESS.* I paid the entry fee, slipped through the gate, and let the fun begin.

Our assigned guide mentioned that every wall there was repainted—nothing was permanent. I stopped at a dripping teal heart half-buried under fresh pink strokes. The piece was titled *Love in Layers.* It was beautiful and messy and profoundly unfinished. I snapped a photo, tempted to send it to Caden with a snarky *work-in-progress.* I didn't. Instead, I noted in my phone—Life can be repainted.

Before I left, I bought a postcard of that mural. A keepsake for Future Me, because Future Me could always use the reminder.

A quick ride-share later, I stood beneath the Pérez Art Museum Miami hanging gardens. Biscayne Bay glimmered like liquid glass beyond the terrace. Inside, the exhibit *Between Memory and Migration* pulled me room to room—in the exhibit, there were textiles woven with family photos, a film loop of waves projected on suitcases. One installation was a cube of mirrored beads suspended from the ceiling. I stepped inside; infinite versions of me shimmered back: younger, older, braver, calmer.

I touched a bead, whispered, *See you in ten years,* and laughed when a nearby guide nodded like this was perfectly normal behavior.

I left the museum and decided to grab lunch. A fifteen-minute walk away was an area of food trucks where I found one that served *the best arepas in Miami!* So of course I had to try one. I grabbed a picnic table, enjoyed the sunlight and the hum of conversation around me. The pulled pork arepa was incredible—the Fanta refreshing and ice cold.

Stuffed to the gills, I let myself relax for a bit before I headed off to do a little shopping and walk off the calories I had just taken in. I found myself at the Bayside Marketplace—an open-air shopping adventure. Listening to the steel drums and feeling the ocean breeze, my feet carried me from one shop to the next—my arms heavier with each door I opened. I bought a breezy teal dress that made my new tan pop and flowed around my legs, landing at my knees. I also found a fabulous new pair of silver sandals that shone in the sunlight.

Making my way back to the hotel, I dropped off all my new purchases—which included a duffle bag so I could get all my retail therapy results home tomorrow. I quickly touched up my hair and makeup, dressed in my new duds, and headed back out the door. I had a sunset cruise to get to.

I arrived just in time for the 7 PM cruise. I boarded the double-decker boat with a coconut water in hand and claimed a rail seat. Families were posing, influencers angling their phones for golden-hour selfies, and children were running around excited for the sunset tour. The skyline ignited in pink and tangerine.

Halfway through, the captain cut the engine for photos. Phones rose up; I closed my eyes and breathed—four counts in, six out—the way I had learned in my yoga classes. Warm wind, salt on my lips, a city buzzing behind me yet somehow far away. For the first time in a long time, the quiet inside my head was louder than the world outside. This was the life. This birthday had been unexpected but, in truth, it might have been the best birthday I had ever had.

Closing out the night, I sat on my balcony back at the hotel. Sandals were askew off to the side, a final glass of wine in hand from room service, I again breathed in and out. I snapped a selfie with my phone so I could seal this memory forever. Changing my phone screen to the new picture, I looked at myself—really looked. And I saw a woman who looked younger than she had when she arrived in Miami just a couple days ago. She was kissed by the sun, cheeks blushing, eyes alight with joy and calm. I saw a woman finally at peace with herself—ready to go home and have the conversation with Caden that needed to happen.

Before going to sleep for the night, I set the postcard I had purchased earlier against the lamp. Stamped and ready to be mailed, I didn't want to forget to send it out in the morning. It would reach me in a couple days, but having the postmark from Miami felt like something special and different for this birthday.

With my alarm set for morning, I climbed into bed and exhaled a sigh of contentment. I drifted off to sleep with the realization that, whatever tomorrow brought, I would face it head-on—no fear and no anxiety could hold me back.

Chapter 13: Lifelines

~CADEN~

Cash picked up on the second ring. "You alive or what?"

His voice was still half-asleep, a low growl that told me I'd woken him up. It was almost 10:00 a.m. on a Saturday! I could practically hear the scratch of stubble as he rubbed his face.

"I need to talk," I said. "Got a minute?"

There was a pause. An aggrieved sigh. Then, a rustle of sheets. "Hang on, lemme get coffee. If you're calling me before noon on a Saturday, shit must be serious."

I waited. Pacing. Trying not to second-guess this.

A minute later he was back. "Alright, shoot."

I let out a long breath. "So... I fucked up. With Felicity."

"Bro. What do you mean, fucked up? Like you cheated on her?"

"What?! Jesus! No! What the fuck? Why would you go there?"

He blew out a breath. "Well, you said you fucked up. That's the biggest fuck-up there is. So then, what did you do? Forget her birthday or something?

I was silent on my side of the line. How did he guess that?

"No man. No way. You didn't."

"Fuck! Yes. I did. I seriously did."

"Caden. Jesus. I'm telling Mom."

"Shut up, man. Mom knowing is the least of my issues. Listen! I'm calling for help. It's more than just her birthday. I've kinda been absentee for a while now. Work got to me. I failed to really pay attention to her and to focus on our relationship. I'm at a point now where I'll be lucky if she gives me the chance to win her back. I'm not shitting you, man. It's bad."

He sighed. "Damn Caden. I'm really sorry. We love Felicity. She's incredible. I hate that this is happening. So, yeah, man. I'll help you with whatever. What can I do?"

"To start with, she's in Miami for her birthday. Alone."

He was quiet. Letting me talk.

So, I told him everything. About the purse. The note. The fight. Her leaving. Macy's tears. The gifts that Jessica had been getting all these years now, the fact that I've forgotten anniversaries, birthdays, you name it. I put it all out there for him to hear. It was hard having to vocalize everything. To hear my own words tell someone how much of an asshole I've been."

When I finished, he whistled. "Damn. You've been busy screwing up, huh?"

"Yeah. I can't even blame her for leaving."

"Look, I could roast you, but you already did that yourself. So I'll say this instead: she didn't leave because she stopped loving you. She left because she stopped feeling loved by you. There's a difference."

That hit harder than I expected. I sat with it.

"You want her back?" he asked.

"More than anything. But I don't want to just win her back. I want to be better. For her. For Macy. For myself."

"Then do the work. Don't half-ass it with flowers and a 'my bad.' You've got to show her you see her again. You remember her. What she loves. What makes her laugh. What made her fall for you."

I rubbed a hand over my face. "That's what I'm trying to figure out."

"Try focusing on your memories. All those things that made her fall in love with you—you need to figure out where it all went. Give her something tangible that helps her remember."

I smiled. "Thanks, man, I'm so sorry. I know me being absentee recently isn't just affecting her. I realize I haven't been around for you all too. I need to figure out where I went wrong and why. I feel awful."

"Good. You should."

"Mom's been asking about you two, by the way. And both Danny and Mikey mentioned they haven't heard from you in weeks. We all noticed you've been MIA, but figured you were just buried in work again."

"Shit. Yeah, I'm sorry, man. I'll reach out to everyone once I get my head straight."

"Do that. You know how the family gets when one of us goes radio silent for too long."

"I know. Thanks, man.""

"Seriously though. Caden, you should try to figure out why it was so easy to just forget about everything and everyone for the sake of your job. It's not like you were sneaking out and drinking. It's not like you were having an affair. You threw yourself into work and just disappeared. People don't just do that for no reason. So figure that out while you're at it."

"I know." I sighed. "Thank you, man. I appreciate you being there for me."

"I will always be here for you bro. And, if you fuck-up even more, then I'll bring the cousins in on either helping you fix it or just helping me kick the ever-living-shit out of you."I laughed, "Yeah, thanks a lot."

"Anytime."

After we hung up, I sat in the kitchen for a few minutes, letting it all sink in. The ache was still there—raw and heavy—but I felt less stuck. I had a direction now.

I walked over to the room where she had been staying. The bed was still made, except for the pillow I had stolen. She had a duffel bag sitting in the corner. I kneeled down and gently opened it, folding the clothes she left behind and placing them in neat stacks on the bed. Not because they needed organizing. Because it felt like a small way to care for her.

Next, I made a list. A real, handwritten one of the things I needed to do before she comes home. First thing to get done—clean the house top to bottom. Second—store and purse with Macy. Third—the box.

Macy wandered in while I was sweeping the entryway later that afternoon.

"What are you doing?" she asked, holding an iced lemonade as she watched me with confusion spread across her face.

I wiped sweat off my brow. "Just trying to make the place as clean as I can before Felicity comes home."

She nodded. "Good. Because you're gross."

"Hey!"

"Dad, your used socks are on the back of the couch. I don't know how Felicity puts up with you. Boys are really gross if they are all like you."

"You just keep thinking that because you're right ... all boys are exactly like that. They fart, and the smell, make awful noises. They leave their socks everywhere, and did I mention they definitely smell?"

She laughed and rolled her eyes. "Yeah, Dad, I think you mentioned that one a couple of times."

"I'm looking forward to Felicity coming back. She is coming back... right, Dad?"

"Yes, sweetheart, she's coming back. She said so. And I'm looking forward to her coming home too." I reached over and tried to give her a hug, but she stepped back and squeezed her nose between her thumb and forefinger."

"Dad! Don't! You stink!"

Laughing, I pulled away. "Fine. Well, will you be ready in an hour to go take care of Felicity's surprise?"

"I'm ready now! You're the one who's all sweaty and smelly. I'm not getting in the car with you until you shower, Dad."

I laughed. "Okay, yeah. I'll shower. Then we can head out and make sure her surprise is perfect."

Chapter 14: The First Step

~Caden~

I took the fastest shower of my life, water still clinging to my hair when I yanked on clean jeans and a lightweight blazer. My pulse felt like it was sprinting ahead of me, pounding in my ears as if it already knew how much today mattered.

Macy and I pulled into downtown, and miraculously I found street parking on the first pass. Normally I'd have circled forever, muttering about the lack of parking in Boston and the ridiculous traffic with nonsensically designed roads. Today it felt like the universe had decided not to stand in my way though. I opened the parking app on my phone, plugged in the space number, and almost typed it twice—I was so keyed up I kept checking to make sure I hadn't reversed the digits. The little green confirmation screen popped up, and I grinned like an idiot at my phone. My success felt like a good sign.

Macy leaned over, eyebrows raised. "Dad, it's just parking. You look like you won the lottery."

I shot her a look, still grinning. "Don't knock it. Perfect parking deserves a merit badge."

She snorted, rolling her eyes and shaking her head. "You're such a dad sometimes." But I caught the way her mouth tugged into a smile before she shoved her hands back into her hoodie pockets.

When I turned, she was already bouncing on her toes, sneakers scuffing the sidewalk as restless energy radiated out of her small frame. She wanted this as badly as I did—maybe more.

The jewelry shop was at the end of the block, its windows shimmered as the sun hit just right. Bright lights and polished glass reflected the world outside in sharp fragments waiting to be pieced together.

Inside, the air shifted—cool, quiet, reverent. The low hum of the A/C was the only sound. A clerk in a crisp gray vest greeted us with professional politeness.

"I called earlier," I said, clearing my throat. "We're here to have a piece engraved."

The clerk nodded and placed a small pad on the counter. Macy slipped the white box from her bag, careful like it might shatter, and set it down. My daughter—who usually tossed her backpack on the floor and left her sneakers wherever they landed—was suddenly careful, reverent.

The clerk opened the box, pulling out the item I'd found a couple days ago following a day of hopping from one store to the next until I'd found just the right thing for Felicity. He pulled out the card beneath it which held something Macy and I had written together. His brows ticked upward in a subtle smile.

"Nice choice," he said. "I'll be right back."

Macy looked at me, wide-eyed. I gave her a small thumbs-up.

We watched as he carried the box into the back. Macy exhaled, the breath shaky, like she'd been holding it since we left the house.

"You okay, kiddo?" I asked.

She nodded but didn't speak. Her hands twisted together, knuckles white. For all her nerves, I could see it in her eyes—this mattered to her. Not just for me, but for Felicity. She wanted this to mean something more than just a gift.

When the clerk returned, he carried the box like it contained something sacred. He placed it on the counter and lifted the lid. The inscription gleamed under the lights, each curve of the script sharp and deliberate. The words felt heavier than a brick of gold.

Macy leaned in, shoulders softening, her fingertip tracing the letters with a reverence that made my throat tighten. A hint of a smile tugged at her lips, hesitant but real.

The clerk closed the lid, tied the ribbon again with practiced precision, and slid the box toward us with a receipt tucked under a small envelope.

"It's a beautiful piece," he said. His eyes met mine, steady. "Good luck."

Two words, but they carried weight. Like he knew what was at stake.

I nodded my thanks and slipped the box into the inner pocket of my blazer. My palm pressed against the fabric once, checking it was secure, like somehow the motion could anchor my resolve too.

Our next stop was a low brick building a few blocks away, the kind of place most people passed without notice. The sign out front listed job-training classes, a food pantry, a clothing closet. Inside, the lobby smelled faintly of coffee and copier paper. A volunteer in a blue polo shirt, hair silver and neat, greeted us with a smile.

I opened my mouth, but Macy spoke first.

"We wanted to... donate. And sign up. For helping," she said, her voice pitched higher than usual, but steady.

The woman listened, nodded, then smiled—an honest, gentle smile that eased the tightness in my chest. No questions. No lecture. Just gratitude.

"Thank you. This will help."

She passed us forms, and Macy scribbled her name with a seriousness that made me ache with pride. I signed next, folding the carbon copy neatly into the folder we were given, careful not to crease it. The original was filed away, part of something bigger than both of us.

On the way out, we stopped at a bulletin board plastered with photos—women in business suits, lined up holding certificates, some grinning so wide they looked like they'd burst. I felt Macy's steps falter. She stood there, staring, lips parted in awe.

"Ready?" I asked softly.

She nodded. "I feel better now."

"So do I."

Outside, the warmth spread across the brick sidewalk. Macy hugged the folder to her chest as though it were treasure. Halfway to the car, she stopped and turned to me.

"Dad... tomorrow, can I be the one to hand her the folder?"

"Absolutely," I said without hesitation.

The smile that bloomed across her face was unguarded, brighter than anything I'd seen from her in days. She hurried ahead, skipping once before falling back into her usual stride.

I followed; one hand pressed against the box in my jacket pocket. The cool weight of it anchored me, a reminder of the promise I was about to make. For the first time in weeks, I felt something I hadn't allowed myself to feel.

Hope.

Chapter 15: Love Changes

~Felicity~

I'd spent yesterday relaxing at the beach and poolside. I read two books and did absolutely nothing else. It was calming. It was rejuvenating. It was mine. But time waits for no man.

I had that weird feeling in my stomach—the one you get before traveling. Sighing, I zipped up my suitcase with a quiet finality. The room was still, the way it always felt after a few days alone—bed mussed, quiet, a little too easy to leave behind. I'd wanted to make the bed out of habit but caught myself—nope. I wiped down the counters—needing to hide the evidence of makeup dust and toothpaste so housekeeping didn't think a slob had been here. I tossed the half-used toiletries in the trash and arranged the wet towels in a pile.

I wasn't sure if I felt rested. Maybe clearer. A little lighter. But I felt like I could almost nap at this point.

The flight home was in three hours. I'd checked in early, paid for my extra bag—annoyed as I thought back to the days when a checked bag was free—and ordered a Venti iced coffee that I pretty much guzzled. I'd probably regret that later when I had to get up and pee endlessly, but the need for coffee outweighed everything else in that moment. My phone was on Do Not Disturb, but I kept checking it anyway—like muscle memory.

There were a few work emails, one from Delia asking if I was okay, and a string of messages from Kelly, who was basically narrating her day in voice memos like I was on speaker in her living room.

In the Uber on the way to the airport, I found myself looking back at Caden's last messages about my birthday. I felt like a lifetime had passed since I spoke with him. I sent him a short one saying, "I'll be home this afternoon." Sitting back, I downloaded my boarding pass, put my phone on airplane mode and locked it.

Going through airport security had to be the worst part of traveling. Luckily, I had Clear—but it seems like everyone else does these days too. Once I was finally at the gate, I took a breath. I found a seat near the window, plugged my phone into the outlet next to me and opened my Kindle. I couldn't seem to concentrate though. Nothing I did let me focus on the book—no matter how hot and steamy it was. So, I sat back and closed my eyes. Meditating, praying, relaxing. Taking time to just ... be. I reflected on this past weekend. I'd had an amazing time—built memories that I never dreamed of. I met a group of women who I know I will see again. It was a unique and surprising birthday. I felt a small corner of emptiness hiding inside though. One I really didn't know how to explain. I breezed past it though, ignoring it felt better than facing it.

The plane started boarding on time. I shoved my carry-on in the overhead and my purse under the seat. Buckled in, I smiled at the woman who slid in next to me. Gray hair, an indescribable shirt that was covered in animal print and flowers. She had a book in hand—definitely a bodice-ripper novel! She politely returned my smile and got herself situated.

As the plane filled up, a shared silence between us settled in. I listened—not really though—to the flight attendant walk everyone through the safety measures. I contemplated that, in reality, I don't think I would actually know what the hell to do if evacuation were necessary—would I really know how to turn my seat into a flotation device? Where was that blow-up thing again? I snickered to myself thinking if we went down, I wasn't sure it would matter. Fuck that was morbid! I actually laughed out loud at my own thoughts then.

My seat companion looked at me a little strangely but still asked "Home or vacation?"

"Home," I said. "I mean—I'm returning from vacation—well, sort of. I was here for a solo birthday trip."

Her eyes lit up. "Oh? Well, happy birthday."

"Thanks." I paused. "It was a big one."

"Let me guess. Forty?"

I smiled. "Is it that obvious?"

"No. I just turned sixty-five, and I've started counting by fives. Forty was a good one. A weird one, but good." She smiled with an almost nostalgic look on her face. She seemed nice.

We made it through takeoff. About twenty minutes in, she tucked her book into the seat pocket and turned slightly toward me, nodding at my ring.

"Left the husband behind, did you? Or wife maybe? You never know these days so figure it could be either one!" she remarked.

I laughed. "Husband." Then I hesitated. "And yes, just me on this trip."

She nodded. Like that answered more than the question. "Been married long?"

"Six years now."

"Mmmmm. Yeah—coming up on that seven-year itch. Supposedly it's when things get real, and life can get in the way more. Crazy, but probably a little truer than not—I'm no scientist though. Just someone with a lot of experience with a husband who was stupid for probably the first ten to twelve years of our marriage and didn't really become wise until maybe the last ten years. We hit forty-five just a couple months ago! I'm still amazed I let him live through it." She laughed at her own joke. I liked her so much that I found myself laughing along. There was something open and approachable about this lady. Unexplainable really.

"You sound like you've seen a few versions of marriage."

"Oh sure. You stay married for as long as I have, you learn that your marriage is something new every year. You grow, you change, kids come and grow, grandkids come and grow, change jobs, change homes—every change comes with almost an entirely different relationship. Though there is one thing that has absolutely never changed—my husband snores like a lawnmower. Years ago, I ordered these strips off of an infomercial, snuck them on him while he was sleeping! He stayed sleeping right through it and snored the whole time. I learned then that, sometimes you have to adapt. My next order was earplugs for myself. Slept like a baby ever since. Sure, he still leaves his socks everywhere—even right next to the hamper sometimes! But we still hold hands at the movies. Still share a bed every night. Still kiss goodbye and still laugh together. That has to count for something."

I genuinely smiled at her monologue. "I guess it does."

She looked at me for a beat, then said, "You look tired. You know, it's normal to feel tired in a marriage. Sometimes resentful. Sometimes angry. But what always got me through was communication—usually me forcing it. Men, at least men of my generation, aren't alway great at communication. So I learned to imitate with Randall. And he learned to give a little and actually talk." She sighed. "There were some tough years. But—you know—nothing's perfect. The question is, if it's real or not. And whether you can decide that trying again when you're sick of trying is worth it."

I didn't respond right away. Just nodded.

"Love changes," she added. "Doesn't mean it disappears. Just looks different than it did at twenty-five."

"I think I'm just... trying to figure out if mine's still in there."

She smiled again. This one softer. "Then you're already doing the work. Most people don't stop to ask the question—they just jump."

We talked a little more—books, grown kids, her trip to visit her niece. She didn't press. Just offered bits of kindness like little morsels. She shared about her family. I talked about mine, including my inherited family with the Barretts as in-laws and the craziness of what came with my mother-in-law's giant family, the Doyles.

By the time we landed, I felt... different. Certainly not fixed, not even better. Just different.

I turned my phone on and opened the messages.

There was a text from Caden.

Caden: Okay. I love you. Safe travels.

I know I had told him not to text while I was away, but I had to admit—while I was gone, there was this weird feeling of disappointment that he hadn't messaged more. Wrong of me, I know. But sometimes you feel what you feel and there isn't rhyme or reason to it. I missed him. I honestly didn't think I would.

I've really been considering everything—not just the purse. I think at some point I'd started to feel like, since he'd forgotten so many major things, that he was never there for anything. Something Barbara said made me think a little deeper. Sure he was always working late—sometimes I did too—but, except the last few nights before Miami, we always went to bed at night together. He always pulled me close while we slept. We still had an incredible sex life. We still kissed goodbye in the mornings and watched TV on Saturday nights. Our marriage wasn't just one moment—it was made up of millions. He fucked up, yes, but I needed to really spend some time reflecting on everything, not just the big things. I had all these mixed feelings rolling around in my head and in my gut.

I know that things are wrong right now. He needs to change. *We* need to change.

Chapter 16: A Thousand Paper Cuts

~Caden~

My phone buzzed just as I was putting the finishing touches on the house. I stood back, surveying the living room. Three bundles of yellow tulips brightened the coffee table, dining room, and kitchen island. The scent of lime and cilantro hung in the air, mingling with the vanilla candles I'd lit on the mantle. In the kitchen, the cast iron skillet waited, filled with layers of corn tortillas, spiced beef, and that sharp white cheese she always corrected me on the pronunciation of. My stomach growled at the memory of us, legs tangled on the couch, fighting over the last bite with our forks clinking against the pan.

I checked my watch. If Felicity made it in time before Macy went home, I'd have just enough time to warm it before dinner time.

Macy was upstairs getting ready when I saw Jessica's name flashed across my phone.

I almost didn't answer. Almost let it go to voicemail like I should have done a dozen times over the past few months. But Macy is here, so I obviously can't. I'm still working on figuring out the balance. I thought it could be something that Felicity and I decide on together...instead of me making another unilateral decision that impacts my wife—without thinking of how it affects her.

"Hey, Jess."

"I need Macy home. Now."

No hello. No pleasantries. Straight to demands. Classic Jessica.

"What's wrong? Is everything okay?"

"Nothing's wrong. I just want my daughter back. You've had her all weekend."

I glanced at the clock. Felicity's flight should be landing soon if my calculations are correct. "Can it wait until tonight? I was hoping—"

"No, it can't wait. Brad's taking us to dinner, and I want Macy there. Family dinner."

Family dinner. The phrase hit like a slap. Since when did Jessica care about family dinners? Last I heard, Brad was the guy who complained about everything related to Macy.

"Jess, Macy was really hoping to be here today. Felicity's coming home from her trip, and Macy wanted to see her before she headed home la—"

"Why's that? Because you're putting Felicity over Macy's interests? Gaslighting Macy into thinking Felicity is some sort of mom to her? I'm her mom. Felicity is nothing but a weekend addition to her life. Enough is enough Caden."

Her words hit like acid, burning through my chest. I gripped the phone tighter, my knuckles whitening. "Hey!" My voice cracked, higher than I intended. "That's—" I swallowed hard, tasting bile. "That's completely unfair and absolutely uncalled for."

"You know what Caden, I have a headache right now and don't have the time or energy for this. Get her ready to come home Caden. I don't need to defend my decisions."

"Jess, I'm supposed to have her for a couple more hours."

"You never cared before if I picked her up early. You start don't now."

I froze. Did she just trip over her words?

"Ugh. Caden, are you dumb? I said you don't get to start now!"

What the fuck? I forced myself to cool my jets. She wasn't completely wrong.

"Look, can we just—"

"No. I'll be there in fifteen minutes."

The line went dead.

I stared at the phone, frustration bubbling in my chest. What the fuck had just happened? I pictured Jessica's face, that tight smile she wore at Macy's fifth birthday when I arrived with Felicity. The same smile from our custody hearing, when the judge granted me weekend visitation. The same smile when she'd "accidentally" forgotten to tell me that Macy's first dance recital was during one of my weekends and I needed to change plans. Now here she was again, yanking the rug out just as Felicity's plane touched down. Maybe it's time for a co-parenting app.

I climbed the stairs. Macy's door was cracked open, and she was sitting on her bed, listening to music.

"Hey, kiddo."

She looked up, grinning. "Hi!" She looked really happy.

My heart sank. "So... your mom called. She wants you to come home."

The smile fell from her face. "But I thought I was staying until after Felicity gets here."

"I know. I thought so too."

"Can't I just call her back? Tell her I want to stay for a little while longer?"

Before I could answer, her phone rang. Mom flashed on the screen.

Macy looked at me, then at the phone. "Maybe I can tell her now."

She swiped to accept. "Hi, Mom. Dad to—"

I couldn't hear Jessica's side, but I watched Macy's face change after she was cut off and the more she heard. The excitement drained away, replaced by confusion, then something that looked like guilt.

"But Mom, I want to—" Macy started, then stopped. Listened. Her shoulders slumped.

"I know, but—" Another pause. Her eyes got watery.

"It's just for a little—"

"No, I didn't mean—" She looked at me helplessly, then back at the phone.

"I'm sorry, mom." Another pause.

"Yes, Mom. I understand." Her voice dropped to a whisper, the words barely making it past her trembling lips as her shoulders curved inward like a wilting flower. She was defeated.

"Okay. I'll get my stuff."

She hung up and sat there for a moment, staring at her hands. I felt helpless. I've never interfered where Jessica's relationship with Macy was concerned. I honestly wasn't sure what the right talking point here was.

So, I went with a basic. "What did she say?" I asked gently.

"She said..." Macy's voice cracked slightly. "She said I'm her daughter, not Felicity's. And that I shouldn't be here for when she gets back."

Macy started gathering her things quickly. "She said if I really cared about our family—about her and me—I wouldn't choose Felicity over her. She said it hurts her feelings when I want to be here more than there tonight. She didn't even let me tell her I wasn't choosing Felicity! But that I still wanted to be here."

I sat down on the edge of her bed. "Okay. Wow. That's a lot. Do you want to take a minute and tell me how you're feeling?"

She sighed, shoulders slumped. "No. It's okay. I don't want to upset Mom. She's been stressed a lot lately and it's probably easier if I just go home like she said."

"She have a lot going on?"

"Um. Yeah—I think it's work, or something. She said that things are tighter right now."

Huh. That seems weird. A memory tickled at the back of my mind where Jess and I had a back and forth about money. As I tried to remember the details though, Macy cut in. "It doesn't matter, Dad. I'll figure it out."

I stood up, pacing to her window. Outside, the neighbor's sprinkler was running, casting rainbows in the late afternoon sun. Such a normal, peaceful scene—nothing like the storm brewing in my chest.

"You know what, Mace?" I turned back to her. "Your mom is wrong."

Her eyes widened. I'd never contradicted Jessica in front of Macy before. Never.

"I'm not saying this to be mean about your mom," I continued, sitting back down. "Just that — well, you wanting to be here doesn't mean you aren't choosing your mom. It also doesn't mean that Felicity is trying to replace her. You caring about Felicity doesn't take anything away from how you love your mom. Love isn't pie, kiddo. There isn't less to go around when you add more people."

Macy nodded slowly. "I know that. I just... Mom has a lot on her plate."

I sighed, choosing my words carefully. "Sometimes adults get scared. We're not perfect, you know. You saw that with me over the last week, right?"

"Definitely."

"Well, maybe your mom sees how much you care about Felicity and worries it means something it doesn't."

"But I want to apologize to Felicity. About the purse. I feel terrible."

"You know it's not your fault. It's still my fault how everything happened."

"Yeah, but dad. I didn't even think about her." She dropped her head. "I only thought about myself and that's what I want to say 'sorry' for."

"Okay, well you should still be able to do that." I stood up, decision made. "Here's what we're going to do. You're going to write Felicity a note—everything you want to say to her. I'll make sure she gets it. And the surprise we prepared? We'll figure out another way to make that happen."

"Dad. No one writes notes anymore. Can I do a video instead?"

I scoffed. "Fine. If notes are too *old* for you, then a video sounds like a cool idea. I bet she'd like that just as much."

"Yeah?"

"Yeah. Your relationship with Felicity matters. And your feelings are yours and yours alone."

Macy hugged me tight. "Thanks, Dad."

"Now go pack up."

"Okay. Mom should be here soon. Can I do the video when I get back to mom's house? I want to think about what to say since all this stuff is different now."

"Sure kiddo. That sounds like a good plan." I reached over and hugged my daughter. I need to figure out how to deal with Jessica. One thing is for certain, I've clearly fallen asleep at the wheel with Jessica's treatment of Felicity's relationship with Macy.

Since we divorced when Macy was just a toddler, I don't think I ever considered the kinds of things that could be going on under the surface. We both met our current spouses years ago. Why there would be such animosity is beyond me.

My jaw clenched, but I forced myself to stay calm. I watched Jessica's car pull into the driveway and felt my fingers curl into fists at my sides. The words I'd swallowed for years burned in my throat, begging to be unleashed. But when I glanced back at Macy's hunched shoulders as she packed, I forced my hands to unclench. Not now. First, get Macy off with as little damage as possible. Felicity would be landing soon, and the house was ready for her return. The confrontation with Jessica could wait.

But I won't be asleep at the wheel any longer. Felicity will know. And this shit won't stand.

Chapter 17: I Didn't Know What to Say

~MACY~

I sat in the car, holding my phone tight in my hands, trying to think about what to say. It was hard to focus though—Mom's been silent the whole ride. When Mom is quiet, she is mad.

Her lips seemed tight, and she just kept tapping the steering wheel.

I turned to face the window so I wouldn't see her mad face. Thinking about what Dad had told me — that it was okay to take my time if I wanted to get the video just right. I really wanted Felicity to know that I was sorry. My cheeks burned hot just remembering the moment I pulled the purse from its wrapping. Sure, it had been hidden in my closet, but I should have thought of her. The way Felicity's smile faltered when she saw me clutching it—my stomach knotted every time I replayed it.

I looked back at my phone, and smiled a little, thinking of the surprise we'd planned. I'd helped dad do the grocery shopping for their dinner and he taught me how to cook it and put it all together. I'd had a lot of fun with that. I don't usually help in the kitchen—mom doesn't really cook, though Felicity always lets me help if she's cooking. Dad also let me pick a bouquet of flowers that are from just me. He did his own too, but I got to have my own picked out for Felicity which was really cool and super fun to do. The lady at the flower shop helped me put some colors and different flowers together for it.

I really hope she likes the bouquet. I was kinda sad, though, that I didn't get to be there to give them to her.

Before I knew it, we had pulled into the driveway. Mom cut the engine fast and got out like she was late for something.

Inside, I followed her to the kitchen.

"Hey, Mom?" I tried.

She didn't look up. "Put your things away."

I hesitated. "Okay. Um... also, Dad said I could record a quick video. For Felicity. Can I do it here?"

That got her attention.

She turned slowly from the counter, face blank. Her eyes looked glassy, unfocused for a second, like she was somewhere else before snapping back to me. "A video?"

"Yeah, for Felicity."

"Why?"

"I didn't get to see her before we left, and I just wanted to say—"

"No."

I blinked. "What?"x

"No, Macy. There will be no video message to that woman."

I stared at her. "What? But—why?"

Mom's eyes got wide, and her look got really sharp like a switch flipped. "Because she is not your family. She's your father's wife—we've talked about this before Macy."

"I know, Mom," I said quietly. "But I really l—"

"That's enough Macy. Can't you see what she's doing? She's making you feel guilty, so you'll fix her problems for her. That's not fair to you or me."

"But Mom! She didn't ask me to do anything!" My voice cracked. "It's something I wanted to do. I feel bad, Mom. I hurt her feelings, and I didn't mean to—"

"Macy! It breaks my heart that you care more about that woman than me. I'm your mother. I'm the one who's been here for you, doing things for you, taking care of you for your whole life." she wasn't yelling, but she wasn't *not* yelling.

I felt my face flush and I know I started to really cry. "That's not fair."

Her eyes narrowed. "Do you want to lose your phone for the rest of the week?"

I opened my mouth to say something else, then stopped. My throat hurt. I looked down at the phone in my hand. "No," I whispered.

Jessica held out her palm. "Give it to me."

"Wait. No, Mom pl—"

"Now."

"But Mo—"

"I said hand it over! Right now!" I handed it over. My fingers were trembling. She snatched the phone from my hand, her nails scraping across my wrist. Her grip was shaky, though—hard and trembling all at once, like she didn't realize how much pressure she was using. I watched four tiny lines appear on my skin where she'd scraped, pale at first, then turning angry pink.

She pocketed my phone, turned on her heel and walked off, leaving me standing in the kitchen with nothing but the sting of her nail marks on my wrist and the hollow echo of her footsteps fading down the hall. I stared at the polished granite countertop, my reflection a watery blur in its surface, while the refrigerator hummed in the silence like it was trying to fill the space where words should be.

I slowly went up to my room, my chest tight and tears flowing down my face. I closed my door and sat on the bed. Lying down, I turned away from my door and stared at the wall. I had never seen Mom like that before. So angry. So... mean. Sometimes I thought she seemed tired all the time, her face pale in a way that made her look older. Tonight, though, it wasn't tired—it was like something else had taken over.

I told Dad I'd send a video. I just wanted to say I was sorry.

Now he might think I forgot.

Felicity might think I don't care.

What do I do?

Sitting there, I kept thinking. And then I remembered—the computer.

"Macy!" I heard Mom yell from across the house. I got up, too scared not to. I walked slowly to my door.

"Macy!" I heard again.

I opened my door and started toward the Den. She yelled again, and I called out, "I'm coming."

"What's taking you so long?"

When I turned the corner she exclaimed loudly, "Are you crying? Why are you crying?!"

"Because you took my phone and now I can't do the video."

"Macy. You better stop crying right now. I've had it up to here with this. Enough!"

"I'm trying. I'm sorry, Mom." I really tried to pull back my tears. The hiccups came though, and I just couldn't control it.

"You know what? You're grounded. I think you need some time to think about what family really means. So, no phone, no hanging out with friends, no video games. I'm doing this because I love you, and I can see she's clearly confusing you."

"What?! But Mo—"

"Enough. Grounded for two weeks. Do you want it to be longer?"

"No." I looked down at my hand and whispered, "I'm sorry," again.

"Brad and I are going out to dinner. You're going to stay in now since you lost the privilege of coming out with us. You'll have to find a frozen dinner or something in the freezer for dinner now."

"Ok."

"Then it's straight to bed. You are not to watch TV and I will be keeping your phone until further notice."

"Ok."

Brad will be home in a few to get me. Go to your room until we've left. I don't want to see you for the rest of the night. I need some space tonight, honey. It hurts too much to see how easily she's turned you against me."

"But Mom, I didn't mea—"

"Enough Macy. Go to your room."

I turned around and walked to my room, head down. Mom's voice kept playing in my head, over and over. "That woman." The way her face twisted when she said it. But this time, her eyes weren't just cold when she talked about Felicity—they were cold when she looked at me too. My chest felt like someone was sitting on it. I wiped my cheeks with my sleeve, but it was pointless. New tears just replaced the old ones, dripping off my chin and making dark circles on my shirt.

Once I got around the corner, I ran to my room and threw myself on my bed. I buried my head in my pillow, not wanting Mom to hear my crying in case it would make her madder.

I decided to wait until she and Brad were gone. Then I could go to the den and use the computer. Maybe I could send dad an email and let him know I was sorry, but I couldn't do the video tonight.

~_~_~_~_~_~_~_~_~_~_~_~_~_~_~_

I heard Mom and Brad walking around in the kitchen, talking and laughing—like she hadn't made me cry all of half an hour before. Waiting for them to leave, I sat on the floor by my bedroom door. I waited and waited. Finally, I heard them head out the door. I raced to the window to watch their car pull out of the garage and leave the driveway.

Once I was sure they were gone, I ran to the computer, doubling back to put something in the microwave from the freezer—in case mom came back and saw me out of my room.

Sitting in front of the computer, I opened an email and tried to think of what to say. I didn't want to tell dad anything that would make him mad at Mom. If I did, then he would tell Mom and then she would get mad at me. Plus, I didn't want to hurt her feelings too. She's just mad right now because she thinks I love Felicity too much. I can fix that. I just need to not talk about Felicity to her anymore. Then she won't worry about it and won't be mad at me.

I watched the cursor blink. I didn't know what to say. I think I started and stopped different versions like ten times before I actually decided what to say. Hands shaking, I sent the following:

To: Dad (Caden@gmail.com)

From: Macy (MacyIsTheBest@gmail.com)

Subject: Video

Hi Dad,

I'm super sorry I didn't send the video yet. I still want to…I just didn't get the chance tonight. I was trying to think of the right words and how to say stuff the way I mean it. I want her to know I'm really sorry, and that I care about her a lot. Could you tell her for now? Just til I send the video, okay?

Oh – and please tell her that I didn't forget. And that I meant everything we planned. I hope she liked the flowers.

I'll try to do something tomorrow if I can.

Love,Macy

I read it over and over again and clicked send. I closed out my email after making sure I signed out. *Should I delete my browser history?* I decided to do it—just in case. Then I closed everything down and turned the computer off. I didn't want Mom to see that I had gone online since she told me to stay in my room. What if he didn't check his email today? My stomach felt weird and nervous. I didn't like feeling this way.

Maybe I should make Mom breakfast in the morning to make it up to her. I don't want her to be mad. Is Mom right? Do I care about Felicity too much?

Going to the kitchen, I got out the dinner from the microwave—Stouffers fettuccini alfredo—and wolfed it down. After tossing the fork in the dishwasher and throwing the container in the recycling, I poured some water and headed back to my room. I had homework that I could work on anyways, so maybe that will distract me until it's time to go to bed.

I really hope Mom still isn't mad at me when she wakes up. And that Felicity and Dad aren't mad that I didn't send the video.

I just wish someone would tell me the right thing to do. So I could stop messing everything up.

Chapter 18: Coming Home

~FELICITY~

The Uber pulled away, leaving me standing in my own driveway with my suitcase and a heart that felt too big for my chest. The house looked the same—white colonial, black shutters, the garden I'd planted three springs ago—but something felt different. I think it was me.

I could see warm light spilling from the front windows. Caden's car was in the garage, but no sign of Jessica's SUV. Good. I wasn't ready for that particular brand of drama tonight.

My key turned easily in the lock, and I stepped inside to the smell of something familiar. Something that made my throat tighten with memory.

"Felicity?" Caden's voice came from the kitchen, cautious and hopeful.

"It's me."

Dropping my suitcase by the door, I followed the scent toward the back of the house. He was standing by the stove, wooden spoon in hand, looking like he'd been caught doing something he'd get in trouble for.

"You're cooking," I said, surprised by how my voice sounded—smaller than I intended.

"Yeah—I...I thought our taco dish could be a good way to—" he paused, almost searching for the words. "I don't know. I guess—it seemed like a good welcome home. Now it feels like..." He trailed off, gesturing helplessly at the pan. "Um. Well I don't know—so, I thought maybe you'd be hungry." He was nervous.

I stared at him. At the clean kitchen, the fresh flowers on the counter, the two forks laid out on a single plate. Just like we used to do—when we were happy.

The flowers weren't white roses. They were vibrant—orange mixed with purple. I wasn't sure what the flowers were, but they were beautiful. I could see there was eucalyptus and some baby's breath mixed in. It was a splattering of colors. It felt like someone had paid attention instead of just checking off a box.

"Where's Macy?"

His face darkened. "Jessica picked her up early. She... there was a situation."

I nodded, not trusting myself to speak yet. The disappointment hit harder than I expected. That felt like a surprise. I'd been looking forward to seeing her, wanted to make sure she didn't think this whole thing was her fault. Because it wasn't.

"She wanted to be here," Caden continued quickly. "She was really upset about leaving. She wanted to apologize to you. About the purse."

"She doesn't need to apologize for anything." The words came out sharper than I meant them to. "She's eleven, Caden. This was never about her."

"I know." He set down the spoon and turned to face me fully. "I know that. I know I screwed everything up. I know I made it worse when you tried to tell me too."

We stood there in the kitchen where this all started, the same kitchen where I'd watched my husband give away the one thing I'd asked for, where I'd finally found my voice and used it to tell him how invisible I felt.

I touched the flowers gently. "These are beautiful."

"Macy picked them out. For you. She spent twenty minutes at the flower shop making sure they were perfect." His voice was soft. "She said the white roses you usually get are pretty, but these ones were happy. Like you."

My throat closed up. An eleven-year-old had put more thought into flowers for me than my husband had in years. That stung.

"I got your text," I said finally. "About my birthday."

He nodded. "I didn't know if I should... you said not to call or text, but I couldn't let the day pass without..."

"Thank you." I surprised myself by meaning it.

"How was Miami?"

"Good." I touched the strap of my purse, thinking of the spa, beach, shopping, the women who'd adopted me for a night. The letter and the postcard I'd written to myself. "Really good, actually. No—that's wrong. It was amazing."

Something shifted in his expression. Relief, maybe. But fear too?

"I'm glad," he said quietly. "You deserved that."

The silence stretched between us, heavy with everything we hadn't said yet. I could feel the conversation coming, the one we'd been building toward for months. Maybe years.

I walked over to the island and set down my purse, my movements deliberate and slow. I was stalling, and we both knew it. But I needed to take a breath and gather myself, to find the words for what felt like the most important conversation of my life.

"The house looks good," I said, taking in the spotless counters, the absence of his usual clutter. "Did you clean?"

"Top to bottom." He almost smiled. "Twice, actually. I kept finding things I'd missed."

"Like what?"

He paused, looking like he was nervous to say. "Your coffee mug. You know, the one I gave you for your promotion? I—um, I found it buried under a stack of paperwork and things on my desk. I'd been drinking my coffee right next to it for well, I don't know how long, without seeing it."

Well, I guess I knew where my mug went. I'd searched everywhere for it the other day, coming up empty handed. "I used to use that mug every morning," I said quietly. "I couldn't figure out where it went. I couldn't find it anymore."

His face fell. "I'm sorry."

I scoffed. "Feels like quite the metaphor, doesn't it?" I looked at him directly. "Me, buried under your stuff. You, drinking your coffee right next to me every morning without really seeing me."

He didn't answer, but I saw the truth of it hit him.

"Caden," I started, then stopped. My hands were shaking.

"What is it?"

"I can't do this anymore." The words fell out of me like stones. "I can't keep pretending that a dinner and some flowers and a heartfelt letter are going to fix six years of me being invisible in my own marriage."

His face went pale. "Felicity—"

"Wait. You need to let me finish." I held up a hand, surprised by my own steadiness. "I'm not saying I don't love you. I'm not saying I want a divorce. But I am saying that something has to fundamentally change, or I'm done."

He nodded slowly, like he'd been expecting this. Maybe he had.

"I've spent so much time making myself smaller," I continued, the words flowing now like water through a broken dam. My voice gravelly, like cracks creating breaks across that dam. "Making excuses for you. Telling myself 'He's just busy, just stressed, things will get better when the next crisis passed, or the next deal closed.' But they never did, did they?"

"No," he said quietly. "They didn't."

"Can you even imagine what it's like to be married to someone who remembers every detail of the things around him except for the details around his wife?" My voice cracked. "To watch you bend over backward for others, for your clients, for your work—but not for me?"

"I didn't realize—"

"I know! That's the problem!" The words exploded out of me. I knew I was yelling. I don't usually yell. But I couldn't control it. "You didn't realize. For years, Caden. You didn't realize that I was right next to you...drowning."

Tears were streaming down my face now, but I couldn't stop. Wouldn't stop.

"I used to feel so loved by you. I was seen. Remember the times we used to go for hikes? Or when you would wake me early for breakfast so we could watch the sun come up together? Or what about when you surprised me that first year with tickets to see Billy Joel?"

His eyes filled. "I remember."

"Where did that man go? When did that man disappear? When did I become just another item on your to-do list, something to be managed by your assistant?"

"I don't know," he whispered. "I lost myself somewhere. In work, in trying to prove something after the company almost went under. I thought I was doing it for us, for our future, but I got so lost in saving everything else that I forgot to save us."

"Let's be clear—You didn't lose me," I said fiercely. "You forgot me. There's a difference."

His tears were flowing now too, and something in my chest cracked open at the sight of it.

"I know," he said. "God, Felicity, I know. And I'm so fucking sorry." He pressed his thumb and forefinger into his eyes as his shoulders began to shake. "I'm sorry for the purse, I'm sorry for the birthdays and anniversaries I missed—and all the gifts I delegated. I'm sorry for making you feel like you had to fight for space in your own marriage, in our lives. I'm sorry for not seeing what Jessica was doing, for not protecting you—for not protecting us and what we have—had. I'm sorry for all of it."

"I don't want you to just be sorry," I said, my voice breaking completely. "I want you to be different."

"I know. I am different." He stepped closer, and I didn't step back. "I can't undo what I've done, but I can promise you that I see myself now and what I'd become. I see you now. Really see you. And I will never, ever take you for granted again."

"How do I know that?" I whispered. "How do I trust that this isn't just another crisis you'll solve and then forget about?"

"Because I'm not the same man who gave away your birthday present. Because I'm horrified by how much I'd forgotten and what I have done—by my failure to be the man you fell in love with. Because I love you, and I almost lost you, and that scared me more than anything ever has in my life."

I looked at him—really looked. Saw the exhaustion in his eyes, the way his hands shook slightly, the stubble that said he hadn't been sleeping well.

"Do you know what I did on my birthday?" I asked suddenly.

He shook his head.

"I had the most incredible day. I pampered myself. I met a group of women who made me laugh until my sides hurt. I danced barefoot on the beach until three in the morning. I treated myself to all the things I wished you'd treated me to." My voice broke. "I had to leave my husband and fly to another state to remember who I was." I decided not to share with him about the letter. It was mine and I didn't want anyone else but me and my future self to know about it. It was sacred.

"I'm so sorry—"

"For fuck's sake—Stop apologizing!" I shouted, startling both of us. I am not a big curser ... well, that's not true—I just don't usually drop F-bombs. So, more quietly I said, "Stop it. I don't want your apologies anymore, Caden. I want your attention. I want your effort. I want you to fight for me—for us."

"I will," he said desperately. "I am."

"The flowers in Miami were beautiful," I said, my voice getting quiet again.

He looked confused. "What flowers?"

"Exactly." I wiped my eyes with the back of my hand. "I sent myself flowers. For my birthday. From a woman who finally remembered she was worth celebrating."

Understanding dawned on his face. "Felicity..."

"I'm not the same woman who left four days ago either, Caden," I continued. "I'm not going to disappear again. I'm not going to make myself smaller to fit into the spaces you've left behind. If we are going to work, you need to make room for all of me. The quiet parts, angry parts, the demanding parts, the parts that need more than you've been giving. You need to see me without me having to tell you or having to give you direction on what I need from you."

"I want all of you," he said without hesitation. "I want to make room for all of you—I *will* make room for all of you."

I walked to the window and looked out at the backyard, at the garden I'd planted and tended mostly alone. The roses needed deadheading. The weeds were taking over the herb bed. Another metaphor for our marriage—me doing all the maintenance while he focused elsewhere.

"Do you remember why I planted that garden?" I asked.

"Because you wanted fresh herbs for cooking?"

I turned back to him. I huffed out a breath. "No. I planted it the year your company almost went under. When you were working eighteen-hour days and coming home exhausted and distant. I needed something that was mine, something that would grow because I cared for it. Something that would respond to my attention."

His face crumpled. "Oh, God."

"I've been tending that garden for three years. Do you know—you've never once asked me about it. Never noticed when I brought in fresh basil for dinner or when the tomatoes were ready. It was right outside your office window, and you never saw it."

"I see it," he whispered.

"Do you? Or are you just saying that because I'm pointing it out?"

He was quiet for a long moment, and I could see him thinking, really thinking.

After a minute I asked, "Caden?"

"Wait—just give me a second?" He looked at his feet, going silent again. And then, "you planted the rosemary in the corner because you read that it's supposed to mean remembrance," he said slowly. "And the lavender along the path because it helps you sleep when you're stressed. The tomatoes are heirloom varieties because you said grocery store tomatoes taste like water. And you put the bench there so you could sit and read in the morning with your coffee."

I stared at him, shocked. "You...wait, what?!" I was speechless.

"I know I'm not always present. I miss things. I've checked out. But I honestly still know you in my heart. When everything happened, I sat and tried to remember all the things you like, all the things about you I should know without trying to dig in my brain." he said simply. "Then I remembered that there is a deeper part of my heart that just knows you. I love you, Felicity. I'm a complete screw up. I know I got so lost in everything else that I forgot to show you. But I see how you take care of everyone around you. I see how you make Macy feel special when she's here, how you give your heart. You leave small notes around for me. You give the most amazing hugs. Your heart is a beautiful thing. I failed to protect it. And I will never make that mistake again."

Tears were flowing freely now. "Then why didn't any of that matter when it came to remembering my birthday? How can you say these things without me now? Where was all this then?"

"Because I'm an idiot," he said simply. "Because I got comfortable thinking you'd always be there, always be understanding, always be willing to wait for me to have time for you. Because I took your strength for granted and forgot that strong people can break too."

"I did break," I whispered. "That night with the purse. I broke completely."

"I know. I saw it happen and I was too stupid to understand what I was watching—even though I was right there in the middle of it."

"I've felt so alone, Caden. Alone in this marriage, alone in this house, alone in my own life. Do you have any idea what that feels like—any idea what it has been like to be me?"

"I don't. And I could never." he said quietly. "You would never put me in that position—not like I did you. But this last week. This time without you—not knowing if you would even come home—if you would give me a chance...they have been heartbreaking. I've never felt lonelier in my life, and just the thought that my small taste of what you experienced over these last few years—I can't even pretend to imagine. I. Am. So. Fucking. Sorry."

I looked around, needing to see anything—anything but the pure sincerity and remorse on his face. "This home of ours—you know it's almost stopped feeling like home," I said. "Almost like a place I was staying. One with memories, but unlikely hope of a future."

"What can I do to make it feel like home again?"

I looked around the kitchen—at the evidence of his effort, at the flowers Macy had chosen, at the meal he'd prepared with his own hands instead of ordering takeout or asking me to cook.

"I don't know yet," I said honestly. "But this is a start."

"There's something else," he said, reaching into his pocket. "From Macy. She emailed me tonight."

He handed me his phone, and I read her message, my heart breaking and mending at the same time.

"She's a good kid," I whispered. "I wish—" I paused, handing him back the phone, and unsure of how to continue.

"What? You can tell me anything. I swear, I'm here to listen now. Now and forever."

"I don't know. I feel this weird sensation. It's hard to explain. I...I feel torn."

"Torn?"

"Yeah. Trying for so long to have a kid. Trying and failing." The tears that had finally dried started again. I knew this was one of those things—one of the issues between us that had no solution.

"Felicity." I heard his sigh. Thinking he was exasperated by the topic, I responded, "I know. I know it's done. I get it. Nevermi—"

"No!" He said sharply, then dialing his volume back he repeated, "no. I don't mean don't talk about it. I meant—I don't know. I guess I just meant that I get it. I feel the same way. Like I wish things had worked out but at the same time I'd hate if there was a little person of our own stuck in the middle of this pain."

Sighing, my shoulders slumped. "Yeah—that's exactly what I mean and how I feel." I looked down at my stomach, the one that had never carried a life to term. The one that had failed me. I laid my hand on across my abdomen, remembering the feeling of life that had been there for only a few moments, never to see the light of day. "Yeah," I whispered.

He reached for me, then pulled back. We both knew that we weren't there yet—in a place where touch was right. Not yet.

I stood up straight and looked around the kitchen again—at the flowers, the clean counters, the care he'd taken to make this space welcoming.

"You know what the hardest part of everything was?" I said suddenly. "It wasn't the forgotten birthdays or the delegated gifts. It was being alone. It was feeling like I didn't matter enough for you to try. Like after you poured yourself into your work, after I poured myself into mourning our loss, what we had together just wasn't enough to hold us together on its own and I didn't matter."

"You matter more than anything," he said fiercely. "You matter more than work, more than anything. I lost sight of that, but I see it now."

"This doesn't fix us," I said.

"I know."

"We have a lot of work to do."

"I know."

"It's work we probably should have been doing already."

"I know."

"So what now?"

He looked at me. "I think we should see someone—like a therapist, I mean."

I know surprised was splashed across my face. "Really? You'd do that? Go to couples' counseling?"

"There is something here that broke between us. Yes, I'm so much at fault, I can't even explain it. But I also recognize that rebuilding what we had—or building something new—I'm not... I just...I don't—I don't want to fuck it up any more than I already have Felicity." His voice was fierce.

I wanted to believe him. That he was willing to do this. God, I wanted to believe him. But wanting and trusting were two very different things.

"I can't," I said quietly. "I can't just take your word for it anymore, Caden. Not after everything."

His face fell, but he nodded. "What do you need from me?"

"Time," I said. "And proof. Real, sustained proof that this isn't just another crisis you'll solve and then forget about when life gets busy again."

"I'm in. I mean it, Felicity. I will do anything and everything for the rest of our lives if that's what it takes to prove it."

I wrapped my arms around myself. "I'll find someone. A therapist. Make the appointments."

"Let me look? Is that okay? I don't want you to have to do it. I fucked up, I should have to do the work. I can call the insurance and get a list. Then how about you and I talk through the list together and decide together."

"That's good. I like that. Thank you."

We stood there in the kitchen, the weight of everything unsaid hanging between us.

"The food smells good," I said finally, because I was hungry and exhausted.

"It's probably overcooked by now."

"I don't care."

But as he moved toward the oven, I added quietly, "I'm still sleeping in the guest room."

He stopped. "Okay."

"For a while. Maybe a long while."

"I understand."

"This conversation—tonight—it's not forgiveness, Caden. It's just acknowledgment that we both see the problem now."

"I know."

We ate mostly in silence. The food tasted like memory and effort and something I couldn't name. When we finished, I stood up.

"I should unpack."

"Do you need—"

"No. I can handle it."

Upstairs in the guest room, I sat on the bed and looked around at the space that would be mine for now. Maybe for a long time. Through the window, I could see my garden in the moonlight—overgrown but still there, still growing despite neglect.

I unpacked slowly, hanging my clothes in the closet. I put the new ones from Miami in the front. They made me smile. No matter what I was feeling right this moment, I could still smile at the thought of what this last weekend meant for me.

At the bottom of my suitcase, I found the receipt from the hotel spa and a few other mementos from my trip. The postcard I'd mailed to myself wouldn't arrive for a few days—with the postmark timestamping the end to my experience there—leaving with me a future reminder of the woman who'd remembered she was worth celebrating.

I thought about that woman, dancing barefoot on the beach, laughing with strangers who'd become friends for a night. She felt both like me and like someone I was still trying to become.

I turned off the light and lay in the dark, listening to him moving around downstairs, and wondered if wanting to fix something was enough when you weren't sure it could be fixed.

Chapter 19: Expensive Revelations

~Caden~

Sitting sat at the kitchen table long after she'd gone upstairs, I found myself staring at the two forks we'd shared and the empty plate between us. The house felt different with her in it—unexplainable, really—not whole, but less hollow than it had been while she was gone.

I pictured her sleeping in the guest room. My fingers itched to touch her—to play with her hair. My lips burned to kiss her face. My arms longed to just hold her. And my heart ached to repair hers.

I scrubbed until the fork squeaked against porcelain, until the soap bubbles thinned to nothing. Maybe if I kept scrubbing, I could scrape away more than pasta sauce. I wanted Felicity to wake in the morning knowing I spent time taking care of this—hoping she would see that I will do this exercise with everything messy and disastrous in our life.

The counters gleamed, the sink was dry, every dish stacked like soldiers in a row. Still, the room felt hollow, like it was waiting for something I couldn't scrub back into place.

I walked to the window and looked out at her garden—really looked at it this time. In the moonlight, I could make out the different areas, including the bench where she would probably sit in the morning tomorrow since the weather was going to be nice.

How many times had I walked past this window without seeing what she'd built? How many mornings had I missed her sitting out there, reading, thinking—just being?

I pressed my hand against the cool glass. The conversation kept replaying in my head—her voice breaking when she explained having to fly to another state to remember who she was. The way she'd looked at me when I listed the plants in her garden, shocked that I'd noticed anything at all.

Then why didn't any of that matter when it came to remembering my birthday?

Because I'm an idiot. I'd said it, and I'd meant it, but it felt too simple. Too easy. I wasn't just an idiot—I was a man who'd gotten so lost in his own priorities that he'd forgotten the most important thing in his life was sitting right next to him, slowly disappearing.

My phone buzzed.

Cash: How'd it go?

I stared at the screen, sighing as I tried to figure out how to answer. How did it go? She came home. She talked. She didn't leave. But she also didn't forgive me, and she shouldn't have.

Me: We talked, but she's still sleeping in the guest room.

Cash: Fuck. I'm sorry man.

Me: No, it's good. I mean, not good... but fair, you know?

Cash: You doing okay?

Me: We're going to try therapy.

Cash: That's something, yeah?

Me: Yeah. Maybe.

I set the phone down and walked through the house, turning off lights, checking the front door. Going through nighttime routine helped settle me—even though nothing about this was normal. At the bottom of the stairs, I stopped and listened. No sound from upstairs. She was probably passed out—exhausted from traveling and from everything we'd just been through.

I wanted to go to her. Not to try anything, not to push. Just to check—does she have enough blankets? Was the room too cold? Did she notice I had swapped out one of her pillows so I could still feel her with me? She probably did—she notices everything.

But I couldn't. I knew she wouldn't want me to come knocking tonight—for any reason. So, I walked by the room, grazing my fingers on the door lightly as I passed.

In our bedroom, I sat on the edge of the bed and looked around. Her jewelry box on the dresser. Her books on the nightstand. Pictures of us from various points over these last years—all scattered around like evidence of a life I'd somehow lost track of.

There was one from our second anniversary. We'd gone to that little inn in Vermont, spent the whole weekend hiking and talking and making love like we were still discovering each other. In the picture her laugh froze mid-burst—her throat arched, hair tangled by the Vermont wind.

When had I stopped looking at her like that—seeing her for this absolutely amazing woman?

The truth was, I did remember. I remembered who I used to be—the man who woke her up early to watch sunrises, who surprised her with concert tickets, who wanted to experience everything for the first time with her. That man was still in me—he'd just gotten buried under deadlines and deals and the relentless pace of trying to prove I was successful enough, important enough, worthy enough.

But worthy of what? I already had everything that mattered. I'd just been too busy to notice.

My phone buzzed again. This time it was Lauren.

Lauren: Saw you were online. Can we talk in the morning? I have something I need to show you?

Me: Yeah. Everything okay?

Lauren: I did some digging into the Visa bill you gave me to research, and found something odd, which sent me down a rabbit hole. I want to review with you in person though. I have a file that we should go through. Nothing burning for the night, but was hoping we could get in early to review before the day gets away from us.

I stared at the message, annoyed that I would have to start my day with some sort of problem I'd probably have to solve already. I should probably get some rest since it seems like the day ahead may be a long one.

I set the phone aside and sat back on the bed, leaning against the head-board, still fully clothed.

Tomorrow I'd call the insurance company, get a list of therapists. To-morrow I'd start the real work of earning her trust back. Tomorrow I'd begin the long process of becoming the husband she deserved instead of the one I'd been. Right after whatever Lauren needed to talk to me about.

I closed my eyes and made a promise to the woman sleeping down the hall, the woman who'd been strong enough to leave and brave enough to come back: I would earn her trust back. I would earn her. I would earn us. And even if Lauren told me that the company would fall apart by the end of the day, I would *not* put Felicity on the backburner—not again—not ever again.

~_~_~_~_~_~_~_~_~_~_~_~_~_~_~_~_~_~_~

My eyes opened to a dark room with the light still on in the bathroom. I turned my neck and felt the telltale crick along it that told me I had fallen asleep in a shit position. I pulled myself up to sitting and looking at the clock could see it was 4:30. I was still in yesterday's clothes, discomfort radiating from my neck down my back. Damn I was too old to fall asleep in such a dumb position. For a moment I forgot—reached for my phone to check emails, started mentally running through my calendar—then it all came rushing back.

Felicity. Guest room. Therapy.

I stood up slowly, listening for sounds from down the hall. Nothing. She was probably still asleep—yesterday had been a long day for both of us.

I showered, dressed, and walked through my morning routine quietly trying not to waking her as I walked by where she was sleeping. In the kitchen, I made coffee for two, left hers in the pot with a note: Good morning. Coffee's fresh.

I'll call about therapists today. – Love you, C

Simple. No grand declarations. No pressure. Just information and cof-fee.

~_~_~_~_~_~_~_~_~_~_~_~_~_~_~_~_~_~_~

At the office by 6:30, I had the place mostly to myself. The quiet felt good—no distractions, no interruptions. Just me and the work I needed to do.

I pulled up our insurance website and navigated to the mental health section. It felt strange typing "couples therapy" into the search bar, but here I was.

The search results populated slowly. Pages and pages of names, credentials, specialties. Dr. Sarah Chen—Specializing in relationship counseling. Dr. Michael Rodriguez—Couples therapy, infidelity recovery, pre-marital counseling. Dr. Amanda Foster—Marriage and family therapy, trauma-informed care.

By 7:15 I had a neat list of fifteen therapists, columns lined up like lifeboats on a sinking ship.

Dr. Jennifer Walsh seemed interesting. I went to her website and found she had evening and weekend appointments available. She specializes in couples rebuilding trust after betrayal. That part caught my eye. Her bio read: "Healing doesn't happen overnight, but with commitment from both partners, even the most damaged relationships can find their way back to love."

I added her name to the top of my list and hit save.

A knock on my door interrupted my thoughts. Lauren walked in carrying two coffee cups and a thick manila folder tucked under her arm.

"You're here early," she said, setting one coffee in front of me.

"Thanks. Yeah, wanted to get a head start on some things."

"Good." She settled into the chair across from my desk, clutching the folder. "How did things go last night? With Felicity?"

"She came home. We talked." I paused, not sure how much to share. "We 're... figuring things out."

Lauren nodded slowly, then leaned back in her chair. "Well, speaking of figuring things out..." She held up the folder. Clearing her throat, she said, "Hold onto your hat, Caden. Your mind's about to be blown with what I found."

I looked at the folder, then back at her face. The expression there made my stomach clench.

"What kind of blown?"

"The kind that involves your ex-wife and some interesting information I came across regarding your expense reports and some discrepancies." She tapped the folder against her palm.

The coffee turned bitter in my mouth. "What are you talking about?"

Lauren's smile was sharp, dangerous. "Oh, we're just getting started. But first, tell me—have you been sending me payment requests from your personal email for the last few years?"

The ice-cold feeling that had been lurking at the edges of my consciousness all morning finally crystallized into pure dread.

"No," I said quietly. "No, I have not."

"That's what I thought." She placed the folder on my desk with deliberate care. "Because someone has. And I think we both know who."

❧

Chapter 20: Parental Controls

~Jessica~

I heard the ding from my phone just as Brad was complaining about the restaurant's wine selection. I glanced at my phone, expecting another client email I could ignore until tomorrow—the housing market never slept, but Monday would be soon enough.

Parental Control Alert: Computer access detected outside permitted hours.

My fork paused halfway to my mouth. Computer access? Well now, Macy was supposed to be in her room. Grounded. No computer. No phone. No privileges. A throb pulsed behind my right eye, the kind that made the light above the table buzz louder, harsher. I pressed two fingers to my temple and forced my smile wider.

"Are you listening to me?" Brad's voice cut through my thoughts.

"Of course," I said, sliding my thumb across the screen to open the monitoring app. "You were saying something about the Pinot."

But I wasn't listening anymore. The alert showed me that Macy had used the computer at 8:47 PM. Logged into Gmail. Stayed on for twelve minutes.

My jaw tightened. I clenched so hard my molars ached. The report blurred for a second, my eyes prickling with the kind of rage that made my hands shake—*breathe... I'll take care of that later.*

I lifted my phone up off the table, hand a little shaky—I'll need to take care of that later. I opened the detailed report—my appetite disappearing as I read. Email sent to Caden. Subject line: "Video."

Perfect. Just fucking perfect.

"Jessica." Brad's tone was sharper now. "What's so important on your phone that you can't focus on our dinner?"

I looked up, forcing a smile. "Sorry. Work email from a client. You know how closings can be."

"On a Sunday night? Must be urgent."

"Just some last-minute paperwork questions. Nothing that can't wait until morning." I slipped the phone into my purse, but my mind was racing.

I mentally went through the monitoring report I'd just read—the email Macy thought she'd sent in secret. Apologizing to Daddy. Asking him to tell precious Felicity she "didn't forget."

Isn't that just so touching...My eleven-year-old daughter, going behind my back to grovel to her father's wife.

I'd clearly been too soft. I was too understanding. The gentle approach I'd taken—explaining that Felicity wasn't family, that loyalties had to be clear—it wasn't working. Macy wasn't getting the message.

Seems like it's time for a different strategy—a new approach to my daughter's thoughtlessness.

I pretended to focus on Brad's wine commentary with renewed attention, nodding at all the right pauses and agreeing to whatever he was blabbing on about. His voice was grating on my already growing headache.

Refocusing on planning for my plans with Macy. If she was reaching out to Caden, if Felicity was somehow making him more attentive to details than he used to be... well, I may need to prepare for the worst. If I've learned one thing over the years, it was that everything was about timing and direction. Most people never paid close enough attention to the details.

Caden certainly hadn't. Felicity needs to stay in her lane.

Macy thought she was so smart, using the computer after we'd left for dinner since I'd taken her phone. She thought she could play the sweet little girl and sneak behind my back.

She had another thing coming.

As a broker, I knew how to read between the lines, and to bury things between lines others don't read. I can see when someone was trying to game the system and I know how to do it better. How my own daughter thought she could outsmart me—she's going to have to learn.

"You know what?" I said, dabbing my lips with the napkin. "I think we should skip dessert tonight. I want to get home to Macy."

Brad raised an eyebrow. "Jess, she's grounded, right. Isn't she supposed to be in her room? Why do we need to get home early?"

"She is. But I think it's time for a mother-daughter conversation about respect. And consequences."

My husband was clearly not happy with me. I'll make it up to him later tonight. The drive home gave me time to plan. Macy was playing little Miss Innocent, probably pretending to be tucked away in bed by now—thinking she'd gotten away with her little rebellion. Looks like she still had no idea I monitored every keystroke and click she made.

Most parents use monitoring software. How else am I supposed to keep an eye on and ensure she doesn't start to have loyalties to the wrong person—to the wrong woman—in the wrong place?

I let myself in quietly, having noted that Macy's light was off when we drove up. Good. She thought she was being so careful.

I walked up the stairs slowly, deliberately, my heels clicking on the hardwood just loud enough to announce my presence. Standing at her door, I could hear the rustle of movement inside—probably rushing to pretend she is asleep.

I knocked once, then opened the door without waiting for permission.

"Mom?" Macy's voice was perfectly pitched—surprised but sleepy, but I could tell she was faking a wake-up voice.

She was good. I'd give her that.

"Hi, sweetheart." I stepped into the room, leaving the door open behind me. "Did you have a good evening?"

"Yeah. I did some homework and went to bed early."

"That's good. Very responsible." I moved closer to her bed, noting how her eyes tracked my movement. I looked around the room casually—her desk chair had clothes draped over it, backpack in the corner—no Dior bag anywhere though. "Where's that beautiful purse Daddy got you? I wanted to see how you're taking care of it."

Macy's face flushed slightly. "It's... I left it at dad's."

"Hmmm. That wasn't smart, Macy. Such an expensive piece—you want to make sure it stays perfect." I smiled softly. "I trust you realize you should bring it home with you this coming weekend. You understand?""Oh. Um. Yeah. Sure." Her voice got quieter, more tentative as she spoke.

Interesting. The hesitation told me something had happened. Either the bag was damaged already—which would be typical Macy—or there was more to this story than I'd been told. I'm betting Felicity was trying to steal it. Like she was trying to steal my baby.

"You know, I've been thinking about our conversation earlier. About Felicity."

I could swear I saw Macy's shoulders tense. "Oh. Okay."

"I realize I may have been too harsh. You're growing up, and you're going to form attachments to people. That's natural."

Hope flickered across her face. "Really?"

"Really." I sat on the edge of her bed, smoothing the comforter with maternal care. "But I also think there are things about adult relationships you don't understand. It's not your fault obviously. It's just that, well honey—sometimes, when marriages are in trouble, children get caught in the middle."

"In trouble? What do you mean?"

"Well, you probably noticed some tension between Felicity and your father. I didn't want to say, but I think it would be good for you to know a little bit—your father and Felicity have been having some problems lately."

Macy's eyes widened. "Problems?"

"Oh, honey," I sighed. "I probably shouldn't be telling you this." I almost whispered, looking down at my hands—as if wrestling with whether to continue. "But I think you're old enough now to understand. Sometimes when couples fight, they use children to send messages. To make the other person feel guilty."

"I don't understand."

"Think about it, sweetheart. These last few months or so, haven't you talked about Felicity trying to do more things with you when your dad had to work? Why do you think she's been doing that? All that special attention, encouraging you to spend more time with her."

I watched confusion cloud her features. Perfect.

"Because she cares about me?"

"Oh, I'm sure she does—in some way. But she also knows that if you're happy there, it makes your father happy." I paused for a moment. "And you know, if your father is happy, maybe he won't leave her."

Seeds of doubt were planted. I could see them root a bit, now I could let Macy's own insecurity water it.

"But...no. Really? No, Mom, she's not like that." Then she whispered, "she's nice to me."

"Of course she is!"

Macy's face reared back at my raised voice. I needed to tone it down. She doesn't understand how things work. God! Why does my head hurt so badly?!

I rubbed my temples as I started again. "Honey, I'm just trying to tell you that's this is how these things work—it feels good at first. It's only later, when everything falls apart, where the kids are left hurting." I brushed a strand of hair from her face with practiced tenderness. "And you're my baby. Of course I don't want you to be the one left hurting. Because things will fall apart, Macy. They always do."

"Dad wouldn't leave her. Would he?"

"I don't know, sweetheart. Marriage is complicated. What I do know is that, when children get too attached, they suffer."

I let that sink in for a moment, watching her process the implications.

"I can't tell you how to feel—I would never do something like that. I just want you to be careful, okay? Guard your heart a little bit. Don't let yourself be used as a pawn in their game."

"Is that why you didn't want me to make the video for her?"

Smart girl. "Partly, yes. I'm concerned that you're telling her you're sorry for something. And whatever it is, I'm sure you're just taking responsibility for adult problems that aren't your fault. And that's not fair to you."

Macy nodded slowly, and I could see the doubt continuing to take root. Good.

"Now, I want you to get some sleep. And tomorrow, we're going to have a conversation about computer privileges. You were such a good girl tonight—following the rules... And hearing me out. I think maybe you've earned some of those privileges back."

I kissed her forehead, inhaling the scent of her shampoo. My daughter. Mine.

"I love you, Macy. More than anyone else ever could."

"I love you too, Mom."

At the door, I paused. "Oh, and sweetheart? If your father asks about visiting this week, why don't you tell him you'd rather stay home with me. You don't have to tell him you know about their problems. It's just until he and Felicity work things out."

"But Mom—"

"Trust me on this one, okay? It's for the best."

I closed her door softly, leaving her alone with her doubts and thoughts.

By morning, she'd be questioning every kind thing Felicity had ever made. By next week, she'd be pulling away on her own, protecting herself from the inevitable disappointment.

I removed my shoes to make my way downstairs, their echo of the heels had made me want to scream. I pressed my hand to the side of my head to help relieve the pressure. It didn't help though. I needed things to work out perfectly, and they would as long as Macy pulled back from Felicity, and any suspicion from Caden about it—well, that would just create more tension in his precious little marriage.

In the kitchen, I poured myself a glass of Pinot. Brad would be waiting for me upstairs, probably still irritated at me for cutting the evening short. I'd need to smooth that over. Maybe I'd tell him I was worried about Macy's behavior lately, that I needed to nip some of this pre-teen rebellion in the bud before it becomes a bigger issue when she *does* become a teenager. He'd understand that—Brad appreciated a firm hand with discipline.

I took a sip of wine and pulled out my phone, scrolling through my work emails. Three new pre-approval requests, one contract question, and a reminder about the Henderson Avenue closing on Wednesday. Normal Sunday night business.

I needed to remember to email Lauren about the credit card replacement. She hadn't responded to my last request, which was unusual. Normally she was so efficient about handling Caden's expenses.

The wine warmed my throat as I finished the glass and poured another glass to bring to our room. Reaching into my bag, I grabbed a pill–I need to get rid of this headache. I took two—it's going to be a busy day and I couldn't afford for it to get worse. At the end of the day, maybe take Macy shopping for school clothes—a little mother-daughter bonding to reinforce tonight's message and ensure her loyalties. It's for her own good, I reminded myself. Even if she hates me for it later.

I climbed the stairs, already planning my approach with Brad. A little wine on my breath, an apology for being distracted, maybe some pointed attention. Men were so predictable.

But as I reached the top of the stairs, I could hear Brad on the phone in our bedroom, his voice muffled but clearly agitated. I paused outside the door, listening.

"—told you, the timeline moved up. We need those permits approved by Friday or the whole deal falls through."

Work call. Perfect. That would put him in a mood, but it also meant he'd be distracted from tonight's dinner drama. I could work with that.

I pushed the door open, giving him an apologetic smile as I mouthed "sorry" and pointed toward the bathroom. I kissed his cheek and left my wine in front of him, my hands still a little unsteady. He nodded curtly, taking the glass for a sip, he remained focused on his conversation.

In the bathroom, I took my time with my cellular rejuvenation routine, letting the familiar ritual calm my thoughts. La Prairie — Platinum Rare. Obscenely expensive, yes—but absolutely worth it. Sleek with a soft scent and clinical, the texture a whisper against my skin. I'd once read about how the formula was designed to restore what age and stress tried to steal. Going through my routine, I also felt shaking ease in my hands.

Good. Let it restore everything.

I dabbed the serum beneath my eyes, smoothing it upward. Felicity could keep her coffee dates and her soft laugh and her stories about books Macy "just had to read." She could keep that garden and her sad little kitchen and her whole pretending-to-be-warm routine.

But she couldn't keep my daughter.

And she wouldn't win.

By the time I emerged from the bathroom, Brad had finished his call and was sitting on the edge of the bed, scrolling through his tablet.

"Sorry about tonight," I said, moving to sit beside him. "Macy's been testing boundaries lately, and I thought it was important to address it right away."

He looked up from his screen. "What kind of boundaries?"

"Sneaking around, not following rules when we're out. You know how eleven-year-olds can be." I leaned against his shoulder. "I just don't want it to escalate."

"Makes sense." His voice had softened. "How'd it go?"

"Good, I think. We had a productive conversation about respect and consequences. I think she understands now."

Brad nodded, setting his tablet aside. "That's important."

"Exactly." I kissed his cheek. Climbed astride his lap. A good distraction may be just what's needed. "How was your call? You sounded stressed," I asked, kissing along his neck.

"City's dragging their feet on a major project. But we'll figure it out." He pulled me close. "I'm sorry I was short with you at dinner. I know you have a lot on your hands."

His hands tightened on my hips. "Speaking of which—did you hear back from your broker friend about that loan? The bridge financing I mentioned?"

My stomach clenched. "Still working on it."

"Jess, we're cutting this close. If the permits don't come through by Friday, and we don't have the capital to carry us through the delay..." He sighed, pulling away a bit. "We could lose everything we've put into this."

"I know. I'm handling it."

"How much more time do you need?" The question hung in the air like smoke.

"Not much. I should have an answer this week."

He kissed my forehead, but I could feel the tension in his body. "Good. I know you know what you're doing."

Chapter 21: Is This for Me?

~FELICITY~

I woke, looking around the guest room—it felt foreign still. I missed my room. I missed Caden—if I was being honest.

The rain was pelting the windows. Great. It's going to be a shit day. It rained every day in Miami, but it was never a dull rain—not like in New England. I heard Caden moving around downstairs. I wanted to run down and talk to him—something held me back though—probably how effing early it was. Why was he out and about already?

Hefting myself out of bed, my bones feeling a little older than yesterday, I rubbed the sleep from my eyes. I think I'm going to head into work. I'd planned another day off, but I actually missed the office. There's something about having interactions with people all day that gives me energy.

Listening to the door close and the garage open, I knew Caden was on his way into work. I showered, got ready and headed downstairs. He'd left me coffee—I love coffee. Pouring it into my favorite mug, I thought back to our conversation last night: "Feels like quite the metaphor, doesn't it?" I looked at him directly. "Me, buried under your stuff. You, drinking your coffee right next to me every morning without really seeing me." He'd left my mug next to the coffee pot—Script facing out—clearly a metaphor of its own, reminding me that he is thinking differently now.

Having forgotten my heels for the day, I ran back upstairs into Caden and my bedroom. Sorting through the closet, I found my shoes and started for the door. A light blue and pink gift bag caught my eye from Caden's nightstand though. Curiosity pulled me toward it.

The bag was from Shreve, Crump & Low—the kind of place where you don't ask for prices and that you don't go to if you have to think about them. Inside, nestled in cream-colored tissue paper, but still visible without digging into it, was a long velvet box.

I leaned back, breath caught in my throat.

Me: (Picture of bag) Is this for me?

Instead of a text back, I saw Caden's name pop up on my screen.

Swiping to answer, I said, "Hi."

"Hi." He cleared his throat. I'd um—yes first of all ... yes, that is for you. It was...I was...we had—Um..."

Silence took over from there for a minute. "Caden?"

"Yes. I'm trying to figure out what to say. You see, I had this whole speech planned, but now I—well, I can't seem to remember any of it!"

This made me laugh. Caden was always so good with words—he could manage a room beautifully. His lack of words and composure was a little endearing to me.

"I know," he said. "Crazy, right?"

"A little, yeah."

"Hang up, open it, and then call me back."

"Are you sure?" I asked hesitantly. "Do you want me to wait until you get home?"

"No. I don't think I could survive the wait knowing you've seen it now."

"Okay." I hung up, laid my phone on the nightstand, and pulled out the box.

My heart did something weird in my chest and my stomach was a mass of butterflies as I opened it.

It was a locket. Long. Stunning. White gold, delicate but substantial. There was an intricate Art Deco pattern etched around the edges and diamonds filled the inside in a cross pattern. It looked like something that belonged in a museum, or at least on someone far more elegant than me. I turned it over in my palm, feeling its weight, and that's when I saw the engraving on the back: "Always Your Family—C & M" and the "Y" was interestingly shaped like a heart.

My throat tightened. C and M. Caden and Macy. A tear fell from my eye.

My fingers were trembling. I must have tried to open the locket a million times before I could control my fingers well enough. On one side was a tiny photo of the three of us from last Christmas—Macy between Caden and me. I'd made them pose for it, hoping to capture a memory to hold onto. Surprisingly, they'd gone along with my request with little to no grumbling and were good sports about it. On the other side, in the same delicate script as the back: "Forever." Then engraved around "Forever" was another heart and a smaller one entwined at the bottom of the larger one.

I sank onto the edge of the bed, the locket cradled in my hands. This wasn't just expensive. It was—I don't know...God it was more beautiful and thoughtful than any gift I'd ever received. This was meaningful. It felt like them saying they wanted to fix this, that they saw me as part of something worth preserving. The kind of gift that takes planning, that takes hope.

But as I sat there, staring at that perfect little photo, something twisted in my chest. How long had they been planning this? Was this some kind of guilt gift, or had Caden genuinely thought I deserved something beautiful? I found myself grateful that he didn't give it to me last night. It would have been difficult to keep my cool and have the conversation we had, while having this in hand. When was he going to give it to me though? Do I put it on?

Deciding to do it, I fastened it around my neck, the metal cool against my skin. In the mirror across the room, it looked like it had always belonged there. And then it began. Ugly crying. I was full on ugly crying. It dawned on me that, during this whole situation, I'd cried, and I'd cried some more. But I had not yet ugly cried. Not like this very moment. I dropped to the floor and sat there—staring into the full-length mirror—seeing myself for what felt like the first time in longer than I could remember.

Moments danced by, flying away at the cost of time—a price that was worth every second. I deserved this cry. I deserved these moments. I deserved to be seen.

I took a moment to just breathe.

I looked back at the bag on the nightstand. It sat atop a manila folder that I hadn't noticed before. I picked it up—not heavy, not light, just substantial. Flipping open the metal clasp, I pulled out the packet of documents inside.

The top page was a schedule showing three-hour blocks, one Saturday each month. For what? I flipped through the pages until I found my answer: donation paperwork from Project Place.

Holy shit. Macy and Caden had donated the purse to them.

As I read through the documents, the scope of what they'd done became clear. The organization had committed to selling the purse and using the proceeds to fund a paid training program for domestic abuse survivors—computer skills, job placement support, career guidance. Everything focused on helping these women rebuild their lives.

But that wasn't all. Buried in the paperwork were volunteer agreements. Both Caden and Macy had committed to donating three hours every month, helping wherever Project Place needed them most.

I paged through brochures, testimonials, sponsoring organization information. It was beyond anything I could have imagined—not just getting rid of something that had caused pain but transforming it into something that could heal others.

I was speechless. Completely blown away.

My phone pinged.

Caden: Did you open it?

I called him. "I did."

He rolled right into an explanation. "The necklace — Macy and I came up with it together. It's supposed to symbolize our love for you, to make sure you know that you are seen. That while I completely fucked everything up ..." Another pause—"Felicity. Honey. I fucking love you so much. I am so sorry. Words honestly cannot describe the way I feel. I'm just so damned sorry." I could hear him crying as he spoke. I started to cry again. Damn it. I'd finally stopped and now I'm ugly crying again.

"God, Felicity. I just—I don't." He sighed. "Will you stay home today?"

"What?"

After a moment of silence. "Stay home. I'll come home. And we could just spend the day together. No phones. No work. Just you, me, and maybe we could marathon our show. Just spend it together on the couch, eating pizza, popcorn, and praline ice cream—like we used to. I know it's a lot to ask. I know you may just want to tell me to go fuck off. But I'm asking you—take a chance on me for today. Will you do that?"

I sat there for a moment—my phone on speaker, staring at the screen. I looked at his name in bright letters across the front, seeing the timer for the call ticking up. Thirteen minutes and eight seconds ... nine ... ten ... eleven ... by the time it got to twenty, I heard myself whisper, almost inaudibly, "Yes."

"Yes?" He practically shouted. "Did you say yes?"

"Yes. I'll let my boss know I won't be in. Come home. Let's spend time together and just—be."

"YES! I'm leaving now." He rushed on, "I'll be there in twenty, depending on traffic. I swear, if I could fly there I would. Don't go anywhere. I'm coming." I could hear banging of things on his desk, I'm assuming he was grabbing his bag and getting his stuff together to come home. And I found myself smiling.

He sounded like a teenager in love, not a man trying to repair a broken marriage. And somehow... I didn't hate it.

"Okay. I'll see you soon."

"I love you, Felicity."

"I love you too, Caden." I disconnected the call. I looked across the room at the mirror while I sat on the bed. It wasn't a solution. It wasn't a fix. But it was a beginning. I still didn't know what tomorrow would bring. But I knew that today, I wanted to believe in this version of us—messy, mending, trying. And that was enough.

Chapter 22: Got Your Favorites

~Felicity~

Twenty-three. That's how many minutes it took before I heard the garage door opening—who was counting though? I'd been pacing between the kitchen and den, touching the locket clasped at my neck over and over. Repeatedly forcing myself to stop touching it—then touching it again. The weight of it felt strange and comforting at once—like wearing someone else's centuries-old heirloom that somehow felt made for me.

The door from the garage opened. Caden's keys hit the hall table with what felt like more force than necessary. I heard his footsteps pause in the kitchen—I could swear he was out of breath.

"Felicity?" His voice carried that same nervous energy from the phone call.

"Right here," I said as I rounded the corner. I'd jumped up from the couch, once I heard him come in. I'd thought the couch would help me look casual, but who was I kidding? My heart was hammering against my ribs and wait—was I the one who was out of breath? I forced myself to calm down. In for five, out for five.

We stood there, facing each other—him in his work clothes, me in a t-shirt and leggings. He looked disheveled in a way that was totally unfamiliar—tie loosened, hair mussed, eyes bright. He was holding a pizza box from Florina's. He must have swung by on his way home. It's been our favorite pizza place since even before we got married. The sight of that box made something flutter in my chest.

"You got the pizza," I said, pointlessly stating the obvious because I didn't know what else to say.

"I stopped on the way. Got your favorite—extra basil, pepperoni, ricotta, and eggplant," he said, setting the box on the coffee table with deliberate care. And yes, it smelled incredible.

"I may have grabbed caramel corn too—it's in the car. I wanted to make sure you were here first."

His vulnerability hit me square in the chest. This man was always so sure of himself, and now he looked afraid I'd vanish before the box cooled.

"I know this isn't an apology," he said, eyes steady. "I'm sorry, Felicity. I forgot your age. I gave away your birthday gift. No excuses. I made you feel invisible, and that's on me. I have a lot to make up for."

He exhaled, shoulders dropping, eyes wet. "Don't leave me, Liss. I don't deserve you, but I want to do the work. Please let me try."

"I'm here," I said softly. "I'm not going anywhere."

Relief washed over his face so completely that I had to look away for a moment. When I looked back, he was staring at the locket around my neck, his expression unreadable.

"It's perfect on you," he said, his voice rough. "Even more beautiful than I imagined."

I touched it instinctively. "Caden, this is—I don't even have words. The locket, the donation, the volunteer work. How long have you been planning all of this?"

He leaned against the side of the kitchen table, leaving space between us but angling his body toward mine. "God, I wish I could say months? But truth? When you left, I sat down and talked to Macy—told her about the purse. I talked to her about what happened. She was so upset that she hadn't even thought of you when she found the purse though—in her defense, it was all my fault ... I am the one who hid it inside her closet." He rubbed his hands down his face and mumbled, "such a stupid mistake."

He stood up straight and continued, "Macy and I talked. We knew you didn't want the purse back; you'd said as much—and I couldn't blame you! I knew it would always come with the awful memories of what happened.

So we talked. She was the one who came up with the idea of donating it for a good cause. Then I thought of the necklace. And we both decided on the inscription—it was her idea for the picture though." He said that last bit with a smile.

"It was?"

"Yes—and I realized something."

I felt tears prick at my eyes again. "What was that?"

"That it was never about the purse. It was about you feeling invisible. About you feeling like your feelings didn't matter to me." His voice cracked slightly.

The space between us felt like an ocean. I wanted to reach for him, but something held me back—maybe I was afraid to break whatever fragile thing we'd just started to repair.

"So, we started researching organizations," he continued. "Macy found Project Place. Did you know they specifically help women rebuild their careers after domestic violence?"

My breath caught. "She found Project Place?"

"Yes. She was looking through different websites, and when she read about Project Place, she got so excited. She said it was perfect because you'd told her once about how important it was to help women who needed a fresh start." He paused, studying my face. "She somehow knew you'd love it. She didn't seem to know details, but I assumed you were talking about Maliyah."

I touched the locket, my throat tight. "Yes. I had mentioned it, but a long time ago. I guess she held onto it." I had to think back—It must have been a year ago. I'd been writing a check to a charity, and she'd asked me about it, having not seen a check before—Gen Z is Venmo, after all.

I'd explained and told her much I admired women who had the courage to start over. I remember thinking of my sister, Maliyah—how far she'd come.

"You're right, though, I didn't mention details—I'd never do that. Macy's just a kid. Plus, it's Maliyah's story, and I don't share the details without her permission." Damn it I forgot I told my sister I'd call her this week.

He nodded. "I figured as much. I know you wouldn't have told her about those details. It's a lot, too much really for someone her age."

He went on. "There's more, though," Caden said gently. "When we contacted Project Place about the donation, we learned about their volunteer program. Macy suggested we shouldn't just give something up for what we did, we should also give our time." A small smile played at the corners of his mouth. "She said she learned in school about 'philanthropy,' and how giving your time can sometimes be as important as giving money.

I was crying again. My sister—what she went through—no one could know how deep this landed.

He continued on, "Macy's not here to tell you herself, but she planned something else too. While we volunteer, she made a little folder with a 'menu' of experiences you could choose from. She wanted you to have options—something just for you."

I sat in silence, absorbing it all. That they chose Project Place felt bigger than coincidence. It felt like the universe trying to tell me something.

"And the locket?"

"That was me." He shifted closer, just slightly. "I wanted you to have something that reminded you every day that you're part of our family. That you're seen. That you're loved." He paused. "The photo was Macy's suggestion though—she said it was a happy memory and could help you."

I smiled through tears. "I remember that Christmas. I forced you both to take that picture. You were surprisingly compliant."

"She thinks we look genuinely happy in it."

"We were."

"I can't believe you two planned all of this together."

"We did. And Felicity—" He turned fully toward me now, his eyes intense. "I need you to know something. This isn't guilt. This isn't me trying to buy my way out of the mess I made. It's me trying to show you how special you are. That I was wrong. That I should have been giving you special things all along, showing you how essential you are."

I touched the locket at my throat again, feeling the weight of it against my skin. "Can I tell you something? About the purse versus this?"

He nodded, waiting.

"The purse—" I paused, trying to find the right words. "It was beautiful. It was something I'd wanted. But it was just a thing, Caden."

I paused to gather myself. "You bought it because I told you exactly what to get. But that's all you did—buy it. You checked a box and moved on. And honestly, after last year's Saks gift card? I was bracing for worse."

His flinched slightly and his face fell, but he didn't look away.

"I know I never said anything. I should have. But part of me wanted to see if you'd notice the disappointment on your own. You didn't. And that kind of broke my heart."

"Felicity—"

"I'm not done," I said, holding up a hand. "I need to say this."

"This—" I lifted the locket slightly, feeling its weight. "The locket isn't about money. It's the kind of gift that says, 'I know you.' Every detail—from the design to the photo, to the engraving—it says you thought about me. You thought about the things that make me feel loved and you made it into something I will wear forever."

Tears were rolling down my face, but I pushed through. "The purse said, 'I bought you something you wanted.' This locket says, 'I see you.' The donation and volunteering say you see what I value. The idea that Macy has a menu of things for me to look at also tells me that she is thoughtful and wants me to know that I matter."

Caden's eyes had filled with tears too. "God, Felicity, I'm so sorry it took me so long to understand that."

"That's what I was trying to tell you that night when I was so upset. I told you then—it was never about the purse alone. It was about feeling like a transaction instead of like someone you love. Like you were purchasing my happiness instead of actually caring about it."

I shifted closer to him. "This locket—I can feel how much thought went into it. I can feel you and Macy talking about what would make me smile, what would remind me every day that I'm cherished. That's what I was missing. Not expensive gifts—though they don't hurt!" I smiled. "It's evidence that I'm in your thoughts in a way that matters."

"I do think about you," he said softly. "I think about you all the time. I just—I got so focused on the company that I forgot about connecting."

"I know that now. I think what I want to see though, is that it's sustained too. That this isn't just a passing moment on the road to forgiveness that will later be forgotten."

"I've been thinking about what you said. About feeling buried under my stuff, about me not really seeing you. And you're right. I got so caught up in providing for us, in building this life, that I forgot to actually live in it with you."

He reached toward me, then stopped, his hand hovering in the space between us. "Can I—?"

I nodded, and he moved closer, taking my hands in his. His palms were warm, slight calluses, familiar in a way that made my chest ache.

"I don't want to just be two people who happen to live in the same house," he said. "I want to be partners again. I want to be the couple who stays up too late talking, who makes each other laugh until our stomachs hurt, who actually sees each other every morning over coffee."

"I want that too," I whispered. "But Caden, I need you to understand—this isn't something that gets fixed with one conversation. Or one beautiful gift, as perfect as it is."

"I know." He squeezed my hands gently. "I'm not expecting everything to turn back time. I get that isn't possible. I'm just asking for the chance to show you, day by day, that I heard you. That I'm committed to doing the work."

I studied his face, looking for any sign of the dismissiveness that had become so familiar over the past few months. Instead, I saw fear, hope, determination, and something I'd almost forgotten—the man I'd fallen in love with all those years ago.

"Okay," I said finally. "But I have conditions."

"Name them."

"First, I want to move back into our bedroom, but I'm not ready for us to be intimate yet. I want to lie next to you, and I really, really want our bed back. I think we need to buy a new bed for the guest room because it is absolutely terrible on the back." I laughed but then sobered. "I still need to take this slow."

He nodded immediately. "Yes. Absolutely—to everything. Whatever timeline you need. Can I hold you though—in bed?"

I thought for a minute. Realized that I really missed his arms around me. The intimacy of being held. I am a cuddler. It's eye-opening how hard it is to be untouched for so long and how lonely it feels. "Yes. But that's our line, okay?"

At his nod, I continued. "Second, we're still doing counseling. Both of us, together. This is not a way out of that."

"Agreed. Completely. I've already researched three therapists," he said, pulling his phone from his pocket. "I thought I would call them today and see if they are accepting new patients. If they are, then we can figure out together where we want to land."

I blinked in surprise. "You already—when did you do that?"

"When I got to the office. I looked through our plan and found a list of people covered, focused on those with experience who were local and with those who mention flexibility in their availability too."

Something warm unfurled in my chest. "Okay. That's good."

Taking a breath, I continued. "The third condition: we establish new boundaries around work. No phones during meals, no emails after nine p.m., and you don't cancel on family time unless someone is literally dying."

"Done." He didn't even hesitate. "Anything else?"

I considered, then smiled slightly. "Pizza's probably getting cold."

He laughed—the first real, unguarded laugh I'd heard from him in months. "Pizza. Right. I'll warm it in the toaster oven. Should I grab the caramel corn from the car?"

"In a minute." I watched him put the pizza in to warm and then led him to the couch where we settled into our spots, next to each other. "What show did you want to marathon?"

"Whatever you want. I know you probably want to catch the new season of Gilded Age. I'd be happy to watch it. I know I complained it was too slow, but I will watch whatever you want."

I raised an eyebrow. "You hate that show."

"I hate a lot of things when I'm not really paying attention to them. But if you're watching, I'm watching."

He got up to get the pizza and plates from the kitchen, and I used the moment alone to touch the locket again. The metal had warmed against my skin, and it felt so right. When he came back, carrying plates and napkins, I noticed he'd changed into a t-shirt and shorts.

"You changed," I observed.

"I wanted to be comfortable. Plus, these clothes don't carry the smell of stress and fluorescent lighting."

I laughed despite myself. "You smell like stress?"

"According to Macy, yes. She said I've been carrying myself like someone preparing for battle instead of someone coming home to his family."

He handed me a plate and settled beside me again, closer this time but still leaving space. The pizza was still warm, the cheese perfectly melted, the basil fragrant. I realized I was hungrier than I'd thought.

"This is good," I said after a few bites.

"It's the same pizza we've been getting for fifteen years."

"I know. But it tastes different today."

He looked at me, a question in his eyes.

"Better," I clarified. "It tastes better."

We ate in comfortable silence for a while, the only sounds the rain against the windows and the quiet hum of the house around us. It felt strange—foreign, almost—to be sitting here together in the middle of a weekday, no rushing, no agenda, no one needing to be anywhere else.

"Can I ask you something?" I said eventually.

"Anything."

"When you were planning all of this—the donation, the necklace—were you scared I'd say no to today? To giving us another chance?"

He set down food, considering. "Terrified," he admitted. "Because I knew that if you said no, it would mean I'd broken something I couldn't fix. And the thought of losing you, of losing us—" He shook his head. "I've never been more scared of anything in my life. I did this to us, and I couldn't turn the hands of time back."

The weight of his words settled between us. I reached for his hand, intertwining our fingers. I knew this conversation wasn't just difficult for me. It was a lot for both of us.

"You didn't do this alone, Caden. I stopped fighting for us too. I started accepting the crumbs instead of asking for the whole meal."

"Why?"

"Because asking meant risking being told no. And somewhere along the way, I got tired of being disappointed." I squeezed his hand. "But I don't want to be that person anymore. I don't want to be someone who settles for being unseen."

"You shouldn't have to be. And I'm going to spend however long it takes proving that to you."

I believed him. Not because the problems were solved—they weren't—but because for the first time in months, I felt like he was really here with me. Present. Engaged. Fighting for us instead of just coexisting.

"So," I said, reaching for the remote, "Gilded Age?"

"Gilded Age," he confirmed.

As the opening credits rolled, Caden got up to retrieve the caramel corn from his car. When he came back, he also had a blanket—the soft throw from our bedroom that I'd always loved but had left behind when I moved to the guest room.

"In case you get cold," he said, settling back beside me.

I pulled the blanket over both of us, and slowly, tentatively, I let myself lean against his shoulder. He went very still for a moment, as if afraid to move and break the spell, then carefully wrapped his arm around me.

We stayed like that for hours, eating caramel corn straight from the container, occasionally commenting on the outfits and the intrigue, scoffing at certain ridiculous scenes. It was ordinary and extraordinary all at once—the kind of afternoon we used to have regularly but had somehow lost along the way.

Around mid-afternoon, I felt my eyelids getting heavy. The emotional exhaustion of the morning, combined with the warmth of the blanket and Caden's steady presence, was making me drowsy.

"You can sleep if you want," he said softly, his voice rumbling in his chest beneath my ear. "I'm not going anywhere."

"Promise?"

"Promise."

I let my eyes drift closed, listening to the rain and the voices from the TV along with Caden's heartbeat beneath my cheek. For the first time in months, I felt safe. Not just physically safe, but emotionally safe—like I could let my guard down without worrying that I'd wake up to find myself invisible again.

Just before I fully drifted off, I felt Caden press a gentle kiss to the top of my head.

"I love you, Felicity," he whispered. "I'm so sorry it took me so long to remember how to show you."

I wanted to respond, but sleep was pulling me under. Instead, I snuggled closer to him, my hand finding its way to rest over his heart.

Tomorrow would bring new challenges, new conversations, new work to be done. But today—today we had remembered how to just be together. And that felt like everything.

Chapter 23: She's Just Sensitive

The first thing I sensed when I woke was Caden's arms wrapped around me—the first time, in fact, since before my birthday. Through the back windows, I could feel late afternoon sun streaming in, touching the skin of my arms as it sunk down preparing to set for the day. The hum of the AC was still lulling me even as I forced myself to not fall back asleep. Laying there, I listened to my husband's steady breathing, feeling the rise and fall of his chest beneath my cheek.

It was surreal, this peace. After everything we'd been through, the fights, the silence, the separate rooms, the separate states even— yet here we were—together. The locket felt warm against my throat, laying between us, a sign of something deeper as it sat touching both our chests.

"Hey," he said softly, and I realized he'd been awake, probably watching me sleep.

"Hey yourself." I stretched slightly, but remaining wrapped in the warmth of his embrace. "What time is it?"

"Almost four."

"Hey—so, Macy will probably be getting home soon, right?" I asked while pulling up to a sitting position. Not waiting for his response, I continued "I want to call her," I said, sitting up slowly. "I need to thank her properly for everything she did. Make sure she doesn't think I blame her for the purse—and that she knows how much everything here meant to me."

Caden smiled, that soft expression I'd missed so much. "She's going to be over the moon to hear from you. She's been so worried."

Caden stood, went to the kitchen. I heard the sound of the espresso machine whirring. Minutes later, he returned with an espresso for each of us in hand. She aroma flowed through my senses. He didn't even have to ask—he just knew I'd want one. I reached for the double he'd brewed for me and smiled as I felt his lips brush mine lightly as I took the cup from him.

Coffee in hand, I reached for my phone on the coffee table. My heart was already lifting at the thought of hearing Macy's voice—at knowing how excited she will probably be. There isn't much more fun than sensing a kid's excitement—at any age, I've come to realize. Getting ready to hear her talk a mile a minute I smiled as I scrolled for her name.

Touching on her contact, I heard the phone rang once, twice, then—

"Hello?" Jessica's voice, crisp and slightly irritated.

My good mood faltered immediately—I double checked and confirmed I'd clicked the right name, "Oh—Hi, Jessica. It's Felicity. Is Macy available?"

A pause that felt loaded with something I couldn't identify. "She's... busy right now. Homework."

"Oh." I glanced at Caden, who was sitting up now, paying attention to my expression. Something in Jessica's tone felt off, but I couldn't put my finger on what. "Could you tell her I called? I wanted to thank her for something."

"I'll let her know." Jessica's tone was dismissive, like she was already ending the conversation.

The brush-off stung more than it should have. This was about Macy, not about whatever issues Jessica had with me. "Actually, could I just say hi quickly? It'll only take a minute."

Silence. I looked at the phone and saw that she had disconnected the call. What the hell? Looking over at Caden, I saw he was just as annoyed as I.

I called again. After a single ring, "Felicity, I said she's busy and can't speak right now." The call was disconnected again.

Caden stood up. "Are you kidding?" He pulled out his own phone and dialed Jessica's cell, placing the phone on speaker.

"Hi, Caden," was the response he got.

"Jessica, did you just hang up on Felicity? Twice?"

"Caden, Macy is busy right now," she says in a placating voice. "I was just trying to help her understand that it's not a good time. It's not my fault that Felicity went crying to you because she is just sensitive."

I mouthed to him, with as angry a face as I could muster, "What the fuck!? Sensitive?!"

"Jessica, I was sitting right here with her when she called. Don't try and play that game. We'll discuss this another time. Put my kid on the phone."

Jessica sighed, "Caden, I'm trying to avoid drama. Macy said she didn't want to talk right now, and I think it's best if we just respect that. I think she feels like she was made to apologize for something you did, Caden. And now she doesn't want to talk to Felicity. This isn't my problem. It's yours. So don't put this on me. I'm trying to be nice h—"

"What the hell are you talking about Jess—you know what? It doesn't matter. Put Macy on the phone."

"No."

"Excuse me?"

"I'm not letting my daughter get caught in the middle of whatever you have going on there. You need to shape up Caden. Whatever is happening is not okay. I don't think I want her over there for a while. It's not healthy."

"Jessica, you better put my daughter on the phone, or so help me God you will be hearing from my lawyer before the day is out."

"Don't you threaten me Caden Barrett!" Jessica barked. Her voice and tone were getting louder and significantly more agitated—way more agitated than the situation called for.

"Jessica, that's enough. I don't know what's going on here, or why you're trying to keep me from my kid, but I will figure it out. We are on our way over."

"Why, Caden? I already told you I don't like how things are unfolding and that she won't be coming over for a while."

"You can't keep me from her, Jessica. She is my daughter, and our agreement clearly states you can't prevent me from seeing her."

"Caden, Macy doesn't want to see you. This isn't about me! It's about you and your wife. You know what? I have a seriously painful migraine Caden, and you're just making it worse."

"I'm coming over and you better have my kid ready to see me or maybe we'll be revisiting our custody agreement!" He hung up, his face flushed with anger.

I stared at him, my mind reeling. "What just happened? Yesterday Macy was planning to help you with my surprise, and today she suddenly doesn't want to talk to me? Something isn't right here, Caden."

"None of this makes sense," Caden said, pacing now. "Jessica's lying. I know she is. But why? What's she trying to hide?"

I felt a chill run down my spine. "Caden, she's been increasingly hostile toward me for a while. I let it be—didn't want to make waves given how much else has been going on. But now she's actively preventing contact with Macy, making up stories about how Macy feels—there's something going on and it can't just be about me. "

He stopped pacing and looked at me. "What do you mean?"

"I don't know exactly, but her behavior feels desperate. Why would she try to keep us away from Macy when she doesn't even really know what's happening between us? Even Macy doesn't know the details—just that I went away for my birthday and the thing with the purse. These are not reasons to separate you from your daughter. There has to be something else going on."

"Like what?"

I started thinking out loud, trying to piece together Jessica's erratic behavior. "Maybe things with Brad aren't going well, or what if she like—lost her job, or there's some other kind of personal crisis she doesn't want us to know about? Could something have happened with Macy that she would try to hide from you? Macy hasn't said anything bad about her mom. I know she feels guilty sometimes but..." I let my words trail off, not really sure how to articulate what I was thinking.

Before he could answer, his phone rang. Lauren. We were making our way through the kitchen where we could enter the garage.

"Lauren," he answered, while walking. He put it on speaker immediately. "I can't talk right now. Felicity and I are heading over to see Macy. Something's seems off and Jessica won't let us talk to Macy, not really sure w—"

"Caden, stop. Don't go to Jessica's house." Lauren's voice was tight with urgency in a way I'd never heard before. "I need to tell you something, and you're not going to like it."

My blood ran cold. Lauren was always calm, always measured. If she sounded panicked, something was seriously wrong.

He jerked to a stop and coming up behind him I didn't have the chance to stop in time. We collided and his phone skated to the floor.

"Damn—sorry!" Scrambling for the phone, I tried to grab it and it flipped out of my hands again. What the hell?

Caden called out, "Lauren—hang on, I dropped the phone."

Out of breath, I finally had it in hand, and brought it up between us. Caden let out a little laugh and I followed suit. He grabbed the back of my neck, pulled me close and laid a kiss on my forehead. "Shit, I think I needed that," he said, laughing a bit.

Sighing, I leaned further into him, "me too."

"Okay, Lauren," his voice more measured now. "What's going on?"

"Are you sitting down?"

"No, but I'm sure we'll survive. Just lay it on us."

"Okay, well—don't say I didn't warn you. So, those financial irregularities we found?" I looked up at Caden, confused. He whispered to me "I'll explain in a minute."

"Go on."

Lauren said, "I took the information over to Jackson over in the Forensic Accounting team. Gave him all the information and the file we put together. He found some major irregularities. He brought Janice from Legal just to have her take a look. I guess Janice found some major concerns and reached out to a contact she has at the DA's office.

"Shit. Really? What did they say?"

"Well, apparently with our current suspicions, there is a huge list of possible crimes. Larceny by False Pretenses, Identity Fraud, Forgery, and even some Computer-related crimes—that's just to name a few, Caden."

Caden pulled out the kitchen table chair and sat down. Motioning for me to do the same, I took the chair next to him. With the phone on the table between us, we listened to Lauren continue.

"No freaking way."

"Yes, way."

"You're serious?"

"As a heart attack, Caden. If it's true then she's been accessing your email account and submitting forged documents for payment in your name, to be paid by the company. Where we thought we were paying a vendor fee or standard operating expense, she was taking that money and using for personal reasons—though I don't know what for."

"What the fuck do I do? Lauren, she has my kid. I want Macy out from under her! Does she know we're looking into this—I mean. FUCK!" He yelled the last, clearly a demonstration of frustration and anger.

I piped up, "Hey Lauren, it's Felicity."

"Hi Felicity. I'm sorry for all this stuff going down."

"I know. And thank you. I think I missed something though—how did we find out about it?"

There was a pause. Then Caden started out...slowly, "so, when everything happened with the purse, I asked Lauren to put together a list of all the things I'd gotten—I mean, she'd gotten for you over the years." He hung his head, clearly in shame.

"I get it Caden, just go on. I know where we were, and let's just focus, okay? It's about Macy right now."

"Yeah, okay. Thank you," he responded, and reached out his hand to lay over mine on the table." So, it was in that conversation where I learned I'd been giving Jessica pretty extravagant gifts in Macy's name over the years. So I asked Lauren to do a full accounting, lo and behold, around the same time she got an email from my personal email address asking her to send a new card to Jessica's house since the existing one had expired. Said I wanted to ensure Jessica had it for anything Macy needed."

What the hell? "That's freaking weird."

"Tell me about it. Regardless, Lauren asked me about it, since she figured I would have just asked her to do it rather than email her. That's when we figured out that, over the years, she had been email in falsified bills. Where the company would send payment to the credit card, but the bills we had on file were being routed through Lauren over to Accounts Payable. That's all I knew though since it was in the infancy stages of research. All this Lauren is sharing is new to me too."

I sat back in my chair. "Holy shit. That's like—diabolical."

"And criminal!" Lauren called out. "So—picking up there, Jackson had done some forensic mojo in technical terms and stuff that I couldn't even begin to explain. Essentially he traced something like an I.P. address back to Jessica instead of to you, Caden."

"I'm completely blown away by this. How could she do something like this? What was she doing with the money?"

"That I don't know, but I do know that the police are very interested in it! All told it's a significant sum—we're talking six figures."

My mouth dropped open, "no way."

"Yes, way."

Caden was staring at the phone like it might explode. "Six figures," he repeated quietly. "She's been stealing from my company for years. How is that even possible?"

"Seems she is quite creative—shaving small amounts at a time so they easily fell into the 'expected loss' and vendor costs without ringing any bells. There may be other means of stealing she took outside of the email address. To that end, do not go into your email. The police want to meet with you both as soon as possible," Lauren continued. "Let me see—here it is. I have information for a—Detective Morrison with BPD. I guess he is the lead handling the case. But Caden, they specifically said not to confront Jessica directly. If she realizes we've discovered the scheme..."

"She could try to destroy evidence or—shit what if she tried to run?" I said, the pieces suddenly clicking into place. Caden jumped up from his chair. "Macy. I need to get to Macy. Fuck the financial shit. What if she tried to take Macy away."

I jumped up with him. "We need to go. We have to go get her."

"Breathe, we don't know anything that for sure," Lauren said quickly. "She has no idea that you know anything. I'm no expert, but my guess is that right now, status quo is best."

Just then, Caden's phone buzzed with a text. He glanced at it, and his face went white.

"What is it?" I asked.

"It's from Macy." He showed me the screen: Dad, I'm fine. Don't come over today. Need space to think about everything. Will call you tomorrow.

I read it twice, my heart sinking. "Bullshit. No emojis or abbreviations? Full sentences, periods included? That's definitely not from her."

"Jessica sent this," Caden said, his voice deadly quiet. "She's using Macy's phone to keep me away."

"Shit. Listen, this is bigger than just one thing—you need to talk to the Detective before you do anything." Lauren said through the speaker. A buzz from Caden's phone showed another text, this time from Lauren. "I just sent you all his contact information. Call him now."

"Okay. She already thought I was on my way anyways. I'll call him and see what he says. But I'm telling you right now, nothing is keeping me away from Macy. I'll get his guidance on 'how' to approach it, but he's not going to get me to back away from getting to Macy."

"I'm with Caden on this. I don't think we should take a chance with Macy's safety."

"Call him. See what he says."

As we hung up with Lauren, I couldn't shake the image of Macy—this young and unassuming girl—potentially caught in the middle of her mother's desperation.

"She's going to be okay," I said, reaching for Caden's hand.

"She has to be," he replied. But I could hear the fear underneath his certainty, and I knew we were both thinking the same thing: what if something happened before we could get there?

Chapter 24: Wellness Check

~CADEN~

I stared at Detective Morrison's contact information on my phone screen. My thumb hovered over the call button—trembling. Every instinct inside me screamed *Fuck this!* Get in the car and go get your daughter! The fear though of what could happen if Jess knows we know—that fear kept me from driving over there immediately.

"Just call him," Felicity said softly, her hand warm on my shoulder. "I'll be here with you, every step of the way. We need to know what we're dealing with, though, so we need to call him—ASAP."

I pressed call and put it on speaker.

"This is Detective Morrison."

"Detective, this is Caden Barrett from B&R Consulting. Lauren Chase called me to let me know you wanted to speak with me about some irregularities we discovered."

"Mr. Barrett, yes. Thank you for calling. I understand this involves your ex-wife and potential theft from your business?"

"That's right. But Detective, there's something else. She's preventing me from speaking to my daughter, and we just received a text from my daughter's phone—but the way it was written, it didn't sound like her at all."

There was a pause. "What kind of text?"

I read him the message, explaining how it wasn't Macy's usual style. "My ex-wife has been acting erratically, and now I can't reach my eleven-year-old daughter."

Another pause, longer this time. "And you believe your ex-wife sent the text from your daughter's phone?"

"I'm certain of it."

"What does your custodial agreement say?"

I explained to him that I get access to her at any time, that she stays with me on weekends and some days after school. I also explained that she can, and has, come over to stay outside of just the minimal agreement we have.

"Okay, thank you. That's helpful. Have you spoken to your attorney yet? I mean about the current issue—given what's going on?"

"Not yet. You were my first call after Lauren let me know how far this issue had progressed."

"Okay, well I think you should start there. Get his perspective on the custodial issue. There's no current evidence of her taking your daughter—right now it seems like she is holing up with her. Furthermore, she doesn't yet know she is being investigated so I'm thinking she isn't going to present much of a flight risk right this second."

I felt some relief at his measured tone, but also frustration. "So, what do I do? I can't just sit here."

"Call your attorney. Have him reach out to her attorney about normal visitation—he can mention the call you had with him. You can share concerns, just make sure that your lawyer knows not to discuss the financial crimes issue since we are still investigating. If she cooperates, you see your daughter and we continue building our fraud case separately. If she doesn't..." He paused. "Then we reassess."

"And if she refuses?"

"Your attorney handles it as a custody matter first. We don't want to spook her about the financial investigation. But Mr. Barrett, if she starts acting more erratically or if there are signs that she's planning to leave the area, call me immediately."

After we hung up, I immediately called my divorce attorney while Felicity gathered the financial documents.

"David? It's Caden Barrett. I need to tell you something confidential, and then I need your help with a custody matter..." I explained the investigation, the issues with trying to contact Macy, my concerns, and my discussion with the detective.

There was a pause. "Jesus, Caden. How much money are we talking about?"

"I don't have exact numbers but it's a lot—Lauren said it's in the six-figure range. And, like I said, she's keeping me from talking to Macy today, which is concerning behavior to say the least."

"Okay, I understand the situation. Let me call her attorney and discuss your call with her and that you just want to see her so Felicity can thank her. We'll keep it simple and like it's a completely normal thing."

"She's been stealing from your company for years," Felicity said quietly as I hung up. "And now she has Macy, and she might know we're getting close to the truth."

Twenty minutes went by. They felt like an eternity. I knocked back a double shot of espresso—thinking I was going to need it to keep my wits about me. Looking over at Felicity, the quintessential stress eater, I saw she was almost at the bottom of the bag of caramel corn.

Lifting my eyebrow at her, I couldn't help but smile— "really?"

"Ugh—you know I eat when I'm stressed!"

"Fuck, I missed you so much. Know that, while all this is going down, I have not and will not forget you. I know we're in a shit place right now, but hear me when I say this—I love you and I will always love you," I reached for her and engulfed her in my arms—burying my face in her hair. I felt her arms reach around me to hold me back. Then I heard crunching—pulling back, I saw she had stuffed another handful of caramel corn in her mouth.

Looking up at me innocently, "I know! And I know we will get to our stuff sooner rather than later. But for right now, I'm worried! You know how I am—sugar will calm my nerves so just get back to holding me and shut your face on the way there!" the last part she said through a mouthful of sticky and sweet popcorn.

I laughed, "yeah, well let's hope you're not sick with it tonight!" She swatted me and laughed. If all this shit wasn't happening right now, I'd be so happy that I was getting the chance to just be with my wife.

My phone rang—we both jumped, looking over at it on the table. David's name flashed on the screen. I swiped to answer, "David, what did you learn? Can we go get Macy?"

"Hi Caden. Okay, so I was able to reach her attorney. Jessica says Macy isn't feeling well and she'd prefer to keep her home tonight. She suggested you can go see her tomorrow instead."

A chill ran down my spine. "She's refusing?"

"Not exactly refusing, just... making excuses. Do you want me to push harder?"

I sighed, "no, not yet. Let me call Detective Morrison back first." I hung up and immediately dialed Morrison.

"Mr. Barrett?"

"She's making excuses. Says Macy's sick and she wants to keep her home tonight."

There was a pause. "That's concerning, given the circumstances. Would you say, as a parent, that you have concern for your minor daughter's welfare?"

"What?! Yes, isn't that what w—"

"Caden, I'm just getting things down for the record."

I paused, following his logic, "Oooooh. Okay."

"And would you say you had concerns for her welfare?"

"Yes, yes I would, Detective."

"Given these factors then, and the depth of your concern, I think a wellness check may be warranted."

"A wellness check?"

"Yes—essentially, we can send a couple officers over—just to ensure your daughter's safety. If your ex-wife is acting suspiciously and given the ongoing criminal investigation, it is reasonable for us to take precautionary methods to provide for the safety and security of your daughter."

"How long before that happens?"

"I can have officers there within half an hour. Meanwhile, I need you and Mrs. Barrett to come to the station. We'll need full statements about the financial crimes, your experiences with your ex, and the more recent custody issues."

Felicity stood up; her face determined. She practically yelled into the phone, "We'll be there in ten minutes."

As we gathered our documents and headed for the garage, I kept checking my phone, hoping for some sign from Macy—a real text, a call, anything. But the silence felt ominous.

The ride was silent—I don't think either of us could muster up the words. The pit of my stomach felt sour.

We pulled into the police station parking lot, and I felt like I was walking from one nightmare into the next. Six hours ago, Felicity and I had been curled up on the couch, finally finding a sort of tentative peace. Now we were about to give statements about felony charges against the mother of my child.

Inside, Detective Morrison was not what I'd expected. Mid-thirties, sharp jawline, the kind of presence that commanded attention without trying. He looked like he belonged on a magazine cover more than in a police station. His eyes held the intelligence and weariness of someone who'd seen enough shit in his day to know that people are exceptionally unpredictable.

While there was something slightly rumpled about the detective, I still felt like I should smooth down my clothes and hair, and probably double check that being in the same room with him didn't somehow revoke my man-card. Honestly—is this guy a cop or a freaking model? His tie was loosened, sleeves rolled up—like he'd been working long hours. He led us to a small conference room and spread some documents across the table with practiced efficiency while loading other documents onto a screen.

"Mrs. Barrett," he said to Felicity, and I noticed the way his voice had a warm, professional tone that seemed to put her at ease, "I understand you've had some concerning interactions recently?"

"Definitely. Jessica has always been a bit of a witch. But she has been increasingly hostile toward me over the past few months. Today she hung up on me twice when I tried to talk to Macy, then told my husband that Macy didn't want to speak to me, which is completely out of character."

Detective Morrison made notes. "And Mr. Barrett, when did you last have normal contact with your daughter?"

"Yesterday. She was excited about a surprise she'd planned for Felicity. She was supposed to stay with me until late in the evening, but Jessica picked her up early, claiming she needed her home."

The detective's phone buzzed. He glanced at it and answered.

"Morrison... Yes... No response at all?... Okay, keep trying. Check with neighbors." He hung up and looked at us with concern.

"The officers are at your ex-wife's house. No one's answering the door, and the house appears empty—no cars in the driveway, curtains drawn."

My heart stopped. "Empty?" I croaked.

"Mr. Barrett, I need you to think carefully. Does your ex-wife have access to significant cash? Other properties? Family out of state?"

"The money she stole," I said slowly. "She could have been converting it to cash. The way she managed it was really around getting my company to pay bills, but in reality I am completely out of touch with the level of fraud she performed and how much actual cash she could have walked away with."

"Well, so far we haven't been able to see how long she has been doing this, so it may be even more than you anticipate." Detective Morrison said grimly.

My phone buzzed with another text. This time it was from Jessica's number.

Caden, Macy and I are taking some time away. She needs space from the drama. She would rather some space from you right now. She told me to tell you that she'll call when she's ready.

Detective Morrison read it over my shoulder and his expression hardened.

"Mr. Barrett, this changes things. Your ex-wife has just admitted to taking your daughter and leaving. Combined with the financial crimes, this is now what we would call custodial interference."

"What's the next step?"

"Since you have documentation that requires agreement for any type of movement out of your local area, her removing Macy without your agreement is problematic. Now that she's confirmed she's left without it, this qualifies as custodial interference. And combined with the fraud, it's more than enough for us to escalate." He leaned away from us.

We should issue an Alert—I'll need recent photos of both your ex-wife and your daughter, license plate numbers, any information about her current husband or partner, family members, anywhere she might go. We'll get an alert out to the surrounding states."

As I started rattling off information, I felt like I was describing strangers. How much did I really know about Jessica's life? Her plans? Her desperation?

As he rushed out to coordinate the alert, I slumped in my chair, staring at Jessica's text. Somewhere out there, my daughter was with a woman who'd been living a double life for years, a woman desperate enough to steal shit-ton of money, and now desperate enough to take Macy and run.

"We'll find her," Felicity said, but her voice was shaking too.

I just prayed we'd find her in time.

Felicity pulled in close. She wrapped her arms around me. How could I ever have let this woman become invisible to me. She is my rock. When all this is over, I will do everything in my damned power to make sure she sees that I can be her rock too. A tear slipped down my cheek—fear for Macy and love for Felicity all tangled together in my chest. Unable to hold it back, a sob wracked my chest. And Felicity was there for every shake of my shoulders.

She was more than I deserved but I'll be damned if I give her up.

Chapter 25: One Crisis at a Time

~FELICITY~

The lights in the police station hummed overhead as I sat in the hard chair, watching Caden pace the small waiting area. Detective Morrison had disappeared twenty minutes ago to coordinate the Amber Alert, leaving us to stew in our own fears.

My phone buzzed. Maliyah's name flashed on the screen, and I felt a pang of guilt. I'd forgotten to call her back earlier this week like I'd promised.

"Hey, it's Maliyah. I should take this," I said to Caden, who nodded distractedly, still staring at his phone as if he could will Macy to text him back.

I stepped into the hallway and swiped to answer.

"Hey, MayMay."

"Finally! I was starting to think you'd forgotten you had a sister." Her voice carried that familiar teasing tone, but I could hear the underlying concern.

"I'm sorry, I've been—" I paused, my voice cracking unexpectedly—unsure of how to even explain this last week. "It's been a complicated week."

The teasing disappeared from her voice immediately. "Hey—Felicity, what's wrong? You sound terrible."

Where did I even start? "So...I'm at the police station."

"What? Are you okay? Is Caden okay?"

"We're fine, but..." I took a shaky breath. "Macy's missing. Her mother took her and disappeared."

"Wait. What? Like took her how?"

"There are a few things happening and—Jesus, Maliyah, I don't even know how to start."

"Okay. Let's just take a minute. How long has she been gone?"

"We don't know exactly. Maybe since this morning? We discovered that Jessica has been stealing from Caden's company for years. We're not talking a few dollars here, May. I mean like a hefty sum."

"Holy shit."

"Exactly. And when we tried to see Macy today, Jessica wouldn't let us talk to her. Then she sent this text from Macy's phone saying they were going away. We don't know if she knows we found out what she's been doing, but why else would she take off?"

There was a moment of silence. When Maliyah spoke again, her voice had shifted into what I called her "professional mode." Maliyah runs a women's shelter down in Orlando and she is an awesome problem solver.

"Tell me about Jessica. What's her behavior been like recently?"

I leaned against the wall, grateful for my sister's steady presence even through the phone. "Increasingly hostile toward me. She's always been...difficult—well, you know—kind of an asshole. But lately it's been different. More intense. She picked up Macy's phone when I called—and hung up on me. Twice. I'd asked to speak to Macy. Caden tried calling her right after. She told him Macy didn't want to see me, which makes no sense. Like a day before—she'd been planning a surprise for me. No way she just flipped a switch when I hadn't even seen her since."

"Control and isolation," Maliyah said immediately. "She's trying to control the narrative and isolate Macy. It's textbook manipulation."

"But why now? Why take this risk?"

"Sounds like maybe she knows she's cornered. Felicity, if she's been stealing for years—and now she realizes something's off, she doesn't even need to know you know everything. In her circumstance, it could just be paranoia. And that paranoia may lead her to make desperate choices. Taking Macy makes her feel in control."

"May, do you really think it could be that bad?"

"I don't know. But in my world, I've grown accustomed to expecting and planning for the worst but hoping for at least better—not best."

"I'm scared. What if she hurts Macy? I feel like neither Caden, nor I really know her. Neither of us would have *ever* guessed she was stealing. She has a job—mortgage broker, you know. And her husband makes good money too. I can't understand where it all went."

"Hey," Maliyah's voice softened. "Listen to me. I've worked with hundreds of families in situations like this. The money and all that—you'll figure it out. Once you get Macy back, she will be okay. Children are more resilient and perceptive than we give them credit for. We don't know what Jessica has told her. For all we know, Macy thinks they are going on a vacation. No matter what though, Jessica can't erase the relationship Macy has with you guys overnight."

"But what if—"

"Felicity." Her voice was firm now. "You have to focus and make sure you don't spiral. I can hear it starting. You can't go down the rabbit hole of worst-case scenarios—it will make you crazy and won't help anyone right now."

She was right. I was already starting to catastrophize, my mind racing through every terrible possibility.

"What should I do?" I asked quietly. "How do I help Caden through this? How do I help Macy when we find her?"

"First, you focus on what is within your control. Support Caden, cooperate with the police, and trust that they'll find her. Second, when Macy comes home, you create the safest, most stable environment possible for her to process whatever she's been through."

"Jesus." I dropped my head against the wall, feeling so overwhelmed by everything. "You know, Caden and I were going through something before all this happened. We'd reached a certain peace, but there is still a lot for us to work through. Add that onto the trauma Macy may be experiencing. It's a lot May. It's a lot."

"It sounds like it. But you know, you don't know what you don't know. Macy may not even be experiencing trauma. Her mom may be acting completely normal with her. She may be completely fine when she gets back. Or maybe she's going to be confused and hurt and angry. Every child responds differently. But Felicity, you and Caden—just remember what it feels like to choose each other, to choose your family. That's exactly what Macy's going to need."

I touched the locket at my throat, feeling its weight. The photo inside—the three of us at Christmas, all genuinely happy—felt like a talisman now.

"Yeah. You're right. And I know I shouldn't borrow trouble."

"One day at a time Felicity."

"I know. So—you said you and Caden were going through something? You don't have to tell me anything, and I know it's shit timing, but know if you need a shoulder, I'm here. And as your sister, I'd like to say—I'll cut any bitch who fucks with you. "I mean, unless someone's listening, then of course any violence threatened is just story telling on my part and not an actual threat...right now." I laughed. She laughed. I needed that moment—where all this turmoil wasn't swirling around me.

"Maliyah, I love you so much."

"Of course you do. I'm awesome," I could hear the smile in her voice.

"You are. Okay—so, the reason we were having some issues..." And I gave her an abbreviated version of what has happened over the last couple weeks from the purse and fight with Caden, the feeling of invisibility for the last few years. My fingers were fiddling with the locket as I told her about the apology gift from him and Macy and how they not only donated the purse but their time too. "They chose an organization that helps women rebuild their lives after abuse. Women like..." my voice trailed off.

"Women like me," Maliyah finished quietly. "Damn. I want to hate him so much for the shit he pulled, but I love what he did to turn things around. I really love that they didn't just throw money at a problem. That's precious."

"I know. It was more than I would have thought they'd do."

"Babes, they did it because they knew you—saw you. I get things broke with Caden along the way, but his actions now say something about his heart. People do dumb shit, but it's what they do on the other side, and how they learn from it, that makes the difference."

"I hadn't thought of it that way."

"I think the big question is whether the change will be sustained, or whether you'll be back in the same spot next year."

"He wants to do therapy. Even found a few therapists—but then all this with Macy happened."

"Damn."

"I know. I think he will still—" my voice trailed off as I saw the door opened down the hall. Detective Morrison emerged with his phone pressed to his ear. He caught my eye and held up one finger—almost done.

"MayMay, I gotta go. The detective is coming back."

"Okay. But Felicity? Call or text me tonight, no matter how late. Just to let me know how things are going, okay?"

"I love you, May."

"I love you too. And I'm praying for all of you."

I hung up and walked back to where Caden was sitting. He looked up expectantly.

"Just Maliyah." I explained, settling beside him. "She had some thoughts about Jessica's behavior."

"Like what?"

Before I could answer, Detective Morrison approached us, his expression carefully neutral.

Morrison appeared in the doorway, looking tired but focused. "The Amber Alert is active across three states," he said, settling into the chair across from us. "But I have some other information that might actually be good news."

Caden looked up from his phone. "What kind of good news?"

"We've been checking out Jessica's husband, Brad, to see if he was involved in the financial crimes. He's clean. No evidence of any connection to the theft, no unexplained deposits, nothing—they even have separate accounts and only use a joint one for their shared expenses."

I felt some tension leave my shoulders that I didn't even realize I'd been carrying.

"So he really didn't know?" Caden asked.

Morrison nodded. "When we questioned him about Jessica's computer habits, her recent behavior changes, he was genuinely shocked to learn about the theft. He talked about her recent behaviors around keeping her devices private, but he thought she was just dealing with work and some other stressers.'"

"He thought it was just work stuff?"

"Exactly. He'd actually been trying to get her help—found searches on his computer for therapists, depression resources. He thought her mood changes were stress-related."

Caden ran a hand through his hair. "So he was trying to help her."

"Looks that way. He did mention she'd been having headaches, trouble sleeping, her moods would swing from irritable to happy and then morose. He'd been encouraging her to see someone."

I thought about Brad at family events—always quiet, always seemed to genuinely care about Macy. "What about Macy? Is he worried about her?"

Morrison's expression softened slightly. "First question he asked was whether she was safe. He's been cooperative about providing information that might help us find them."

"So where does that leave us?" Caden asked.

"Well, for now it seems isn't a threat or a flight risk. It also means Jessica was operating completely alone, which might actually make her easier to predict."

"To that end, we've been able to trace more of Jessica's activity. The good news is that she's left a clear digital trail. The bad news is that she seems to be acting unpredictably. Her activity seems to be all over the place from going to multiple gas stations to food stops, she's stopped at various places multiple times, using her card—a few dollars here and a few dollars there."

"So, you don't think she's been planning this?" Caden said, his voice hollow.

"It's too hard to make a judgment right now with what we have, but preliminarily I think it's a good guess."

"I feel like I'm in a really bad dream right now."

I looked up at Morrison. "It feels like tracing her cards has us playing catch-up. When can we get a break? I mean, people notice an eleven-year-old, right?" I asked. "Hotels, restaurants, gas stations?"

"Normally, I'd say yes. The issue is that Jessica is her mom. And we don't know what Macy knows—so she may not realize the depth of what's going on. Jessica's car is on the alert, and we have banners going across the highways with the description of her car."

Detective Morrison's phone rang. He glanced at it and held up a finger. "This might be something." He accepted the call, "Morrison... Yes... Where?... How long ago?" His expression shifted, becoming more alert. "Keep me posted. I'll have someone call the local station."

He hung up and looked at us with cautious optimism. "We have the card companies on notice and are tracking her real time now. Jessica's credit card was just used at a gas station out in Western Mass. State police are en route, but..."

"But?" Caden leaned forward.

"It's getting close to the border where Connecticut, New York, and Mass meet. She's still technically in Mass, but if she crosses into New York or Connecticut, this becomes a multi-jurisdictional case, which complicates things."

"What does that mean for finding Macy?"

"It means more agencies get involved, which can help with resources but slow down decision-making and present issues around process. The important thing is that we have a confirmed sighting and direction of travel."

My phone buzzed with a text. My heart jumped, hoping irrationally that it might be from Macy, but it was from Maliyah.

Maliyah: Thinking of you. Remember what I said about focusing on what you can control. Love you.

I showed the message to Caden, who squeezed my hand.

"Your sister is amazing," he said quietly.

"She is. She said children are more resilient than we think."

Detective Morrison was doing something on his phone. "Sorry to interrupt. So, we found Jessica's computer at the house—given everything that's happening, we got a warrant—seems her husband wasn't the happiest, but he kept out of the way. Something a bit weird about that guy, but nothing on his record pops.".

"I just got confirmation that, when they did a cursory review of her computer and data, our forensics team found some concerning searches. It's just preliminary for now, but it was enough to be eye-catching."

"What kind of searches?" Caden asked, though his tone suggested he wasn't sure he wanted to know.

"Searches about leaving the state without co-parent consent and custodial interference." He paused. "All today and yesterday."

The room felt like it was spinning. This wasn't a panicked flight. This was a calculated kidnapping.

"So, Forensics searched their home computer. We can only assume the searches we found were made by Jessica—for the time being, until we can speak with her." Detective Morrison paused, his expression growing more serious—looking down at his phone again to read something. When he looked up, it was with almost regret in his eyes, "Caden, are you aware of Jessica having issues with prescription drugs?"

"Prescription drugs?" We both looked at Morrison in confusion. "Wait, what? What do you mean?"

"I mean drugs like Oxy or Norco. Anything like that?

"What?! No way!" Caden stood up from his chair, facing the Detective. "You're serious?"

"I am. Your ex has her devices connected, so we can see what she has searched on her phone, which is mirrored on her personal computer. We found evidence of what may indicate a possible substance abuse problem and what the team thinks could be a shopping addiction. There are multiple searches for online pharmacies, ways to obtain prescription opioids without a prescription, and she has significant purchasing activity around luxury goods."

"Opioids?" Caden's voice was hollow.

"While she tried to erase her browser history, we all know that's really just skimming the surface. It's something forensics will dig into—no real details right now, but we have a general idea of what we are looking at. Given the current exigent circumstances, we will limit our current search to focus on what we need to help us get Macy back."

I felt sick. "I'm just so—I can't even explain it. I mean, I guess the drugs could explain the paranoia, and her recent behavior."

"That's definitely possible. For now, let's focus on what we do know. We know she left with Macy. She is traveling by car and is headed west. We have local units heading out to intercept. And we are working to locate her phone."

Continuing, he said, "In the meantime, I think you need to talk to your attorney again. See if he can get an ex parte emergency custody hearing given the circumstances."

His phone rang again. While Morrison answered, Caden began scrolling. "I'm going to text David. Send him some of the new info and see if he can file for an emergency hearing."

Morrison was a few feet away. I couldn't make out the details, but I could sense the urgency in his body language. As he approached, I heard him say, "How long ago?... We're on our way."

He hung up and looked at us with barely contained excitement. "We have a confirmed sighting. A clerk at a rest stop saw the Amber Alert and positively identified both Jessica and Macy from the photos. Said they bought snacks and used the restroom less than an hour ago. It's in the same direction where her last charge pinged."

"That recent?" Caden jumped up. "Then they can't be far."

"State police are setting up checkpoints on the major highways heading south and west with a twenty-mile radius intersecting the two points."

"What did the clerk say about Macy?" I asked, almost afraid to hear the answer.

"Said the little girl seemed tired and quiet, but not scared or distressed. She was holding her mother's hand and that Jessica seemed scared—keeping Macy close to her."

Relief flooded through me. None of this was ideal, but 'tired and quiet' wasn't the nightmare scenario my mind was conjuring.

"What happens next?" Caden asked.

"We wait for the checkpoints to report back, and we hope Jessica makes another mistake. Using her credit card was sloppy—especially if she has cash on her and she's really been planning this. She really should have known better. I would think she's either not as smart as she thinks, or the pressure is too much for her. Too many unanswered questions here."

He rubbed the back of his neck and continued, "The important thing is that we're closing the gap. She's got a very narrow head start from that truck stop, and we know her general direction of travel."

My phone buzzed. Maliyah.

Maliyah: Love you chickadee.

Me: We might have found them!

Maliyah: Thank God. Is Macy okay?

Me: We think so. They were seen recently. Said Macy seemed tired but not hurt.

Maliyah: That's good news. Take a deep breath.

I looked around the room—at Caden's anxious face and at Detective Morrison coordinating with what seemed like half the state police force.

Me: I'm breathing.

Maliyah: I'm praying she makes a mistake, and it helps get Macy home.

Me: Me too

Maliyah: and remember one crisis at a time...you and Caden will figure all the other stuff out.

Me: you're right...one crisis at a time

Chapter 26: Broken Dreams

~Caden~

Detective Morrison was hanging up from another call, and his expression had shifted to something I couldn't quite read.

"What is it?" I asked immediately.

"Good news and less good news. The good news is that we have another confirmed sighting—a McDonald's about thirty minutes from the gas station—they went in and got what I'm assuming is dinner. One of the staff noticed them when they came in. Says he'd seen the Amber Alert we sent out in the area."

"That's good, right? Did he do anything?"

"It is good. But he said Jessica seemed 'agitated'—she was shaky and... I don't want you to worry, but he said she was yelling at Macy. Apparently, he tried to make small talk with Macy, Jessica cut him off abruptly and hurried Macy back to the car."

Felicity whispered, "Could she know we're looking for her?" My stomach plummeted.

"Honestly, I don't think so. If she did, she wouldn't be using her credit cards. You mentioned your lawyer said she agreed for you to see her tomorrow. She may think she is in the clear for the night."

I stood up abruptly, pacing to the window. How could this be happening? I needed to do something! "We have to find them—find Macy—now."

"We're doing everything we can. We have units moving into the area. I truly believe it won't be long."

He paused, looked me in the eyes and continued, "Amber Alerts are very effective. Between the alert, the checkpoints, and the teams we have moving to get to her, we will find her—and I don't use those words lightly. She's driving a specific car with a specific license plate, and she has an eleven-year-old with her. She is not invisible."

The Detective's phone buzzed again. "Morrison—What? Can you patch it through? I'm with her dad now." Morrison walked over to the desk phone in the room and started rattling off information. I was freaking out—I didn't know what was happening!

The phone rang and he answered on speaker. "Morrison"

"Detective Morrison, as I said, I have a 911 call from Macy Barrett who is asking for her father."

I ran to the phone, "I'm here!"

"Put her through," Morrison responded.

"Patching her through now. Our calls are recorded, per protocol I will remain on the line with you. Macy, can you still hear me?"

"Yes," my little girl's voice whispered.

I fell to the floor on my knees, my face as close to the phone as I could get it. Felicity dropped to the floor beside me, wrapping her arms around me. "Baby, I'm here. Daddy's here." I was trying to remain calm and keep her from hearing me cry. She needed me to be strong for her right now, she didn't need me to fall apart.

"Daddy!" I could hear her excitement even through her whisper. Felicity's hand flew to her mouth, tears streaming down her face as she heard Macy's voice.

"Baby, where are you? Are you okay?" I croaked out, my hands clenched into fists against the floor.

"I'm okay, daddy. Mom's acting weird. We're at the Sleepy Inn but I don't know where. It was dark and there's lots of trucks around us."

Detective Morrison was on his cell repeating the information to someone quietly.

"Where's your mom, honey?"

"She's in the bathroom. I think she's taking a shower. Daddy, I stole someone's phone. I thought I'd try to text you, but I couldn't open the phone. But it let me call 911. I'm sorry!" She started to cry.

"Don't cry, honey. Don't be sorry. You did good kiddo."

"The shower stopped," she whispered. "I took too long trying to call!"

"It's okay, honey. It's going to be okay. Daddy's going to come get you, okay?"

"Okay daddy."

"Macy?" Detective Morrison said softly but firmly. "This is Detective Morrison. I'm a friend of your dad's and I'm just helping him out right now, okay?

"Okay," she responded slowly.

"Honey, can you leave the phone on and hide it somewhere? Somewhere your mom won't see?"

"I think so?"

"That's good, honey. Hide it somewhere she won't look for it. We're going to stay on the line but we're going to be really quiet, so your mom won't hear. If anything happens that makes you uncomfortable, you can say something out loud so we can hear you. Sound okay to you?"

"Yeah, okay. I can do that. I'll put it upside down on the floor under the bed so you can't see the light."

"That's a great idea."

"I hear her coming."

"Okay—quickly hide it. You did so good, sweetheart." I swallowed hard, trying to hold it together.

"I love you, Macy," I called out, just as I heard the phone sliding on the carpet.

Detective Morrison pressed the mute button on the phone and stood up straight.

Felicity embraced me, kissing my forehead and my cheeks—holding me. "She's going to be okay. She is a smart kid. Look at what she's done."

"How did we even get here? It's surreal—like I'm watching someone else's life. This can't be real. Things like this don't really happen!"

Morrison spoke up, "Unfortunately, you'd be surprised how often these kinds of things happen. Amber Alerts exist for a reason. It's a painful fact that abductions happen much too frequently. Getting to hear Macy's voice, having that phone on, we're talking about miraculous stuff here. They traced the phone using the number she called from, and we have pinpointed her location. We've got units on the way—maybe twenty minutes out. We're going to get your girl."

"How far for us?"

"It's a few hours away–where they are.."

"Can we go now?"

"Yeah—I'm working on getting the call transferred to my department cell. Once I have the call on my line, we're moving. Fast."

"Okay, yeah—that's good. Thank you, God."

I unfolded myself from my position on the floor, stood up, and helped Felicity to her feet. I looked into her eyes, placing my hands on either side of her face. I leaned in, forehead to forehead. This woman. *I can't believe I almost lost this woman.*

~ ~

~Jessica~

The shower wasn't helping. I'd hoped that the hot water, which usually calmed my racing thoughts, would settle me. Instead, I felt like I was suffocating. Through the shitty motel walls, I could hear trucks rumbling past, each one making me jump. In this Podunk town with no real hotels anywhere near me, I can't believe I'm stuck in this hell-hole.

Having my attorney get Caden to back off for a day was genius. Tomorrow we'll say she's still sick and that he can pick her up on Saturday. By then we'll be long gone. It's not like he could know, right? No one knows we're gone. Brad's got that thing later tonight. He'll probably be too drunk to notice I'm not even in bed.

Maybe I should text him. No, better to stay off his radar for the night.

My hands wouldn't stop shaking. I knew what would help—the pills in my purse would steady them, would make everything clear again. Just one. Maybe two.

No. I'd already taken... how many today? Where was I when I took the last one? Was it at McDonalds? Before that? *Why can't I remember?*

I turned off the water with trembling hands. The McDonald's employee—the way he'd looked at us, tried to talk to Macy. Creep. Trying to talk to my daughter. I shouldn't have stopped there for dinner. What's one meal? We could have skipped it and just eaten the chips from the gas station.

Stupid, stupid, stupid.

"It's okay," I whispered to my reflection in the foggy mirror. My eyes looked wrong—pupils too small, shadows too dark. When had I gotten so thin? "She's your daughter, not that woman's. It's your job to protect her. They can't tell you what you can do."

But through the haze, I didn't really know why I cared anymore—*if* I cared anymore. My head was pounding. I need to make it stop.

I wrapped myself in the threadbare towel they provide and opened the bathroom door. Macy was sitting on the bed, her back to me, unnaturally still.

"Macy? What are you doing?" Her stillness made me pause. She was quiet. Too quiet.

"Just sitting." Her voice was strange. Guilty?

My heart began to race—or maybe it had been racing all along. The pills did that sometimes. If I hadn't run out earlier this week before I could get my refill yesterday morning, it wouldn't be this bad. It's always worse then. *It'll get better. It'll be better.*

"We need to get a good night's sleep. We're going to leave early tomorrow, for our adventure."

"I want to go home."

The words hit me like a physical blow. Home. Where Caden was probably sitting with that woman, playing happy family in my house, with my daughter.

No. I couldn't let him poison Macy against me too.

"That's not... we can't..." My voice cracked. I was so tired. Why is there so much pressure inside my head? When had I last really slept? The pills kept me going but real sleep... I wish I had a glass of wine—that would help too. "Why don't you watch some TV while I figure things out?"

I clicked on the television, some cartoon filling the room with artificial brightness. Macy settled back against the pillows, but I could feel her watching me.

I started pacing. Five steps to the window. Five steps back. The room was so small. Why was it so small? I needed to put some clothes on. The AC was making my skin itch. I threw on my Eberjey pajamas, needing the soft comfort of the jersey fabric. Rubbing my arms, my hands were shaking. I need to go lie down. Maybe that would help.

Crawling under the covers, I looked over at Macy. Why does everything have to be so complicated? I wonder what Brad is doing. He's going to be so mad I just took off. Or maybe he just won't care. No one fucking cares.

Fuck! My head is killing me! The pills help—thank God I found them. Before I started taking them, everything was just noise. Now at least I can breathe.

I stood up again. I need something. What do I need? Oh—yeah. Pills. Okay, get the pills, get the pills. Just one. This is why I—where's my water? Damn it. "Macy! Where's my water?"

She looked at me, shock on her face, and whispered "I don't know, Mom."

I started tossing things around. I need water to take my pills. Fuck it, I'll use the water from the bathroom sink tap.

I took one. That should be enough to take the edge off. I went back and took a second. Settling in on my bed, I watched TV with Macy. Within fifteen minutes I felt like a new woman.

Tomorrow we'll drive to the next state. Maybe find a nice town where nobody knows us. I have enough cash for a few weeks, maybe a month if we are careful. Long enough for Caden to realize what he's lost—if he wants to see Macy again, then he needs to pay for it. If that fucking card hadn't expired, if Lauren hadn't started sniffing around, this all wouldn't be happening.

I bet Felicity planned for all of this. She just wants Macy.

Focus, Jessica, focus!

I sighed, looked over at my daughter. "We'll leave first thing in the morning, okay honey? Get some sleep."

"I'm not tired."

"Please, Macy. Just... please!" I felt tears dropping down my face. When did I start crying? "Let's just get some sleep, okay? I promise things will be better in the morning." I hated the desperation in my own voice.

Now I was begging my eleven-year-old daughter to pretend everything was normal—while we hid in a roach motel that smelled like cigarettes and broken dreams.

I have enough pills to last about another week... I think. I need to figure out how to solve for that.

I closed my eyes and could feel myself nodding off.

Then I heard it... *Bang, Bang, Bang!*

"Jessica Jensen, this is the Police. Open up!"

Chapter 27: Sirens

~MACY~

The knocking was loud—and heavy. I could swear I felt my bed move against the wall.

The scratchy bedspread had been annoying me. I wasn't even watching the cartoons on in the background, but I was scared to say anything. Mom seemed like she could get mad at any second, so I decided to just stay quiet. I'd just wait for Dad to come get me.

Sitting and waiting, I could hear Mom mumbling to herself. Not to me—to herself.

"I know, I know," she'd whispered to herself. "But I can't let them take her."

I don't know why she's acting so weird. She wasn't always like this. I tried to remember when things changed. She used to like to hum. When she met Brad though, things became about him and less about me. I thought of all the times recently when she would nap after coming home from work. That didn't start until the last year...I think. I squeezed my eyes closed. How long until my dad gets here?

And then, I heard banging on the door. "Jessica Jensen, this is the police. Open up!"

Mom's eyes flew open. She sat up so fast it looked like it hurt, her hair all messy from the pillow. Her face went completely white, but then she looked toward the window and nodded like someone was telling her what to do.

"They're here," she whispered.

"Police! We need you to open the door, ma'am!"

"I KNOW!" Mom suddenly screamed at the door. Then she looked at me with wild, unfocused eyes. "Macy, they found us."

I sat up on the bed, scared. "Mom, what's happening?" Why are police here? I thought my dad was coming.

She scrambled, stumbling out of her bed—falling to her hands and knees. Her movements seemed crazy and scary. "They want to take you back to him. Back to that house. To her." She started frantically digging through her purse. "I need... where the hell are my pills? I need them. Just one to help me think straight!"

Items were falling from her purse as she searched—scattering across the carpet. "Just give me a second!" she yelled at the door, then immediately back to her purse.

"Got 'em!" As she pulled a bottle from her bag, she tried to open it. I saw all kinds of pills scatter across the carpet. She dropped down and tried to pick them up. There were white ones and a couple blue.

"Mom, you're scaring me."

"It's fine, honey. Everything is fine. I took some an hour ago." She was looking between me and the carpet as she tried to pick them all up. "It just wasn't enough. I should have known that. It'll be okay though." She found a pill and dry-swallowed it. Then another. Then she was gripping her head, pressing on the sides of her temple.

I kept looking at the carpet. It had weird red and green swirls all over. Someone had left a chip bag right near where my mom's foot was. I thought about the pills my mom was taking, wondering if there was dirty stuff on them now. Why would she want to take them? What about the police?

The knocking came again, harder this time. "Ma'am, we need you to open this door now or we will enter by force."

Mom grabbed my arm, her grip too tight. I cried out and asked her to stop. I don't think she heard me though. Her eyes were really bright. She was sweating too, but it was so cold in the room. Why is she so sweaty?

"Macy, listen, listen. You have to listen." She shook me. "When they come in, you tell them you want to stay with Mommy, okay? Tell them your dad is just angry because he didn't want to give me the money he owed me."

"Money?"

"Yes, Macy! The MONEY!" she shouted.

"What money, Mom?"

"The money I had to take! It was mine anyway—I earned it! It wasn't a lot. Just a little. You know—to help out. Things are so expensive. And there was so much noise, so it helped with mommy's medicine. You understand, right, honey?" Her words were getting slurred.

Before I could ask what she meant, there was a loud BANG. I looked up and the door flew open.

All of the sudden it felt like a hundred police officers came into the room really fast. One of the policewomen tried to come straight toward me, but everyone else went to Mom.

"Get away from her!" Mom screamed, stumbling backward. When she tried to put me behind her, I fell and then she fell on top of me. I screamed out—my arm caught underneath me. Pain like I'd never felt before climbed up my arm from my wrist to my elbow. Mom tried to get up, but she fell on me again and caused more pain. When she fell, my head bumped into the corner of the bed frame.

Tears were streaming down my face. Everything hurt. So bad. "Mom, stop! Please stop!"

Finally, she was up off of me—she yelled to the police, "I have custody! Check the papers! She's MY daughter!"

"Macy?" the woman officer asked gently, dropping down to the ground to help me up. She had kind eyes and brown hair pulled back. "I'm Officer Lidia Martinez. You can call me Lia. Can you move your arm, sweetheart?"

I tried to move it, but it hurt so much I started crying harder. "It hurts!"

"Okay, honey, let's get you checked out. Just sit still for now. Did you bump your head too?"

"Yes, against the corner of the bed here." I used my good hand to show her where I hit the side of my head. When my hand came away, it was sticky. I think it was blood. I looked at the officer and showed her. "Am I bleeding?"

"Oh boy. It looks like you are. It's okay. Everything is going to be okay now." She looked at the other officers. "We need paramedics for the child too, ASAP."

"I didn't do anything wrong!" Mom shouted from across the room. Two officers were holding her arms as one cuffed her—she kept trying to come to me.

"Ma'am, we need you to calm down," one of the officers said to her.

What's happening? My arm and my head hurt really bad, and Mom was acting so weird—weirder than normal.

"What kind of pills did your mom take, honey?" Officer Lia asked me really quietly.

"I don't know. She had lots of them. White ones and blue ones. She said they help her think. There are some on the floor and I think some in her purse too." I wiped my nose with my good hand. "Is she sick?"

"Yes, sweetie. Your mom is very sick right now. Those pills probably aren't good for her."

I looked over at my mom—sitting on the floor now because the officers made her sit down. She looked so sleepy, and she was hanging her head like she was super falling asleep, her eyes looking tired... and sad.

I could barely hear her through her mumbling, but I think she said, "I was trying to protect you." Her words sounded funny. "Your dad... he doesn't understand. The pills—they clear things for me. "

I don't get it. If the pills helped her think, why was she acting so confused?

"Am I in trouble?" I whispered, not wanting my mom to hear—*would she be mad if she found out?* "Because I took someone's phone."

"Absolutely not. You're not in trouble at all. You did exactly the right thing by calling for help." She was pushing on my head with a towel from the bathroom. It made it hurt, but it was more of a dull hurt than the pain from when I actually banged it.

A man in a uniform came in with a big bag. Officer Lia told me he was a paramedic, and he was going to look at my arm.

"Hi there," he said. "I'm Mike. Looks like you got hurt, yeah?"

"Yeah. My mom fell on me—on my arm. And then I hit my head." I started crying again because talking about it made it hurt more.

Mike was really gentle when he touched my head, peeling back the towel that Officer Lia was using. He replaced it with some gauze and wrapped it tightly—so tight it hurt a little, but it still felt better. Then he looked at my arm. "I think you broke your arm when you fell. We'll need to have you get an X-Ray." I cried harder at that. Everything seemed like a lot. I wanted my dad. I wanted my mom too... just not like this. "We're going to wrap it with this splint, just to keep it still and make sure you don't get hurt anymore. Then we'll put it in something called a sling to keep it safe, okay?"

While Mike was fixing my arm, I could hear the other paramedic talking to my mom. She kept saying weird things like "it's all too much," and asking him to make it all stop.

"Officer Lia?" I said.

"Yes?"

"Is my dad really coming?"

"He is. He's driving here as fast as he can. It might take a couple hours though because he was far away."

"Can I wait for him?"

"Of course. We're going to take you to the hospital to make sure your arm is okay, and your dad will meet us there."

"What about Mom?"

Officer Lia looked sad. "Your mom needs to go to the hospital too, but she'll be in a different area. The doctors need to help her with the pills she took."

I nodded. I felt really confused and scared, but also kind of better. With the police here I wasn't as scared as I was before—plus, Dad was coming. Maybe things would be normal again.

As they helped me walk to the ambulance, the officer was putting Mom in the back of a police car. I grabbed Officer Lia's hand with mine, wishing it was my dad's hand. Normally I'd feel like I was too old to hold someone's hand. But I didn't care right now.

Mom looked so sleepy. Even though she scared me and hurt my arm, she was still my mom. I hoped the doctors could get her the right pills. Maybe she just didn't have the right ones.

"Will this be the first time you're in an ambulance?" asked Officer Lia.

I nodded, "yes. I've only seen them driving or on TV. I've never been inside one before."

"Well, this will be your first time then!" she responded with a smile. "Normally I'd ask if you want to turn on the sirens, but you're probably too big for that now."

"No, I'm not! I would totally turn on the sirens. Do you think Mike will let me?"

Mike was a little bit in front of me and said, "you bet, kid!"

"Okay cool! Thanks Mike!"

"You're welcome Macy."

I saw Mom again. I could see her lips move but couldn't hear anything she said. There was no one with her though in the back seat, so I think she's talking to herself.

"Will she be okay?" I asked Mike as we got in the ambulance.

"The doctors are going to do everything they can to help her," he said. "Sometimes when people take too many pills, it takes time for their bodies to get better."

"Officer Lia?"

"Yes, Macy?"

"My mom said she took some money. Do you know what she means?"

"Oh honey, don't worry about that right now. Your dad can figure all that stuff out. Right now we should just focus on getting your arm fixed up. Okay?"

I leaned back against the stretcher thing and closed my eyes. "Okay." My arm still hurt, but I felt safer now. Dad was coming, and soon this whole scary thing would be over.

I wonder if he'd hug me right away or if he'd look me over first. I hope he isn't too scared. He will probably cry when he sees me. *I won't cry when he sees me, that way he won't be scared anymore—he'll see I'm strong, so he won't worry.* I felt tears roll down my cheeks. Better to cry now instead of when my dad is here.

Chapter 28: Not Completely Broken

~Felicity~

The emergency department at Berkshire Medical Center was quiet—we were definitely not in Boston. The makeshift room separated Macy from other patients with surrounding curtains. When Caden and I had entered the hospital, looking for her with Detective Morrison, my stomach was in knots. Still trapped in the whirlwind of the night, it was too hard to even unpack everything that had happened so quickly.

When we found Macy, she was lying back on a hospital bed that would be small for me, but looked like it was ready to engulf her little body. She looked over at us and her eyes lit up. Caden broke down into a blubbering mess of emotions. He ran to her bed and pulled himself up short, stopping before he might hurt her if he embraced her. He ran his hands lightly over her arms, shoulders, and head.

The hospital had called to get verbal consent to treat her when we were on the way, so we knew what her injuries were already. But seeing it in real life is so very different. It was hard to even describe. She had a bandage on the side of her head, bruising that ran down her temple close to her eye. Her arm was in a cast, from fingers almost to her elbow. She had an IV in the other arm—the nurse explained that Macy was somewhat dehydrated, so they were giving her fluids.

Caden leaned forward and kissed his daughter's forehead. "I am so sorry, honey. I'm so sorry for everything you have been through." He laid his head on top of hers, I could tell he was trying to be careful of all her injuries. "We love you so much. Everything is going to be okay."

We sat quietly as the nurse came in and took her vitals again. Once we were alone, I asked, "Does it still hurt, sweetheart?" adjusting the blanket around her for the third time in ten minutes.

"Not really—not anymore, that is. The medicine they gave me helped. It was so bad before, Felicity." She looked up at me with droopy eyes that were fighting to stay open. She whispered, "but it's much better now."

"That's good, honey. You tell us if that changes, okay?"

"Okay. Felicity?"

"Yes, honey?" I leaned closer.

"Are you and Dad still fighting?"

Caden and I exchanged glances over her bed. The question took me aback for a minute, though it shouldn't have.

"We're working on things," I said carefully. "But right now, we're just focused on you."

"Good. Because I was scared you might not want to be my family anymore."

My throat tightened, and I tried, and failed, to blink back tears. "Oh, honey. Nothing can change that. You're stuck with us, whether you like it or not."

She smiled sleepily, the first real smile I'd seen from her since we'd arrived at the hospital. "Even if my mom did bad things?"

"Especially then," Caden said firmly, his voice thick with emotion. "What your mom did wasn't about you—and it has nothing to do with how much we love you."

"Did she really take a lot of money, Dad?"

Caden's jaw tightened, but his voice stayed gentle. I could tell he was trying to figure out what to share and how. He looked to me, I nodded in response—at this point, with all she has been through, it didn't seem right not to tell her at least something. "Yes, she did. But that's not something for you to worry about, okay? The grown-ups will figure all that out."

"Is that why she was acting so weird? Because she was scared about money?"

I looked at Caden, both of us struggling with how much to explain. "We don't know everything yet, honey. I think we have a long way ahead of us before we understand all the things that happened and why your mom was acting the way she was. What we do know, is that your mom was taking medicine that wasn't good for her," I said finally. "The doctors said that the types of medicines and the amounts she had been taking probably made her confused and scared, and she made some bad choices because of it."

"Like taking me away?"

"Like taking you away," Caden confirmed. "She thought she was protecting you, but she wasn't thinking clearly."

A nurse came back in with some food for Macy, her soft-soled shoes squeaking against the linoleum. The hospital felt smaller than the ones I was used to in Boston—more personal somehow.

"How are we feeling, sweetheart?" the nurse asked, checking the monitors again and scanning her bracelet. Her name tag read "Patricia" and she had the kind of gentle manner that made you feel like your grandmother was taking care of you.

"Tired. And my head feels weird."

"That's normal after a bump like you had. I thought you might want something to eat now, we don't have much up here, but I brought you a turkey sandwich, some graham crackers, and a pudding. I also found a ginger ale in our fridge that I thought you might like to have." Winking at Macy, she started to lay everything out in front of her on the bedside tray. Thank God for nurses. I swear they do angels' work.

Going to the computer, she took down some notes. "Now don't worry, the weird feeling should go away in a day or two." She made notes on her chart. "Try to get some rest, okay? You've been through a lot tonight. You're a brave little girl." She lightly tapped Macy's shoulder, smiled, and left the room.

As Patricia left, Caden's phone buzzed. He glanced at it, and I saw his expression shift.

"David," he said quietly to me, showing me the text.

David: Emergency custody petition filed. Hearing is 9 AM tomorrow. You don't need to be present—stay with Macy. Police reports and hospital records will help. Send me pics of what you have just for the time being, I will work on official records later.

Relief washed over Caden's face like a physical thing. "He's moving fast."

"That's good," I said. That's exactly what we need—I thought... though I could tell from his expression it was very good.

"Very good. This means we'll have legal authority to make decisions for her by morning. No one can question our right to be here, to make medical choices, nothing."

"What's that about?" Macy asked, her voice small.

"Just my lawyer making sure you're protected," Caden said, moving to sit on the edge of her bed. "He's working to make sure you can stay with us."

"I want to stay with you and Felicity," she said, and something in my chest cracked open.

"Absolutely, honey."

Through the window, I could see the parking lot of the small hospital, mostly empty except for a few cars scattered under the streetlights. The mountains of Western Massachusetts rose in the distance, dark silhouettes against the night sky. It was so different from Boston—quieter, more peaceful. Had it really only been six hours since we'd raced through the night to get here? It felt like a lifetime.

I thought about Jessica, somewhere else in this same building, probably in whatever passed for a psychiatric unit in a hospital this size. I want to say I'm a bigger person and not angry at Jessica—that having a substance abuse disorder is its own trial, but I can't. I am fuming inside.

I know it isn't the same thing, or even on the same wavelength—but I think of how often Caden and I tried for pregnancy, the rounds of IVF, knowing that my body is broken. I was diagnosed with Primary Ovarian Insufficiency years ago. After IUI and then five rounds of IVF, we had to accept that no amount of intervention would ever be enough for us.

I think of how much I have always wanted to be a mom. That it was a dream of mine to someday hold a baby of my own in my hands, watch them grow up, be a part of their lives and see something so beautiful in my child as joy or love. Then I see someone like Jessica—she had that. And she used manipulation to get what she wanted, she stole a significant sum over time, she exposed her eleven-year-old to drugs. My God! Macy could have taken something, just following what her mom did.

I think of how her actions led her where she was. I look at Macy and see her, bruised with a broken arm—this little girl shoved into a scenario and a situation that she should never have to have experienced. No, I can't find pity or empathy in me. Not right now. Not in this moment. Maybe later, maybe I'll see Jessica as something else later. But not today. Today, I'm angry. Angry at Jessica, and angry on behalf of Macy.

"Felicity?" Macy's voice pulled me from my spiraling thoughts. "You look sad."

I forced a smile and moved closer to her bed. "I'm not sad, sweetheart. I'm just thinking."

"About what?"

How do you tell an eleven-year-old that you're thinking about how much you want to knock some sense into her mother? That you're thinking about the unfairness of life, about lost hopes and dreams?

"About how glad I am that you're safe," I said instead, which was also true.

Macy picked at her sandwich, taking small bites. The ginger ale seemed to be helping—there was more color in her cheeks now. "Felicity, can I ask you something?"

"Of course."

"Do you think my mom loves me?"

The question hit me like a physical blow. Caden's head snapped up from his phone, and I saw the same pain reflected in his eyes that I felt in my chest.

"Oh, honey," I said, sitting on the other side of her bed. "Of course she loves you—so much. Even when people make bad choices, even when they're sick like your mom is, that doesn't mean they don't love you."

"Then why did she hurt me?"

The innocence in that question nearly undid me. How do you explain addiction to a child? How do you make sense of something that doesn't make sense?

"Sometimes when people are really sick," Caden said carefully, "they do things they would never normally do or that they don't even realize they're doing. It's like... imagine if you had a really high fever, and you said things you didn't mean, or do things that were scary. Your mom's sickness is like that, but in her brain."

"Will she get better?"

Caden and I exchanged another look. The truth was, we didn't know. It's clear Jessica had been struggling with prescription drug abuse for a while, this is not something that just happened yesterday. Who even knew what recovery would look like—or even what Macy will be exposed to given the legal ramifications of everything Jessica has done.

"We hope so," I said finally. "But that's going to take a long time, and I don't know that we have all the answers right now, but I think that's okay, right?"

"Yeah, I think you're right." Macy looked back and forth from me to Caden, "you promise I can stay with you guys, right—not just weekends like before?"

"Honey, of course you'll come home with us." Caden said. "We want you with us, Macy. We are your family, and we love you."

Macy nodded, then settled back against her pillows. She was quiet for a moment, picking at the crust of her sandwich. "Will I have to see her? My mom, I mean."

The question hung in the air between us. Caden and I exchanged another look, this one full of uncertainty.

"I don't know, sweetheart," Caden said honestly. "That might depend on a lot of things—how she's doing, what the doctors say—I just don't know. Do you *want* to see her, Macy?"

"I don't know. I don't think so. Not right now. Is that okay?"

My heart broke a little more. An eleven-year-old shouldn't have to make decisions like this. She shouldn't have to be afraid of her own mother.

"Of course it's okay. But Macy, these aren't things you have to decide right now." I said firmly. "We'll figure it out."

Macy seemed to consider this, then nodded slowly. "Okay. I'm really tired now."

"Of course you are, honey," Caden said, adjusting her blanket. "You've been through so much today."

"Will you both stay here tonight?" she asked, her voice small and vulnerable.

"Absolutely," I said without hesitation. "Wild horses couldn't pull me away."

As if those were the words she'd been waiting to hear, Macy's eyes finally began to close. A minute or so later, I heard her say, "Hey Felicity?"

"Yes, Macy?"

Still sleepy with her eyes closed, she responded "Did you hear I got to turn on the sirens in the ambulance?"

"No way, that's awesome!" I whispered back.

"Yeah," Her breathing evened out, and within minutes, she was asleep.

Caden and I sat in the quiet room, listening to the soft beeping of monitors and the distant sounds of the hospital corridors. The adrenaline that had carried us through the night was finally wearing off, leaving behind bone-deep exhaustion and the crushing weight of everything that had happened.

"I can't believe we're here," Caden said quietly, his voice barely above a whisper.

"I know." I watched Macy's chest rise and fall steadily. "This morning feels like a lifetime ago."

"This morning, I was worried about finding a way to get you to forgive me and give us a second chance." He ran his hands through his hair. "How did I not see this coming?"

"Caden, stop. You can't blame yourself."

"Can't I? I'm her father. I should have protected her better."

I looked at him next to me in these uncomfortable hospital chairs. I could see the guilt written all over his face—filling every line. The way his shoulders curved in, like he was holding the burdens of everything across them.

"Jessica is an adult who made her own choices," I said quietly. "You trusted her. That's not a character flaw."

"I barely spoke to her, to be honest. I missed the signs because I didn't care to look."

"Signs of what? Addiction? Mental health struggles? You're not a mind reader—even if you were looking, who's to say you'd know what you were seeing? You're not a doctor. Even Brad didn't see everything that was happening. Caden, I don't know a lot, but I do know that addicts usually hide their addiction—at least, until they can't hide it anymore."

He was quiet for a long moment, staring down at his hands. "I don't know. But something. Anything."

I reached over and took his hand. "The only thing that matters right now is that she's safe. We found her, she's going to be okay, and she's coming home with us. That's what counts."

He squeezed my hand gratefully. "I keep thinking about what could have happened. If her fall had been worse when Jessica broke her arm, if the police didn't get there when they did, or if Jessica had..."

"Don't," I said firmly. "Don't go down that road. She's here. She's safe. That's reality."

A soft knock on the door interrupted us. Detective Morrison peered in, his expression apologetic.

"Sorry to bother you again. I just wanted to give you a quick update." He stepped into the room and lowered his voice. "Could we talk outside?"

We both looked at Macy. She was fast asleep, so we stepped outside but cracked the curtain to keep an ear and eye out for her.

In the hallway, Detective Morrison continued, "Mrs. Jensen is stable. She's been admitted for psychiatric evaluation and will likely be here for several days at minimum—at least seventy-two hours."

"What happens after that?" Caden asked.

"That depends on a lot of factors. The DA will decide on formal charges, but given the evidence we have..." He glanced meaningfully toward Macy, then back at us. "She'll be facing serious felony charges. Child endangerment, theft, drug possession. Even if she gets treatment, she's looking at significant jail time."

The reality of it hit me like a cold wave. Jessica wasn't just going to disappear into rehab for a few months and come back ready to resume her role as Macy's mother. This was bigger than that. This was life-changing—this was permanent.

We talked more about planning, the need to give statements, and the jurisdictional issues that Morrison would take care of in partnering with the local police department. After he left, Caden and I went back to sit with Macy while we sat in silence again, waiting for them to release us so we could take her home—a long night, even though it was almost morning at this point. The weight of everything we'd learned was settling over us like a heavy blanket.

"Are you okay with everything? I know this is a lot. I know we still have a lot to manage and deal with, and taking this on is huge. I can't even begin to tell you how sorry I am for all of it, and now for all this too." Caden said eventually.

I looked at Macy, sleeping peacefully despite everything she'd been through. Her face was relaxed in sleep, making her look even younger than she was.

I turned back to look at Caden and said, "We aren't fixed, but we aren't completely broken. We have a lot to work on. I believe you when you say you want to work on it. I'm not going anywhere. Not right now. Not if we continue to work on us."

We were still gathering the fragments. But for the first time in a long time, I believed we might finally make something whole.

Chapter 29: She's So Strong

~CADEN~

The call from David came early in the morning, just as I was getting Macy settled with her food tray. I was annoyed that we still hadn't been released, but I also get that overnight staff is sparse. The nurse had said we should be out by noon. I really wanted to get Macy home—and shower. Damn did I need a shower.

Stepping out of the Emergency Department area and out of Macy's hearing, I answered David's call.

"Caden? It's done. Emergency custody granted, effective immediately. The judge reviewed everything—police reports, hospital records, Jessica's circumstances. She called it 'a clear case for child protection.'"

My legs were suddenly weak with relief. "Great. I don't want any decision-making left with Jess. Thanks, David."

"You now have full physical custody, for now. To make it permanent, we need the judge's formal order at the final hearing."

"What's that mean? Why isn't it permanent yet?"

David continued, "Well, the emergency hearing was just for the present circumstances. There still needs to be a full custody hearing. That's where we'll request sole custody—so you'll get physical custody and full legal decision-making capability."

"How long will that take?"

"I'll start the process to file for permanent custody. Our first step is a temporary custody hearing in the next couple of weeks. Then we'd get a final hearing. All told, probably 3 or 4 months start to finish."

My stomach plummeted. That felt like forever, "Okay. You'll get everything started?"

"I'm on it. Go take care of Macy and Felicity. I'll keep you posted on how things go with the case."

"Thanks, David."

I walked back toward Macy, entering her space.

"Can we go home yet?" she asked.

"Soon, honey."

"I'm so boooooooooored!"

Felicity and I both smiled. Damn kids are resilient. I'm still freaking out, meanwhile she's bored. I don't know if I will ever be bored again given how my heart hasn't stopped pounding for the last eighteen hours.

Dr. Patel arrived an hour later for final discharge instructions. Six weeks for the cast, follow-up with her doctor at home, keep the stitches dry, go to the local emergency department if she experienced dizziness or increased pain. All standard stuff, but I found myself taking meticulous notes on my phone as if I were studying for the most important test of my life.

"She's been through significant trauma," Dr. Patel said quietly while Macy was in the bathroom with Felicity. "Physical recovery will be straightforward, but watch for her emotional response. You may find she has nightmares, anxiety, starts to get clingy. All normal, but she'll need support."

"We're setting up therapy," I said.

"Good. I hope I'm not overstepping, but I'd recommend family therapy too. This affects all of you."

"Already on it."

"Good. I wrote her out of school for the rest of the week, but I'd recommend getting back to routine as soon as you can."

"Got it."

The drive home felt surreal. Three days ago, I'd been desperately trying to save my marriage. Now I was bringing my daughter home from the hospital after her mother had kidnapped and hurt her. How the hell was this real?

"We need to stop at the drug store," Felicity said. "Need to pick up her prescriptions—and maybe some treats for her," The last part Felicity whispered.

But Macy had perfect hearing for things she loved, "Treats!? Treats like what? Can I have a Snicker's bar? Oh, oh, oh I want nutter butters! Wait—no, not nutter butters—Reese's Peanut Butter Cups! Yeah -definitely peanut butter cups." Felicity laughed.

"You have sonic hearing kid!"

"I know. It's true. It's my superpower."

That moment—where my kid could joke in the face of all she'd been through—that was a moment for the record books. I'd get her all three treats if she wanted. Fuck, she could have the whole store with what she experienced—just to see that smile stay on her face.

I watched Macy in the rearview mirror as we drove through town. She'd gone silent for a bit. Felicity had given Macy her phone so she could watch a show while we drove. I'd catch her looking out the window at times—with an expression I couldn't quite read. I'm sure there was a lot going through her head. Need to get that therapist scheduled ASAP.

At CVS, I would have left my girls in the car, but Macy wanted to come in. Felicity and she wandered around, filling their basket with everything from snacks to nail polish to markers to decorate her cast. I waited in line for prescriptions.

Finishing up, we all climbed back into the car—me with a small brown bag of prescriptions, them with three giant bags of I-don't-t-know-what. The girls were chattering away talking about colors for toes and nails or some such thing, and I had this feeling of calm wash over me. It's going to take a lot of work, but we're going to be okay. I'll make sure of it.

Walking into the house, the quiet came with the reminders of our rush out the door. The empty caramel corn bag still sat on the kitchen table. Our coffee cups with the dregs of coffee were on the counter. The lights were still on in the kitchen. You could tell we left in a hurry, but it was good to be back home.

I turned to Macy, and said "why don't you head upstairs, and get settled. I want to grab a shower and then I can make all of us something to eat. Sound good?"

"That sounds good. Thanks dad."

Felicity responded, "Ugh, I need a shower too."

"Okay, how about this—you grab the first shower. I'll get lunch started. Then we can tag team?"

"That's perfect," she leaned forward and in for a kiss. I deepened it, enjoying holding my wife close and just being with her. "It's a good thing we both smell otherwise I'd have to tell you that you smell ripe."

"Ha!" I swatted her ass while she walked away laughing. "Roses, Felicity! I smell like roses."

Her laughter followed her up the stairs, "sure! Keep telling yourself that!"

I thought back to that night when I watched her walk up the stairs after our argument about the purse. It resonated with me what a different feeling it was today, even after how tumultuous the last few days have been, the sense of belonging and rightness was a major juxtaposition of the sense of dread I had that night.

Feeling content, I turned to start prepping some lunch. Grilled cheese and tomato sandwiches were definitely called for.

I was still processing everything when I heard Felicity's footsteps on the stairs. She appeared in the kitchen doorway, hair damp from her shower, wearing comfortable clothes and looking more relaxed than she had in days.

"Macy fell asleep," she said softly, coming over to sit beside me on the couch. "Poor thing was exhausted. Probably the adrenaline wearing off—she's been through so much."

"Good. She needs the rest."

I put my arm around Felicity and pulled her close.

"Gross, you still smell! Go shower." She laughed.

I sat forward, elbows on my knees—sighing loudly.

"Hey—I'm sorry—I was just teasing," she said while rubbing my back.

I grabbed her hand and held it. "No, it's not that. I know you're teasing—and I do actually smell." I smiled.

Felicity leaned back against the couch cushions. "Hey—so, you know we will need to go to Jessica's house and get some of Macy's things. Her school stuff, most of her clothes and—well, pretty much everything that she needs is there."

"Shit. I didn't think about that. I'll call Brad in a bit and see if it's okay for us to come and gather Macy's things." I looked toward the stairs, where Macy was sleeping peacefully for the first time in days. "Whatever we do, I know I want to do everything I can to protect you and Macy. Everything else, we'll figure out.

"All right—go shower and I'll finish lunch."

I reached for my wife, ignoring her laughing protests about my B.O., and pulled her in close. I held her and kissed her deeply—passionately. Pulling back, seeing that dazed look in her eyes—knowing the same was reflected in my own, I felt grounded. "I love you."

"I love you too. Now go wash up."

I laughed and headed upstairs; running the list of things to do through my head as I climbed.

Rounding the corner at the top of the stairs, I walked past Macy's room. I doubled back, peeking through the door she'd left cracked open. She usually closed it if she was in her room, but I'm guessing she wasn't quite ready to be all alone. I don't think I was either.

I thought of when she was just a baby—her first smile, first laugh, first uncontrollable giggle. I remember her first big fall when she tumbled from her bike and scraped up the whole side of her leg. I thought back to when she was little, how she was so young when we got divorced and then later, when I met Felicity.

For as long as she could remember, Macy has always lived in two places. Being full time with Felicity and me is probably going to be a major adjustment. With one last look at my daughter's face, expression soft with sleep, and relief from the last twenty-four hours, I turned and continued on.

I took out my phone before heading to the shower. Scrolling through the list I had saved, I searched for a therapist specializing in family support.

Lifting the phone to my ear, I responded to the answering service, "Hi, I need to book an appointment . . ."

Chapter 30: Not Fixed, Not Broken

~FELICITY~

The house quiet. Different. There was a new sort of stillness in the air—with Macy upstairs permanently. Things had shifted, and I knew it was for the better.

We'd spent the evening getting her settled. We brought in a nightlight because she was scared to sleep in the dark—that was new, and clearly related to the circumstances.

"Can we paint this weekend?" she'd asked as I set a water glass on her nightstand.

"You want to paint your room?"

"Yeah. Well, the pink was okay because I wasn't here every day, but I'm older now and thought it would be cool to have something different, like—I dunno ..." her voice trailed off at the ened.

"We can paint if you like, but I don't know about this weekend. Why don't we see how your feeling? We'll have to go to the store, pick out some colors, get some samples and try them out. It can be a big job—and you're still recovering. I don't want you to overdo it, okay?" I'd said, smoothing her hair back from her forehead.

"I feel fine. My arm doesn't even hurt anymore."

But exhaustion was written all over her face as she fought sleep. She was clearly worn out. She'd been through a major trauma, and it wasn't over yet.

Caden and I both planned to take the rest of the week off of work to stay with her and look after her. I'm pretty grateful Mass has such robust leave laws that give me time, with pay, to stay home with her and make sure she's okay. Caden could do some work from home, reviewing new contract bids.

"Okay, well, we'll talk more this week. Sleep tight, sweetheart," I whispered, kissing her forehead. "We're right down the hall if you need anything. I'll convince your dad to do pancakes in the morning, sound good?"

In response, she whispered, "paaaaaaaaaancakes!" I laughed quietly given that her eyes were closed, and she was inches away from sleep, yet pancakes could elicit a smile and excitement from her.

Now Caden and I were finally alone in our bedroom for the first time since before I went to Miami. It felt strange, and I was actually nervous—like we were both trying to remember how to be a couple. So much had happened.

"She seems to be adjusting well," Caden said, sitting on the edge of the bed to pull off his socks.

"She does. I didn't know what to expect, honestly." I was brushing my hair, watching him in the mirror. "I have to wonder how long she's been dealing with things at home and kept quiet. Like was Jessica like this for a while? Was this spiral new?"

"It's a good question. I'm hoping a counselor can help her with whatever she's feeling, and if it's been more long term than we realized, they can help her cope. The doctor did say kids are resilient and can sometimes do really well right after a trauma but to watch for delayed reactions, right? "

"It's true. Said she could have nightmares, too."

Caden stood up and walked over behind me, his arms settling around my shoulders as he put his chin on my left shoulder. Quietly, he said, "and what about you? How are you doing with all this?"

I leaned back against him, closing my eyes. "Honestly? Terrified I'm going to mess it up. Afraid I'm going to get lost in all of this. Scared we're going to fall apart. Worried that I won't be enough for her. She's never been here full time, you know?"

"Firstly, we are going to work on us—I won't fall back into old habits, and I already put calls out to the therapists we looked at to see who has availability."

"Really?"

"Really."

I looked at him in the mirror—locking eyes. "Thank you. I'm glad we aren't getting lost in everything."

"Honey, we may have a lot going on around us, but I am committed to making sure I never lose sight of you and what we have—ever again."

I turned my head, brushing my lips across his. I felt his arms wrap move from my shoulders to wrap around my waist. He deepened our kissed me, passion pouring from him—and I matched it. It was a war of hunger and desire wrapped around the conclusion of fear and anxiety we'd been fighting for the last two days. It was every emotion we'd been carrying—anger, love, worry, joy. Fire, and ice, clashing and melting at the same time. Everything was in this moment.

Breathing heavy, Caden pulled back first. "We need to stop. You asked for us to reconnect, but no sex. We keep this up, well, you and I both know the idea of stopping will be a distant memory for us both.

Panting, I responded, "shit, you're right. I know, you're right. It sucks—it was *my* rule, but I think we both know fun in the bedroom was never an issue for us—it was everything else. So, yeah, you're right."

He responded, "*We're* right."

I smiled, leaned in, and laid my cheek against his chest. After a minute I stepped back, told him I would get ready for bed, and headed into the bathroom to wash up and dress in my least sexy pajamas possible—we're talking full length pants and long-sleeved top, zero cinching, extra baggy.

I walked back into the bedroom to find Caden walking in from the other side at the same time. He told me, "I did the rounds, made sure everything was locked up, and I set the alarm."

I don't know why, but I was comforted by that more than usual. He always does the last walkaround, it's routine for us, but tonight, it felt a thousand times more soothing on my nerves than normal.

I climbed into bed, wrapping myself in all the layers. I like to be warm when I sleep, so layers are my best friend. Caden likes to be cold, so we are perfect at sleeping since, by morning he has kicked the covers off and I have stolen all of them into my cocoon.

He made his way to the other side and under the covers. Pulling me close, he nuzzled his face into the side of my neck—making me giggle. This. This feeling and this moment—I wish I could stop time right here. Our breathing evened out as we both fell into a comfortable quiet. Soon, I felt myself drifting off, safe in Caden's arms. I sensed him doing the same. Glad Caden was never a snorer, I contented myself in the feel of his body heat warming me down to my soul and allowed my dreams to take me.

~_~_~_~_~_~_~_~_~_~_~_~_~_~_~_~_~_~

A blood curdling scream rocked my world and ripped me out of my sleep. Glancing around, the room was silent and pitch black except for the Echo where I could see the time in dim blue showing it was 3 a.m. My heart was pounding and Caden was sitting up now too.

"What happened?" he said.

"I don't know. Maybe I had a dream? I could swear I heard screaming, but now I don't know if it was me or if I actually heard it—everything's so quiet. I want to go check on Macy." Just then, the scream happened again—it was Macy, and I hadn't dreamt it. That scream was very real.

Caden and I rushed to her room, Caden turned the hall light on as he passed it. The night light in her room added enough lighting to see her clearly. I ran to her bedside and dropped down to my knees. She was thrashing and whimpering, her movements putting her arm at risk of getting hit against the nightstand. I firmly grabbed her shoulders, at least to stop her from hurting herself.

"Macy. Macy. We're here." Caden was on the other side of her bed brushing her hair back from her face.

"Honey, wake up. Can you hear us? Wake up."

Her body movements started to slow, and her eyes began to open. She jolted awake—covered in sweat and holding her cast as if her arm was broken all over again.

"No, no, it's okay. It's just us," I said, putting my hand on the other side of her head to gently hold it.

She was crying, tears running down her face.

"I—I was bas back in the room and Mom was falling on me again. I swear I felt my arm break again." She started to sob, and I climbed in bed with her, engulfing her in my embrace.

"I'm going to go get her some Tylenol and warm milk. She loves the milk, maybe it will help."

"Good. Good. Yeah, good idea," I responded.

Making soothing sounds as I rocked her, I felt myself tearing up with her as she sobbed. How to help a little girl who went through everything she experienced. How we got here, was beyond me.

I felt her body start to relax and her sobbing ease just as Caden returned with her milk and meds. They gave her prescription strength acetaminophen for her pain. She took the pill and held her mug of milk close to her.

"Thanks, Daddy."

Leaning his head into hers, he kissed her forehead and said, "you're welcome, honey. Are you feeling any better?"

"Yeah. A little."

"Okay good. You want me to stay the night with you in here?"

"Yeah—would you both stay with me?"

We looked at the twin bed and I responded, "I'm not sure we'd both fit with you, honey."

"Oh... yeah, I guess you're right."

"Why don't we have a slumber party," Caden said. "I can throw some blankets on the floor next to your bed. You and Felicity can share the bed together. How does that sound?"

"That sounds great!"

"Your dad can grab the blankets and I'll go help with the pillows. You'll be okay for a minute?"

"Yeah, I'll be okay. Thanks Felicity," she said—a small smile starting to blossom on her face.

Caden and I walked back into our room.

"Damn, that was terrifying," he quietly mumbled.

"Tell me about it. Let's get our stuff and get back in there."

I approached the bed and pulled the pillows off, looking at them I noticed there were different cases on them. "Caden?"

"Yeah?"

Holding up the pillow from my side, I asked, "is this the pillow from the guest room that I was using?"

"Oh—um," he cleared his throat. Rubbing the back of his neck, he was looking down and, I swear he was red from his cheeks down past his neck. "Yeah. So, I grabbed the one from the guest room while you were in Miami," he said. "It still smelled like you. I actually wondered if you noticed it missing," he laughed lightly with his response, embarrassment written all over his features.

"I didn't." I looked at the bed, the pillows, and then back to him. I was touched. I felt my eyes start to water. It meant something to me that he needed me in those—that he missed me.

I walked over to him and wrapped my arms around his waist, burying my face in his chest. Still holding both of the pillows, one in each hand, they rounded to his back. I mumbled into his chest, "I missed you too," I whispered. "Every night."

We brought the pillows and the extra blankets from the closet, creating a makeshift bed on Macy's floor. It wasn't the most comfortable arrangement, but as we all got settled into our respective spots—Macy curled up against me in her twin bed, Caden stretched out below us—it felt right.

"This is nice," Macy said sleepily, her voice already getting heavy again. "Like camping, but inside."

"Yeah, it is," I agreed, stroking her hair. "You feeling better, sweetheart?"

"Mmhmm. Thanks for staying."

"Always," I whispered. "We'll always stay when you need us."

Within minutes, her breathing had evened out into the deep rhythm of sleep. I lay there listening to both of them—Macy's soft breaths above, Caden's steady breathing from the floor. My family. Our family.

"Felicity?" Caden's voice was barely a whisper.

"Yeah?"

"I love you."

"I love you too."

The house settled around us, quiet and peaceful.

As I drifted back to sleep with Macy's small hand tucked in mine and Caden's presence steady beside us, I felt something I hadn't felt in a long time: complete peace. We were exactly where we belonged.

Tomorrow will bring its own challenges—therapy appointments to make, routines to establish, the ongoing legal situation with Jessica, and collecting her belongings from her mom and Brad's house. But tonight, we were together. Safe. Healing.

All of us.

Chapter 31: Macy's Things

~CADEN~

I'd woken up this morning to a texts from pretty much every family member, but most importantly one from my Aunt Patty, telling me she'd arranged for a grocery delivery, and it was on the front porch. Perfect!

I quietly left the room so as not to wake Felicity and ran down to bring the bags inside so nothing spoiled. In the bags, I found the makings for pancakes, various cereals, milks, pre-made meals and sides—you name it, she sent it. My family was amazing.

Not long after, I found myself standing at the stove, groceries unpacked and the makings for breakfast unpacked and prepped, I was flipping the second batch of pancakes and bacon—Macy's favorite breakfast. I only bust out the giant cast iron griddle a few times a year, but it was worth every penny for mornings like this. I love this thing and it makes the pancakes taste out of this world. Well, that, and my super-secret recipe. The smell of breakfast permeated the kitchen, and probably the whole house by now. This was morning comfort food at its finest.

"More syrup and strawberries, please," Macy said, holding up her plate. She looked better this morning—she had a little pink back in her cheeks, and she seemed more like herself.

"How's your arm feeling?" I asked, adding another pancake to her stack. I placed the bowl of sliced strawberries and the bottle of maple syrup in front of my daughter.

Today, she could have as much as she wanted—we'd all just have to plan for a nap. A carb-and sugar-loaded breakfast like this was definitely going to knock us into a food coma sometime in the next two hours.

"Good. It doesn't hurt at all anymore. Can we still go get my stuff today?"

Felicity and I exchanged glances. We'd planned to retrieve Macy's belongings this morning, but after last night's nightmare, I wasn't sure if it was the right timing.

"We don't have to rush it," Felicity said, gently. "We could wait a few more days if you want."

"No, I want to get my things. Especially my art supplies and my books. I miss them."

"Okay," I said. "Or we could just buy you all new supplies for now."

Macy paused, looked down, and very quietly said, "but I need Lamby too."

"Oooooooh," responded Felicity. Lamby is Macy's stuffed animal. She has loved it and slept with it since she was a baby. I'd thought maybe by now she had outgrown it, but she must still sleep with it. If ever there was a time for your emotional-support-stuffie, now was it. Felicity reached over and placed her hand on Macy's back, smiling softly at her.

"Okay honey, we'll go get your stuff today. Don't worry," I responded.

"Okay. Thanks, Daddy."

"But if you change your mind at any point, we leave. Deal?"

"Deal."

An hour later, we were getting in the car,

~Felicity~

As we arrived, we rang the doorbell and waited for Brad to come to the door.

The door swung open silently with Brad standing there, clearly at a loss. We all just stared at each other, no one really knowing what to say or do first.

Brad broke the silence when he cleared his throat and said, "Ahem, Macy. I—" then he shuffled his feet, hands settling on his hips. "I mean, how are you?" He looked pointedly at Macy's cast.

"I'm okay." Macy didn't seem to know what to say in response. She leaned her head into her dad.

"Yeah, okay." Brad ushered us in. "I'll just hang down here while you guys do what you need to do. I don't want to get in the way.

We walked into the house, the silence was almost deafening. The front door led us to the stairs. Climbing to Macy's room, I looked around, amazed at the gaudiness of the house. There was gold painted trim on columns, a naked African style bust when you reached the top of the steps, ornate pieces all along the hallway. It was like a museum rather than a home.

I felt uncomfortable here. There was definitely something wrong about this place. "Macy, why don't you show us what you want to take," I said, placing my hand lightly on her shoulder.

Macy's bedroom was its own type of museum. Well decorated, almost like a guest room. No pictures on the walls. Everything curated specifically to almost be on display. There were a few toys strategically positioned, not a piece of clothing anywhere in sight. It lacked the lived-in feeling of a child's real space.

"Lamby!" Macy rushed to her bed and grabbed the worn stuffed sheep out from under her pillows, clutching it to her chest. "I missed you so much."

Watching her reunite with this ugly, well-worn-stuffed animal made my throat tight.

"What else do you want, sweetheart?" Caden asked, pulling out the duffel bags we'd brought.

As Macy pointed out the things she wanted to come home with her, I found myself collecting the items from her closet. In my hands was an assortment of items when I looked up and saw myself in the full-length mirror on the back of her closet door.

I caught my reflection and, just as suddenly, saw hers in my mind. Macy—standing in this same spot, twirling, maybe modeling that purse the way I never got to. I felt a pang in my chest and my stomach twisted at the thoughts of the purse. I'd never even had the chance to touch it or hold it. I hadn't been able to model it. I don't blame her, but I do have a little resentment sitting there under the surface. I couldn't even make sense of the emotions churning inside of me. I looked away, trying to put the visual out of my head.

It didn't matter anymore—the purse was gone now, donated to provide for women who needed the proceeds more than I did. I was glad it was gone. I was proud that we'd done the right thing, that it had gone to a good purpose. But God help me, I still wanted that fucking purse. Even knowing it had been Macy's, even knowing I wouldn't actually want that specific purse anymore—I still felt that hollow ache of want.

What was wrong with me? Was I selfish?

Here we were, so soon after Macy's trauma, sitting in her room and gathering her belongings, where she has to say goodbye to a major part of her life, and part of me was still thinking about that damned purse. I told Caden last night that I was afraid I would get lost in all of this, that I was afraid we would fall apart. I can't help but feel like those fears are coming true and I don't know how to articulate it.

A tear sprung to my eye, but I looked away, afraid Caden might see. I stopped myself though—maybe I need Caden to see. Maybe he needs to see that I was struggling still, that this whole situation was hard for me in ways I didn't know how to explain. Part of our issues, I know, were exacerbated by me not communicating—expecting him to change without telling him that I wanted him to change.

"Felicity?" Caden's voice was gentle. "You okay?"

I turned around, still holding Macy's clothes. "Yeah, just... taking it all in, I guess."

But I wasn't okay. Why can't I bring myself to tell him?

Looking around this sterile room that was supposed to be Macy's space, I felt overwhelmed by everything we were dealing with. Macy's trauma, our marriage, becoming full-time parents overnight, and somehow, underneath it all, my own selfish wants that I couldn't seem to shake. Honestly, I wish my mom were still with me. I feel like I could talk to her, and she would know what to do.

"Can we get my art supplies too?" Macy asked, pointing to a desk in the corner. "They're in the bottom drawer."

Caden walked over and pulled out a sketch pad, some colored pencils, and markers. "This it?"

"Yeah—it's not a lot but I love drawing. Mom said when I go through that sketchpad she'd see if she could get me another."

The reminder of Jessica hit me like a punch. Focus—just get this done and you can think these things through when we get home.

"That's great, honey, maybe with the move we can get you some more." I said, kneeling down next to the desk. "We can set up a really nice art station in your room at home."

"Really?"

"Really."

Macy's face lit up. "That would be so cool!"

As we continued packing, I found myself watching Caden with Macy. He was so patient, asking her about each item, making sure she felt heard about what mattered to her. This was the man I'd fallen in love with—attentive, caring, present. It made me wonder why it had taken a crisis to bring this version of him back. And then it made me aggravated. At him. At myself. At the situation. Tamp it down, Felicity. Let's not lose it in front of everyone, yeah?

"I think that's everything," Macy said after we'd filled two large duffel bags and a box with her books.

"What about your school stuff?" I asked. "Notebooks, backpack?"

"Oh yeah!" She ran to her closet and pulled out a purple backpack. "I'll need this for when I go back to school."

Well that felt a bit weird. We'd never had her for school drop off before. Could that really be? Damn, that can't be right. But as I thought back, it was just weekends and vacations, so dropoff at school really hadn't been a thing.

What time is drop off? Am I supposed to make her lunch? Does she need anything special? I don't even know her teachers! Internally, my wheels started to spin. I had this crushing feeling in my stomach—Am I even ready for something like this? This is bigger than we'd experienced with Macy before. Sure, we went to events and supported her for things, but this is routine stuff that I have absolutely no idea how to do.

I took a breath. Reminded myself that there was a time and a place to have my freak out and that was not here.

Brad helped us carry everything to the car while Macy did a last run through inside. As we loaded the bags, I caught Caden looking at me with concern.

"What?" I asked.

"You've been quiet. More quiet than usual."

I glanced back at the house, then at Macy who was arranging Lamby in the backseat. "Just processing, I guess."

"Okay. You want to talk?"

I looked at him like he was crazy, whispering, "not here, Caden. Yes—I want to talk, but not right this second."

"Yeah. Sorry. I'm not really thinking straight."

I sighed, realizing I needed to give a little on this one. "It's okay."

Brad approached with the last bag. "Hey Caden. Can I talk to you for a minute?"

Caden looked between us, and, at my smile, he nodded. They stepped off to the side and I could hear them talking. Brad asked if he could still see Macy, take her to dinner or out for ice cream here and there. Caden promised to talk to Macy and let him know.

Macy came down the steps, carrying a few more things with her. She hugged Brad, and while she teared up a bit, she seemed okay, which was a relief.

The drive home was quiet. Macy sat in the backseat, staring out the window. Even with everything on her plate and all the emotions that today must have caused, she was still looking more relaxed than I'd seen her in weeks. But as the adrenaline from everything at Jessica's house started to wear off, I felt my earlier confusion settling back in.

I wanted to be grateful for everything we had—and I am. We're all safe, we're working things, life is still moving along. But I still had this nagging voice in my head that reminded me of what I had been through these last few years.

"You're thinking really loud over there," Caden said as we pulled into our driveway.

"Sorry."

"Don't apologize. Talk to me. What's going on?"

I looked back at Macy, who was already unbuckling her seatbelt, eager to get her things settled in her room. "Later," I said. "When we're alone tonight."

At home, Macy went upstairs to unpack her belongings while Caden and I made lunch. I went and checked on her upstairs, to see how she was doing. She had arranged her stuffed animals on the windowsill and put her art supplies to the side of her dresser—just until we had a desk for her to put in the room.

I looked around her room, feeling a kind of loss in my soul. Caden and I had started trying at the very beginning of our marriage. If we'd had a baby then, they would be around five—around the same age Macy was when we got married. I pictured a little girl—she'd probably look a little like Macy did back then. Macy didn't have much of her mom's look—taking mostly after Caden.

Macy interrupted my thoughts, "this feels more like home now," she said, sitting on her bed with Lamby.

"Good," replied Caden who had just entered the room. He went to her, kissed the top of her head. "Because it is home."

I had a quick snapshot in my head of Caden holding our little girl and felt my heart crack a bit. I walked out of the room before I lost it, leaving them to their moment.

After dinner, and what had to be the thousandth time Macy has watched Moana, she went to bed early, exhausted from the emotional day. Caden and I were alone in the living room, and suddenly I found myself unable to figure out how to explain or even start the conversation I knew we needed to have.

"So," he said, settling beside me on the couch. "Talk to me."

I pulled my knees up to my chest, staring at my hands, trying to find the words through the silence. "I feel terrible about this, but... I'm struggling."

"With what?"

"With being grateful enough. With being happy enough. With not feeling selfish when I should just be thankful for what we have."

Caden frowned. "What do you mean?"

I took a deep breath. "Today, in Macy's room, I kept thinking about that damn purse." I stopped—trying to figure out how to say what I was feeling.

"Okay, first, I'd like to say that I'm happy you donated it—I honestly would not have wanted that purse anymore. Too many bad memories attached to it. So, I just want to put that out there."

"Okay," he said, drawing the word out.

I started to tear up—annoyed with myself that, sometimes when I can't get my frustrations out, I cry, not even meaning to! "So—yeah, I know it's stupid and petty, but I can't seem to help being resentful about it. I know she is a kid, and she didn't mean anything, but I hurt over this. It's stupid that I looked in the mirror on her closet and found myself thinking about how she probably modeled it for herself, she wore it, and got to use it—meanwhile I never even had the chance to touch it. I never even got within ten feet of it!"

I held up my hand, saying, "I get that it seems ridiculous, but I can't seem to hold back my feelings on the issue. We are finally in an okay place, and maybe the adrenaline of the last couple days has worn off or something. I don—"

"Felicity—"

"Wait. I'm not done," I said quickly. "I'm ashamed of feeling this way. The locket is absolutely beautiful, and it's thoughtful. It is exactly what I would have wanted you to give me without needing to be prompted. And, yes, that purse obviously had to go. But I don't know how to change my feelings. I don't know how to turn this part of me off that still feels like I lost something in the process—even after losing so much of my voice for the last few years." I rushed on, "which I know is not your fault. Nothing you did made me uncomfortable to say something to you about how I felt and yet, I couldn't bring myself to talk to you."

Caden was quiet. Waiting. Processing.

"I feel like it's wrong to feel this way," I continued in a whisper—needing to fill the silence. "But I can't change how I feel."

I didn't know how to fix what still felt broken inside me. But for the first time, I wasn't hiding it.

Chapter 32: Apology Tour

~Caden~

I sat there listening to my wife, seeing the struggle in her as she tried to explain her feelings and how she thought they made her selfish. She was apologizing. For her feelings. For being human. Fuck, this is all my fault.

"Felicity," I said quietly, waiting until she looked at me. "Please. Please, stop apologizing."

"But I—"

Softly, but firmly, I said, "No. I'm begging you to stop." I turned to face her fully, my heart breaking seeing her try to hold back tears. "You don't have a single thing to apologize for. Not one thing."

She leaned her head back, as if resigned to not know what to do with her feelings. Reaching forward, I placed my hand along the curve of her cheek. I felt love wash over me as she nuzzled her cheek into my hand, letting me give her comfort in this moment, something I was so deeply undeserving of.

"Can I tell you something?" I asked. "About the last few years?"

She opened her eyes and gave a slight nod.

I dropped my hand a bit, blowing out a breath of air while I worked to find my words. "When the company almost went under a few years back, I was terrified. Not just of losing the business, but of losing everything. The pandemic almost broke it. I mean, I know you know, but thinking back on how we skated by in the black through most of it, and then when business didn't pick back up right away, we were so deep in the red that I really didn't think we would have a choice but to close the doors."

I took a deep breath, rubbing my eyes with my thumb and forefinger. I moved so I could face her completely, sitting on the coffee table in front of her—my hands on her knees, elbows on mine. "I was terrified of all the jobs that could be lost, of having to start over. I became afraid of not being able to provide for you, for us." I paused, trying to catch my thoughts as they ran through my head a mile a minute.

"When we met, I had already had the company—for a number of years in fact. I couldn't imagine what it would be like if I was suddenly not just an unemployed failure, but possibly buried under debt and bankruptcy filings, and all the turmoil that would come with me being such a catastrophic disappointment."

"You never said anything." She placed her hands on top of mine. "Why didn't you tell me how bad it was? You told me that there were struggles and that you were trying to keep everything from folding, but you didn't tell me how close you were to completely shutting down." Her words came out as a whisper.

"I know. And I think that is where I started to go wrong. I didn't talk about it, allowing embarrassment to steal my words—trying to keep my work and my home lives separate—which was obviously the wrong choice," I offered a chagrined half smile.

"If you had included me, I would have been there for you. I would have told you that I didn't marry you for your damned company. I married you because I love you and it had nothing to do with the dollars in your bank account."

"I honestly think that the humiliation of telling you how bad it had kept me from saying anything." I looked her in the eyes and said, "and that was wrong."

I took a beat and just stared into her eyes, letting her see everything in my soul—my sorrow, my regret, my love, my heart. I wanted her to see it all. No holding back.

"I lost sight of you," I said, voice cracking and tears starting to fall. "I let my own self-consciousness about my failure bleed into our marriage and I broke something between us. It was me who let you become invisible. You shouldn't have to tell me the things you needed in order to feel loved. Seen. I made assumptions that I'd take care of things at work, and you'd always be there, always be understanding, willing to wait for me to have the time for us."

She was crying now, silent tears streaming down her face.

"The purse," I continued, my throat tight. "I know it wasn't about the purse alone. It was about three years of me making you feel like an afterthought in our marriage. Three years of you sitting and waiting for me to notice you. Three years of you feeling smaller and smaller until you fit into the parts of our life left behind."

"I should have said something sooner," she whispered.

"No." I turned my hands up to intertwine our fingers. "You really shouldn't have had to. I'm your husband and I should have noticed when my wife is disappearing. You said it yourself, a husband protects his wife, her gifts, her heart. I should have made you feel cherished, not like you were in competition for a place in my life."

I squeezed her hands gently. "You know what kills me the most?"

She shrugged lightly, encouraging me to continue.

"You think you're being selfish for wanting something you never got to have. But I'm sitting here realizing it's my fault you feel that way. I made you feel like your wants didn't matter. Like you didn't matter."

"But the locket—"

"The locket is beautiful, and I'm glad you love it. It is an expression of my love—of the love both Macy and I have for you. But Felicity, I also know it doesn't erase three years of me failing you. One great gift doesn't replace the countless forgotten moments and missed chances to show you how much you mean to me. I know that, and I want you to know that I truly understand that."

I felt like I was rambling now, but in for a penny..."There's only so much I can say about the past though. I can apologize until kingdom come, but it is completely meaningless if I don't back it up with action. It's not lost on me—not like the last three years have been," I gave a little laugh, trying to lighten the moment for her, looking back up at her, I asked, "too soon?"

She laughed. Through her tears, I could see a small spark, "yes!" Still laughing she continued, "too soon, but not too soon. I can use a small moment of relief from all the stomach swirling, you know?"

With a light huff, I looked down and responded, "yeah, honey. I know. And I'm going to give you that relief. Come hell or high water, I will find a way to make things right with us."

She looked at me. Really looked at me. "I believe you. I believe you are going to try. I don't know how, but I believe you will put the effort in."

"I will. And therapy is still happening. But I know I have to do work before our appointment next week. I know I can't just rely on someone else telling me where I went wrong. I know it's up to me to help you see my heart."

She reached for my hands and started to play with my fingers. It was a nervous habit—one that I realize we haven't done in a long time. She used to do this, almost like the itsy-bitsy-spider, moving finger to finger with hers. It made me smile that we could still have this moment in the midst of all this uncertainty.

"Okay," she said quietly.

"Tomorrow, starts my apology tour."

"Apology tour?"

"Yup."

"What does that mean?"

"Well, when you were in Miami, I talked to Cash."

"Ooooookaaaaay... about, what?"

"About my complete fuck up."

"Seriously."

I smirked. "Seriously. I talked to him about what an absolute shit husband I had been. He made me think about how I need to show you my heart and help you see my love for you. So, I began the work of figuring out how to bring together something that would really demonstrate that, and show you how I heard you."

She sat up. Looked at me critically. "What does that mean?"

"That, my love, will have to wait for tomorrow. And the following days ahead. This is not a one-and-done. It's the start of a life with us where I remind you daily how deeply rooted you are in my heart." I cleared my throat, unable to help myself, I continued, "and that's the only hint you'll get from me."

"Wait! What was the hint? Say it again!"

"Nope! You're going to have to just wait and see!"

"That's crap! I hate waiting!"

"I know." I smiled at her. "But I love you so much that I'm going to help you with that waiting."

She looked at me quizzically. "What do you mean?"

"Why don't you wait here for a bit. If you'll let me, I'd like to go get a bath ready for you. I know it's always been one of your favorite things to decompress with. So, how would you feel about a bath with your favorite salt stuff that you drop in—you know, the pink thing—and a glass of wine?"

While I saw a light in her eyes, I still rushed on, wanting to make an important point, "and before you think anything differently—this is not me avoiding. I meant what I said. We are going to work through things, and I have a lot of work to do. But in the meantime, while I do that work, I'm going to also do the work of showing you—actions *and* words.

She looked at me softly, "yeah. Okay—*and* it's called a bath bomb, not a pink thing."

I smiled. "Duly noted."

"Honestly," she said, while stretching. "I could really freaking use a bath. It's always been one of my favorite things."

"Babe, I know—you had me pipe in speakers to the bathroom, along with a massive renovation, when we first moved in—including the giant jacuzzi tub. Believe me, I know you love it." I smiled, remembering our discussions about what would be best in the bathroom. It was at the beginning of our marriage, and we'd gone back and forth on decisions.

Then, one day she dropped a printout of all the things she wanted in the bathroom, gave me the puppy-dog eyes, and told me how much it would mean to have the giant list of things to make the 'best bathroom of all time.'" So, of course, I ripped out the whole bathroom—redoing the whole thing.

From the Venetian plaster on the bathroom walls that reminded her of her father, to the double sinks, linen closet, standing shower that overlooked the jacuzzi tub—it was a major job and came out awesome. She was so happy with everything that I can almost feel the memory imprinted in my soul.

"I know you do," she acknowledged. "And I love my bathroom that came out of it. Isn't it so much better now?"

"Yes, love. Sooooo much better." I winked at her.

Smiling at me, she said, "well?"

"Well, what?"

"Why are you still sitting here? I distinctly remember you promising me a bath and wine, like three minutes ago."

I coughed a laugh out, pulled her to her feet, and kissed her soundly. She responded in kind, deepening the kiss and opening her heart to me—just a little bit, but it was a small stitch she let me sew in the brokenness I had placed there. And I prayed to God she would let me keep stitching and mending the fragments together.

Chapter 33: Deeper Roots

I woke the next morning wrapped in Caden's arms, feeling a small bit of peace. It wasn't overwhelming. It wasn't perfection. But it was something—it felt new. A bit of quiet in the storm.

The conversation last night had been a start. I'd needed his honest apology—not the apology from the night we fought about the purse. Last night felt like he understood a part of where I was coming from. The way he'd seen my pain and called it valid instead of calling it selfish. It gave my anxiety some ease.

"Morning," he murmured against my hair, his voice still rough with sleep.

"Morning." I turned in his arms to face him, but I was cocooned in all the blankets and him. As I tried to turn, I got stuck and ended up flopping around like a fish out of water.

"Wait, wait—" he called out—the both of us laughing hysterically, "you're gonna go overboard!" He was grabbing me, trying to keep me from falling off the bed.

"I'm stuck!" I was laughing so hard that I started snorting. Then I shot up, still wrapped, but now sort of sitting upright. "Oh my God, Caden, get me out of here!" I said, with a bit of panic starting to flow through.

"Okay, okay. Hang on—"

"Hurry, hurry, hurry!"

Finally clearing me, I jumped from the bed, running to the bathroom. The sigh of relief—from actual relief, and from not peeing myself in bed, was almost tangible. Jesus, forty certainly comes with new experiences—I thought, laughing to myself.

Going back to the bedroom after washing up and brushing my teeth, I climbed in bed. He reached for me, "Nope!"

"What?"

"I just brushed my teeth! *I'm* clean—you have morning breath!" I playfully dove under the covers and hid my face. He burrowed under trying to blow his nasty breath on me. "Nooooooo!!!!"

Laughing, he nuzzled my neck after digging deep enough to find me, saying, "fiiiiine. I'll go make myself presentable. Can I get a raincheck?"

Muffled, I replied, "yes, as long as you brush away all that yuck."

"On it, babe."

He grabbed his phone, put on some music, and went to the bathroom to clean up. I climbed out of bed and went to the mirror on the other side of the room. Looking at my reflection, I could see a very small light in my eyes. I hope it keeps getting brighter.

"Felicity?" I heard him call out.

"Yeah?" I responded.

"Don't go down without me, okay?" He seemed a little uncertain when he asked, but I could swear I heard a bit of hope in there.

"Um, okay. I was going to head down now."

"No! Wait for me! Please?"

"Um," I looked around and decided to sit on the small bench in front of our bed. "Okay."

A couple minutes later, he came out of the bathroom, texting with someone.

"Who's that?"

He looked up, responded with a small, nervous smile, "you'll see."

"Okay, can we go down now?"

"Nope! Need four more minutes."

"Seriously? Caden! Why?! I need coffee!" I was a little exasperated. Coffee was my liquid gold and starting my day without it could be dangerous—to others.

His smile grew, but his face was pleading with me to agree. "I know, but it'll only be a few more minutes."

I blew out a breath, "Okay," flopping my hands out at my side, "well what will we do for four minutes?"

"I could think of a few things!" he responded with a wink as he meandered closer to me.

Backing up, I laughed, "get outta here."

"Hey! You gave me a raincheck!"

"I did?" I feigned surprise.

"Yes! I distinctly remember that from just a few minutes ago!" He winked, clearly remembering my words from last night about the bath.

Sighing with resignation, I responded, "Well, a raincheck is a raincheck, I guess I'll have to pay up."

"Damn straight."

With that, he ran his hands along either side of my neck, pushing his fingers through my hair. Massaging my scalp, he looked me in the eyes with honesty, lust, regret, pain, joy, love—all the feels.

Leaning forward, he touched his nose to mine, gently rubbing his nose back and forth over mine. He touched his lips to mine. He kissed me softly at first—so softly I almost missed it. His lips traced around mine before finally settling, until I couldn't tell where his stopped and mine began. I felt his passion and his love pouring from him into mine, warming my soul and feeding my own passion.

Wrapping my arms around him, I felt my fingers run down the curve of his back to the tops of his buttocks, grabbing the edges of his shirt—just to hold on, almost for dear life.

This was a kiss. This was probably a kiss for our record books. As we stood there, we were lost in each other—in the moment. I couldn't tell you how long we were there. Definitely more than four minutes, that's for sure.

And then I felt the buzz. His phone was buzzing with a call in his back pocket. He pulled away, breathing heavily, "damn," he whispered.

"You got that right. Haven't felt that in a long time, you know." I whispered back.

Quietly, he responded, "I know. And I hate that, but not anymore." He reached back with his right hand, keeping his left buried in my hair and his forehead leaning on mine.

Bringing his phone to his ear, he breathlessly said, "yeah?"

I could hear the voice on the other side of the line, "what are you doing? You running a marathon? You know what? Never mind, I just realized you're in your room with Felicity, and I really don't want to know what you and my sister-in-law are getting into right now."

I laughed, recognizing Cash's voice. I heard a few laughs in the background too though and looked at Caden questioningly.

Caden laughed a bit too, "no, no you do not!"

I blushed, dipping my head. I looked at him and said, "coffee!" trying to make sure he remember my desperate need for the nectar of the gods.

He asked Cash, "is it ready?"

"It is."

Caden looked at me while saying into the phone, "Okay, we're on our way."

He ended the call and stepped back, looking down at my feet, "you may want to put some shoes on."

"What? Why? Where are we going?"

"Just outside into the back yard."

I was confused, "the yard? What did you do?"

Smiling, he said, "you'll see soon enough."

Huffing, I did as he suggested, and threw on some tennis shoes.

"Okay, I'm ready," I told him, heart beating a mile a minute.

I padded out of our room, Caden following. I felt his hand at the small of my back. We walked past Macy's door, still slightly ajar from the night. I peeked in just to check, and saw she was still knocked out. Looking at my watch, I saw it was only 8:30a.m. She's almost twelve and isn't in school this week, my guess is she will be sleeping for a few more hours—if her weekend sleep schedule—and the week she's had—is any indication.

I clicked her door closed just to make sure we didn't wake her with any of our movements.

At the bottom of the stairs, I turned away from the kitchen, heading to the back door of the house. I looked longingly back at the kitchen—where my coffee would be. Feeling Caden slip his hand in mine, I turned my head up toward him and met his eyes. He leaned forward and said, "Coffee in a few minutes, I promise."

I grumbled, "okay, but I'm holding you to it."

"Hold away."

He pulled me toward the back door. Through the glass, I could see a couple of guys cleaning some things up—a tarp, some burlap netting, a shovel, and a few other items. I looked back at Caden, with a knowing smile, he told me to open the door and head outside.

At the entrance of the garden stood my brother-in-law Cash, and a few other guys in jeans and t-shirts. Everyone was staring at me, and, after a moment, I saw why. I had what I feel is a pretty large garden, fairly nondescript though. It's off to the side of my yard but runs the entire length—so around fifteen feet deep and forty feet long.

There's a bench off to the side when you walk in, and a dirt path that takes you from the entry down the middle all the way to the end. I plant everything from lavender to basil, cucumbers to eggplant. I thought it would be terribly overgrown since I haven't tended to it in over a week now, but it looked like someone had been caring for it, pulling weeds and watering—I glanced at Caden, thinking it must have been him.

Looking back over, I saw that at each end of the garden sat two newly planted trees—stakes holding them up, so the trunks remained straight, each about 6 feet tall. There was red mulch covering the ground around both and probably about thirty feet or so between them.

My breath caught. These weren't just any trees hastily picked up from a nursery. This was well planned—from the matching trees, and their placement, to their meaning.

Confused, I looked to Caden.

He looked over at the trees, but spoke to me. "Did you know that the gift for a fourth anniversary is fruit or flowers?" he asked.

I shook my head—I hadn't.

"Three years ago, I missed our fourth anniversary. I was so focused on what was going on at work, that I lost sight of celebrating us on that night. When I cancelled, I didn't explain what was going on, and then I failed to focus back on you and our life together."

"Okay..." I said, waiting for the explanation, because he wasn't saying anything I didn't already know.

"I did some research, and I learned that the sweet cherry tree symbolizes renewal and love."

I whipped my head toward the trees, noticing then that the yard had emptied of everyone by Caden and me. I eyed the trees, seeing for the first time what they were—young cherry trees.

"Eventually, these trees will give both flowers and fruit every year. And for each year that passes, they will grow stronger—their roots deeper." He paused, turning his head to look down at me, love very clear in his eyes. He said quietly, but meaningfully, "The cherry tree is also said to represent new beginnings."

With those last words, I could feel his eyes boring into my soul.

He shifting his body to face me. "Felicity Barrett, I am so far from perfect that I'm almost in another solar system. I have messed up so much in our marriage and I know without a doubt, that I am so deeply unworthy of you. I cannot promise you perfection, but I can promise you that I will work every day for the rest of our lives to keep our roots growing deeper and our marriage growing stronger."

He placed his hands on either side of my face, and said, "I'm not asking for you to forgive me and merely give me a second chance. I'm asking for just one day at a time from you, and I swear that by the end of every day I will have shown you my love, and at the beginning of the next day I will begin the work on earning your love again. Every day another chance of loving you, for the rest of our lives—this is my promise to you. Just give me one day at a time—and I will give you the rest of my life."

By this time, I was sobbing. So much anger and so much resentment had been filling the corners of my heart. With those words, it felt like he was stitching something back together—just one stitch, but it felt like it would hold.

I whispered to him, nodding, "you can have one day." By the time I finished the sentence, he had already leaned in to nuzzle his face against mine, pulling my body in close to his, I could feel his desperation to hold me closer than he ever had before.

I heard him whisper, "you think the trees are nice, just wait 'til tomorrow."

Chapter 34: A New Light

~FELICITY~

It was evening, and we were sitting outside on the garden bench, the air cooling but quiet. Macy was upstairs in her room, working at her new desk with her art supplies—still decompressing after her first therapy appointment.

Dr. Maggie Chen, Macy's new therapist, had met with us first. She had a kind face and an easy, steady way of speaking that immediately made me feel like she was the right choice. She explained her process and the approach she planned to take with Macy. Her priority, she told us, would be building a relationship where Macy could begin to feel safe enough to trust her. That meant some conversations would stay just between them—unless there was a safety concern.

She also let us know that Massachusetts law is fairly strict when it comes to confidentiality, even with children, which meant her ability to share details with us would be limited.

Honestly? We didn't care. We didn't need to know everything. We just wanted Macy to have someone—someone safe, someone steady, someone who could help her hold the weight of everything she's been through. As someone who works in HR, I understand how important psychological safety is in the aftermath of trauma. I can only imagine how much more essential it is for a child.

We told Dr. Chen to share only what she needed to. But Caden had one caveat—and I was grateful he said it out loud.

"Dr. Chen," he said, his voice calm but lined with restrained fury, "as you know, the circumstances surrounding her mother were... highly concerning. If you learn anything suggesting Macy's safety with her was ever at risk—or if something needs to be reported to the court—can you share that with us?"

Dr. Chen nodded. "Yes. I'm a mandatory reporter. If I have reason to believe Macy has experienced abuse, neglect, or exploitation—or if there's substantial risk to her safety—I'm required to report it to DCF. That includes formal documentation and notification through the appropriate legal channels. I also reviewed your emergency custody paperwork. Macy has a Guardian ad Litem assigned to her, so any serious concerns I uncover would be shared with them as well."

She said she'd always let Macy know when something needed to be shared, and why. That transparency, she explained, was part of how she protected the therapeutic relationship. It wasn't about keeping secrets—it was about giving Macy a safe space that belonged just to her. Still, she promised to keep us in the loop on big-picture things: patterns she noticed, progress toward goals, and anything she thought we could help support at home.

It felt both like a relief and a letting go—knowing we wouldn't know everything, but that maybe, for once, Macy wouldn't feel so alone with it all. Macy may not be my biological daughter, but she's been my step-daughter for more than half her life, and I want nothing but good things for her.

After the meeting, we left Macy there for her session. Caden and I walked down the street to grab a coffee. Exiting the front entrance, Caden reached for my hand just as I had unconsciously found myself reaching for his. We walked to the nearby shop close to Broadway Station called The Grind.

It had a chill atmosphere. I grabbed us a table while Caden ordered—black coffee for him, cappuccino for me. Before finishing, he looked back at me and nodded toward the pastry case. I mouthed "YES, you pick" with a smile. I hoped he would go for the ridiculously sized slice of Chantilly lace cake—one of my absolute favorites. I watched as the barista went straight to the cake and pulled it out of the case. Something in me twittered—excited for the cake, but also pleased he'd chosen it. It spoke to my heart as a small thing he knew about me.

We sat for about half an hour, speaking about our discussion with Dr. Chen. Eventually we came to the topic of our appointment coming up next week.

"I feel a little nervous, but I'm glad we are going," I admitted.

"Me too. I know we are going to be seeing someone together, but I think I should also plan to see someone myself." Caden's words surprised me—in a good way.

"Really?" I asked. "I have to admit, I've been thinking of doing so too. These last few weeks have brought up a lot for me, and I think I may want to talk to someone about it all too."

"Whatever you want, sweetheart."

I smiled at him and took a sip of coffee. We sat back and enjoyed our time before having to go get Macy.

Back at the house, sitting in our garden, I looked at the cherry trees and said to Caden, "They look good out here."

"They do. Jake said they may not bloom this year with the transplant process, but there's still a chance they could."

"Makes sense, but I hope they do. I can't wait to see it."

"I keep thinking about what you said before," I murmured, pulling my sweater tighter around my shoulders. "About wanting to remember how to see each other again."

"What about it?"

"I think we're doing it. Right now." I gestured to the space between us, the comfortable silence that had settled over the garden. "This feels like seeing."

Caden's phone buzzed in his pocket, the sound almost mingling with the chirp of the crickets. Pulling it out, he glanced at the screen with a slight frown. "It's my mom. Should I—?"

"Take it," I said with a smile, stretching my legs out and feeling the satisfying pull from my ankles to my hamstrings.

He swiped to answer, his voice immediately shifting to the warmer tone he always used with Sandy. "Hey, Mom."

I could hear Sandy's voice through the speaker, warm and animated as always. Caden got his easy laugh from her—along with his pancake recipe.

"Hi, sweetheart. Is Macy still with you tonight?"

"Yeah, she's inside probably raiding our snack cabinet as we speak. Why?"

"Well, I'm driving down to Providence tomorrow to visit Gladys for the night. Angie and Alex are coming up from Hartford." Gladys is Sandy's sister; Angie and Alex are her grandkids—adorable twins just a bit younger than Macy.

Caden smiled, and I could see him picturing the chaos those three created when they set their minds to it. The last time everyone was at my in-laws', the kids were upstairs while we were in the family room. Things got quiet—we all know what happens when kids are quiet. Caden and the twins' dad, Andy, went up to check. Lo and behold, the three of them had decided they wanted to see how the upstairs armoire was put together—so they found tools and took the whole thing apart. Every piece, from the shelves and drawers to the doors, was completely disassembled.

I started laughing to myself, remembering my mother-in-law's reaction. Troublemakers, the bunch of them. Caden looked over at me questioningly. I just shook my head, still smiling.

"Oh! Nice, Ma. You have enough quarters for the rounds of poker you're sure to lose to them?"

"Quarters!" she laughed. "More like dollars now. They've progressed from amateurs to pure sharks."

Caden let out a solid belly laugh, Sandy following suit.

"Anyway," she said, "I thought Macy might like to come along. Gladys always spoils them rotten, and you know how much Macy loves hanging out with them. Plus, she's been asking about them since Easter."

I watched Caden's expression shift, becoming more thoughtful. "That's really thoughtful of you, Mom, but are you su—"

"Plus," Sandy continued, not letting him finish, "I thought it might be nice for you and Felicity to have some uninterrupted time together. You know, without an eleven-year-old's ears and eyes around the house. Just for a couple of days."

Caden looked at me, eyebrows raised in question. His mother was about as subtle as a Mack truck, but her heart was always in the right place. Honestly, the idea of a full day with just Caden sounded almost too good to be true.

I found myself nodding before I'd even fully thought it through.

"Actually," he said into the phone, "that sounds perfect. Let me ask Macy, but I'm pretty sure she'll be thrilled. Those kids always have the best adventures together, and I think she could use a little fun and mischief right now."

"Wonderful! I can pick her up around ten tomorrow morning. Pack enough for a few days, then. I'll bring her back Sunday or maybe Monday. We'll see how things go. With everything going on, I think she could use a little grandma time, and I could use a little time with my grandbaby. Plus, your father will want to see her when I get back from Providence, so we'll just plan to keep her another night unless she grows tired of us."

Not two minutes after hanging up, Macy's voice exploded from the kitchen.

"YES!" she shouted. We heard some unintelligible sounds and squealing, then through the back window, "Daaaaaaaaaaaad! Felicity!"

Caden scoffed. "Here we go," he said to me. Then he called toward the house, "Yes?!"

"Grandma said I'm going to Providence tomorrow!"

"Yup! So I heard!" he yelled back through the window.

Getting up, both of us groaning a bit from stiff muscles, we headed toward the house. Following her voice toward the stairs, we found her practically bouncing a couple steps up, the remnants of a sandwich in her hand quickly disappearing into her mouth.

She started to rattle off questions but found her mouth too full. Unprepared for the moment, she stomped her foot, looking at the ceiling, chewing as fast as she could while clearly dying to talk. When she finally swallowed, Caden and I both laughed at her antics.

After swallowing, she took a deep breath and began at a rate just shy of the speed of light. "Grandma said she's picking me up in the morning. We're staying at Aunt Gladys's house. She said Alex, Angie, and I can bunk together. Do you think they'll take us to that ice cream place with the weird flavors like last time? Do you think they'll remember the magic trick I taught them at Christmas? Oh my God, I need to pack my art supplies in case Aunt Gladys takes us on a hike again. Oh! And I can bring my bathing—"

"Slow down," Caden laughed, holding up his hands. "Grandma won't be here until ten. That gives you exactly"—he checked his watch— "fourteen hours to pack and repack your bag three times."

"I need to text Angie!" Macy was already heading up the stairs. "She probably doesn't even know I'm coming yet!"

"Don't forget to check the laundry," I called after her. "I just did a load."

"Thanks, Felicity!" came the muffled yell from upstairs, followed by the sound of drawers opening and closing.

After the whirlwind of Macy's excitement settled into the background noise of her getting ready, I settled beside Caden on the couch with a contented sigh. "Your mom's pretty transparent, you know."

"Subtlety was never her strong suit," he agreed, pulling me closer. "But she means well. And she's probably right—we could use some time without having to wait until Macy's asleep to have real conversations."

"The timing is perfect," I agreed, leaning against his shoulder. "We could use some time to just... be together without a filter."

"So, what do you want to do with our unexpected freedom?"

"Sleep in," I said immediately. "Then maybe we could drive out to Ipswich?"

~ ~

We spent the following morning puttering around the house—Caden catching up on some work while I dug in the garden, deadheading roses and checking the herb beds. Just after ten, we heard Sandy come through the front door.

"Grandma's here!" Macy called from upstairs, and within seconds she was thundering down with her overnight bag, practically vibrating with excitement.

Sandy appeared in the kitchen with her usual warm smile and what I was sure was enough snacks for a cross-country trip waiting in her car—gotta make sure Macy doesn't starve for that hour-long drive.

"Ready for an adventure, sweetheart?"

"I've been ready since yesterday!" Macy announced, giving us each quick hugs.

"Hope you guys have fun. Don't miss me too much! I'll be partying with ice cream and the A-team"—her favorite name for her cousins since both their names start with A.

"Have the time of your life," I said as she turned toward her grandma, still bouncing on her heels.

After they left, the house settled into a different kind of quiet—not the tense silence we'd grown used to during our rough patch, but something expectant and peaceful.

"So," Caden said, wrapping his arms around me from behind as I stood at the kitchen window, watching Sandy's car disappear. "Beach day?"

"Beach day," I agreed, leaning back against his chest. "But first, more coffee. And maybe those chocolate croissants you think I don't know about."

"I have no idea what you're talking about," he said with exaggerated innocence.

"Caden Barrett, let's not pretend you don't have croissants hidden away."

He laughed and headed for the freezer. "Fine. But only because it's a special occasion."

The drive to Ipswich took just over forty minutes, windows down, our road trip playlist playing.

We found a spot near Crane Beach and spent the day doing exactly what we'd promised ourselves—being completely present. We ate overpriced lobster rolls at a picnic table overlooking the water, walked the length of the beach twice, and let our feet skim the cold surf along the sand.

"You know," I said around three o'clock, looking up from my book, "this might be the most relaxed I've felt in months."

"No schedules, no crisis calls, no one needing anything from us," he agreed, settling beside me in the sand. "When did we stop doing this?"

"I think we both know," I said, meeting his eyes.

"Yeah. We do." He looked down at his feet as we walked.

"That wasn't fair. We were having a good time," I said quickly. "I know you're trying, and it means the world to me."

"No, it was fair. That it hurts my heart to know it was my fault doesn't make it any less true. But Felicity, it's moments like this that keep me grounded—and remind me of what I almost lost. I love you."

He reached around me, hooking his arm over my shoulders and intertwining our sandy fingers. "I've missed this version of us."

"Me too."

We stayed until the late afternoon sun started slanting low across the water, then packed up and headed home. I dozed for the last twenty minutes of the drive, waking as he pulled into our driveway.

"Good nap?" Caden asked, his voice soft.

"Mmm." I stretched, feeling pleasantly tired and sun-kissed. "I'm going to feel that sun tomorrow, but it was worth it."

"Definitely. Want to grab showers and then maybe order dinner? I'm thinking Thai food and a movie night."

"Perfect." I started gathering our beach gear. "Though I call dibs on the shower first. I've got sand in places sand should never be."

"Deal. I'll bring the stuff in and check a few things while you get cleaned up."

As I headed upstairs, I heard Caden's phone ring. He answered quickly, his voice dropping to a quieter tone that made me pause on the landing.

"Hey. Yeah, we just got back... Everything's ready? ... Perfect. Thanks for all your hard work. Thank the guys for me too. I'll send pics."

I smiled to myself, curiosity piqued but not wanting to eavesdrop—okay, maybe I wanted to eavesdrop—but whatever he was up to, it sounded like it involved more than one person. A project of some kind. I hummed my way toward our bedroom.

The cool water felt amazing after hours of salt and sand. I took my time, letting the pulsing water ease the pleasant tiredness from the day. When I finally emerged, I dried off and slathered on my homemade body butter—a mix of mango and coconut butters, aloe, sweet almond oil, and beeswax. It's my little ritual every other month, and it works wonders for turning my pink skin into a solid tan by morning.

I pulled on a long-sleeve and sweats—late summer days might be hot here, but the nights still drop into the fifties.

"Your turn," I called down to him.

I met him at the top of the stairs as he came up. "Great! Hey, when I'm done, want to take a quick walk through the garden? I want to check how everything did today, and the evening light should be perfect."

"Sure," I said, though something in his tone made me suspect this wasn't just about plants. "I'll make us some tea."

Before he could speak, I held up my hand. "Don't worry—I won't go out without you." I smiled and headed down while he hopped in the shower.

The sound of running water drifted into the kitchen. I smiled, settling into the den with my tea, his mug waiting on the coffee table. It took every ounce of willpower not to peek outside.

I heard him padding down the steps. Standing, I turned toward him and handed him his mug.

"Okay, sir. Lead the way."

"It would be my honor." He offered his arm, and I slipped my hand through it.

As we approached the back door, I noticed dim lights glowing through it—right where the garden entrance was—but I couldn't make out details. Interesting. There aren't usually lights there.

Switching his tea to his other hand, he reached for the door handle. "This is just the beginning of what you'll see in a moment. For now, welcome to seeing us in a new light—literally."

The warm glow spilling through the doorway revealed what looked like thousands of white lights woven throughout the garden. Too far to make out the details yet, but from here, it already looked magical.

Chapter 35: A Concrete Foundation

~Felicity~

I stepped through the doorway and gasped.

The garden had been transformed into something from a fairy tale. Countless tiny, warm, white lights were strung up everywhere. Along the outside of the garden, at each corner and then maybe six or so feet between, were tall lampposts. Strings of lights ran from each lamppost, connecting them.

As we approached, I saw there was a new arbor, white and covered with tiny little lights that wrapped around each slat from top to bottom.

"Something to know about the lights," Caden said softly. "They're all solar—they recharge during the day and pour out their light at night. Just like I want to do with loving you—each day I'll have a new chance to pour out everything I have, to spend the whole day showing you my love, and then recharge overnight so when we wake and you give me another day, I can do it all over again, for the rest of our lives."

Dear Lord, that was beautiful—if not a little on the nose.

I kept walking toward the entrance and realized it wasn't just the lights that were new. As my eyes adjusted to the soft glow, I realized the garden path itself had gotten a complete overhaul.

"Caden," I breathed, stepping forward to get a better look. "What is all this?"

Where once there had been worn dirt paths that I'd never taken steps to improve, there was now a beautifully paved walkway. The path I'd worked around when building my garden had been rudimentary—meant for access more than aesthetics. When you entered, my bench sat just off to the side. Then, walking in about six feet, you were faced with a runner path that stretched the full forty feet of the garden—basically cutting the length in half so I could access both sides of all my plantings easily from the main pathway.

These stunning wood pavers—rich, warm, perfectly fitted planks, all came together to create this long pathway and smaller ones that jutted out in between the garden beds. In the fairy light glow, they seemed to pulse with life. It made my space look refined and exciting—like spending time out here would be a luxury even though gardening was hard work.

"Do you like it?" His voice was soft, uncertain in a way that made my heart squeeze.

"Like it?" I turned to him, wonder, and awe the only emotions I could seem to collect in that moment. "Caden, this is... I don't even have words."

He reached for my hand, his fingers intertwining with mine. "Walk with me?"

I nodded, clearing my throat, not trusting my voice. Together, we stepped onto the new path, and it was so solid and firm as we walked.

"I know this space means a lot to you," Caden said as we walked slowly toward the center of the garden. He paused and brought me around by the hand to stand in front of him. He lifted his head to look around us. "You built this when you needed something that I wasn't giving you. When I was working and focused on things that weren't you."

I squeezed his hand, remembering those long, lonely months that Spring as I had moved to set my garden up—I'd never done anything like it before. "I needed something different—new. I spent hours at the local nursery, annoying the owner with every question under the sun, but she was so kind and answered everything I brought to her."

He smiled—small and sad, "I'm so sorry you had to create this beautiful space alone, and learn all of this without me by your side." His voice caught slightly.

In front of us was the herb garden, where lavender and rosemary released their scents into the evening air. The fairy lights made everything look magical, it actually felt like a dream.

"But in that loneliness, you created this beautiful sanctuary. You are the architect of something that was meant to console you in your pain."

I leaned into his side, overwhelmed by the emotion in his voice. "It helped me do something productive in that year. Gave me somewhere to put all the energy, so much so that I could honestly say that first year wasn't so hard for me. This place wasn't a place of loneliness by the end. It was a place of joy for me."

"I know. And that's why..." He gestured to the transformation around us. "I wanted to honor what you built here, but also give you new memories. I wanted to take this space that was born from a dark time for us, that you turned to joy, and I wanted to show you how I see you—to give you something that recognizes what this place has come to mean to you."

As we continued walking, I noticed details I'd missed in my initial enchantment. Solar lights had been installed along the path's edges, subtle enough not to compete with the fairy lights but providing a gentle ground-level glow. There were some new plants too in plots I hadn't filled with anything yet—white flowers that caught the moonlight, and I could smell them—fragrant and beautiful.

"The pavers—they are called Basalite Wood Grain Concrete," he said, a slight smile in his voice. "I know it sounds technical, but I chose it instead of wood for a reason." Instead of finishing that thought, he turned me to face the entrance—fifteen or so feet away now.

"That arbor—it's made of cedar. In some traditions, cedar has different meanings—it can symbolize sanctuary, offering refuge to those who seek it. It can also mean purification and healing—cleansing away negative energy and past pains. And it's enduring enough to weather our harsh New England storms and sun alike."

My eyes widened as his explanation came to a close, and he turned to face me. "It felt like the perfect representation of us. Of our marriage. Of the work I need to put in, but also the future we have and the past I hope to cleanse."

"The reason this is so important in our story isn't just because of the symbolism behind the wood though. You see, wood is the traditional fifth anniversary gift."

Aware now of where he was going with it, I finally caught on to the background on how it all came about.

A little breathless, I said "I see." I left it there, not wanting to interrupt. Feeling like I should hear what he has to say on this—I deserved it.

"I said it the other night, this is my apology tour—starting with our missed anniversaries. I never made it up to you, those failures. And while I apologized, what is an apology with no context or comprehension behind the meaning of the loss you experienced?"

I felt his thumb brush over my knuckles as he continued. "The arbor—the wood in it, as I said, represents so much with regards to our past and our future. What you may not realize though, is that this arbor—while in a different wood—is actually the same design as the one we were married under.

I gasped. "No way."

Caden grinned. "Yes, way. Took me forever to find a photo in all our wedding pics that didn't actually blur it out when the focus was on us—as it should be. Finally, though, I found one. So, the same day you went to Miami, I'd asked Marvin, our carpenter, if he could recreate it—he was all too happy to help.

I walked over to it, marveled at the sight and I was touched by the thought behind it. There was true meaning here—not just an empty gesture.

"So, that's the wood."

I responded, "but the pathway isn't wood though?"

"Exactly," he said.

I looked at him quizzically—"but it looks like wood."

"I know," and he explained. "The pavers look like wood but are actually made of concrete. In time, wood will fade and become weathered." Caden continued, "but I chose concrete pavers because they're what you use for foundations. For building something that will last. I wanted the path itself to represent the foundation we're building for our future. Something solid. Something permanent."

The symbolism hit me like a physical force. Well, shit. I'm going to cry. Damn, he put some thought into all of this.

I stopped walking and turned to face him fully.

"Felicity, in this garden, I'm trying to take something that came out of my own thoughtlessness and offer you pieces of what our future will be—if you let me—one day at a time," he said, his voice thick with emotion. "I can't go back and be the husband you deserved back then. But I can acknowledge what I missed, what I failed to celebrate, and I can make the changes that you deserve—that our marriage deserves."

"Caden..." I was crying in earnest now, but they were good tears. Happy tears. "This is more thoughtful than even I could have imagined myself," I said, laughing through my own sniffles.

"But wait," he said softly and with a wink. "There's more."

He led me off to the side of the entrance, to the bench where I spent my mornings reading and thinking. But even the bench area had been transformed. What used to be packed earth was now a small patio of the same wood-grain pavers, creating a defined seating area that felt intentional and beautiful.

I settled onto the bench, still overwhelmed by the transformation. The fairy lights in the trees above cast dancing shadows across the new patio, and I could see the careful thought that had gone into every detail.

He held my hand and said, "look down."

Chapter 36: Forged in Iron

~Felicity~

I looked down at the pavers directly in front of the bench and saw it—an iron plaque embedded seamlessly into the concrete. In the soft glow of the fairy lights, I could just make out the elegant engraving:

"You are my heart, my life, my one and only thought." (ACD/C)

I stared at it for a long moment, tracing the letters with my eyes, then looked up at him with a puzzled smile. "ACD/C?" I asked, trying to keep a straight face, but unable to keep one of my eyebrows from raising. "Is this like a play on lyrics? 'Thunderstruck' or something? God, okay—please don't tell me you put an ACDC lyric in the garden and are going to say it's because you were 'thunderstruck' by me. That may be taking it a bit far."

He threw back his head and laughed—like a full-on-belly-laugh. I couldn't help but laugh a bit—mine a little more awkwardly. Fuck, he better not have put a lyric from Highway to Hell or some shit in my garden. "Love, the ACD/C stands for Arthur Conan Doyle/Caden," he said, his eyes bright with mischief. "Honestly—I couldn't resist the play on the letters."

Now *that* was funny. "You are an absolute dork," I said, laughing. "I'll admit, though, it's a good play on the letters."

He wrapped his arm around my shoulders, pulled me in close and kissed the top of my head. He pulled back and settled beside me on the bench. "But the iron plaque—that's for our sixth anniversary. Iron is the traditional gift, and I wanted it to mean something more than just a piece of metal."

My heart clenched as the memory came flooding back. "Last year's anniversary. The one where you had to leave town at the last minute."

"And I sent you flowers from an app with a note saying we'd celebrate when I got back." His voice was heavy with regret. "But when I got back, there was another crisis, then another project deadline, and we never did celebrate. I let it slip away like it was just another day."

"But it did matter," I said quietly, my arms crossing over my chest, defensive at the memory.

"It mattered so much. Every anniversary matters. Every milestone we reach together matters." He wove his fingers into the hair at the nape of my neck, massaging as he played with it. My posture released a bit and, while my arms stayed crossed, my body leaned unconsciously into his hand.

"Iron represents strength, Felicity," he said. "The strength to weather any storm. The strength to build something that lasts. The strength I should have shown our marriage instead of letting other priorities get in the way of the important moments."

I leaned forward slightly, his hand dropping to my shoulder, as I read the quote again in the dancing light. The words seemed to shimmer with meaning—not just Doyle's words about love, but Caden's promise embedded in permanent iron at my feet.

"Your one and only thought," I said. "And now it's literally set in stone," I gestured to the plaque. "Well, iron and concrete, but you know what I mean." Pausing, I added, "The real question, Caden, is whether it's true. And whether you can keep up with it—or will you fall back on bad habits again?"

"It. Is. Forever." He said it with firmness. He believed it. Truly. Now, I needed to as well. His next words did a lot to help me get there. "No matter what storms come, no matter what distractions try to pull us apart, those words will be here, and they will always be more than just words. In this place that you created, in this space that saved you when I didn't, these words will be marked for all time. But in my heart, in my words, and in my actions, they will be demonstrated for all time—one day at a time."

The quiet took over then. A moment for both of us to reflect on the words he'd spoken aloud.

Sometime later, Caden spoke.

"You know, I came in that night, that anniversary, rushing to get out and save the high-rise project. I remember seeing how amazing you looked, and I hated to leave you. Hated to have to run up and pack a bag." He turned to look at me. "It's something I've been thinking about—how in certain circumstances, different choices could have meant the difference between your feelings of being forgotten and the possibility of you being part of it all."

"What do you mean?" I asked.

"Well, hindsight is twenty/twenty, but I think about how I could have asked you to come with me. Sure, I would've been stuck in a conference room early the next morning, but I see now what a lost opportunity it was for us—for you to see how much you were still in my heart. And for you to see firsthand the work I was buried under. I could have involved you and included you in what I was going through."

He blew out a breath. "I could have booked us first class, gotten us champagne, taken you to a fancy restaurant as soon as we landed—made a weekend out of something that was painfully exhausting. Let you in. So much of my mindset was focused on putting the fire out that I didn't realize I was just transferring the fire from work to our marriage."

Caden's face crumpled. "God, Felicity. I'm so sorry. I can picture you in that dress—it was blue and had little flowers on it, I think. You looked so beautiful, but sad."

I was surprised he remembered. "You noticed what I was wearing?"

"I did. And your hair was up in that big fancy bun on the top of your head." His voice broke slightly. "You looked beautiful. You are beautiful."

I felt something shift inside me at his words. Not just that he remembered, but that he'd truly seen me that night—even in his rush to leave. "I'd spent two hours getting ready," I admitted. "I kept thinking maybe if I looked perfect enough, you'd find a way to stay."

"You were perfect. You are perfect." He cupped my face gently. "And I'm so sorry that I made you feel like you had to compete for my attention."

I placed my hand over his, leaning into his touch. "The iron quote—it's beautiful. Caden..."

"Yes, love?"

"This whole garden transformation, the thoughtfulness behind every detail—it's showing me who you really are when you're present. When you're focused on us." I gestured around at the fairy lights twinkling above us. "This is the man I fell in love with. The one who notices details and creates magic."

"I want to be that man every day, not just when I'm making up for mistakes."

"I know you do. And I can see that you're trying." I looked down at the iron plaque again, then back at his face. "I need you to actually embody these words. I need you to know that it's about being worth your thoughts. Worth your time. Worth your love."

"You are. You are worth more than all of it combined, Felicity."

I stood up and walked a few steps away, taking in the full scope of what he'd created here. The path that connected every corner of my garden, the lights that transformed it into something magical, the cedar arbor that welcomed us into this sacred space. Then I turned back to him.

"Caden, I need to tell you something that I've been thinking about since Miami."

He waited, patient and attentive.

"When I was on that trip—sitting on the beach by myself, touring the city alone, and celebrating my birthday with strangers...aweso me strangers though. One day, I'll tell you all about the. I digress though—in all of that—I realized that I'd forgotten how to be happy. Not just content or okay, but actually a happy person. That's not on you. That's on me." I sat back down beside him. "It's not your job to make me a happy person. It's my job to do that. It's your job not to get in the way of it. It's your job, as my husband, to give me joyful moments and memories. Just as it's my job to do the same for you. But my happiness, and how I feel about myself, that isn't contingent on you and shouldn't be."

"That said, you lost sight of me in the last few years—on some of my needs and my wants. But I also recognize that you weren't *never* there. You just missed the things that should have been big moments in our lives. That lack of attention contributed to my own lack of focus on myself. So, I stopped talking. I didn't tell you when things weren't well with my soul. I expected you to notice and change."

Caden gave me the space to think and to continue on, so I did. "I listened to this podcast recently about expecting versus hoping—essentially that expectations, even with communication, will likely end in disappointment.

Hope, with or without communication, can go either way but ultimately won't ruin you when things don't pan out."

I paused and let the silence sit between us again, giving weight to the moment. "Caden, I want for us to work, and I want to forgive you—I do forgive you. I didn't fall out of love with you because you stopped celebrating us, but I did lose a piece of my joy." I turned my body so one leg was hiked up on the bench and the other foot rested on the ground.

"What you did here," I said, motioning all around us, "this gives me joy again. Real, honest joy. I have a ways to go to find my happiness, but this—this makes me see that you and I are not done." I reached for his hand. "I'm choosing you, Caden, one more day. I say one more day because I truly believe you will continue to work on us every day. In return, I will commit to telling you when things aren't right with me, when I'm not feeling seen or valued. If things get tough with work, bring me along for the ride—or at least invite me and let me choose if I can handle it or not. Fair?"

Caden leaned forward and buried his face in the crook of my neck. "Felicity, it is more than fair. I will do anything and everything in my power to never stop showing you that you are valued in every inch of my heart."

As we sat there, embracing one another—just holding on in the stillness of the evening—a gentle breeze stirred the lights above us, making them dance in the darkness. The iron plaque caught the light, the engraved words seeming to shine with promise. This garden had been my refuge when I needed it most, but now it was something more—it was ours. A place where we'd chosen each other, where we'd committed to building something beautiful together.

"So," I said, settling more comfortably against his side, "what's our next adventure going to be?"

"What do you mean?"

"I mean, we've got this beautiful garden, we're talking honestly with each other, we're making plans for the future. What do we want to do next?"

Caden was quiet for a moment, then smiled. "I have some ideas—one of which was already planned, so while I want to plan things with you as partners, this one has to be exempt," he said, turning the smile into the sweetest, most boyish grin.

"Okay, Sir Mystery—you can keep your plans." I leaned back into our embrace, enchanted by the scents in the air mingling with his own. This. This finally felt like home.

Above us, the fairy lights continued their gentle dance, and somewhere in the distance, I could hear the quiet hum of tomorrow's possibilities already beginning to charge. I knew we were on the mend, but we weren't finished yet—there was still work ahead. And not all of it would be easy. Jessica lingered at the edges of my mind, like a storm cloud you keep watching on the horizon, unsure when it will break. I tightened my hold on Caden, choosing—for tonight at least—to focus on the warmth of his arms and the promise of what we were building together.

$$\sim\!\!\infty\!\!\sim$$

Chapter 37: Call Declined

~CADEN~

It was early when I heard the buzz from my phone on the counter. Sunday tradition called for fried egg sandwiches—the ones with the oozing warm yolk, hot cheese (that isn't really cheese, but we don't talk about it), and slice of ham or bacon. Felicity was still upstairs, but as soon as I heard her milling about and getting in the shower, I put that griddle on the heat.

I reached for my phone—no caller listed. Weird. I answered though. With everything happening these days, I was almost afraid to screen my calls and miss something important.

As soon as I answered, I heard a long beep and then "This is a call from Jessica Jensen at MCI-Framingham. This call is from a correctional facility and may be monitored and recorded. To accept this call, press 1. To decline this call, press 2 or hang up."

I pulled my phone away from my ear. What the fuck. Do I answer? Hang up?

I thought of everything that's happened in the last week. We don't owe her shit. I hit the #2 on the screen dial pad and hung up.

I opened a text message and sent a quick note to my attorney, David.

Me: Just got a call from Jessica.

David: What do you mean? Like she's out? I would have been told if they released her.

Me: No, sorry—it was from her at the correctional facility. It was weird, I thought that calls in from jail came in collect, but it just asked if I wanted to accept or hang up.

David: Mass passed a rule a few years back that people who are incarcerated should be able to call family without charges. Helps them keep relationships with family. Still all recorded though. Did you answer?

Me: Hell no. Was I supposed to? I don't feel like we owe her a conversation.

David: Totally up to you. Since I'm sure you are concerned about Macy's emotional wellbeing and have pending charges against her for the theft and child endangerment, I think avoiding conversations is wise. Probably a good idea to let the detective know.

Me: Okay good. Will do. It's a good idea.

The smell of burning hit my senses. "Shit!" I ran over to the stove and started scraping the remnants of what could have been breakfast, off the griddle.

As soon as I had everything cleaned up, I heard, "I'm baaaaaaaaack!"

I walked toward the front of the house and found Macy dragging an overstuffed duffel bag across the threshold. Her hair was piled in a messy ponytail, her whole face and shoulders were bright red and pink from whatever adventures she'd had with her cousins. Mom followed behind, carrying what looked like enough leftover food to feed us for a week.

"Hey, kiddo." I wrapped her in a hug, gently though, looking at my mom I said, "I see we had some beach time."

My mom responded, "don't look at me! I swear I covered her in sunblock!"

"Really," I responded doubtfully.

"Really! I swear. I had a bottle in the car from the last time we went down."

"Okay," I laughed. "Well, I'm guessing it went bad sitting in the hot car for like the last month, and it's probably even expired."

My mom's response told me everything I needed to know, "oh come on, that's not a thing."

I smirked, dropping, and shaking my head, "um, yeah ma, it's a thing."
My poor kid—note to self, stick sunscreen in Macy's bag whenever she
goes with mom.

"Can I use some of Felicity's cream?" Macy asked.

"Of course you can, honey," that came from Felicity as she walked into
the room, appearing in one of my old college t-shirts and jeans, hair
still damp from her shower. The sight of her still made my heart skip
and breath catch, especially after yesterday's breakthrough for us.

"Ohhhh, that looks like it hurts!"

"Yeah, it's a little hot, but not too bad," responded Macy. Look what
happens when I push on it! At that, Macy made finger spots on her
shoulder so we could all see the white left behind in the indentation
of her fingers. Just before her skin pinked back up right away.

Felicity shook her head and held her arm out for Macy to walk into it,
"come on, love. Let's go upstairs and I'll see what I can do. You're going
to have quite a lot of skin peeling soon enough. Maybe we can save you
from too bad of a peel, but I'm not really sure."

As Macy and Felicity disappeared, I turned to my mom, "other than
her sun exposure and future state of freckle constellations, how did
everything go? I know you mentioned last night that she was having a
good time with the cousins. Anything else?"

My mom sighed as we walked into the kitchen. "She seems completely
unwilling to talk about her mom and everything that happened. I
swear Caden, if I could slap that woman for what she did, I would.
I'm just so angry with Jessica and I'm pissed on behalf of Macy."

I looked at my mom, understanding her frustration. "What do you
mean she won't talk about it?"

"Okay, well—she's not completely silent, but when Angie asked her
why she was living with you full-time now, she just said 'some stuff
happened but I don't think it's forever—just til my mom gets better.'
That was it. Changed the subject immediately." Mom set the containers of food on the counter and turned to face me fully. "Caden, that
child is processing something huge, and she's doing it all internally."

My God. She doesn't think it's forever with us. My stomach plummets. I
need to talk to Felicity. Get her thoughts. I remember something Dr. Chen
mentioned too though. "Her therapist said that this is normal. Something
about how kids can often compartmentalize trauma. That they want to

maintain some sense of normalcy." I ran my hand down my face. "We have another appointment with her this week."

"Good. Because I'm telling you—there were moments this weekend where my little grandbaby was like her old self, laughing and playing with everyone—giving us a run for our money. But then she'd get this look, like she was somewhere else entirely. She'd stare off into space and then just disappear. Gladys and I were just brought to tears about it."

Before I could respond, my phone buzzed again. Same unknown number. My stomach dropped.

"Shit, that's probably her."

"Who? Jessica?" Mom asked, but I was already declining the call and texting David again.

Me: She called again. Declined again. Is there a way to block these?

David: You can ask the facility to put you on a no-contact list, but given she's Macy's mother, that might complicate things. Might be better to just decline for now and document each attempt. Meanwhile, I'll add this to the list of things for our next hearing.

"Caden?" Mom's voice pulled me back. "What's going on?"

"Jessica's trying to call from prison." I showed her the declined call log. "This is the second attempt in ten minutes." I turned my phone back towards myself and said, "hang on a sec, mom. I just want to make sure to give Felicity a heads-up." At this, I texted her. While she was just upstairs, I wanted to be discreet so I didn't upset Macy, and I know that Felicity reading her messages would give her a few minutes to process instead of being bombarded by issues.

Me (to Felicity): Sweetheart, Jessica has tried to call multiple times this morning. Comes from unknown number. I know you're still upstairs with Macy, but didn't want you blindsided. Maybe ignore her calls if she gets through to you, for now. Let's talk later when alone.

I put my phone down and turned back to my mom, whose expression had hardened. "That woman has some nerve. After what she put Macy through, and what she did to your company—"

"I know, Ma. Trust me, I know." I pocketed the phone. "But I need to handle this carefully.

Footsteps on the stairs announced Felicity and Macy's return. Macy's shoulders now had a light coating of what looked like Felicity's homemade aloe cream, and she seemed much more comfortable.

"Better?" I asked.

"So much better. Felicity's magic cream works on everything," Macy said, settling at the kitchen table. "Can we have those egg sandwiches now? I'm starving."

"About that..." I glanced at the cleaned griddle. "I may have had a small cooking incident while you were upstairs. How do you feel about cereal?"

"Dad!" Macy laughed. "Who burns egg sandwiches?"

"Apparently your dad!" Felicity said with a grin, but I caught the slight tension around her eyes. She'd gotten my text. "Good thing your grandma brought enough food to feed an army. How about some of whatever's in these containers?"

We unpacked Mom's care package—leftover fried chicken, pasta salad, and what appeared to be homemade brownies—and set about to dig in.

I didn't respond right away. My gaze stayed on Felicity's hand resting lightly on Macy's back. They were both leaning over their plates, giggling about something. That image was everything—and I'd do anything to keep my girls happy and safe.

Chapter 38: A Salve For The Burn

~Felicity~

Seeing Macy with her dad, sporting that sunburn, brought about my tendency to nurture. I held out my arm for her to walk into it, "Come on, love, let's go upstairs and I'll see what I can do. You're going to have quite a lot of skin peeling soon enough. Maybe we can save you from too bad of a peel, but I'm not really sure."

Letting Macy go first, I fell into step behind her as we climbed the stairs.

"It doesn't hurt that much," she said, though I could see her wince slightly when the fabric of her shirt shifted against her sunburned skin.

"I know, but trust me—in a few hours when that heat really sets in, you'll be grateful we took care of it now." We approached my bathroom, where I kept my collection of homemade remedies. "Your dad thinks I'm crazy for making most of my own skincare stuff, but days like this prove it's worth it."

"What's in it?" Macy asked, settling on the edge of the bathtub while I gathered supplies from the linen closet.

"Hmmm. Well, the green stuff here is just plain organic aloe." I showed her the glass jar filled with the slightly green gel. "I buy the leaves from this little market downtown and extract the gel myself. Much better than the store-bought stuff that's loaded with all kinds of chemicals and unnecessary additives—many of them would just dry your skin out more."

Then I handed her a separate glass jar that has a white whipped-cream texture body butter. "This is my recent batch of body butter that I made for summer. It has mango butter, coconut oil, some beeswax, sweet almond oil, a little shea, and a couple other secrets in it. It's like magic for sun damage."

"Will you show me how to make all this?"

"Sure! Started a few years ago when I got tired of spending ridiculous amounts of money on lotions that didn't work as well as what I could make in my kitchen." I sat down on the small bench across from where she sat on the bathtub edge. "Okay, let's see the damage."

Macy lifted her over shirt off—it was large and off a shoulder, but was still bulky enough that it was hard to tell how far the burn reached. Sitting in her tank top, I could see the sunburn was worse than I'd initially thought—angry red patches mixed with areas that were even brighter. Shit this was going to be really painful for her in the next couple days.

"Oh, honey," I murmured, gently touching an unburned spot on her shoulder blade. "This is definitely going to peel. But we can make sure it heals well."

"Will it scar?"

"No, no scarring. But you might have some interesting tan lines for a while, and you'll want to stick with cool showers." I opened the aloe gel and scooped some onto my fingers. "This might feel cold at first, but it'll help with the heat."

The moment the aloe touched her skin, Macy sighed with relief. "Oh wow, that feels amazing."

"Right? Nature's air conditioning." I worked the gel gently across her shoulders, careful not to press too hard on the more tender areas. "So, tell me about this weekend. Your grandma told us some of the highlights, but I want the good stuff. What was your favorite part?"

Macy's face lit up. "Probably the pottery place. Aunt Gladys took us there the other day, and it was so cool—you get to pick out whatever you want to paint, and they have like a million different colors and brushes and stamps." She gestured excitedly with her hands, then winced as the movement pulled at her sunburn. "I made you and dad something, then I did something little for my mom, but I also made this really cool bowl for my room. It's purple and blue with these swirly patterns."

My breath caught at the mention of her mom. I wondered to myself how we were going to talk to her about all of this stuff. I can't imagine she has any idea of the consequences that Jessica is going to have to face. I don't even really understand what her home life was like—how long all the issues were going on and what it was like to live with Jessica. So much that I'm sure her therapist will work through with her. I filed my thoughts away to talk through with Caden and probably with Dr. Chen.

"That all sounds beautiful. I can't wait to see."

"Angie tried to paint this super detailed flower on her plate, but she kept messing up and getting frustrated. Alex just painted his entire plate black and called it 'his expresionisticism.'" Macy giggled. "I told him that wasn't a word, but he was so sure and the lady who worked there said 'art is in the eye of the beholder,' which I don't really get, but Alex nodded along like he did, so I guess it makes sense."

I laughed, smoothing more aloe along her shoulder blades. "Alex has always marched to his own drummer. Remember at Christmas when he decided to wear that suit jacket with his pajama pants to dinner?"

"Oh yeah! His 'formal lounge-wear!'" Macy dissolved into giggles. "He's so weird, but like, in the best way."

"Exactly. Weird in the best way." I moved to her other shoulder, working the cooling gel into the heated skin. "What else did you do?"

"Yesterday we went hiking and then to the beach, and then to the park today—I think that's how I got this sunburn. Aunt Gladys said the trail was mostly shaded, but there were these big open meadows where we stopped to eat lunch and look for wildflowers." Macy's voice took on the animated quality it always had when she was truly excited about something. "We found this stream that had these tiny fish in it—like, seriously tiny, maybe an inch long—and we spent forever trying to catch them with our hands."

"Did you succeed?"

"Definitely not me—since I have the cast on, I could only do one hand, but it was fun to try, and the fish felt all funny when they swam through my fingers." She was showing me how she tried to catch them—jutting her hand into the bathtub like there were fish in it. "Oh! Angie almost caught one! But it was really hard, and it got away. Alex claimed he caught three, but I think he was teasing because I never saw them." She shifted slightly so I could reach a spot near her shoulder blade. "Oh, and Alex had a tick on him! That was scary. And gross!"

"Oh no! Did you check yourself?"

"Grandma did. She said I was good."

Ticks give me the heebie-jeebies. I needed to move on before I started unreasonably searching her bags, clothes, and hair—I completely understand it's not a thing, but there's just something about ticks that make me lose my damned mind and automatically begin to spiral. Ticks, bed bugs, and lice—oh my God, I need a new topic to think about before I go insane.

Relief washed over me when I heard Macy continue, "then we went to the beach, obviously." She gestured to her sunburned state. "Grandma Sandy packed this huge picnic, and we built sandcastles and played with a frisbee. Well, tried to play with it. Turns out none of us are very good at it. Have you ever played with a frisbee? It was my first time, and you only need one hand, so I didn't have any issues throwing it. It was a lot of fun, but also a lot of running since the wind kept sending it all over the place."

"I have played frisbee. It's been quite a while though. I'm glad you had so much fun!"

I reached for the jar of body butter, warming some between my palms before applying it over the aloe. "This will help lock in the moisture and start the healing process."

"It smells really good. Like... sweet maybe?"

"That's probably the coconut oil." I worked the cream gently into her skin, watching the angry red fade slightly under the nourishing oils. "Did you miss being home at all?"

Macy was quiet for a moment, considering. "A little bit, I guess. But not in a sad way."

"Well, we definitely missed you too."

"Really?"

"Really. Everything was so quiet. And there was no one to help me make fun of your dad when he did something funny."

Macy smiled at that. "I'm glad I went, though. It was fun to hang out with Angie and Alex, and I don't get to see them very often. Plus, Aunt Gladys taught us this card game called Spit that's really fast and crazy. We played it for like two hours yesterday morning. It was a little hard to move really fast with the cast on, but I got the hang of it."

"Oh man! Spit! I played that one when I was your age!"

"Really?! Do you think Dad knows how to play too? Will you guys take turns playing with me? It was so much fun!"

"I'm sure he does. Though we both may need lessons since I'm not too sure I remember the rules."

Macy looked back at me excitedly, "yeah! I can teach you! It's simple. We'll have so much fun!"

"Sounds like a plan. Maybe tonight, we can play before dinner."

"Yes!"

Silently, I finished up with her back, doing one last check to make sure I didn't miss any spots from her neck, even down her arms. The backs of her arms were almost lily white—like I said, she's going to have interesting tan lines.

"I'm really glad you're home." I capped the jar of body butter and sat back to admire my handiwork. "There. That should help a lot. You'll want to reapply the aloe a few times today, and definitely tonight before bed."

"Will you help me reapply?"

"Of course. We should probably do this again tomorrow morning too, before you go back to school. Just to make sure everything's healing well."

Macy nodded, then carefully pulled her shirt back on. "Felicity?"

"Yeah?"

"Do you think people at school know what happened?" she asked quietly—nervously.

The question caught me off guard, and I could hear the vulnerability beneath it. I set the jar down in the linen closet and turned to give her my full attention.

"I don't know, honey. Maybe some people do, maybe they don't. Are you worried about it?"

She nodded, picking at the hem of her shirt. "What if they ask me questions? What if no one wants to talk to me anymore? I haven't talked to any of my friends from school in the last week. What if they think I'm weird or different now?"

"First of all, you're not weird or different. You're the same amazing kid you were before any of this happened." I moved to sit beside her on the edge of the tub. "But if people do ask questions, you don't have to tell them anything you don't want to. You can try changing the subject, or you can tell them pieces of what happened if you want to—it's completely up to you."

"What if I don't want to tell anyone but they keep asking?"

"Then you walk away if you want, you can find a teacher or go to the office. You can always call me or your dad. We'll come get you if you need us to."

Macy looked up at me with relief. "You'd really do that?"

"Without hesitation. Macy, you never have to handle difficult things alone, okay? You, your dad and me—we're a team."

She was quiet for a moment, processing. "I think... I think most kids probably don't know. It's not like it was on the news or anything, right?"

"I don't think so. And even if some people do know, that doesn't define you. You're still the same they knew before it all happened."

That earned me a small smile. "They'll probably ask me about my cast."

"You're probably right. You can just say you broke it when you fell. We bought all those markers too. So, everyone can sign it. So, maybe bring the markers and have them set out so people can pick whatever colors they want to use, right?

She stood up carefully, testing how the shirt felt against her treated skin. "This feels so much better. You really do have magic potions."

"Years of trial and error. And a few minor kitchen disasters while I was learning."

"Kitchen disasters?"

"Let's just say melted beeswax and stovetops don't always mix well. I may have accidentally created a waxy volcano once."

Macy burst into giggles. "Did Dad freak out?"

"He was surprisingly calm about me essentially waxing half the kitchen. Though he did suggest smaller batches after that."

"That's smart."

I nodded sagely, "He has his moments."

As I went to stand, I felt my phone vibrate in my pocket. Pulling it out, I read:

Caden: Sweetheart, Jessica has tried to call multiple times this morning. Comes from unknown number. I know you're still upstairs with Macy, but didn't want you blindsided. Maybe ignore her calls if she gets through to you, for now. Let's talk later when alone.

I felt my stomach start to churn. Closing my eyes, I got my expression under control and stood up. Turning toward Macy, I asked, "ready to go see how your dad and Grandma are doing?"

As we headed toward the stairs, I could hear Caden's voice from below, talking with his mom.

In the kitchen, Caden asked Macy, "better?"

"So much better. Felicity's magic cream works on everything," Macy said, settling at the kitchen table. "Can we have those egg sandwiches now? I'm starving."

"About that..." I looked over at Caden and definitely got a whiff of something burnt. He told us, "I may have had a small cooking incident while you were upstairs. How do you feel about cereal?"

"Dad!" Macy laughed. "Who burns egg sandwiches?"

"Apparently your dad!" I said—to her, and the room. So many things to worry about, egg sandwiches seemed like such a non-starter. "Good thing your grandma brought enough food to feed an army. How about some of whatever's in these containers?"

As we unpacked Sandy's containers—some fried chicken, pasta salad, and what appeared to be homemade brownies, I grabbed a brownie to start—secreting it away, don't want to be a bad influence, but a brownie and coffee felt like the right next step for me at the moment.

Caden's phone rang, and he looked at his phone, showing me it was someone from the office. He announced, "Work thing, give me two minutes." I nodded, and as I turned to go brew myself a cup of coffee, I heard Alexa announce:

"Someone is at the front door." I turned toward the screen to look at who it could be and was shocked.

Not caring who heard me in my shock, I said aloud, "No fucking way."

Chapter 39: I Missed You Too

"No fucking way," I breathed, staring at the Echo Show screen in disbelief.

I ran quickly to the door, throwing it open—tears already starting to spring to my eyes. There, on my front doorstep, stood my sister Maliyah with a duffle in one hand and two backpacks in the other. Behind her, I could see my niece and nephew—Zoe had her curly hair up in the cutest little pigtails. She was clutching a stuffed elephant like her life depended on it. Standing to her right was Lucas. He was slightly taller, but twice as energetic. You could almost see the energy trapped within him as he stood there bouncing on his toes, a toy truck in his hands.

"What's wrong?" Macy asked, coming up beside me at the door. "Who's here?" She gasped as soon as she saw them. "Aunt Maliyah?"

Sandy rounded the corner at the same time, exclaiming, "Maliyah? Oh, my goodness!"

I looked at her, saying, "What are you doing here?" Peeking behind her at the car, I realized it was her actual car—not a rental—which meant that she drove all the way here—from Orlando. With two really young kids, it must have taken her days!

Before Maliyah could answer, Zoe dropped her elephant and launched herself at my legs with a squeal. "Aunt Fliss!"

"Oh my God, Zoe!" I scooped her up immediately, spinning her around as she giggled. She smelled like strawberry shampoo and joy. "Look how big you've gotten! And these pigtails are adorable!"

"Mommy did them last night in the hotel!" she announced proudly, patting her curls. "She said I looked like a princess!"

"That's because you *are* a princess," I agreed, settling her on my hip. Over her head, I caught Maliyah's eye. "Seriously, May. What are you doing here? Not that I'm not thrilled to see you all, but this is—"

"A thirteen-hundred-mile surprise," Maliyah finished with a tired but satisfied grin. "We left Friday afternoon. Spent Friday night in Savannah—which was an adventure with these two—then we drove all day Saturday. When I say we, obviously it was me—I drove all day Saturday."

Maliyah pushed past me with Lucas, throwing all the bags at the foot of the stairs. She continued rambling, telling me all the fun times she had with the kids while driving all day. They stayed in Connecticut last night and got up early to drive here this morning. I'm still dazed while I'm listening to her chatter.

At this point, Lucas had hugged my legs and run over to Macy to hang out. Lucas is six and has a minor crush on Macy. She's always a trooper about it though.

"Come on Lucas, I'll teach you a new game I learned. It's called 'spit!'" Lucas followed after her like she hung the moon and stars.

Zoe was still hanging out with me, perched on my hip—arms wrapped around my neck. God I love this kid.

"Aunt Fliss, I missed you so much," Zoe whispered in my ear, squeezing tighter around my neck.

"I missed you too, sweet girl. How was the big car ride?"

"Long! But we had snacks and movies and Lucas threw up in Georgia."

"I did not!" Lucas called from across the room while following Macy toward the kitchen. "I just felt sick!"

"You threw up McDonald's nuggets all over me," Zoe announced matter-of-factly. How she even explained this without throwing up herself was beyond me.

I looked at Maliyah, mortified on her behalf. She grimaced, clearly remembering her experience. "That was a fun stop. Nothing like cleaning vomit off a four-year-old in a gas station bathroom at midnight."

"Oh honey," Sandy said, immediately switching into grandma mode. "You poor thing. Come here, let me get you something to settle your stomach."

"I'm fine now!" Lucas protested. "Macy, what's spit? Is it gross? I like gross games!"

"It's a card game," Macy explained patiently. "Really fast and fun."

I watched Lucas's face light up like Christmas morning. His crush on Macy was adorable and so very obvious—the way he hung on her every word, tried to copy whatever she was doing. Macy handled it like a champ, treating him almost like a little brother.

"May," I said, still trying to wrap my head around this surprise. "I can't believe you just packed up and drove here. With work, and the kids' schedules, and—"

"Felicity." She stopped unpacking random kid items from her bag and looked at me. "You're my sister. With all that's happened recently, I just can't—." She leaned back, looking like she was searching for the words. She looked me in the eyes and said, "you were there for me with everything. I wouldn't be anywhere else than right here with you. I just can't imagine not paying it forward." She smirked then and continued, "besides, you know you're my favorite sister."

"I'm your only sister Maliyah."

"Semantics."

Zoe patted my cheek. "Mommy said Aunt Fliss was sad and needed hugs."

"Did she now?" Zoe nodded before I continued, "well, I feel like you've got a lot of work to do. I counted only like ten or so hugs so far. A trip from Florida feels like it's supposed to come with closer to like seven or eight hundred!"

"Eight hundred! Auntie Fliss, I'll have to hug you like forever!"

"Better start now!" At that, Zoe threw her arms around me and started counting every squeeze.

Once she hit the thirties, Caden rounded the corner. It looks like he finished his call with Morrison. "What's going on over here?!"

"Uncle Caden!!!!" Zoe started to push me away and climb down from my arms, all memory of hugs forgotten. Caden has a swing and toss that Zoe loves and, let's face it, I don't compete.

Caden swooped her up into his arms, hugging her and then throwing her over his shoulder. He leaned forward and gave Maliyah a kiss on the cheek. "Maliyah, it's great to see you. Not sure about what made you think to come, but I'm fairly certain your sister is over the moon to see you right now."

He looked between us and continued, "why don't I steal this munchkin away!" As he said the word 'munchkin' he pretended to nibble on Zoe's side sending her into screams of delight. Looking back over to me he said, "go spend some time with your sister. Mom, Macy, and I will handle things with the kiddos for a bit. I'm sure Maliyah could use a break too."

He turned away, tickling Zoe's side and through the giggles I heard her squeal and yell out, "I have to pee!!" Caden switched course, dropped her to her feet and sent her off yelling out to her, "okay kiddo, you do that, and Uncle Caden will go make you a snack."

"Okay!" Zoe yelled back.

With all the sounds of chaos and happiness we could hear from every corner of the downstairs, Maliyah and I took ourselves upstairs to help her get settled, laughing the whole way up the steps.

Zoe and Maliyah will take one room. Lucas will get the other guest room. Macy has a twin daybed and a trundle, and while I'm guessing Zoe will want to start the night off staying with her, the last time we tried that, she ended up scared in the night and called out for her mom before ultimately settling in with Maliyah.

"This is exactly what I needed," I said, opening the door to the larger guest room. "I didn't even know I needed it until you showed up."

Maliyah dropped her duffle on the bed and turned to face me. "Okay, now that we're alone—how are you really doing? And don't give me the 'fine' answer. I want the real story."

I sat on the edge of the bed, suddenly feeling the weight of everything that had happened. "It's been... a lot. But also, good? Does that make sense?"

"Not really. Start from the beginning."

So I did. I retold her some of the stuff with Caden from before my trip to Miami, and some of the highlights she already knew about everything with Jessica and Macy. I showed her the text I'd received from Caden from earlier when he was downstairs and me upstairs. I shared what we knew so far about Jessica, even talking through the custody of Macy. We talked about Macy starting therapy and Caden and me doing so too—essentially unloading weeks'—years' worth of craziness in what felt like no time at all.

But then I told her about the garden and all the work Caden had been doing. I told her about how it wasn't just doing things, it was about how he was acting too—talking with me, sharing, going back to the days when we were truly partners. I mentioned Macy's therapy and the permanent custody situation. About the garden and the locket and the slow, careful work of rebuilding trust.

"Jesus, Felicity," Maliyah said when I finished. "No wonder you sounded overwhelmed. That's like a lifetime of drama crammed into two weeks."

"The weird thing is, though—Caden and I are better than we've been in years. Like, really better. Not just crisis-better, but actually better."

"It sounds like it. This is all huge, Fliss."

"Macy goes back to school tomorrow. Caden and I go back to work. I guess time will only tell for us—and now that we are going back to normal scheduling, I wonder how everything will unfold.

"That's what I'm here for," Maliyah said firmly. "To help you figure it out while things get back to a more normal cadence. I'm off for the next couple of weeks, so let me help you with whatever you need."

"I can't tell you how much that means to me." I twisted my wedding ring around my finger. "I keep waiting for the other shoe to drop, you know? Like things are going too well, and something's going to come along and mess it all up again."

"Like what?"

"Ugh, I don't know. Like Jessica finding some way to manipulate the situation to her benefit." I shrugged helplessly. "Like me screwing up this whole stepmom thing because I have no idea what in the hell I'm doing. Like Caden getting overwhelmed with work and reverting back to his old patterns—though I'm worrying less and less about that last one."

Maliyah was quiet for a moment, then said, "You know what I think?"

"What?"

"I think you're borrowing trouble. You've got a good thing happening here—Caden's stepped up, Macy's safe, your marriage is healing. Instead of waiting for it to fall apart, maybe just... enjoy the moment?"

From downstairs came the sound of something crashing, followed by Sandy's voice calling out, "It's fine! Everything's fine! Just dropped the syrup!"

We looked at each other and burst out laughing.

"See?" Maliyah grinned. "This is what family chaos looks like. Messy and loud and perfect."

"Should we go rescue Sandy?" I asked, standing up.

"Probably. But Felicity?" She caught my hand. "Whatever happens next, you've got this. And you're not alone."

I squeezed her hand back. "Thank you. For making the drive with two little ones—all by yourself. For dropping everything. For just... being here."

"That's what sisters do. Though a glass of wine tonight wouldn't get declined. I can promise you that—early though, I'm going to need an early bedtime. I have to sleep off the trauma of the drive and the kidney kicks I experienced from sleeping with both of my kids these last two nights—apparently, hotels are scary so everyone sharing a queen-sized was necessary to avoid bad dreams." Maliyah rolled her eyes at this and started making her way to the stairs.

As we headed back down, I could hear Lucas trying to explain the rules of spit to Caden while Zoe demanded to be tossed around like a "sack of potatoes"—a game he liked to play with the kids when they visited. The sound of my family—expanded and chaotic and wonderful—filled the house with exactly the kind of noise I'd been missing without even knowing it.

Whatever challenges tomorrow would bring, at least I wouldn't face them alone.

Chapter 40: I Can't Keep It

~FELICITY~

Monday morning felt surreal. After two weeks of crisis mode and chaos, the simple act of putting on work clothes and heading into the office seemed almost foreign.

"You okay?" Caden asked from the doorway, buttoning his cuffs. Damn, he was hot in a button down and slacks. Something about a man all dressed up is a righteous turn-on. Looking at his face though, I could see the tension around his eyes. Going back to work meant facing the reality of Jessica's theft, the missing money, the potential impact on the company.

"Yeah, I'm okay—just feel weird, you know? Like we're playing dress-up as our old selves."

He stepped into the closet and wrapped his arms around me from behind. "We're not our old selves, though. We're better—well, I'm doing better. You are just as amazing as you've always been."

I leaned back against him, drawing comfort and warmth from his presence.

He pressed a kiss to the top of my head. "Maliyah going to hang out at the house while we're working today?"

"Yes. I gave her a key, figured she could take the kids to the museum or just out and about if she wanted—not sure she will want to be cooped up with the kids all day."

"That's a good plan. Maybe she can come up to your office and grab some lunch."

"Not a bad idea," I responded. "I'll see what she thinks." I smiled at him and kissed his cheek. It was a good morning, and I liked the experience of starting it off on a positive note.

Downstairs, the kitchen was controlled chaos. Maliyah was making pancakes while Macy packed her school bag. It's amazing how easily kids adapt—her cast didn't even seem to be holding her back as she pulled all her stuff together.

Lucas sat at the counter, truck in hand, explaining the differences between dump trucks, backhoes, and front loaders to anyone who would listen. Zoe was methodically eating strawberries, sorting them by size, and making them dance on her plate before each bite.

"Aunt Fliss!" Zoe called out when she saw me. "Do you have to go to work today?"

"I do, sweetie. But I'll be back later this afternoon."

"Will you bring me a present?"

"Zoe," Maliyah warned gently. "We don't ask for presents."

"It's okay," I said, sitting down next to her. "What kind of present would you want?"

"An elephant! A real one!"

"Hmmmm, I have a feeling like a real elephant might be a little big for our house, and pretty hard to find on short notice," I said seriously. "How about I see what I can find that's elephant-adjacent?"

"What's that? Elephanjesscent?" Lucas asked, momentarily distracted from his truck discussion.

I held my laugh back and repeated, "elephant-adjacent," sounding it out with him.

Once he had the new word mastered, I explained, "elephant-adjacent is something that's almost like an elephant but not exactly an elephant."

"Like a hippopotamus!" Macy suggested.

"Or a rhino!" Lucas added.

"Or a really big dog!" Zoe giggled.

I laughed at the three of them. *Man, they were cute.* I looked up at Maliyah and caught her eye, sharing a smile together. This was exactly what we'd needed—normal family chaos, kids being kids, the kind of noise that made a house feel like a home.

"Alright, everyone," Caden announced, grabbing his coffee and brief-case. "Time to get this show on the road. Macy, you ready?"

"Ready." She shouldered her backpack carefully, mindful of her cast. "Aunt Maliyah, will you be here when I get home?"

"Absolutely. Lucas, Zoe and I have very important plans around fort-building activities."

"Can I help when I get back?"

"I promise that we'll save the best part for you," Maliyah promised.

As I headed in to work, I tried to shake off the almost surreal feeling I had. Just a couple weeks back, this commute had been routine, automat-ic. Now everything felt so different—from my trek in, to the audiobook I had going, even the taste of my coffee. I felt as if I were experiencing something new yet rote. It made me wonder if this was what it felt like for people who had been on leave and were returning after a long absence.

Walking in, it took all of thirty seconds before I heard, "Felicity!" Sud-denly, Callie appeared as the elevator doors opened on my floor. "Wel-come back! How are you feeling? Did you have a good time on vacation?"

Shit. Well, I hadn't really thought about how I'd respond to people. What was I saying to Macy just yesterday? "Hey Callie, how's it going? Did everyone miss me?" Avoidance it was!

"Of course! I imagine your team has lots to catch you up on. I'm guessing they'll have some good HR fodder for you now that you're back!"

I nodded, smiled, and said, "HR is never boring!" Definitely not sharing the details of my personal life of chaos with her or the rest of the team up here. I'm not interested in becoming the topic of conversation. The sounds of Dori ran through my head, Just keep swimming, just keep swimming.

Tossing my stuff on my desk, I sat down and sighed. I'd barely settled in when there was a knock on my door.

"Welcome back."

Ethan stood in my doorway, looking polished and professional in a charcoal gray suit. His smile was warm but somehow different—more reserved than usual.

"Thanks. How was New York?"

"Productive. Mind if I come in for a minute?"

I gestured to the chair across from my desk. He sat down, but there was something in his posture that felt formal, careful.

He gave a small smile when he said, "I hope your time off was restorative. You seemed pretty stressed before you left."

I kept my expression neutral. "It was... eventful. But good to get some much-needed time away."

"Good. I'm glad." He shifted in his chair awkwardly, seeming to gather himself. "Have you cracked open the book? I was thinking about it, and you, while you were away." He cleared his throat and continued, "you were missed, you know."

Here it was. The conversation I'd been dreading.

"Actually, I was hoping we could discuss that too." I opened my desk drawer and pulled out the Handmaid's Tale. "This is amazing, Ethan, and I want you to know that I'm grateful for the thought behind it. I know I said it when you gave it to me, but I should have been firmer—I really can't keep it."

He looked at the box but didn't reach for it. "Oh," he said quietly before pausing and then asking, "may I ask why?"

"Honestly? Because it feels like more than something a colleague would give another colleague. I also feel awkward accepting it—I'm married, and I can honestly say that, if a coworker gave my husband something like this, I wouldn't be happy. I'd like to avoid any confusion for everyone involved here, so I think it's best I not accept it."

Ethan was quiet for a long moment, his hands clasped in his lap. When he looked up, his expression was rueful but not surprised.

"You're absolutely right," he said simply, but I could see his hands trembling slightly as he clasped them in his lap. "It was more than a colleague gift."

The honesty in his voice made my chest tighten. "Oh. Ethan—"

"No, let me finish." He held up a hand. "I've been telling myself for a while that we were just friends, just work colleagues who got along well. But the truth is, I've had feelings for you that went beyond that. And I think part of me was hoping..." He shrugged. "Well, it doesn't matter what I was hoping."

He trailed off, looking down at his hands. "This is mortifying. I feel like I'm fifteen again, getting shot down at a school dance."

"I'm sorry," I said quietly. "I really hope I didn't give you the wrong impression."

"You didn't. That's the thing—you never said anything or led me on. You definitely never did anything inappropriate. This was all on me." He gestured toward the pen box. "But you should keep it."

"I can't."

"Actually, it isn't really returnable." His laugh was shaky, self-deprecating. "Turns out rare books aren't like department store purchases. I asked when I was buying it. The dealer looked at me like I was insane."

I stared at the box. "Ethan..."

"Look, I get it. I understand why you can't keep it as a gift from me. But it's yours now, practically speaking. So maybe you know someone you could give it away to."

Despite everything, I found myself smiling. "Really expensive office supplies?"

"The most expensive pens in the building, probably." He stood up. "Maybe you could give it away—give it to a friend or something. Whatever works and entirely up to you."

He turned to walk away, paused, and turned back toward me. "For what it's worth, Felicity, your husband is a lucky man. I hope he knows that."

"Thank you Ethan. He does."

"Good." Ethan moved toward the door, then paused. "I should tell you that I'm already planning to transfer to the Chicago office. I wasn't completely sure until this conversation, but I think it's for the best."

"You don't have to—"

"Felicity—I really mean it. This was already in the works. After my trip to New York, they offered me a senior director position to lead the mid-west out of the Chicago office. It's actually a great opportunity."

I felt a mix of relief and sadness. Ethan was a good colleague and, despite the complications, a good person.

"I'm happy for you. I'll miss working with you, but this sounds like an awesome opportunity and is much deserved." I said honestly.

"I'll miss working with you too. But this is better. For both of us."

After he left, I sat staring at the pen box for a long time. I'll figure out what to do with the set. At some point, I'll need to tell Caden though, this I know. No more secrets. Maybe tonight when we have some privacy.

The rest of the morning passed in a blur of emails, catch-up meetings, and project updates. Everyone was welcoming about my return, but I could feel myself struggling to get back into the rhythm. The professional facade felt like a costume I'd forgotten how to wear properly.

By lunch, I was mentally exhausted. I texted Maliyah to see if she wanted to meet up, but she responded that they were at the children's museum and having too much fun to leave.

I called Caden instead.

"How's your first day back?" he asked, and I could hear the stress in his voice.

"Surreal. Yours?"

"Like walking through a minefield. Everyone's being polite, but I can feel the questions they're not asking."

"About what?"

"Stability. Job security. Word travels fast."

I felt a pang of worry. "Are their jobs secure?"

"For now, yeah. We're going to be tight for a while, but we'll survive." I could hear him blow a breath out.

"What can I do?"

"Exactly what you're doing. Be with me through this. Let me hear your voice when my own gets too loud in my head. Just knowing we're together in this—it's a lot Felicity."

"I'm here."

"I love you."

I responded, "I love you too."

The afternoon dragged by. I tried to focus on the stack of reports that had accumulated during my absence, but my mind kept wandering to everything that wasn't work related.

By four-thirty, I was more than ready to get home. Walking into the house, I was thrilled by how alive with energy it was. Giggles sounded from the living room. An exceptionally elaborate blanket fort had been constructed using the couch, dining room chairs, kitchen stools, some cushions and pillows, sheets, blankets, lamps, and tables. If it was in my house, it was somehow being used for this fort. I was torn between being impressed and anxious at who the hell was going to clean all this up.

"Aunt Fliss!" Zoe's head popped out amidst the chaos of sheets. "Come see our spaceship!"

"It's not a spaceship, it's a castle," Lucas corrected from somewhere inside the fort.

"It can be both," Macy's voice came from the depths of the construction.

I crawled inside the section of the fort that looked safe—and big enough to house someone taller than four feet. Okay, well—admittedly I was surprised at how spacious and well-engineered this thing was. Maliyah was clearly behind this fascinating monstrosity.

"This is incredible," I said, settling cross-legged on the cushioned floor. "Very professional architecture."

"Aunt Maliyah helped," Macy said. "She's like super good at building things."

"Years of practice with these two," Maliyah said, appearing in the entrance and crouching down with me. "How was your first day back?"

"Complicated. It was okay, but I'm glad to be home." I looked around at the cozy fort. "This looks like way more fun than budget reports and employee complaints."

"It was. Though I think we're going to need to disassemble before dinner. This thing has gotten completely out of hand."

Caden arrived home soon after carrying ice cream for the family. Of course—sugar before bed seemed like a great idea. Should probably address my addiction, but not today!

Chapter 41: Not Quite Ready

~CADEN~

The calls started again the following morning while I was at work.

I was in the middle of reviewing a contract for new business with Lauren when my phone buzzed with an unknown number. The automated message was becoming depressingly familiar: "This is a call from Jessica Jensen at MCI-Framingham. This call is from a correctional facility and will be monitored and recorded. To accept this call, press 1. To decline this call, press 2 or hang up."

I declined and turned back to the documents in front of me.

"Again?" Lauren asked.

"Yeah. I have a call out to our family law attorney to discuss it. Really hoping it's something we can stop, but I don't know if we can until we have the next hearing in the custody process later this week."

Lauren and I had been going over this contract all morning and she had seen how frequent the calls came through.

We'd found a sort of peace, Lauren, and me. Even so, I wasn't all that surprised she had come in that morning and told me she is planning to take a break from working. She talked with her husband, and they are going to spend a year touring the US in an RV starting this Fall.

Honestly, it's probably for the best at this point. She agreed to stay while I find someone to replace her and agreed to train them. It's rare for someone to be willing to do that and I appreciated her offer. The mere thought of having to recruit and train someone at this stage felt exhausting.

My phone rang again. Decline.

Then again an hour after that. Decline.

Sitting at the table for breakfast the next morning, I was listening to Macy's story about a book report she had to write. She was complaining about how much effort it was to have to flip screens from her e-book to the paper she had to write—on her computer.

I looked at her and laughed, telling her about the 'olden days' when we did things with pencil and paper. She looked absolutely horrified. Getting up, she put her dishes in the sink and went to grab her stuff for school.

My phone rang again. Looking down, I saw it was from the correctional facility—again. I was done.

"I'm calling David again. I can't figure out why he hasn't called me back." I told Felicity over breakfast, after declining the call.

"Good," Felicity said simply. "This can't continue."

I stepped into my home office and dialed David's number.

"Caden," David answered, then coughed.

"You good?"

"Yeah, somehow I came down with a righteous cold and was down for the count yesterday."

"Oh man. I'm sorry. I wondered why you hadn't called me back."

"Yeah, I'm really sorry about that. Checked out for a bit. When the fever hit yesterday, everything pretty much flew out of my mind."

I sat down behind my desk, leaning my head on the back of my chair. "That's awful. Are you back to work now?"

"Yeah, but taking it a bit easy—working from home for a couple days. Everything okay?"

I sighed and told him about everything going on. "Jessica's been calling constantly from prison. Multiple times a day. We're not taking the calls."

"How many calls are we talking about?"

"Nine to me already, a few more to Felicity. It's disruptive, and honestly it feels like harassment."

David was quiet for a moment. "In custody cases involving incarcerated parents, courts can impose communication restrictions, especially when there are pending criminal charges. We could petition for supervised communication only, or request no direct contact until the custody hearing."

"What would you recommend?"

"Before we file anything, we need to know what Macy wants. This is about her relationship with her mother, and she's old enough now that the court will want to know her wishes."

He was right. Any decision about Jessica's contact had to start with Macy.

"Do you have any thoughts about what I should tell her? Like what options she could have? I guess I'm not really familiar with what could be allowed given the circumstances."

"Well, you've got a few. First up, she could have supervised phone calls through the court system. Another option is to keep communication to letters that go through a supervisor. She could also choose no contact for now. But Caden – this decision has to be hers. Don't lead her toward any particular answer. The judge will ask her, and you want her answer to be completely her own."

"Completely get that and already planned to keep my own thoughts to myself. I'll talk to her and let you know what she decides."

After I hung up, I went back out and caught Felicity's eye. Macy was in the living room with Lucas and Zoe, building what appeared to be a Lego city.

"How did it go?" Felicity asked quietly.

I relayed the conversation with David to her.

"That's a huge decision for her."

I replied, "Because it is. But she deserves to make this choice herself."

"Macy," I called. "Can we talk to you about something?"

She looked up from her construction project, immediately alert to the serious tone in my voice. "Is everything okay?"

"Everything's fine," Felicity assured her quickly. When she came over to the kitchen, Felicity continued, "but your dad wants to talk about something. Come sit sweetheart."

We all gathered at the table, and I began, "Macy, your mom has been trying to call us from where she is now."

Macy's face went carefully blank.

"Oh," she said quietly.

"We haven't been taking the calls," I continued gently. "But we wanted to ask you what you want to do. Do you want to talk to her? If you do, we can arrange for that to happen safely. If you don't, that's okay too."

The silence stretched for what felt like an eternity.

"I don't know," Macy said finally. "I mean... I think about her. But also ..." She shrugged, a gesture that seemed too heavy for an eleven-year-old.

"It's okay not to know," Felicity said softly. "This is a big decision, and there's no right or wrong answer."

"Can I think about it?" Macy asked. "Maybe talk to Dr. Chen about it first?"

"Of course," I said, relief flooding through me. "That sounds like a really smart idea. You have an appointment tomorrow, right?"

"Yeah. Can I tell you what I decide after that?"

"Absolutely. Take all the time you need."

The next afternoon, I picked Macy up from her therapy appointment. Dr. Chen asked if she could speak with Felicity and me for a few minutes.

"Macy and I had a good conversation about the situation with her mother," Dr. Chen said once we were settled in her office. "She's processing this very thoughtfully."

"What did she decide?" Felicity asked.

"She asked me to tell you that she's not ready to talk to her mom right now. She said she needs more time to feel... and I'm quoting here... 'better inside' before she has that conversation."

I felt a mixture of pride and heartbreak. Pride that my daughter was learning to recognize and articulate her emotional needs. Heartbreak that she had to navigate something so complex at her age.

"But," Dr. Chen continued, "she also wanted you to know that she might want to talk to her mom eventually. She said if her mom is getting help and getting better, maybe someday she'd be open to it."

"Wow," said Felicity. "That feels like a really mature perspective for someone so young."

"You're not wrong, but it's also completely age-appropriate. Children often need time and psychological safety before they're ready to engage with a parent who's caused them trauma. The fact that Macy is setting her own boundaries is actually a very healthy sign."

Dr. Chen turned to address both of us directly. "I'd recommend supporting her decision completely and I'll be writing a letter for her to that effect. The best thing you can do is support her decision. Let her know the door is always open when she's ready—that if she changes her mind – whether that's next week or next year – you'll help her figure out what that looks like safely."

That evening, after I'd updated David on Macy's decision and he'd agreed to file for no direct contact during the custody proceedings, Felicity and I finally had a chance to decompress.

"You know what I realized today?" she said, curled up next to me on the couch.

"What's that?"

"Six months ago, if Jessica had been calling like this, you would have answered. You would have tried to manage her emotions, tried to fix whatever crisis she was having."

I thought about that. She was right. The old me would have felt responsible for Jessica's desperation, would have taken those calls out of some misguided sense of obligation or guilt.

"And now?" I asked.

"Now you put Macy first. You asked her what she wanted before making any decisions about her own mother. That's huge growth."

She was right about that too. The calls still bothered me, but not because I felt compelled to answer them. They bothered me because they represented a threat to the peace we'd built, the healing that was happening.

"Speaking of putting our family first," I said, "are you ready for tomorrow?"

Tomorrow was our first therapy session together. We'd talked about it, scheduled it, rescheduled it once because of work conflicts, but somehow it had felt abstract until now.

"I think so," Felicity said. "Are you nervous?"

"A little. But also... eager? Does that make sense?"

"It does. I feel the same way."

We'd been doing so well, communicating better than we had in years, working as a team through all the crisis and chaos. But we both knew that real change required ongoing work, not just good intentions during emergency situations.

"What do you want to get out of it?" she asked.

I considered the question seriously. "I want to make sure I have tools to keep myself from slipping back into old patterns when things get less crisis-mode. I want to learn how to be a better partner during normal, boring Tuesday kind of life, not just during emergencies. What about you?"

"I want to learn how to ask for what I need instead of hoping you'll figure it out," she said. "And I want to make sure we keep talking to each other, really talking, not just managing logistics."

Later that night, lying in bed with Felicity's head on my shoulder, I thought about how much had changed. A month ago, our marriage had been hanging by a thread. Macy had been living with an unstable mother who was slowly destroying her sense of security.

Now Jessica was in prison and could only reach us if we let her. Macy was safe, healing, and making her own thoughtful decisions about her relationship with her mother. We were in a good place as a family—Macy felt safe with us.

Felicity and I were not just surviving but actually growing stronger.

Tomorrow we'd start couples therapy, another step in making sure we kept choosing each other, kept doing the work, kept building something stronger than what we'd had before.

My phone rang again. Same facility, same response—decline. And I was at peace with it.

Chapter 42: Our Turn Now

~Felicity~

The waiting room for Dr. Sarah Mitchell's office had a calming atmosphere to it. It was decorated in soft blues and grays, with comfortable chairs and calming music in the background. There was a wall between the front desk and the waiting room seats. It was made of glass and had water in it, with bubbles that floated to the top on a cyclical basis—almost hypnotic in a sense.

Even with all that, I was a wreck. I was anything but calm while we waited, hands clasped together on the armrest between us.

"You okay?" he whispered.

"Yeah. Just nervous for some reason."

It was strange, being nervous about therapy when we were actually in a good place. Six months ago, if someone had told me we'd be in couples therapy, I would have assumed it was because we were on the verge of divorce. Shit, six *weeks* ago, I would have said the same thing. Instead, we were here because we wanted to stay together.

"Mr. and Mrs. Barrett?" A woman appeared in the doorway—tall, probably in her fifties, with kind eyes and graying hair pulled back in a simple ponytail. "I'm Dr. Mitchell. Why don't you come on back."

Good Lord. Her office was even more soothing than the waiting room. I wish it would start working to calm my nerves. There was warm lighting and two comfortable chairs positioned at an angle to each other, with Dr. Mitchell's chair completing a triangle. No couch—I'd been wondering about that.

"Thank you for coming in," Dr. Mitchell said as we settled into our chairs. "I know taking this step isn't always easy, even when you're motivated to be here."

"Actually," Caden said, "we're both pretty nervous but also eager to be here. Which probably sounds weird."

Dr. Mitchell smiled. "Not weird at all. Some of my most encouraging work is when couples come in proactively, wanting to strengthen what they have rather than waiting until crisis hits."

"Well, we've had our share of crises," I said. "But we've been working through it, and we want to make sure we keep doing that well."

"Okay. Well, let's start with what brought you here specifically?"

Caden and I looked at each other, having one of those wordless conversations that had become more frequent lately.

"We had some rough years," I started. "I felt invisible in our marriage. Caden was consumed with work, and I was... well, I just kept making myself smaller and smaller, hoping that if I ignored it all, everything would somehow get fixed on its own."

"I buried myself in work to the detriment of my marriage," Caden added bluntly. "I thought providing financially was the same as being a good husband and father. I was wrong."

"What changed?" Dr. Mitchell asked.

"Crisis, honestly," he said. "It started with me failing to realize how much I'd missed about my wife and finally everything hit the fan when I..." Caden's voice trailed off.

Dr. Mitchell encouraged him, saying, "Caden, this is a safe space. This is the place where you put it all out there and we work through it. Consider this—Not saying it doesn't erase it, Caden. It already happened. Talking about it is how we work through it."

He sighed, "You're right." Clearing his throat, Caden continued, "I gave my wife's birthday gift away—a very expensive custom purse that she had designed herself and asked me for. I hid it in a stupid place—my daughter's closet. She lived with us on weekends and, not realizing she would search her closet for her ballet shoes, I had tossed it in there to keep it away from prying eyes. Hindsight's 20/20 and I now realize how dumb that was."

"Okay, how did it lead to you giving it away?" Dr. Mitchell's approach was clear, open, and without judgment, which I appreciated.

"My daughter found it and, since it was in her own closet, she thought it was for her—a gift for her first day at her new school. When she found it, rather than explain the situation, I agreed it was for her when she asked."

Dr. Mitchell turned to me and asked me how I found out.

"When I got home, Macy was all excited to show me, not knowing it was supposed to be mine."

"How did that make you feel, Felicity?" she asked me.

The question hung in the air, and I felt that familiar tightness in my chest. Even now, after all we'd been through, remembering that moment still hurt.

"Invisible, forgotten, small, heartbroken, unloved," I said quietly, feeling the words tumble from me like an avalanche. "I felt like I didn't matter enough for him to just tell the truth. Like it was easier to let me be disappointed than to have an uncomfortable conversation with Macy."

"I was devastated," I continued, the words continuing without exception. "Because it wasn't just about the purse. It represented everything wrong with our marriage. I'd asked for something, after being forgotten, and then it was just out of reach—like I'd felt Caden had been over the last few years."

Dr. Mitchell nodded thoughtfully. "Caden, how did you feel when you realized what had happened?"

"Like the worst husband in the world," he said immediately. "But also defensive, which made it worse. I tried to justify it instead of just owning how badly I'd screwed up."

"What happened next?" Dr. Mitchell asked.

We spent the next half hour unpacking all the things that had happened through to when Jessica had taken Macy. We put it all out there, without holding back. I felt broken almost like I'd had to relive everything—giving me somewhat of an emotional hangover by the time I'd said my piece and listened to Caden's.

"This feels like a good place to pause on talking through the events and to instead focus on some homework."

"Wait," I said, and all eyes fell on me. I turned to Caden and said, "I want to tell you about a gift I received from my coworker." And I did. I explained the book and the conversation with Ethan. I told him about how we resolved it and shared the details of my last discussion with him.

"I just—I don't feel anything for him and there's nothing there at all. I explained to him that it wasn't appropriate, but I wanted to tell you because—well, if someone at work gave *you* a gift, I'd be pissed."

Caden sat quietly for a moment, eyes glassy. "It's a gift I wish I'd thought of. It was a beautiful idea, and while I don't love that he gave it to you—or his motives—I can't begrudge him. You're the most amazing person I've ever known, Felicity. And honestly... I'm torn. I'm jealous he knew what would mean something to you, but I also feel this weird sense of pride."

"Pride?"

"Yeah—like. I don't know. This sense that I have you and, while I don't deserve you, it's still you and me. I don't even know how to explain it. But I guess I feel a bit bad for him."

I hadn't expected that. After everything we'd unpacked, I felt emotionally drained—like we'd just run a marathon through our entire history. Caden looked the same.

Dr. Mitchell smiled gently. "That feels like a good place to pause and talk about the homework."

"Yes. From what I've heard today, you've both been through quite an ordeal. I know you mentioned that a lot has changed, and we can't really get there in good time today. So I want to see what we can do to make sure that walking through today's trauma doesn't become your sole focus for the next week, after leaving here."

I asked, a little hesitantly, "Okay, what do you have in mind?"

"Today is Thursday. Before you go to sleep tonight, and every night until our session next week, I want you to do something—no phones, no TV, no kids interrupting, no distractions." Nodding at our hands clasped together, "since you don't seem to have an issue with touch, I'd like to keep that as an anchor for you. I'd like for the both of you to sit with each other, hold hands, and ask each other three questions."

We both responded at the same time with, "okay."

"Caden, your questions are: How did you feel about our relationship today? Was there a time when I wasn't there for you today when you needed me? Was there anything today that I did that made you happy or feel seen?"

Caden pulled his phone out and took them down in his notes section, looking up at the Doctor and saying, "I promise to have them memorized and not to have my phone out during our time."

Dr. Mitchell smiled and responded with, "Nicely done, Caden."

From there, she continued, "Felicity, your questions are: How did you feel about our relationship today? Was there a time you felt like I wasn't being open with you about my own feelings or response to something? Was there anything that I did today that helped you see me or how I felt about our relationship?" Just as Caden had, I took the notes on my phone and made the same promise he did, smiling as I did.

"That sounds manageable," I said, though even the thought of going through this exercise every night felt slightly overwhelming.

"The key is consistency and openness. I want you both to keep in mind that while these questions may feel like yes/no questions, they are meant as dialogue openers, so while you'll respond with yes or no, you should both plan to expand upon *why* the answer is yes or no," she said.

After we both agreed, Dr. Mitchell proposed we do weekly meetings for the next two months and reevaluate after that. We both found that to be reasonable.

Walking out to the car, I felt like we'd just turned our entire emotional life inside out and examined every piece.

"That was intense," Caden said, starting the engine.

"Yeah. But good intense?"

"I think so. It felt like... like we were being honest about everything for the first time."

We drove in silence for a few minutes, both processing.

"You know what struck me in there?" I said finally.

"What?"

"How much we've both changed already. Before all of this unfolded, I never would have been able to say those things about feeling invisible and unloved. I would have just... swallowed it."

"And I would have gotten defensive and made it about how hard I work instead of hearing what you were actually saying."

"But we didn't do that today."

"No, we didn't."

As we pulled into our driveway, I could see through the kitchen window that Maliyah was cooking dinner while the kids set the table. Normal family life, continuing on while we'd been dissecting our marriage and putting it back together stronger.

"Ready to go back to real life?" Caden asked.

"With our homework assignment and everything?"

"Especially with our homework assignment."

I looked at our house, warm with light and filled with the people we loved. "Yeah. I'm ready."

As we walked into the house, Caden paused and reached into his pocket. Pulling it out, he showed me the caller ID flashed Morrison's name.

Answering with the phone on speaker, he said, "Morrison, everything okay? You've got me and Felicity here."

"Hi Caden, Felicity. Sorry to call unexpectedly, but I wanted to let you know Jessica's been moved out of Framingham."

I looked at Caden, and I knew the surprise I saw on his face was mirrored on my own. I said out loud, "What's going on?" at the same time he said, "What? Why?"

"Staff reported she'd begun to have erratic outbursts, paranoia, and confusion. At first, they thought it was withdrawal, but by today her behavior should have evened out. They did a tox screen too and it didn't show new substances either. Concerned about her behavior, they moved her to McLean Psychiatric Hospital for evaluation. She'll be under observation there while they run more tests."

Holy shit.

Chapter 43: They Found Something

~Caden~

"Holy shit," I said.

"I know it's a lot to process," Morrison continued through the speaker. Felicity and I both took a seat on the front steps of our porch. Both of us clearly realized we couldn't go inside before our conversation was finished—not with the chance that Macy could hear before we knew what to do. "The facility staff said her behavior had been escalating over the past few days. She was having violent outbursts, confusion about where she was and why, and she kept yelling that people were plotting against her."

Felicity and I looked at each other. The expression on her face told me we were both stunned by this news. I was ashamed to admit though, I had a small thought—could she be faking it to try and get out of the charges?

"What does all of this mean?" Felicity asked.

"Not really sure yet. We'll have to wait and see what the psychiatric evaluation reveals. Could be anything from severe withdrawal complications to underlying mental health issues that were masked by drug use."

"How long does something like this take?" I asked.

"Depends on what they find. Could be a few days for observation, could be longer if they determine she needs treatment, and they need to figure out how to stabilize her behavior. I'll keep you posted as I hear more."

After Morrison hung up, Felicity and I stood in our driveway, trying to process this latest development.

"Should we tell Macy?" she asked.

"Let's wait until we know more. No point in worrying her over something that might be nothing. Given what she shared with Dr. Chen, I think it's safe to say that sharing with her right now could cause her undue stress for something she can't do anything about."

But even as I said it, I had a feeling like there was something we weren't thinking of.

The next few days passed in a strange limbo. We went through our normal routines—work, school, dinner, homework—but there was an undercurrent of tension, like we were all just sitting here, waiting for the other shoe to drop.

True to our promise to Dr. Mitchell, Felicity and I did our nightly check-ins. The first night was awkward, both of us self-conscious about the formal structure of it. But by the third night, it was starting to feel natural. More than natural—helpful.

"How did you feel about our relationship today?" I asked on the fifth night, holding her hands as we sat on our bed, cross legged and facing each other.

"Good. Solid. I felt like we were really working together, especially when Macy had that meltdown about her math homework." Felicity dipped her head and shook it back and forth lightly, clearly thinking back to the screaming fit Macy had. It was obvious that math wasn't the cause, but we gave her space to have her moment and then, together, we sat and talked with her about what was going on.

"Was there a time when I wasn't there for you today when you needed me?"

"No, actually. You were really present today. Honestly, this one answers this question and the one you would ask next about me feeling seen."

"Okay, hit me."

Felicity continued, "Well, you remember how when we were making dinner together, we were talking about my presentation at work when you got a call from the contractor?"

"Yeah?" I responded, nodding, and thinking back to that moment.

"You got stressed about the call and stepped into the other room to take it. At first, it felt a little weird—we'd been cooking, and you had to disappear. But I stepped away from my feelings and looked at the actual scenario. I realized that, first you'd let me know first—not just walking away. Second, the kitchen would have been a distraction—pots and pans, movement, music and all the things going on."

She took a deep breath and continued, "so, I realized that, in reality you were looking for a quieter, less distracting space to take the call, not to just get away from me. But the big thing for me was, when you came back into the room and you gave me a quick insight on what the call was about, let me know why it was a stress point, and *then* you jumped right back to our conversation about my presentation at work."

I smiled. Hearing her say it made me consider how effortless it had been to include her in everything. I was happy we were together for the moment because it was clear how much more powerful our relationship was when we did life together.

As we talked, we let each other in on ourselves—working through our questions and hearing one another. When we finished the conversation, Felicity bent forward and laid her head on my shoulder. My arms wrapped around her, and I basked in the settled feeling of love and gratitude I had.

The following morning, as we were getting ready to head out, Morrison called.

I answered, "Hey Morrison, we're heading out to drop Macy at the bus stop. Can we call you right back together?" I caught Felicity's eye and she nodded, shuffling Macy out to the door so we could walk her to the corner.

"Yeah. That works. Call me back soon though, it's important."

"Okay. Will do."

As soon as we were alone, Felicity and I called Morrison back together, putting the phone on speaker as usual. He answered and his voice sounded different. More serious, if that was possible.

"Hey—thanks for calling me back," he answered.

"Of course. What's up?"

"Honestly, I'm actually already almost to your house. I'll be pulling into your driveway in just a couple minutes. We can talk when I get there."

I looked at Felicity, my head rearing back a bit at the surprise I felt from his words. "Okay, we'll be here." I hung up and grabbed Felicity's hand.

"Let's head back inside. It feels like this is going to clearly be bigger than something we talk about while standing in the driveway."

Felicity texted her boss to let her know that she'd be late in. I did the same with Lauren and asked her to reschedule my morning meetings—just in case.

When Morrison arrived, he looked like he'd aged five years since our dinner earlier in the week. He declined Maliyah's offer of coffee and asked if we could speak privately.

We settled in the living room, the kids' laughter from the backyard creating an odd juxtaposition to Morrison's somber expression.

"I got a call from the medical team at McLean this morning," he began. "Jessica's been undergoing a series of tests—blood work, psychological evaluations, brain scans."

"And?" Felicity prompted when he paused.

"They found something. A mass in her brain. Specifically, in her frontal lobe."

The words hit me like a physical blow. "A mass?"

"The preliminary diagnosis is Glioblastoma." She had a Glioblastoma? What the hell does that mean? My fingers were itching to Google it.

Morrison continued after he let the news sink in. "It's an aggressive brain tumor in her frontal lobe. It can cause exactly the kinds of behavioral changes Jessica's been experiencing. The paranoia, the erratic behavior, the poor judgment—it all fits."

Felicity's hand found mine. "Is it... is it treatable?"

Morrison's expression told us everything we needed to know before he spoke.

"Well, Glioblastomas are aggressive. Depending on the size and location, the prognosis can range from months to a couple of years. They're still running tests to confirm the grade, but... they already know it's in her frontal lobe, and it's large. With how far it's spread into surrounding brain tissue, the doctors believe it's likely inoperable."

Leaning back, he dropped an even heavier bomb. "If it's inoperable, you should know we're looking at months instead of years."

"But it's not good," I finished.

"No. It's not good." Morrison blew out a breath and looked at us both, saying, "I wish I had better news for you."

We sat in silence for a moment, the sound of children playing outside suddenly feeling surreal.

"What does this mean legally?" I asked, my mind already racing through implications.

"It complicates things significantly. If Jessica's behavior over the past months—including the embezzlement and the kidnapping—was influenced by an undiagnosed brain tumor, it changes the legal landscape entirely."

"Changes it how?"

"Well, it raises questions about her mental capacity at the time of the crimes. It doesn't excuse what happened, but it could affect sentencing. And regarding custody..." Morrison paused. "Given her diagnosis, it's possible she'd never be in a position to care for Macy again."

I felt a strange mixture of relief and sadness. It felt wrong, but I had a sense of relief that Macy's custody situation would likely be resolved definitively. Then, I had an immense sadness because, despite everything Jessica had put us through, she was still Macy's mother—she was still someone I used to have feelings for. And now she was dying.

"Does Jessica know?" Felicity asked.

"They told her this morning. The medical team said she took it... about as well as you'd expect. She's asked to speak with you, Caden."

"Me?"

"She wants to see Macy too, but the doctors think it's better to wait until they have a better handle on her condition and treatment options."

I looked at Felicity, who squeezed my hand.

"You don't have to decide right now," Morrison said. "But I wanted you to have all the information."

After Morrison left, Felicity and I sat on the couch, both of us struggling to process this latest development.

"Holy shit," she said finally.

"Took the words right out of my mouth."

"Do we tell Macy?"

I thought about what it would be like, as a little girl, to be in her situation. She'd been doing so well, settling into our routine, feeling safe and secure for the first time in months.

"We have to. But carefully. I think we should talk to Dr. Chen and get some perspective."

"She's going to want to see her."

"I know."

"And you? Are you going to go see Jessica? She wants to talk to you."

I considered the question. Six months ago, I would have gone immediately, driven by guilt and some misguided sense of responsibility. Now, I found myself thinking about what was best for our family, for Macy, for my marriage.

"I don't know, I think so? Not for Jessica's sake, but for Macy's. Someday she's going to ask me if I did everything I could for her mother. I want to be able to say yes."

Felicity nodded. "I think that's the right choice."

"Will you come with me?"

"If you want me to."

"I do."

That evening, during our check-in, I found myself especially grateful for the structure Dr. Mitchell had given us.

"How did you feel about our relationship today?" Felicity asked, settling cross-legged facing me on our bed, hands clasped in mine.

"Solid. Like we were really facing this together instead of me trying to handle it alone," I said. "Even with something this huge and complicated, it felt like we were a team and would face it as a team."

"Was there a time you felt like I wasn't being open with you about my own feelings or response to something?"

I thought about the day, about Morrison's visit and the hours afterward. "No, actually. I appreciated how you let me see your reaction in real time. When Morrison said 'Glioblastoma,' I could see the shock on your face, and then when you squeezed my hand—it felt like we were experiencing it together instead of me having to guess what you were thinking."

"Was there anything that I did today that helped you see me or how I felt about our relationship?"

"When you offered to come with me to see Jessica. You didn't hesitate, you didn't make it about anything other than us, doing this together. It showed me that you're really in this with me, even when it's complicated and messy."

"Of course I am," she said softly. "We're partners—in everything, partners."

Later that night, lying in bed with Felicity's head on my shoulder, I thought about how much had changed. If this had happened last year, even six months ago, I would likely have tried to carry the burden alone, tried to figure out how to handle everything by myself.

Now, I saw Felicity as the partner she is, that she had always been. Someone who faced the hard things with me instead of expecting me to manage them alone.

"We're going to be okay," I said into the darkness.

"Yeah," Felicity agreed quietly, sleepily. "We are."

Chapter 44: Okay, I Want To

~Macy~

I sat in Dr. Chen's office by myself. Felicity and Dad came in to help me get settled but left to go to the waiting room until Dr. Chen said it was okay for them to come in too. Dr. Chen said she wanted to talk to me alone first about Mom.

"How are you feeling about everything we discussed last time, Macy?" Dr. Chen asked. "About your mom being sick?"

I picked at the edge of my cast. It was getting gross and smelly, and I couldn't wait to get it off later this week.

"I don't know," I said, which is what I always say when I don't know how to put feelings into words. "Confused, I guess."

"Confusing how?"

I thought about it for a minute—then another minute, dragging the time out while trying to search for words. "Well, everyone keeps saying Mom has been sick, and that's why she's been acting weird. But she's been acting weird for a really long time. Like, maybe since I was nine or ten?"

Dr. Chen nodded. "Can you tell me what you mean by weird?"

"She used to be really fun, like when I was little. We'd make pancakes on Saturdays, and she'd let me help crack the eggs, even when I was even littler—I'd get shells in the bowl, and she wouldn't yell at me. She'd read me stories every night and do different voices for all the characters."

I could feel tears starting, which was annoying. I'd been crying too much lately.

"Those sound like really nice memories," Dr. Chen said softly.

"But then she started getting mad about everything. Like, if I left my backpack on the floor, she'd yell at me for an hour about being irresponsible. Or if I asked her to help with homework, she'd get frustrated and say I should already know how to do it."

"When do you think that started happening?"

I thought back to the first time Mom grounded me and took away all my art supplies after I hadn't put my laundry away before starting to sketch after school. "Maybe when I was going into like sixth grade? It got worse this year. I got really good at making my own TV dinners too."

I wiped my nose with the back of my hand. Dr. Chen handed me the tissue box.

"This year, she got like really different. She'd say Dad was trying to turn me against her, or that Felicity was trying to replace her. She'd ask me weird questions about what Dad and Felicity said about her when she wasn't around. Every day, it seemed like she was different."

"That must have been really hard for you."

"I guess. It was just like—I don't know—something was always happening, so I guess I didn't see it as like overnight? You know? I don't really know how to explain it."

Dr. Chen was quiet for a minute, which usually means she's thinking about something important.

"Macy, it's okay not to have all the words right now. What the doctors found in your mom's brain—this tumor—it's probably been growing for a little while, likely for the last year. I want you to think back to the memories that were good—before things started to change."

"Okay." Before Mom started changing. *She was always fancy, always spending money, so that's not it.* "Do you mean like when she was nice?"

"Yes, let's think about that time."

"So that would probably be before she met Brad. I was little when my parents divorced, but it was just me and Mom for a while. She met Brad like when I was, I don't know, like six?" *Yeah, six*—I thought to myself.

"How were things different with him?"

"Well, she had less time for me, and she shopped—like a lot!"

Dr. Chen sat silently and waited for me to keep going.

"So, like before Brad, we had an apartment—it was cool. Just Mom's room and mine. And mine was decorated like with princess stuff—I was little, you know—not like now."

Dr. Chen smiled and told me to continue.

"Okay, so then when she met Brad, he was fancy and stuff. He liked stuff. Then we moved into his house. It's so big, you know? And like...I don't know... Fancy. That's really the best word for it. Super fancy."

"So, when she met Brad—is that when you think she started to spend a lot of money but less time with you?"

"Oh yeah—for sure. But then, like in the last year—that's when she got really super different, you know? Like, mad, and really focused on Felicity and stuff."

"Okay, well it's possible that the tumor was growing in her brain for the last year, so I want you to think about her personality—not her spending or her time—but how she treated you. Think about who she was before all the changes happened in her being mad."

"Okay, yeah."

"I want you to consider that mom. You mentioned your mom used to kiss you goodnight and, even if she was going out to an event or a dinner, she would still make sure you were settled, right?" When I nodded, Dr. Chen kept talking. "Okay, well that mom, the one who kissed you and told you she loved you—the one who still hugged you and made sure you were doing okay—that was your real Mom. That was the one you should try to hold onto when your memories get hard."

"So I should try and forget about what happened over the last year?"

"No, not forget—those memories will always be part of your history. Instead of forgetting them, try to think of them as something different than the memories you had *before* they happened. You can still think of them, but put them in a different space of your mind and heart. Let the mom who you knew from before those memories take up more space, and the one who was there in the last year take up *less* space."

"Um, okay, I can try that—I think."

"In time, it will get easier. The point of the exercise is to realize that you don't have to forget the difficult times in order to remember the good ones, okay?"

"Okay."

"Have you gone to see her yet?"

I looked down at my fingers and started to pick at my nails. "No," I said quietly.

"Is there anything holding you back?"

"I don't know."

"It's okay to go see her, Macy. You're not doing anything bad by seeing her before she passes away."

We've talked about my mom dying a couple times now. I see Dr. Chen three times a week these days, so this has come up before.

"I'm still scared."

"It's okay to be scared too. You're allowed to have your own feelings." She leaned forward and looked at me, making eye contact. "I don't usually do this, but I think that the circumstances call for it."

"What?" I asked.

"I think you need to go see her."

"I thought I got to choose!"

"You do. And I'm not forcing you to go, Macy. But I am saying that you should. This may be the last chance you have to say goodbye. It's called closure. This is a defining moment in life, Macy. A decision not to see her is something you cannot un-decide or un-do. I want you to consider that and take the step to see her."

The tears were flowing down my face. Dr. Chen had never told me to do something, not like this. I pulled my knees up to my chin and held onto my legs, curling into a little bit of a ball on the couch. I nodded and said I would try. Dr. Chen gave me some tissues and let me have a minute to get it out—all the tears and all the pain. It all hurt so much.

After a few minutes, Dad and Felicity came in. I could tell they'd been talking in the waiting room because they both looked worried.

"How are you doing, kiddo?" Dad asked, sitting down next to me.

"Okay," I said quietly.

"Dr. Chen says I should go see Mom," I said, not looking up from my hands.

"Only if you want to," Felicity said quickly. "You don't have to do anything you're not ready for."

"But Dr. Chen thinks I need to. For the door close."

"For closure," she said.

"Oh, closure, I mean."

I looked up at them. "She said if I don't see her, I can't undo that decision later."

Dad and Felicity exchanged a look.

"She's right about that," Dad said gently. "But it's still your choice, Macy."

"I want to see if any of my real mom is still there. The one who loved me before all the stuff happened with her brain." I wiped my nose with another tissue. "Dr. Chen helped me remember that she wasn't always different. Just the last year or so."

"That's a very brave thing to want to do," Felicity said.

"What if she's mean to me? What if she says something mean?"

"Then we can leave," Dad said firmly. "The moment you feel scared or uncomfortable, we're out of there."

"And it won't be your real mom saying those things," Dr. Chen added. "It would be the tumor."

I took a deep breath. "Okay. I want to go see her."

"Then we'll make that happen," Dad said. "Together."

Chapter 45: What If She Doesn't Remember?

~Felicity~

The twenty-minute drive to Brigham and Women's felt endless. Macy sat in the backseat, quiet, her fingers twisting the hem of her shirt. The silence was deafening. She was so nervous getting ready this morning. I'd helped her pick something out and she changed countless times before we settled on her favorite purple sweater and jeans—the outfit we'd actually started with.

Jessica had bought the outfit for her this past Christmas—well, the sweater and jeans. The shoes were too small, so we went with a new pair of boots. Macy's realization that her shoes were too small resulted in a minor meltdown which ended with the both of us on the floor, crying while I rocked her.

"You okay back there, kiddo?" Caden asked, glancing in the rearview mirror.

"Yeah," Macy said, but her voice was small. "Just thinking."

I turned around to look at her. "Anything we can help with?"

"I don't know." She pulled her knees up to her chest on the seat and leaned against the door of the car, head resting on the window. I barely heard it, but I was able to catch her asking, "What if she doesn't remember me?"

Fuck. There is no way out of this without all of our hearts breaking—Macy at the loss of her mother, Caden and I in watching Macy's heart break and the utter unfairness of a kid getting such a raw fucking deal.

"Then we'll remind her," I said gently. "And if she can't understand or remember, that won't be your fault. It won't mean she doesn't love you."

"But what if she says mean things? Like she did before?"

Caden pulled into the entrance, turning the car over to the valet. "Then we remember what Dr. Chen told us—that's not your mom talking. That's the tumor."

At the front desk, we asked for directions amidst the loudness of the hospital setting. Patricia, the concierge, helped us with where to go. Before heading up though, Caden had placed an order at the Panera in their lobby and picked us up some coffees and waters which were already ready in the to-go area by the time we were heading up.

Jessica had been transferred from the Neuro-oncology department at Mass General Hospital to the Palliative and Hospice care unit at Brigham and Women's. She had to remain in hospital while under guard and, due to her circumstances with the charges, she couldn't be transferred to a private facility or for homecare for end-of-life care.

We were told her condition was deteriorating more rapidly than initially expected.

"She has good moments and difficult moments," the Doctor had said. "She asks for Macy and Brad intermittently, but her words get jumbled easily. The tumor is putting pressure on the areas in her brain that impact her speech and memory."

Making our way to the elevators, we followed Patricia's directions and ended up in a small unit area. We knew we were in the right place when we saw the on-duty Police Officer stationed outside the unit entry. After checking our visitor badges, he radioed to someone else, and we were ushered in.

Walking down the hall, we passed another two officers before reaching her room. Two additional officers were placed outside her room—it felt excessive to be honest. What do they think she's going to do? Make a run for it? I put my sarcasm away though and opted for silence. In all fairness, I haven't seen her, so I don't really know what her circumstances look like right now.

Caden bumped elbows with me, checking to make sure I was okay. I was on his right and he was holding Macy's hand on his left.

Arriving at her door, I maneuvered behind Caden and leaned down toward Macy. She was shaking. "We don't have to do this," I whispered. "We can leave right now if you want."

"No," Macy said, squaring her small shoulders. "I need to see her."

Caden approached one of the officers stationed outside her door. "We're here to visit Jessica Jensen. We're on the approved visitor list."

The officer checked his clipboard and nodded. "You can go in. Just knock first."

Caden knocked softly on the door. "Jessica? It's Caden. I have Macy with me."

"Come in," came a voice from inside, but it sounded different than I remembered. Weaker, more uncertain.

We stepped into the room, and noticed Brad was with her, holding her hand. He looked haggard. You could tell that, no matter what she did, he still loved her. He stood and approached us, shook Caden's hand, saying, "I'll go grab some coffee and let you guys spend some time with her." At this, he touched Macy's shoulder gently and left the room.

Looking back toward Jessica's hospital bed, I had to work to keep my expression neutral. Jessica was propped up, positioned near the window. She looked like she'd aged years in just weeks. Her hair, once perfectly styled, hung limp and unwashed around her face. Her skin had a grayish pallor, and there were dark circles under her eyes that spoke of sleepless nights and pain.

But it was her eyes that were the most shocking. They had a vague, unfocused quality, like she was looking through us rather than at us.

"Macy?" Jessica's face lit up, but there was something off about her facial expression—there was almost a delay, like her emotions weren't keeping up with the moment. "My beautiful... my... you came to see me."

"Hi, Mom," Macy said quietly, not moving from her spot near the door.

"Come here, baby. Come... come..." Jessica gestured vaguely her bed, but her hand trembled and she seemed to forget what she was doing in a moment. I think she even may have forgotten we were even here.

I felt Macy hesitate, so I walked with her to the chair. Caden followed behind like he was on guard or something.

"You look so... so pretty," Jessica said, reaching out to touch Macy's hair. But it seemed like she lost the strength when she reached the cup and, instead of grasping it, she ended up knocking it over on her table. The water flowed over the table and onto the floor.

"Oh, I'm sorry. So sorry. I'm so... stupid fucking stupid..." She looked at me as if noticing me for the first time and just stared. Moments ticked by and she was still just staring.

"Mom?"

Surprised, Jessica looked over at Macy and said, "Macy! You came. Come, come sit with me." Her words were slurring as she rolled over the consonants.

Macy's eyes filled with tears as she watched her mother remember her, realizing she'd forgotten the minutes before when we came in. She reached for my hand, clearly scared.

Jessica's eyes skated to where our hands were clasped and said firmly, "Macy, come here."

I leaned to my side and told Macy, "It's okay, Macy. I'm right here. I'm not leaving your side, okay?" She nodded at my encouragement and shuffled toward Jessica's bed.

"My daughter doesn't need help from some nurse. You can go now." Jessica must not recognize me. To keep from antagonizing her, I stepped a little outside her line of sight and into Macy's instead.

Macy leaned toward her mother, settling her hip a bit on the bed.

Jessica reached for Macy's hair but struggled to get her arm up high enough. Macy grabbed her hand and held onto it rather than watch her keep trying.

"I'm so-so-so-sor-sorry," she said, stuttering out her words. "I...I...I am ha-ha-hav-ing a ha-ha-hard ti-ti-time some-sometimes. It co-comes and goes." Jessica blew out a breath, pausing for a minute, she appeared to be struggling to focus, and after a bit, she continued. "Okay. I think I got it."

"It's okay, Mom. I understand."

Jessica nodded. "I know what I did was wrong." Jessica's voice became urgent, almost panicked. "I just couldn't stop. They said that it was because my brain and my pills. I hate you." She pressed her palms against her temples, frustrated. "No! The words are wrong. They're all wrong."

"Mom, take your time," Macy said gently, and I was struck by how mature she sounded, how she was comforting her mother instead of the other way around.

"I love you," Jessica finally managed. "That's...that's the right words. I love you so much, baby girl."

"I love you too, Mom."

Jessica's eyes suddenly focused on me with startling clarity, and I saw a flash of the woman she become in the last year, before her deterioration—sharp, calculating, angry.

"You," she said, pointing at me with a shaking finger. "You took... you took my..." Her face contorted with frustration as she struggled to find the words. "My family. My life. Everything."

"Jessica," Caden said firmly, stepping forward.

"No, it's okay," I said quietly, holding my hand out to my husband to stop him from proceeding. I looked at Jessica. I no longer saw the the woman who had tormented our family. Instead I saw a sick, dying woman whose body and brain was betraying her. "I know you're scared and confused."

Jessica stared at me for a long moment, then seemed to deflate, the anger draining out of her face as quickly as it had appeared.

"I'm sorry," she whispered. "I don't... I can't think straight anymore. It's eating my brain."

Macy said gently, reaching out to take her mother's hand. "But it's not your fault, Mom."

Jessica looked back up at me again and said, "Can you come closer?"

I was hesitant at first, not sure if she would be volatile or not, but given her lack of strength, I wasn't as afraid. So, approaching her bed, I stayed on the other side of Macy—just in case I needed to keep her out of the line of fire.

Jessica leaned toward me and said, "I'm dying."

At this, a sob escaped from Macy. Jessica glanced back to her and squeezed her hand slightly. "It needs to be said."

"Jessica, it's okay. I know."

"No—know don't you." She dropped her head and blew out a breath, grunting at the effort and tapping her forehead with her free hand.

She spoke more slowly. "I mean—no, you don't know. I need you to do something."

"Okay. Tell me what you need." I thought she would say something like, bring me a new water or cover my feet because this room is freaking cold! That is not, however, what she said.

"Macy is yours now. It's what you always wanted—to steal her away. So now you'll have her."

I paused, shocked but realizing that this is part of the paranoia she has been experiencing, I measured my response. "Jessica, I don't want to steal her. She will always be your girl and you will always be her mom."

She shook her head, but I continued, "Jessica. You *will* always be her mom. No matter what, and I will remind her of you all the time. We won't forget you. We will talk about you, and help Macy remember good things about you.. And one day, she will tell her children about you. And her children's children. I promise you this. You will *not* be forgotten or replaced."

We were all crying now. Fuck this was so hard. She nodded her head and laid it back on the pillow.

"Macy..." Her voice was thin and breathy. She turned her head toward her daughter.

Macy's breath caught and she held back another sob. Through her tears and sniffles she said, "I'm here, Mom."

For a moment, Jessica just looked at her, really looked at her, as though taking in every detail. Her expression was soft, and her eyes were heavy.

"I always loved you. You were the best thing I ever had." She licked her lips, her mouth clearly dry.

Caden approached the bed. At some point he had gotten another cup and straw for her because he had one at the ready. As he stepped closer, he held the straw to her lips and helped her so she could drink.

"I love you too, Mom."

Jessica's eyes closed, but a faint smile lingered on her lips. In mere seconds, she had slipped into a restless half-sleep. She muttered something, but it was too incoherent for any of us to understand. The moment was gone, but I knew that Macy would keep those words with her forever.

There is no easy solution here. There is no easy way out of this. No one wins in this scenario. I stepped to the side of Macy, placing my hand on her shoulder. Caden had already moved behind her and rested his head on top of hers.

Tears shone in his eyes. He cried for the woman Jessica had been and for the daughter they had together. Macy cried for the loss she was experiencing and the pain she felt in the depths of her soul. I cried for the future that was forever changed and the lives that would never be the same.

And in that moment, as the three of us stood there by Jessica's bedside, I saw tears stream from her eyes. I knew that she cried for the life she didn't get to live and the daughter she wouldn't see become a woman.

Chapter 46: What if I Don't Remember?

~CADEN~

The drive home from the hospital felt different this time. It was heavier. There was a weight of finality settling in the car all around us. Macy sat in the backseat, her legs curled up as she hugged the door, head resting on the window. She was focused on the scene passing by us in the drive.

"You okay back there, kiddo?" I asked, my voice gravelly. Watching her in the rearview mirror, I could see her lips move, but she didn't turn her head to face me—keeping focused outside.

"Yeah," she said softly. "I'm fine."

Felicity reached back and squeezed Macy's knee. "It's okay to be sad."

"I know. I just wish..." She trailed off, then shook her head. "Never mind."

"What, sweetheart?" I prompted.

"I wish she could stay. It's not fair. I just feel like so much has happened and it's so hard." She broke at this, sobs pouring from her—wracking her body.

Felicity hiccupped with her own sob. I looked over and saw her unclip her seatbelt and crawl through the center console area into the back seat. That's my wife—my fucking amazing wife. She saw when she was needed and put everything to the side to be there for Macy. This woman is the kind of woman people dream of finding. Even the mere thought that I could have lost her sent moments of panic through my system.

I watched Felicity throw herself into the back seat. She put her arm around Macy's shoulders, and when I saw my daughter turn toward my wife, my heart jumped in my chest. This moment when Macy allowed Felicity to engulf her and comfort her told me how much love there was in this car.

Tears flowed. Cries sounded. Hearts broke.

How does one comfort a little girl through something like this? How do you not want to give her the world for just one moment to forget the circumstances that landed us here?

I pulled over at the next safe spot, putting the car in park and turning in my seat to face them both. We weren't going anywhere until Macy was ready.

"I'm so tired of everything being sad," Macy whispered against Felicity's shoulder. "I'm tired of being scared and worried all the time."

"I know, baby," Felicity murmured, stroking Macy's hair. "I know you are."

"She's really dying, isn't she. Like, this is really happening—no changing it."

The directness of the question caught me off guard, but I knew she deserved honesty.

"Yes, sweetheart. She is."

"Soon?"

"I think so."

Macy sniffled; her sobs having subsided. I felt helpless watching her, not knowing what to do to comfort her—to help her through the grief for a mother she'd already lost in so many ways—more than once, but this time she would lose her for good.

"What if I forget her voice?" Macy asked suddenly, her words muffled against Felicity's shoulder. "What if I forget the sound of her voice?"

"Then we'll help you remember," I said. "We have some videos on my phone from when you were little. We can watch them whenever you want—I think I can even save them on a drive or something for you."

"What if I only remember the scary parts? The yelling and the stuff that happened this past summer?" She paused then and quietly, oh so quietly whispered, "and how she looked today?"

Felicity lifted Macy's chin gently. "Sweetheart, what a mom and a daughter have is unique. That kind of love—it's part of who you are. The good memories are stronger than the scary ones, even when they don't feel like it." Felicity ran her hand over Macy's hair, stroking it to help comfort her. "You know, I lost my mom many years ago."

"Mmmhhhmmmm." Macy acknowledged this with a muffled assent.

"Even after all these years, I can still remember her. I can remember the smell of Sunday sauce that she would cook starting early in the morning. I can remember her laugh and the way she would answer the phone with a sing-song tone of voice. I remember her hugs and hunting through book-store stacks with her to find just the right book to read that week."

"Really?" Macy asked, pulling back to look Felicity in the eyes, almost like she was checking to make sure Felicity was being honest.

"Really." She assured her. "So don't worry about not remembering her. I can promise you—your heart won't let you forget her. And if there are moments you can't recall right away, your dad and I will help you." Felicity returned Macy's look, providing reassurance that she meant what she said.

My phone rang, the sound jarring in our quiet bubble of grief. I glanced at the caller ID: Brigham and Women's Hospital.

My blood went cold.

"I need to take this," I said quietly, stepping out of the car.

"Mr. Barrett? This is Dr. Patel from The Brigham."

"Yes?"

"I'm calling about Jessica Jensen. Do you have a moment where I can speak with you in private?"

I looked back at the car while standing on the sidewalk. Keeping my wife and daughter in my sights, I responded, "I do." My voice cracked. I knew what this was.

"I'm very sorry to have to tell you this, but Jessica passed away about ten minutes ago."

The words hit me like a physical blow. I gripped the car door for support.

"What happened?"

"She went into cardiac arrest. She had a DNR, so we couldn't attempt to resuscitate her. The nurses stayed by her side in her last moments. She wasn't alone."

I stared at the ground, trying to process what he was telling me. "She's gone."

"Yes, I'm very sorry for your loss. I know this is difficult news, especially since you were just here visiting."

"Does... do we need to do anything right now?"

"Not immediately. There are arrangements to be made, but those can wait until tomorrow. I wanted to call you personally since I'm sure you will want to tell your daughter yourself."

"Thank you. I appreciate that."

After hanging up, I stood by the car for a moment, gathering myself before climbing back in. Felicity took one look at my face and knew.

I glanced meaningfully toward Macy, who was still curled against Felicity's side.

"Let's talk when we get home," Felicity said quietly, understanding immediately.

The rest of the drive passed in relative quiet, with Macy eventually falling asleep against Felicity's shoulder. When we pulled into our driveway, Maliyah came out to meet us, taking one look at our faces and immediately stepping in to help.

"How did it go?" she asked softly.

"We can talk inside," I said. "Can you keep Macy occupied for a few minutes?"

"Of course."

Once Macy was settled in the living room with Lucas and Zoe, watching a movie, Felicity and I pulled Maliyah into the kitchen.

"Jessica passed while we were on our way home," I said without preamble.

Maliyah's eyes widened. "Oh no. Does Macy know?"

"Not yet. We thought we should get her home to a comfortable place before we told her."

"How do we tell her?" Felicity asked. "It happened all of what—twenty minutes after we left Jessica's side?"

"And now she has lost her," Maliyah finished quietly. "Poor baby."

We stood in silence for a moment, all of us processing the weight of what this meant.

When we finally called Macy into the kitchen to talk, she took one look at our faces and knew.

She sat down at the kitchen table and said, "Mom's gone, isn't she?"

The question was so matter-of-fact, so resigned, that it broke my heart all over again.

"Yes, sweetheart. She passed this afternoon."

Macy was quiet for a long moment, staring at her hands folded in her lap.

"Did it hurt?"

"No, baby. She wouldn't have been in any pain and the doctor said her nurse was there with her."

Macy nodded slowly, tears starting to fall again, but quieter this time. "I'm sad, but also... is it okay that I'm a little bit okay?"

"Of course it's okay," Felicity said immediately, moving to put her arm around Macy. "You've been watching her suffer. It's natural to feel relieved that her suffering is over."

"What now?" Macy asked.

We talked briefly about the process for the funeral. Macy decided she wanted to pick out the flowers and wanted to help with the planning. Already I felt the weight of the decisions we will need to make.

Exhausted after talking and crying, we decided to call it a night soon enough.

As we said good night to Macy, she asked if she could fall asleep with the light on and if we would wait until she was completely asleep before turning it off. We didn't hesitate. As we looked in on her later, curled up in her bed,

I thought about how our family had been through so much—from crisis to crisis, and now sealed by loss.

I took a moment to say a quick prayer over my daughter, asking the angels to watch over her tonight. Praying for comfort and a sleep filled with dreams of wonderful things—that she would have peace tonight, without the burdens of pain.

Chapter 47: This is Family

Blinking, the first thing I noticed when I woke was the feeling of Caden's arm tightening around me. I was warm, safe, and it felt glorious. Caden squeezed lightly a few times, pulling me against his chest and cuddling me close. For just a moment—that blessed space between sleep and full consciousness—I forgot all the events of yesterday. I just felt the safety of my husband's arms and the comfort of our bed.

"Morning," he murmured against my hair, his voice still rough with sleep.

"Morning." I turned in his arms to face him, studying his face in the early morning light coming in from the windows. "How did you sleep?"

"Better than I expected. You?"

"Same. I was just so exhausted that there was no other choice but a deep sleep."

We lay there quietly for a few minutes, neither of us ready yet to face the day ahead. Yesterday felt surreal—honestly, the last few months had been surreal. The whole thing felt like it had happened to someone else.

"We need to call Morrison, though I'm sure he already knows," Caden said eventually.

"I know. And Dr. Chen. Macy will probably want to see her this week."

Caden's phone rang, and he reached for it, showing me Brad's name flashing on the screen.

He answered, "Hello?"

I couldn't hear Brad's side of the conversation, but I knew what he was asking—he was asking for help. Neither Brad nor Jessica had any family to speak of, I think it was just Brad's father and brother left. My guess is he had no idea what to even do for something like this. Knowing what he wanted, I nodded to Caden communicating without words that we'd be happy to help.

After he hung up, Caden said, "Damn, there so much to do."

"One thing at a time," I said, pressing a kiss to his collarbone. "We don't have to figure it all out right moment."

"Yeah, I'm going to text my mom and see if she's willing to lend a hand."

"That's a great idea."

Just as Caden shot off his message to Sandy, a crash from downstairs sounded, followed by what was definitely Lucas yelling about something.

"Sounds like the kids are up," Caden said with a sigh.

Another bang, then Zoe's voice carrying up the stairs, though I couldn't make out the words.

"Maliyah probably has her hands full," I said, reluctantly pulling away from Caden's warmth. "We should get down there."

"Shower first?"

"You go ahead. I'll brush my teeth and then switch with you."

We moved around each other in a practiced morning routine—him stepping into the shower while I washed my face and brushed my teeth. The normalcy of it felt both comforting and strange given everything that had happened.

"Your turn," he said, emerging from the bathroom with a towel around his waist.

"Thanks. Is it getting louder down there?"

"I think so. But I think I smell breakfast, so that's something."

When I emerged from the bathroom ten minutes later, Caden was dressed and checking his phone.

"Anything important?" I asked, pulling on jeans and a sweater.

"Just work stuff. I'll deal with it later. According to Lauren, her replacement, Nathan, is doing well. Picking things up quickly, and will be ready to be on his own soon. I think I agree since, when I checked my phone this morning, he sent me an email with essentially a rollup of everything that happened yesterday when I was out of office. Then—check this out." He leaned over and showed me his phone.

"He already sent a list of everything he rescheduled for today and tomorrow and he rafted an email to the team about me being out for the next several days. It's only just eight in the morning!"

We made our way out of our bedroom together, and I noticed Macy's door was open, her room empty. She must have already gone downstairs with the other kids.

"At least someone's cooking," I said as the smell of pancakes and bacon grew stronger. "Maliyah must have gotten up early."

But as we reached the top of the stairs, I heard a door slam somewhere below us, followed by sudden quiet. The yelling and banging had stopped abruptly.

"That's weird," Caden muttered.

We made our way down the stairs, and when we rounded the corner into the kitchen, I stopped short.

Caden's mother, Sandy, was standing at our stove, flipping pancakes on a griddle I didn't even know we owned. The counter was covered with what looked like enough food to feed a small army—bacon, eggs, hash browns, fruit salad, and a stack of pancakes that was already taller than seemed reasonable for our family.

Before either of us could say anything, the front door banged open, and we heard Cash's voice boom through the house.

"I brought bagels! Everything bagels, sesame, plain, and some of those fancy ones with the cranberries!"

"I'm making pancakes!" Sandy yelled back from the kitchen, not turning around from the stove.

Caden and I stood frozen in the doorway, staring at the scene unfolding in our kitchen. We hadn't even said good morning to anyone yet.

Sandy finally noticed us and immediately threw her hands up, spatula still in one of them.

"Oh, honey!" she exclaimed, rushing over to envelop both of us in a fierce hug. "I may have hated that C you next Tuesday, but even the devil wouldn't keep me from being there for my Macy."

I found myself pressed against Sandy's ample chest, breathing in her familiar scent of hairspray and vanilla perfume, completely overwhelmed by her sudden presence in our kitchen.

"Mom," Caden said when she finally released us, "what are you doing here? How did you even get in?"

"Maliyah let us in, of course. Sweet girl, that one. She's out back with your father keeping all the children in line."

She turned back to the stove, continuing her pancake production as if this were the most natural thing in the world.

"Now, I got your message, Caden, and I've already called the funeral home," she continued, flipping another pancake with practiced efficiency. "Henderson & Sons on Elm Street. I've been to enough funerals over the years to know which ones are crap and which ones aren't, and Henderson's is good people. They'll treat our family right."

"Mom, I like texted you two seconds ago. Caden said. "how did you—"

"Honey, there's no time to waste. I scheduled you an appointment for noon today, so everyone better get moving to eat breakfast and get ready. You can't make these kinds of decisions on an empty stomach."

Cash appeared in the kitchen doorway, carrying multiple bags of bagels.

"Morning, kids," he said, as if showing up unannounced at seven in the morning were perfectly normal. "Sorry for your loss. That woman put you all through hell, but nobody deserves to go like that."

I looked at Caden, who appeared as shell-shocked as I felt. His entire family had apparently mobilized overnight and descended on our house to help us navigate Jessica's death.

"Where's Macy?" I asked, suddenly realizing I hadn't seen her yet.

"Outside with Peter and the other kids," Sandy said, adding another pancake to the already towering stack. "She seemed to be holding up okay this morning, poor thing. Asked if she could help make breakfast, but I told her today was a day for adults to take care of her."

"She's okay with all of you being here?"

"Are you kidding? She lit up when she saw us. Kids need family around them at times like this."

I felt a sudden rush of emotion—gratitude mixed with overwhelm, relief mixed with the strange sense that our quiet family grief had suddenly become a very public affair.

"Sandy," I said carefully, "this is incredibly kind of you, but—"

"This is what family does, love." she interrupted, waving the spatula for emphasis. "You think you can handle a funeral and a traumatized child and all the legal nonsense that comes with a death and custody without help? Please."

She had a point. I looked at Caden again, who shrugged as if to say, "This is how my family works."

"Now," Sandy continued, "we need to talk about what kind of service Jessica would have wanted. I know she wasn't religious, but the girl deserves something dignified. And we need to think about what's appropriate for Macy to see and do."

The practical nature of her planning was somehow both comforting and jarring. While we'd been lost in the emotional aftermath of Jessica's death, Sandy had apparently spent the night making lists and phone calls.

"Coffee," Cash announced, having apparently located our coffee maker. "Everyone needs coffee before we start making big decisions."

As the kitchen filled with the smell of brewing coffee to join the pancakes and bacon, I realized that this was what family looked like in crisis—not the quiet, processing time I'd imagined, but this loud, overwhelming, practical love that showed up without being asked and took charge when you couldn't.

Chapter 48: Love in the Chaos

~FELICITY~

The funeral was smaller than I'd expected. The funeral home had done exactly what Sandy promised—treated the family with dignity while keeping things simple. The wake had been modest, with soft lighting and flowers that Macy had helped choose earlier in the week—white roses and wildflowers, beautiful and colorful.

Brad and his family sat in the front row to the right while Macy sat between Caden and me in the opposite row. As we sat, Macy's small hand gripped her dad's tightly while the minister spoke about Jessica's life before the illness took hold, before the addiction and all the changes. Macy wore the black dress we'd bought together yesterday, paired with the pearl necklace that had belonged to Jessica's grandmother—one of the few family heirlooms Jessica had kept.

The service was brief, and sad. I looked around and realized how small Jessica's world had become. In addition to us, Caden's family and mine were here—including everyone from the Barrett side and the Doyle side. But for those representing Jessica specifically, there were just a few coworkers, and friends. Most came and left soon after.

The minister held the service and then Brad spoke for a few minutes, and that was it. No fun stories, no eulogies, just quiet.

After the service, we made our way to the cemetery for the burial. It was a gray day, overcast but not raining, which felt appropriate somehow. Macy was too afraid to approach the casket alone. She asked me to come with her. When I bent down, Lucas reached for her hand and said, "I'll go with you."

Funny how little moments can really change your outlook. In that moment, Lucas looked strong though he was just six. Macy looked down at him and his hand. Something shifted inside of her, like a realization that if Lucas could be strong, so could she.

So, the two of them approached the casket where it stood in front of her. She reached a hand toward it and placed a rose on top. Lucas leaned into her on her other side, holding her hand close to himself and leaning his head on her arm, not quite reaching her shoulder height.

Lucas looked up at Macy, as if she ruled the world. Macy looked down at Lucas as if she had a purpose—to care for something more than her own pain. It was beautiful to see this friendship become stronger than it had. I could already tell that, while Lucas had a childhood crush right now, this could be the start of a true friendship—despite the age difference.

Back at our house afterward, Sandy and Cash had somehow managed to transform our home into what looked like a restaurant buffet. The dining room table was completely covered with casseroles, sandwich platters, salads, and desserts. Who did they think was coming? There wasn't anyone at the funeral!

"I didn't realize your mother was going to organize all of this," I murmured to Caden as we watched Sandy direct traffic in our kitchen like a general commanding troops.

"Years of practice," he said. "She's been the unofficial coordinator for every family crisis since I was a kid. Death, divorce, job loss—Mom shows up with food and hugs."

I approached her—with caution, "Sandy, I don't know if this food will all get eaten. There wasn't this many people at the funeral."

"Oh, don't be silly, Felicity. The whole family will come over to be here for Macy."

"The whole family?"

"Oh sure. You know, everyone—those who could make it to the funeral and the rest of Caden's cousins, aunts, uncles, and the like. All coming to be here with Macy now that we're in a place she can let loose and be with her loved ones."

"Oh." I was kind of dazed by it all. I hadn't expected anyone else to come in. It's been a while since I've seen Caden's full family—usually it was the cousins he would hang out with for Sunday football and such, but having everyone here at once, that was usually reserved for holidays or events once a year or so. But I guess this counted as an event? Sandy is one of six and Peter one of six or seven, I think. Regardless, they both have really big families. It's a wonder they only had two themselves—Caden and Cash.

As I was standing there, I heard the front door open and voices soon after.

"I told you to park on the street!"

"What does it matter! The driveway is a fine place for parking."

"It is if you are actually on the driveway, Danny!"

"It's only a small section of grass, Tommy. Shut up."

I looked at Caden with raised eyebrows. "So, everybody?"

"Not everybody!" Sandy called from the kitchen, not even turning around from where she was orchestrating the food situation, "Just my brother Tom and his crew. Probably my sister Gladys and hers, and maybe Billy—he wasn't sure if they'd all make it but said some of them would try. Chris and Jimmy won't be here with their broods though—too much going on. That's okay though, with everyone we have showing up, it'll be a wonder if we get any leftovers!"

Before I could respond, Patty Doyle's voice filled the house, loud enough to also be heard from the kitchen too—so glad for that open floor plan... "Sandy, where the hell do I put this lasagna? This kitchen looks like it's been hit by a food tornado!"

"Patricia Anne!" Sandy shot back immediately, spatula in hand. "Watch your language in front of the children!"

I smiled despite everything. Some things never changed—Sandy and her sister-in-law, Patty, had been bickering like this for as long as I'd known them, but they could organize a small army if needed.

Tom appeared in the doorway behind his wife, carrying what looked like enough beer to stock a small pub. "Sorry for the loud invasion, Felicity," he said, giving me a quick hug. "We tried to leave the kids at home, but they weren't having it. Turns out, you stop having any say-so when your kids become adults." He shook his head when he said it, as if he was disappointed, but the smile on his face belied his words.

Behind him came the parade of people he was referring to—Tommy with Rachel and their kids, the twins Mike and Joey carrying coolers. Coolers? Why in the hell do they have coolers? Then came Danny. The house instantly filled with the chaos of a Doyle family gathering.

"Macy!" Danny called out, spotting her in the living room. "Come here and give your favorite uncle a hug!"

"You're still not my uncle," Macy said, but she was smiling as she walked over to him. I remember when she was younger, she would run to him. I don't know if it's time, or the circumstances, but she seemed so much more withdrawn from the little girl she used to be.

"I keep telling ya! I'm your dad's cousin, which makes me your Cuncle—practically the same thing," Danny said, scooping her up in a bear hug. "Besides, I brought you something."

From his jacket pocket, he produced a mid-size, wrapped package. "Made this for you. Nothing fancy, but I thought you might like it."

Macy unwrapped it carefully, revealing a small wooden box, about seven or eight inches wide by four or five long, with her name carved into the lid. "It's beautiful," she said softly.

"It's for keeping special things. Memories, pictures, stuff like that." Danny's voice was unusually gentle. "Sometimes when we lose someone we love, it helps to have a special place to keep the good memories safe. Tommy stained it and did the engraving." At this, Macy ran her fingers over the engraving of her name, clearly in awe of the handiwork.

"Thank you," she said in a hushed voice, "I'll put Mom's necklace in here."

"You can put whatever you want in there, kiddo. It's yours."

"Aunt Felicity," Samantha, Tommy's daughter, appeared at my elbow. "Dad said we should ask before we set stuff up in the backyard. Can I put some games up? Like cornhole and stuff?"

"Of course, sweetheart. Whatever you need."

Within the hour, our quiet, grief-heavy house had been transformed. The Doyle energy was like a force of nature—loud, warm, and completely overwhelming in the best possible way. Kids were running between rooms, adults were debating the proper way to heat so much food at once, and someone had started a card game at the kitchen table. Brad had come in a few minutes ago and seemed to be blending in, though he appeared to be quiet and reserved, unsure of what to make of all the crazy around him in the midst of his mourning.

I found myself standing in the middle of it all, watching Macy move from group to group, being passed from cousin to cousin, each one making sure she felt included and loved. This was what she'd needed—family, love, fun—a reminder that she was part of something bigger than her grief.

"You doing okay?" Maliyah appeared beside me, shoulder bumping me.

"Yeah, I am." I nodded my head toward where Macy was helping Tommy's wife Rachel arrange sandwiches on a platter. "Look at her."

"The Doyle effect," Maliyah said with a smile. "They don't know how to do anything quietly, but they sure know how to be there for one another."

The front door opened again, and I heard a woman's voice calling out, "Sorry I'm late! Had to drive around the block three times to find parking with all these cars!"

"Andi!" Macy called out, apparently having already met her at some previous family gathering.

Andi Doyle, Caden's other cousin, appeared in the living room doorway, wild curly hair escaping from what had probably started as a neat ponytail, carrying what appeared to be to-go boxes of coffee. She took one look at the scene—kids everywhere, adults passing plates of food, conversations happening all around—and grinned.

"Well, this looks about right for a Doyle family crisis response," she said. "Who needs caffeine?"

"Everyone," Danny called out from the kitchen. "Especially if we're going to keep up with this chaos all day."

"On it." Andi made her way toward the kitchen, stopping to ruffle Macy's hair as she passed.

"How you holding up, sweetheart?"

"Better now," Macy said, and I could see she meant it.

The doorbell rang, cutting through the comfortable chaos. Mike, being closest to the door, went to answer it.

"Uh, Caden?" he called out, his tone shifting. "You might want to come out here."

The noise in the kitchen died down. Caden appeared in the living room doorway, curiosity written all over his face.

"What is it?" he asked.

Detective Morrison stepped into view behind Mike, looking somewhat shell-shocked as he surveyed the scene—kids everywhere, adults passing plates of food, the kind of organized chaos many never see in their lives.

"Detective Morrison," Caden said, immediately alert. "What's going on?"

"It is. I just came to pay my respects."

Relief flooded Caden's face, I don't think either of us could take any surprises at this point. "Please, come in."

With Morrison entering, he made his way around, fitting in well with the family. Turns out, Caden's cousin Danny already knew him since Danny works for the Boston Fire Department.

I approached him with a plate from the kitchen, "I thought I'd make you a plate."

"Thanks, I'm actually starving."

My sister joined us and I introduced them. "Morrison, meet my sister Maliyah. Maliyah, this is Detective Morrison."

"Reed," he said as he reached out to shake her hand. "You can call me Reed." I could swear his cheeks pinked up when he looked at her.

As soon as she placed her hand in his, I could see interest spark in her eyes and a shy smile tip up the corners of her mouth. Oh boy.

⌘

Chapter 49: You're My Family

~CADEN~

After everyone left, I felt like I could breathe again. Aside from the emotional exhaustion a day like today brings, there's something to be said for the energy that goes into hosting a bunch of people and feeling like you have to be "on" the whole time.

The Doyle family had descended like a tornado—a loving one—but a tornado nonetheless. bringing casseroles, opinions, and enough noise to wake the dead. Tommy had insisted on moving furniture around "for better flow," Danny had given Macy a forty-minute dissertation on the proper way to throw a curveball, and Mom had decided to dig in on reorganizing Macy's bedroom with her and telling Macy they would go shopping for some "wall art" the coming week. I loved them all fiercely, but damn if they didn't leave me feeling like I'd run a marathon.

Cleanup was a bitch, but after getting everyone out, and getting the house and yard cleaned up, we all vegged out in front of the TV for a bit and just sat in silence. The reverence of the day finally sat on our shoulders, Macy at the center of our thoughts.

I found myself watching her during those quiet moments. Her small frame disappeared into the corner of the couch, knees drawn to her chest, fingers loosely curled around the edge of Mom's old afghan—the pastel one with the uneven border she'd tried fixing countless times before giving up. Macy's eyelids fluttered every few minutes, her breathing deepening before she'd catch herself with a tiny jerk of her chin. For the first time in weeks, her shoulders weren't hunched toward her ears.

Felicity had her feet tucked up under her, reading something on her phone while occasionally reaching over to smooth Macy's hair. Every few minutes, our eyes would meet across the room, and she'd give me that small smile—the one that said *we're okay*. After everything we'd been through, those moments of normalcy felt like gifts.

"I think I'm ready for bed," Macy had announced around nine, stretching and yawning dramatically.

"You sure? No second wind tonight?" I'd asked, knowing how she sometimes got a burst of energy right before bed.

"Nope. I'm beat. Today was... a lot." She'd looked between Felicity and me. "But good. It was good to have everyone here."

After helping her get settled upstairs—tucking the comforter just how she likes it with one corner folded back, placing her water glass within arm's reach, adjusting the nightlight until it cast just enough glow across the carpet—I'd come back down to find Felicity in the kitchen. Steam curled from her mug of tea, the string from the tea bag dangling over the side. I slid my arms around her waist, pressed my nose into her hair, and eyed the amber liquid. "Mmm," I murmured, reaching one hand toward the mug. "Is that chamomile?"

Her shoulders shook and eyes crinkled at the corners as she ducked forward, amber liquid sloshing dangerously close to the rim of her mug. She twisted her body away, one elbow out to block me, she stuck her tongue out at me. "Get!" Her free hand flicked toward the counter. "Yours is over there, by the coffee pot. Already has honey in it."

My palm connected with the curve of her pajama shorts with a soft pat, and I reached around her for the steaming mug waiting on the counter—the blue one with the chip on the handle that I refused to throw away.

She'd leaned back against me, and I'd felt some of the tension leave her shoulders. "I love your family," she'd murmured. "Overwhelming, but wonderful."

"They love you. And Macy." I'd kissed the top of her head. "Though I think Tommy might have given himself a hernia moving that dining room table around."

"He means well."

"They all do. Sometimes I think they mean a little too well."

"Mmmmm. Well, be grateful we have them." Her voice vibrated against my chest, the words warm and sleepy.

I leaned into her, nuzzled my face against her temple where a few strands of hair had escaped her messy bun. The scent of her lavender shampoo mingled with the earthy aroma of chamomile. "I am. More grateful for you though."

As she turned, we both set our mugs down on the granite countertop with soft ceramic clicks. Her arms slid around my waist, fingers pressing into the small of my back through my worn t-shirt. I pulled her closer until I could feel her heartbeat against mine, our bodies fitting together like puzzle pieces worn smooth from years of finding their way back to each other. We stood there in the kitchen's dim light, holding onto each other with the quiet desperation of people who had nearly lost everything.

At bedtime, I locked up while Felicity made her way upstairs. I found myself looking around me, being thankful for all I have and all the blessings that I'd been given. The house still smelled faintly of the various foods and the flowers that had littered the house.

Standing in the kitchen, I thought about how different this felt from just a few months ago. Then, the house had felt hollow even when all three of us were home. Now, even in the quiet aftermath of a crowd, it felt full. Complete.

Shaking my head, I ascended the stairs, checked on Macy, and headed to my bedroom.

Macy's room was dark except for the small nightlight. She was already fast asleep, Lamby clutched to her chest, her breathing deep and even. In sleep, she looked so young—too young to have been through what she'd experienced. But she was healing. We all were.

As I walked into our bedroom I stopped and stared at my amazing wife. She was propped up in front of *all* our pillows—no pillow was safe when Felicity was around. Sitting up with her Kindle laid out in front of her, set on top of *my* pillow, she looked incredibly content.

She was wearing one of my old college t-shirts, the fabric soft and thin from years of washing, and her hair was still pulled back in a messy bun that had even more strands escaping than there were when we were downstairs. This was my favorite version of her—relaxed, unguarded, completely herself.

However, after watching her for a second, she looked up at me and I could swear I'd heard the sound of a wrapper crinkling. I walked over to my wife, leaned down to kiss her and smelled it—chocolate. And at the back of her Kindle case, there was the tiniest corner of orange peeking out.

"Felicity. Love-of-My-Life. Owner-Of-My-Heart."

"Hmmm?" She tried to look innocent, but there was mischief in her eyes.

"Curious. Are you eating in bed?" I was trying so hard to hold back a smirk, but it was a feat in and of itself.

She blinked at me with exaggerated confusion. "Hmmm?" she repeated again, clearly waiting for whatever was in her mouth to melt away.

"I asked if you were eating in bed?" I pressed my lips together, the corners of my mouth twitching upward despite my best efforts to furrow my brow.

"Hmmm?" she repeated, doing her best impression of someone who hadn't heard the question.

"Felicity. You wouldn't be eating peanut butter cups right now, would you?"

Finally, after a clearly visible swallow, she gave in and spoke. "What? Of course not!"

Clearly she thought she had gotten rid of the evidence, however there was a small bit of chocolate on the corner where her lips met, and the telltale scent of Reese's Peanut Butter Cups—my wife's kryptonite.

I laughed loudly, tackled her, and stole her e-book. Out came the wrapper which I waved in front of her face. "Not eating peanut butter cups...hm mm?"

"What? Who knows how long that's even been there!" She was giggling now, trying to grab her Kindle back. "That could be from yesterday! Or last week! It could even be *yours*!"

I couldn't help but tickle her until she finally gave in. "Okay, okay!" She squealed, laughing, and trying to fend me off from tickling her further. "You got me! Uncle! I call Uncle!"

"I thought you gave up sweets after dinner," I said, still holding her Kindle hostage.

"I did! This was a... post-dinner emergency snack. Very different thing entirely."

"Emergency snack?"

"Yes. A chocolate emergency. Very serious condition. Could have been life-threatening if left untreated."

I nibbled on her neck, tracing my way up to her jaw, her chin, and then landing on her lips. Kissing her lightly—gently I said, "yup, I can taste it on you." I smiled through my kiss, unable to hold my love for her back. "I love you my little sugar-addict."

She sighed and smiled back, her arms coming up to wrap around my neck. "It can't be helped. You know I eat when big things are happening! I'm going to be as big as the Pillsbury dough boy."

"I've always had a thing for blue hats and soft bellies. I think you'll make a great dough girl." I squeezed her side, loving the softness I found there.

The playfulness faded for a moment as something more serious passed between us. After everything we'd been through—the separation, the crisis with Jessica and Macy, the uncertainty about our future—moments like this felt precious. Sacred, even.

I wouldn't let anyone or anything steal these moments from us—not anymore. The work stress, the family drama, the constant pull of obligations that used to take me away from what mattered most. This was what mattered. This woman in my arms, our daughter sleeping safely down the hall, the life we were rebuilding together one day at a time.

Kissing her deeply, we made quick work of our pajamas. I love this woman with every ounce of my being. The gratitude I felt was indescribable.

As I took my wife in my arms, I was swept away in the moment, knowing that blessings like her don't come around more than once in a lifetime and I was one lucky bastard that she let me love her.

I kissed my way up and down her body, not leaving an inch of her unloved. She gave me her body, gave me her heart, gave me the greatest gift of all, and I gave her my soul.

Afterward, we lay tangled together in the mess of pillows she'd commandeered, her head on my chest, my fingers playing with her hair. The house was quiet around us, the kind of peaceful quiet that comes after a day well-lived.

"Thank you," she murmured against my skin.

"For what?"

"For today. For being present. For..." She paused, searching for words. "For being the man I married."

I tightened my arms around her. "I should be thanking you. For giving me another chance. For not giving up on us when I gave you every reason to."

"Yesterday is gone, Caden. What matters is that we've chosen each other and keep choosing each other every day."

Outside, I could hear the wind picking up, rustling through the trees in our backyard. But inside, we were warm and safe and whole. Tomorrow would bring new challenges—Macy's continued healing, the daily work of rebuilding trust and intimacy in our marriage.

But tonight, none of that mattered. Tonight, we were exactly where we belonged.

One day at a time.

Epilogue:

The Gathered Fragments of Us

Day One—(Felicity) "Are you sure you'll be okay?" I asked Macy for the third time, watching her help Zoe with a puzzle at the kitchen table. It had been six weeks since Jessica's funeral. She'd been doing great. The most resilient kid I've ever heard of, yet the thought of leaving her felt like abandoning a bird with a broken wing.

"Felicity, I'm fine," Macy said, not looking up from the puzzle piece she was examining. "Aunt Maliyah is here. Dr. Chen says you guys need time together and—well I need time away from you guys!" At that, she looked up at me, eyes wide—making a point. Okay, got it. We're smothering.

"Point taken." I smirked and sighed at the same time.

Maliyah appeared in the doorway, coffee mug in hand. "We're going to have the best time. Movie marathons, pancake dinners, maybe even some late-night ice cream if certain people finish their homework."

Lucas looked up hopefully. "Even me?"

"Especially you, buddy." Maliyah smiled at her son. It was so good to have her home. I can't wait to see what the future will bring for her.

Caden wheeled our suitcases to the door, and I noticed how amazing this felt. Doing life together, not watching him rush off to a business trip, and neither of us running for our lives!

"Two weeks," I said, still hardly believing it. Walking up to my husband, I said, "We're really doing this."

"Fourteen days," he corrected with a small smile. "Two days for every year we've been married. I figured we had some catching up to do." He leaned forward, placing his forehead on mine, and smiled.

His words and the gesture hit me square in the chest. This wasn't just a vacation—it was a promise. A commitment to making up for lost time, one day at a time.

Then we heard Macy's voice call out, "If you're going to make out, could you do it on the other side of the door? Gross."

Day Two — Vermont (Caden) The inn near Stowe was everything I'd hoped for—rustic but elegant, there was a stunning fireplace that didn't just look nice, but it actually worked. Our room had a view of mountains painted in shades of October garnet, coffee, and gold. Felicity had spent the morning on the small balcony with her coffee, just watching the leaves dance on the wind, drifting down, as they fell from their branches a little at a time.

I'd been carrying the sweater in my bag since we left Boston, wrapped in tissue paper like it was something precious instead of the slightly lopsided disaster it actually was. I'd started it soon after Jessica had passed, teaching myself from YouTube videos during lunch breaks—and truth be told during conference calls that droned on. The first attempt looked like it belonged on a scarecrow. The second wasn't much better.

"I have something for you," I said, pulling the package from my bag.

She looked surprised. "Already? We just got here."

"It's not... it's not what you'd expect." I handed her the tissue-wrapped bundle, suddenly nervous—my hands sweating. "I made it myself."

She unwrapped it carefully, and I watched her face as she held up the navy-blue sweater. It was wool, as tradition called for on our seventh anniversary. It was clearly handmade by someone who was horribly unfamiliar with how to hold knitting needles.

"Caden," she said softly, running her fingers over the uneven stitches—one of her fingers catching in a loop. My God, what was I thinking—it was awful. "You made this?" She asked.

"I know it's terrible. I spent weeks on it at work—Nathan kept finding me in my office with yarn everywhere. But I wanted to give you something I'd actually put time into. Real time."She slipped it on over her shirt. It was slightly too big in the shoulders and a little short in the arms—one arm seemed shorter than the other. Damn it. But she didn't seem to care and instead wore it like it was cashmere.

"It's perfect," she said, and I could hear she meant it. "You're right when you said it was something I wouldn't expect. It's much better than I would expect. This shows your heart and tells me where you invested your time."

"There's something else," I said after clearing my throat. "But that's for a different day."

"I don't need anything else. I love this." She looked down at my handiwork, running her hands along the stitching, smiling the whole time. My heart couldn't even fathom this woman and the love it felt for her.

Day Five — New Hampshire (Felicity) The Kancamagus Highway was everything the travel guides promised—a tunnel of red and gold stretching through the White Mountains. We'd stopped at every scenic overlook we could, taking pictures of every kind—silly, fun, serious, scenic. You name it, our phones captured it.We breathed in the crisp October air every chance we could. October weather in New England isn't the most predictable, but the sunny days were worth a hundred of the gray ones, and we had so many sunny ones that it was like a down payment on the winter to come.

Caden had been different on this trip. Not just attentive, but wholly and completely present. No phone calls with work. No distracted conversations. When I spoke, he listened like my words were the most important thing in his universe.

We were walking along a trail near the Swift River when he stopped suddenly.

"This feels right," he said, pulling a small velvet box from his pocket.

My heart jumped. "Caden, we're already married."

He laughed. "Not that kind of box. Though I like that your mind went there." He kissed me first, then stepped back and opened the box. I leaned forward and saw the most delicate earrings I'd ever seen—tiny forget-me-nots crafted from black onyx petals with opal centers that caught the light like captured fire.

"Forget-me-nots?" I whispered, taking one from the box to examine it.

"For remembrance. And onyx for our seventh anniversary, opal for October." He took the earring from my hand and gently brushed my hair aside. "But mostly because I never want you to forget that you are seen. You are remembered. You are loved."

I put them in my ears, feeling the slight weight of them, as he explained, "I found a local artist who makes jewelry. I asked if she could make something custom with the shape and stones I showed her. It took her a little while, but I think she knocked it out of the park."I smiled at the thought behind the time he spent on even this gift.

"How do they look?" I asked.

"Like you," he said simply. "Beautiful."

Day Eight — Maine Coast (Caden)

The sailing trip on Casco Bay had been Felicity's idea—she'd seen the brochure at the resort and mentioned how peaceful it looked. We'd booked it immediately.

Now we were out on the water, the October wind filling the sails, and I was watching my wife laugh as spray misted over the bow. I was grateful we were decked out for a cold day because it was freezing. And even in the cold, covered in layer after layer, with a hooded anorak, she was the most stunning thing I'd ever seen. Her hair was escaping from the ponytail and out the sides of her hood, yet nothing stole her smile.

"Take the wheel," the captain said to me. "She's all yours."

I'd expected to be nervous, but it felt natural. Felicity and I worked together to adjust the sail, her hands covering mine on the wheel, both of us learning something new, but thanking God we weren't alone since I'm pretty sure we weren't cut out to be sailors in real life.

"I love this," she said, closing her eyes and lifting her face to the sun. "I love being here with you. I love everything about this trip."

"What else do you want to do?" I asked.

"Everything," she said without hesitation.

"Everything?"

"Why not? We have time. We have each other." She looked at me with eyes bright from wind and possibility. "We have our whole lives ahead of us."

Day Twelve — Acadia National Park (Felicity)

Cadillac Mountain at sunset was Caden's surprise for our actual anniversary date. We'd hiked up the easier trail in the afternoon, and now we were sitting on the granite summit with the entire Maine coast spread out below us.

He'd secreted a few small champagne bottles into his pack. He broke out wood cutting board and covered it with cheese and fruit, poured us some champagne, and set out a blanket for us to sit. I swear it was like something out of a movie.

"You really thought of everything," I said, gesturing at the setup.

"I tried," he admitted. "I wanted our anniversary to be something we'd never forget. I intend to never forget a single moment with you ever again."

"Hard to believe how we almost lost this," I said quietly. "All of it."

"But we didn't." He reached for my hand, running his thumb over my wedding ring. "We fought for it. We chose each other. We chose our family—one day at a time, you chose me, though I was so deeply unworthy."

His words held truth—hard truth, but truth, nonetheless. I thought of that conversation I'd had with the woman on the plane, realizing something she'd said still resonated with me. She'd mentioned something to the effect that love changes through the years. That it doesn't mean it disappears, but that it does still look different.

I looked at my husband. Looked at the years on his face that hadn't been there years ago. I looked at the love in his eyes—a love that looked so different from the love I'd seen for so long. I saw the truth in his words. I chose him—one day at a time. And I was glad for it.

The sun was setting behind us, painting the ocean in shades of pink and gold. In the distance, I could see the lighthouse at Bass Harbor, its beam beginning to sweep across the darkening water.

"I have something to tell you," I said.

Caden looked concerned. "What?"

"I'm happy," I said simply. "Really, truly happy. Not just content or okay, but actually happy. And it's not because of this trip, though this has been incredible. It's because of us. Because of the 'us' we've become."

Day Fourteen — The Drive Home (Caden) The two weeks had passed too quickly and not quickly enough. We'd visited covered bridges and maple syrup farms, taken the cog railway up Mount Washington, spent hours walking through Mystic Seaport. But more than the sights, I'd discovered my wife—the wife of today.

I'd watched her try lobster for the first time (she hated it and said she'd be happy to stick to crab legs any day), seen her bargain with a vendor at a craft fair in Vermont (she won), listened to her sing along badly to classic rock songs as we drove the scenic routes (she was borderline tone-deaf and didn't care—neither did I though).

"I don't want to go back to real life," she said as we crossed into Massachusetts.

"This is real life," I said. "This is what we're choosing. Maybe not fourteen-day trips every month, but this—" I gestured between us, "—this attention to each other, this presence. This is our real life now."

She was quiet for a while, watching the familiar landscape of home appear outside the windows.

"Macy texted," she said finally. "She and Maliyah made dinner for us. And Lucas apparently helped Zoe make us dessert."

"Is that a good thing? Or are we looking at a creative dessert?" I asked, eyes wide and a little nervous about the possibilities.

"Ha! I think we'll have to wait and see."

We both laughed, and I realized how natural it felt now, this easy back-and-forth between us. The trip wasn't meant to be a fix—but it had reminded us who we were together when we paid attention.

<u>Two Weeks Later (Felicity)</u>The package arrived on Saturday morning while Caden was at the farmer's market with the kids. I recognized the return address—the photography shop in Bar Harbor where we'd stopped on our last day.

Inside was a leather-bound photo album with "Seven Years" embossed on the cover in simple gold lettering. I opened it carefully, and my breath caught.

Every moment was there. The two of us laughing at that ridiculous scarecrow in Vermont. Caden looking terrified as he tried to steer the sailboat. Me wearing his lopsided sweater while feeding chickadees in New Hampshire. I love this ugly ass sweater, I thought, as I looked down at myself wearing it.

But it wasn't just the scenic shots. He'd somehow included the quiet moments too—me reading on the inn's porch, him studying a map with serious concentration, a selfie we'd taken after we'd collapsed in laughter over something I couldn't even remember now.

On the last page was a photo I didn't remember him taking. It was of our hands clasped together, with what looked like the trail in the background. He must have snapped it quietly during one of our hikes. I looked at the edges of our sleeves and realized it was probably from the day where he'd brought a picnic lunch for us. Damn he was slick.

Underneath, in Caden's handwriting: "Seven years down. Forever to go. All my love ~ Caden."

I closed the album and held it against my chest, listening to the sounds of my family coming home—I could hear laughter from everyone and each of their voices through the door—though I couldn't hear what anyone was actually saying.

What a year it had been. What a blessing today was. What an amazing gift this life will bring.

I heard Macy calling, "Felicity! We got the most amazing apples!"

"Coming!" I called back, setting the album on the front hall console table, I turned and almost knocked the album over. I watched the cardboard from its carrier package hit the ground though. As I was picking up the box and packing material I saw the corner of something bright peeking out from behind the wide leg of the table. Carefully grabbing the corner, I felt my heart soar as I pulled the postcard out that I had mailed from Miami.

The front had a stunning sunset off the coast of Miami Beach—with palm trees and sand, painted by gold pink sky. When I flipped it over, I found the message I'd written for myself that couldn't have been more right:

Life can be repainted.

Yesterday's sunset became today's sunrise and

Tomorrow is a blank canvas.